Rogue Mission

Book 7 in the Dan Stone series

A Novel

By
David Nees

Rogue Mission, Book 7 in the Dan Stone series is a work of fiction and should be construed as nothing but. All characters, locales, and incidents portrayed in the novel are products of the author's imagination or have been used fictitiously. Any resemblance to any person, living or dead, is entirely coincidental.

To keep up with my new releases, please visit my website at www.davidnees.com._Scroll down to the bottom of the landing page to the section titled, "Follow the Adventure".

You can visit my author page and click the "Follow" button under my picture on the Amazon book page to get notices about any new releases.

Manufactured in the United States
ISBN 9798374624762

For Carla

You always inspire me to be my best.

Many thanks to Eric who not only encourages, but gives critical feedback that makes a rough text shine. Your generous gift of time and attention is very much appreciated.

Further thanks go to my beta readers. Brian, Paul, Ed, Alex, Joyce, Bruce, and Bob. These are people who have enjoyed my stories over time and unselfishly contributed to this book's success with their critical reads. You have made this novel a better one.

Rogue Mission

"If something can corrupt you,
You're corrupted already."—Bob Marley

"Diapers and politicians should be changed often.
Both for the same reason."—Unknown

"Desperate diseases must have desperate remedies."—
Proverb

Chapter 1

The lab in Saskatoon, Saskatchewan, run by the Vaccine and Infectious Disease Organization for the Centre for Pandemic Research, was connected to the University in the city. It carried a high safety ranking but was not part of the International Experts Groups of Biosafety and Biosecurity Regulators, or IEGBBR. This organization set standards for biosafety and biosecurity. Not being a member didn't mean the lab had inadequate security, but it might not be of the latest levels as recommended by the organization.

The building was set out with one long wing where the secure labs were located. This was connected by a segment to another shorter wing that housed the administration offices and main entrance. Fortuitously, there was a large clump of woods near the building, which made for a perfect place to assemble the assault team.

The night was chilly this far north, even in late summer, as the days were getting shorter and the sun lower in the sky. The men Zhōu had assigned watched from the tree line with night vision optics. By 9 pm, all the workers had gone, and the only cars left in the parking lot belonged to the overnight security detail.

A van pulled up on the adjacent street. It had multiple antennas on it. The assault leader waited for the word that the men in the van had jammed the phones, so no calls or alarms could go out.

"You are all clear," came the disembodied voice.

"Good. We will begin. I will update you. Have the second van ready to pick us up."

The men emerged from the trees and quickly dashed across the dark parking lot. The security cameras would not record their passing. They stopped at the front doors and pulled hoods over their faces. They were all carrying Zastava AK47 pistols, the shortened version of the rifle with a pistol grip, short barrel, and collapsible stock. It was a compact and deadly weapon for close engagements.

"We're going in." The commander radioed to the men waiting in the electronics van.

A small explosive charge was placed on the doors. The team stepped back, and the leader triggered the explosion. They ran through the lobby, with two men taking control of the guards while the others ran up the stairs to the security office. Inside, the men were vainly trying to call out for help.

"There's no connection," one of them shouted. "The lines are dead!"

"My cell phone doesn't work either," said another.

Just then, the assault team broke through the doors.

"On the ground, or we'll shoot!" One of them yelled.

One of the guards tried to pull his sidearm and was immediately cut down with a short burst from an AK. The other men obeyed the command.

After securing the guards, the assault team went through the building to the inner part containing the bio-pathogens. They donned hazmat suits and shot their way into the inner containment section. With the schematics of the building memorized, they quickly located the storage containers. The anthrax was stored in four leak-proof plastic cylinders. These were removed from their storage locker and placed into four larger containers which were then sealed. Finally, they put the larger containers into two ballistic cases, which were locked shut.

After leaving the bio-hazard area, the men removed their suits, packing them in an empty bag before making their way out of the building, leaving the guards tied up. Except for the commands when the intruders entered, no words were spoken.

Later, when the police interviewed the guards, no one could recount whether the thieves had any accents. Given the lack of any clear foreign accent, the investigation immediately looked towards domestic terror. The first focus of the investigation in the subsequent days would be on domestic terrorists who might want to destroy the Canadian beef industry. When that produced no results, the investigators would turn to various right-wing organizations. Due to the left-wing bias of the current liberal party and bureaucracy, this would seem to be the natural path to pursue. Last would come a look into leftist-leaning separatist groups. The theft would not be considered a threat to the U.S.

† † †

Zhōu Ming was a member of the CCP and was involved in the country's research on pathogens. He had been associated with the Yuntau laboratory, but distanced himself from the institution when the pandemic broke out. There were suspicions regarding its origin along with the lab's involvement and Zhōu could not be tainted by such conjecture. He was a high-level bureaucrat in the massive spy agency run by the CCP.

Zhōu had an agent positioned in Franceville, Gabon, where the Level 4 lab was located. His agent had identified and made the acquaintance of a worker who had been passed over for promotion in favor of the supervisor's nephew. Nepotism was a continual source of corruption and inefficiency throughout much of Africa.

While Gabon ranked as the fifth highest economy in Africa, twenty percent of the population earned ninety percent of the income, leaving a large segment in deep poverty. Politics had also become increasingly tumultuous and unstable. In these conditions, it was not hard to find, even among the workers at the lab who earned more than most of the population, someone who could be bought.

Hsu Jiang was an agreeable fellow and the lab worker, Doukas, quickly succumbed to his friendship and favors. By playing on the man's resentment, he won his confidence and then, with the promise of riches, his acquisition into helping steal the anthrax.

"Doukas, I have an exciting business opportunity for us," Jiang said when they met for drinks after Doukas' shift was over. "It will overcome your unhappiness at not being promoted."

"You think so? I have stopped rising in my career. What will my family do if I can't increase my wages? I worked hard for this job, and I do good work. But you think that makes a difference? The supervisor has chosen family over me." Doukas shook his head. "It is unfair, but I understand it. There are just not many other opportunities for me."

Jiang smiled. "Ah, but that's just it. There *are* other opportunities for you." He paused for dramatic effect. "And I have just come across one."

His face beamed with a bright smile. Doukas looked at his friend. He'd known him for three months, but they had become close. Unlike the few other Chinese he had come across in Gabon, Jiang was not standoffish but welcomed his company. He had even helped Doukas at one time, providing access to a Chinese doctor when his father had become ill.

"So, what is this opportunity? A new job with your company?"

Jiang shook his head. "My company hires few local people, you know that. But I am not so constrained. No," Jiang's face turned serious, "someone I know knows a person who is willing to pay a lot of money to acquire a certain item. And that certain item resides in the lab where you work."

"We don't sell our inventory. It is all bio-pathogens. We do research on them. That is what I do. You know that."

"I know. But this person is interested in one of those pathogens." Jiang shrugged his shoulders. "I don't know why. I think he may be a wealthy businessman who wants to get into tech research and produce new compounds. Maybe he thinks he will take a shortcut."

Doukas thought for a moment. "The only way he could get something from our lab is to steal it."

Jiang smiled back.

Doukas gave Jiang a cautionary look. "Are you suggesting theft?"

"There is a lot of money to be made. For both you *and* me."

"But we could go to jail. Have you seen the jails in Gabon?"

"I can plan a way to do this so we will not get caught."

"But you will need me to actually do this deed."

Jiang nodded. "That is why we will share in the payoff. Fifty-fifty split."

"What is it this rich person wants from the lab?"

"One kilo of Anthrax."

Doukas looked out of the window to the bustle on the street in downtown Franceville. "That is a dangerous substance. How much money are you talking about?"

"Five hundred thousand U.S. dollars."

Doukas' eyes opened wide, and he gasped. "That is more than 300 million CFA."

Jiang nodded. "And you get half of that. It is enough money to secure you and your family for the rest of your lives."

Now doubt began to spread across Doukas' face. "I could never hide that much money. People would wonder where I got it and then connect me to the crime."

"Doukas, I have traveled much, and this posting is only my latest job. I have found ways of doing business all over the world, including things like hiding money. I can help you with that. Your challenge will be to keep this a secret, even from your family, and to not get greedy and spend it too fast." He paused for a moment. "You could even take your family to the U.S. with that much money. A new life for your children in America."

They conversed quietly for the next half hour, with Doukas casting cautious glances around to make sure they were not overheard. He finally agreed, and he and Jiang made a date to meet later to discuss the details.

† † †

Zhōu's agents arranged to meet with members of the Communist Party of India. One of the numerous communist groups operating in the country, but considered to be the most dangerous. They, like all the other Indian communist parties, believed in and participated in direct violence to advance their aim of spreading Maoist ideology throughout India. Violence was part of the agenda, considered even more important than politics.

With guidance and funding from Zhōu, the group planned an assault on the Poojapra Central Prison. The prison was conveniently located near the Rajiv Gandhi

Centre for Biotechnology, a Level 4 lab located in the southern Indian city with the tongue-twisting name of Thiruvananthapuram.

Once the bomb went off and the prisoners began escaping, Zhōu had locals ready to attack the lab. With the floor plan already acquired, they proceeded much like the team in Canada. In this attack, they killed the guards and went straight to the inner building. After suiting up, they removed the anthrax and received their payoff of 250 thousand U.S. dollars.

Chapter 2

Two months earlier

The man came to his suite late at night. It was cold and gusty. A night that continued the dreariness of the earlier day which has been gray and chilly with a wind blowing off the desert to the west, bringing clouds of sand and dirt.

Rashid was sitting on a couch with a glass of Turkish Tea in hand. It was grown on the banks of the Black Sea and known for its pungent taste. He enjoyed it with a teaspoon of sugar added.

He didn't like Beijing in any season. If he were honest, it was more that he didn't like the men he had to deal with. But as with Scorpion, his past assassin, now dead by another assassin's hand, he put up with distasteful people for the sake of jihad.

He had come to China under the cover of developing business. China was heavily involved in its Belt and Road program which helped developing nations build out their infrastructure. The Chinese helped, but with the price of debt laid upon the recipients; debt by which they hoped to enslave these other nations, grabbing control over their infrastructure, and making them beholden to China. Rashid had managed to grab a piece of this program through his companies. He had a large construction firm which specialized in a wide array of projects from high-rise office buildings to road and rail construction. Rashid also provided the machinery for various mining operations which were of interest to the Chinese.

He had been in meetings all day trying to sift through the opaque language the Chinese used in order to glean their true intent in the negotiations they were finalizing. It was as much diplomacy as business and the conversations reflected that reality. Now he waited for another visitor; one he hoped would be more direct. It was this visitor and the discussion they would have which had been the driving motive for Rashid to attend these meetings directly instead of leaving them to his lieutenants.

He was staying in a large suite in the Hotel Éclat. It was a luxury establishment in a prime location near the embassy district and catered to rich businessmen doing deals in China. With its iconic glass pyramid, it had become an instant landmark since its construction. The hotel boasted an impressive collection of modern art by Salvador Dali, Andy Warhol, and Zeng Fangzhi. It provided a comforting oasis apart from the crowded environment of the city. The rich could insulate themselves from the hectic bustle of the capital. The density of the people in the city was hard to avoid, except in the few quiet and luxurious oases such as provided by this hotel and its rooms.

The door rang with a simple chime. Rashid's servant and bodyguard rose to open it. A man stepped in. He was dressed in an immaculate designer suit that looked freshly pressed even this late in the evening. The guard blocked his path and carefully checked him for weapons before admitting him and then retired to an adjoining room. He kept the door slightly ajar.

"Zhōu Ming, welcome," Rashid said. He spoke in English, the *lingua franca* of the business world.

"I am happy that you agreed to meet with me." The guest took a seat across from the couch that Rashid pointed to.

"Coffee?"

Zhōu Ming nodded and a servant girl came in and poured a cup for the visitor, placing cream and sugar on the table.

"I was interested when you contacted my staff about a meeting," Rashid said. "Curious about what you might want."

"Well, I have some knowledge of your activities and interests."

Rashid smiled at the man. "Maybe you should start by reciting what you know about me and my interests." The statement was as much an order as a request.

Zhōu took a sip of his coffee. "I know that some years ago you pursued three cannisters of weaponized anthrax left over from the Soviet era. Apparently two of those cannisters were captured by the Americans." He paused to take another sip and then looked at Rashid. "That was accomplished by a lone agent as I understand it. Someone who may have interrupted your plans in other areas."

Rashid kept his face immobile, not giving his visitor any hint that he was surprisingly correct. "And you know what happened to the third cannister?"

Zhōu nodded. "My information is a bit vague, but as near as I can tell it rests on the bottom of the Caspian Sea. I do know there was an expedition a few years ago. A deep diving exploration in the Sea under the guise of searching for seabed minerals. It apparently was unsuccessful."

Rashid smiled but didn't comment. He was surprised that Zhōu also knew about the attempt to recover the cannister. Of course, the expedition couldn't be kept from scrutiny, but Zhōu had been able to go beneath the cover story and link it to the missing anthrax which indicated more knowledge of his operations than he was comfortable with.

"Maybe you are surprised by my knowledge," Zhōu said with a cautious smile. Rashid could see the man knew the answer to his own comment.

"My efforts at exploration are not always publicized. Looking for resources is sometimes best done quietly. Finding them can be a great asset which is best kept to oneself. I am a businessman, after all."

His guest nodded.

"But maybe it is time to tell me the reason for your request to meet," Rashid said.

"I have some sense of what you are trying to accomplish. Not so much in your businesses, but in your...shall we say...private endeavors."

"Continue."

"I may be of some help to you in these matters, especially since your expedition came up empty."

Rashid didn't answer. He knew where this conversation was headed, but needed Zhōu to tell him in his own words. It was always best to not help the other person finish their thoughts. You might mislead yourself and give them the opportunity to deceive.

"Your country and mine are involved in a growing relationship between our increasing purchase of your oil and partnering with you on development projects. Your business profits from such construction opportunities as far as I can tell. While we may not agree on all things, there are areas where our interests overlap."

"I am well aware of those areas. That is why I am at this meeting, even though I find Beijing not the most pleasant city to spend time in."

"But there are other areas as well...more private areas which we should discuss."

Rashid nodded as if to say, "proceed."

Zhōu paused for a moment as if he were getting ready to plunge into a deep pool. “You are interested in advancing the cause of Islam which for you seems to translate into bringing the west, the U.S. in particular, to its knees.”

Rashid didn’t respond, but held the man’s eyes in his steady gaze.

“We also have an interest in bringing the U.S. down. In this area our interests align. What is the saying you have? The enemy of my enemy is my friend? That is not to say we are enemies but if we have differences, they disappear when we consider this goal.”

“I make no secret of my criticism of the west and the U.S. in particular.”

“I believe I can help you with more than just criticism.”

They had been talking for an hour. Rashid had finished his tea and his guest’s coffee had grown cold. He looked at his watch.

“Zhōu Ming, we have been dancing around this subject for some time. It is late. Please come to the point.”

Rashid needed to get whatever this man was going to offer out in the open. He would not volunteer any information that could later be used against him. Zhōu might be acting on his own, or with party approval, or looking to trap him with his own words so he could be manipulated.

“The cannisters you lost. You know they are not the only ones in existence. What would you say to the possibility that I could put into your hands others of the same quality?”

“I would say that you should explain yourself further.”

“I am in position to do just what I said. I assume you would be interested in such an offer.”

“All offers come with a price. I’m not saying I’m interested, but what would the price of such an unusual offer, perhaps a dangerous offer, for you and the recipient, be?"

Zhōu shrugged. "It is all negotiable. What would you consider the offer to be worth?"

Rashid smiled and stood up. "Thank you for coming to see me. I have learned that you are far more interested in my activities than I realized. I am not going to commit anything to you to be used later against me. If you wish to consider more conversation on our mutual areas of interest, I suggest you find reason to travel to my country. I will be happy to host you in a most luxurious manner as befitting your status. Meanwhile, we should end tonight's discussion. Or, should I say, pause it for another time?"

Rashid could see the surprise slip into Zhōu's face. He stood; almost reluctantly. Rashid shook his hand and both men bowed slightly. As if on cue, Rashid's servant entered the room and led Zhōu to the door.

"You are sure you don't want to continue our conversation while you're here in Beijing?"

"Quite sure. I will be happy to hear from you later, when I am at home, if you want to continue."

The door was opened and Zhōu left.

Chapter 3

Dan Stone was up at dawn for an early bike ride. He loved to crank along the flat ground near the canals, urging himself to top his most recent speed as well as his average for the ride. It was a game he would eventually lose, with his wins coming by ever-smaller margins. Still, it gave him a benchmark to compete against.

He was a contract killer for the CIA—an assassin; quite a successful one. He worked for Jane Tanner, who had recruited him years ago. She ran a deeply hidden black operation within the CIA. Since his recruitment, Dan spent his time eliminating terrorists, defeating their plots, and causing them to lose sleep over worries about whether he would show up and end their lives.

He had always been fit; training intensively since middle school for sports. In that effort, he had discovered martial arts and delved into some of the more esoteric ones. He started with Karate and then added various forms of Kung Fu along with Aikido and, later in the army, he trained in Krav Maga. Throughout his training, he developed his own technique for working on his core strength which gave him a powerful body that didn't appear particularly muscular. He was a deadly opponent both with or without a weapon.

For his morning rides, he rode a Trek Tarmac SL6 carbon racer with Shimano Dura-Ace Di2 electronic gearset. The wheels were carbon fiber with disk brakes. It was a fast, smooth bike that Dan could push and abuse to his heart's content. After an hour's hard ride, he cooled off at a more leisurely pace as he approached the parking area just outside of Venice. After locking his bike at the car rental shop whose owner he knew, Dan boarded a *vaporetto*, or water bus, to take him into the city proper. He disembarked at St. Mark's Square and walked to his favorite coffee shop for water, coffee, and a *torta sabbiosa*, or "sandy cake". A soft and fluffy creation made with, flour, butter, sugar, eggs, and potato starch.

Life felt good. He had acquired enough money to live as he desired. He was not extravagant but could purchase the best of whatever item he wanted. His wounds were healed from his last mission to Yemen. It had been a harrowing, painful expedition, but he had avenged Carrie's horrific death. Evangeline, the girl he had rescued, still kept her distance. She harbored the feeling that Carrie's death was Dan's fault, even though she recognized the struggle he had gone through to track down her killer and send him to hell. Jane had helped Evangeline to better understand the dynamics in play. She counseled Dan the young woman would come around and that he just needed to give her time.

Dan's relationship with Jane had taken its next step. Now that they had consummated it, there was less tension about showing how they felt for each other. Of course, they kept their feelings suppressed when Dan visited her at headquarters. But since he hated going there, they more often met away from the agency, allowing them to indulge their passion along with business.

He smiled and relaxed. Right now, he was a man at peace, content. How long would that last? He didn't know and didn't bother to dwell on the question. Over the years, he'd learned to just enjoy these moments of calm and tranquility—a sense of normality—when they appeared in between the dangers of his missions.

Dan sat at the window of the coffee shop and looked out on St. Mark's Square. The morning sun painted a bright light on the pavement and splashed off the walls facing to the east. The Square was growing more active, setting up for the day's business.

Dan could sense the anticipation in the air. Vendors were opening their stalls on the square, and shops were being unshuttered. Soon they would be competing with one other for the tourists who would leave their money behind in exchange for some cheap mementos of their trip to this exotic city on the water. As Dan observed the pace of activities slowly increasing, his gaze wandered past a gypsy woman opening her stall of scarves. She looked at him through the coffee shop glass and stopped his eyes from roaming. It was the arresting look of a Watcher, the same woman who had talked with Dan years ago. There she was, undiminished by age, still with that penetrating gaze.

She nodded once. Dan sighed and got up. After leaving a generous payment for his indulgences, he walked out into the growing sunlight. The morning's peace and reflection were soon to be ended.

† † †

Henry Mason sat in Roger Abram's office. Roger, head of SAD, Special Activities Division of the CIA, was his immediate boss. Roger was a retired military colonel who had successfully transitioned to the world of espionage and, more importantly, the world of bureaucracy. He was an adroit player in the interface between government and operations. Henry felt he could count on Roger's support for the missions he ran. They both wanted an effective counterforce to the terrorists that threatened the U.S. around the globe.

With Garret Easton, the DDO and Roger's boss, willing to look the other way, Roger had let Henry set up a deeply hidden task force of assassins that operated outside the normal CIA channels. Both men saw it as a risky operation but felt such a force would be an excellent method to blunt terror operations. Henry had chosen Jane Tanner to lead the group. She was a tough, experienced handler, having done fieldwork in the middle-east for five years. She had successfully recruited Dan, her first and most effective agent.

Now, sitting in Roger's office, Henry began to wonder about the future of his operation.

"You didn't call me up here to tell me what a great job I'm doing," Henry said.

Roger shook his head and smiled.

"I know what you do," Roger said. "I'm grateful that you run your operation anonymously. You've been good at keeping some distance between the two of us. But if the reformers in congress uncover our work, we'll both go down with the ship, so to speak."

"I do what I can."

Roger leaned forward towards Henry. "We both know you've been effective. I don't want to know the details, although that probably won't help me if the shit hits the fan. And the fan is on full blast right now. The admonition I gave you earlier, about this administration, about lying low for a while? I need you to know we're still in that mode, only more so. We got a congressman—"

"Greely?"

Roger nodded. James Greeley was a congressman from California who had a chip on his shoulder regarding all espionage activities and the CIA in particular. He had the support of the party now in power and had recently been made chairman of the House Permanent Select Committee on Intelligence with full support from the Speaker of the House.

"The heat is increasing. He's asking for hearings, trying to uncover any clandestine operations that he thinks may be 'off the books' as he calls it. He's had Garrett up on the Hill to brief his committee. It was informal, not under oath, but that could change."

Garrett Easton, the DDO, had oversite of Roger and, hence, Henry. He was an Ivy League man with deep connections to the power elite in Washington.

"Garrett's a good man," Roger said, "but he's not going to fall on his sword for you or this program. He knows almost nothing of what's going on and likes it that way. But he could point them to me, and that will be a problem if I'm put under oath."

"Can Greely close us down?"

"Not directly. But he could make your operation untenable...toxic enough that Garrett would be forced to have me dismantle it."

"Just by fiat? By edict?"

"Purse strings. If he uncovers how things are funded, he gets that shut off. Plus, the press would have a field day writing about the, quote, bad guys in our own agency who go about the world flaunting the norms of civilized countries to kill people."

"It's okay to do that with drones, but not assassins?"

"It's all about how the public can be made to perceive it."

Henry noticed the language Roger used. The public could be manipulated with the right slant on news reporting. It happened all the time. This would be no different and probably easier. Most civilians didn't want to know about the hard men who fought to keep them safe, the men who kept the wolf from the door at night.

Chapter 4

Alejandro Mendoza was the nephew of Jorge Mendoza, the past leader of the Sinaloa cartel. Jorge had been killed by Dan Stone years ago. Dan's assassination of other drug kingpins in the same operation had caused chaos in the drug business and triggered a steep drop in the quantity of drugs smuggled into the U.S.

Now Alejandro, after careful maneuvering and timely assassinations of his own, had emerged as the cartel's leader. He had rebuilt the cartel's business back to its dominant position. However, the recent legalization of marijuana in the U.S. had caused the prices and profits earned from smuggling the drug to drop.

"The freighter just came into port," Sergio, Alejandro's chief lieutenant, said as he entered his boss's office. "We can separate out our product tonight after the ship's unloaded."

Alejandro nodded.

"You look worried, *jefe*. Is something wrong?"

Alejandro shook his head. "It's our finances. Income is down. You know that. But if it stays down for too long, we'll start losing the politicians and the police. We can't have that."

Sergio shrugged his shoulders. "Marijuana profits have dropped so much. But the fentanyl is helping."

"It is. But we need something more."

"We can take over the people smuggling operations. Put the coyotes under our control or out of business."

"Do we have enough men to do that?"

"*Si*. Most of the coyotes are small operators, small organizations. I can make them see it's better to align with us than face destruction. Besides, we can protect them from others who are looking to muscle in."

Alejandro got up and paced the room. His suite was on the tenth floor of an office building in the downtown area of Mazatlán. He had leased the whole floor with his personal office in the northwest corner, giving him a view not only of the city but the port and the fantastic sunsets over the Pacific. He stopped at the window to stare out over the city's skyline. Mazatlán was a major destination for the smuggled fentanyl coming from China, and Alejandro had made it his home base.

"Los Zetas," said Alejandro. His voice registered tension. The two cartels bumped against each other, with a band of disputed territory between them running through Mexico up to the Texas border.

"*Si*."

"Go do it. We need to find ways to branch out, just as my uncle was doing when he was assassinated."

† † †

One month after the Beijing visit, Rashid was in his office in Riyadh when his phone rang. It was Zhōu Ming. He wanted to meet with him when he traveled to Saudi Arabia. Zhōu promised a much more frank talk about their mutual interests.

Rashid knew Zhōu's predicament. Most of the hotel rooms in Beijing were bugged. He could not speak openly. If he were offering to help him with his jihad, he had to do it without his government knowing, so they could deny any connection if he was discovered. Rashid smiled. They probably wanted Zhōu to succeed, but they would sacrifice him to maintain the illusion that China was not an outright foe of the U.S. They were fine with the label of a fierce competitor. They had enough friends in high places in the U.S. government to protect them. It was all about leverage, something his own government knew well how to practice with their dominance of oil resources. So long as the U.S. was foolish enough to let them have the leverage, the Saudis would use it to keep the U.S. on their side and look the other way as they competed with Iran in the middle-east and suppressed democratic currents in their own country.

And like Zhōu's masters, the Saudi government did not want to know or be a part of Rashid's efforts. If they weakened the U.S., that was fine as they were selling an increasing amount of their oil to China. But his government was walking a narrow path between opposing forces. In effect, they didn't want Rashid to be too successful. That would be disruptive, which was why he had to keep his current plans deeply hidden.

The silver Mercedes Maybach waited outside Terminal 1 of the King Khalid Airport in Riyadh. When Zhōu emerged, a man walked up and introduced himself. He was dressed in a white *thawb*, the traditional robe worn by so many Arab men. He took Zhōu's bag and escorted him to the car. After he settled in, the man drove off to the downtown area. There was no conversation. The man who attended to his bag and the driver said nothing. The phone in the car rang, and the man picked it up. After listening for a moment, he handed the phone to Zhōu.

"Welcome to Riyadh." Zhōu heard Rashid's voice over the phone. "We will have a late lunch in my offices. They are secure, and we can talk freely."

"Thank you for picking me up," Zhōu said. "It is quite hot in your city."

"Yes, it is, but we'll keep you comfortable during your stay here."

The phone went dead.

Rashid greeted Zhōu as he emerged from the private elevator that took him to Rashid's executive office and apartment on the top floor of the fifty-floor office building that housed Rashid's many companies.

With lunch being the main meal in Saudi Arabia, there was a sumptuous spread of food laid out for Zhōu. It consisted of *Kabsa*, a rice dish mixed with beef, along with *Mugalgal* lamb and a meat stew offering. There were a variety of fruit juices ranging from hibiscus to orange to mango. These were set on a sideboard along with tea, coffee, and a plate of dates.

After eating, the serving girl cleared the food and departed, leaving Rashid and his guest alone. Large windows ran along one of the room's walls. The view overlooked the skyline of the city and further, into the desert. The overall tone was brown and dry. Heat waves shimmered up from the desert floor. Zhōu guessed that with a sufficient breeze, the city would be enveloped in dust that rivaled Beijing.

"We can talk freely here. These are my offices which are not only sound-proofed but swept for bugs daily."

"Let me begin by going back a few years," Zhōu said. "I don't know if you are aware of it, but two of our highly placed generals were assassinated in Africa, just outside of Goma in the DRC."

Rashid nodded but didn't speak.

"It was the work of a single sniper. He may have had help, but it was only one shooter."

He paused to let that fact sink in. Rashid waited for him to continue.

"Shortly after that, a local warlord was killed, again by a sniper, only this time there was additional help directly involved. No one found out who it was. The shooter and his accomplices seemed to have just disappeared."

"What does that have to do with our conversation?"

"The similarities indicate that we both may have been impacted by the same assassin. The one you have been looking for...unsuccessfully, it seems."

"Again, what does this conjecture have to do with our previous conversation?"

"I bring it up only to point out that we may have a common enemy who has been quite adept at thwarting our plans." He hunched forward in his seat as if warming to his theme. "Now, I learn of an interest on your part in bio-pathogens. It is in this area that I can help."

Now we come to the point, thought Rashid. "Please continue."

"I've been involved in such research for some years now. I had to separate myself after the spotlight was put on the laboratory at Yuntau. My connections reach out to many other Level 4 labs around the world. They are sources for what you seek, and I can help you get them."

Rashid thought for a moment. This man did not operate without some level of CCP approval and knowledge. But China was not going to allow itself to be connected to any terrorist operation. They worked on a much more subtle level. It might be effective, but it was too slow and did not have the ability to incite the minds of potential jihadists—fighters who would die for their cause. Rashid understood that mentality and exploited it.

He could also play the game of high-level diplomacy, but it was too subtle for the fighters he could recruit. While China maneuvered to gain financial and military leverage, playing a long game as they described it, Rashid could unleash destruction that would bring the U.S. to its knees in a quick and deadly attack.

How much of his efforts would get back to Zhōu's masters? And how much might they interfere if they thought he was being too radical?

"You are willing to work outside of your boss's approval? Are you telling me that you can do this separately from them? Without their knowledge or support?"

"There are layers in our system. The layers insulate those above from accountability, but they also make them blind to some of the activities below them."

"Nothing important happens in China without the CCP knowing and approving." Rashid smiled. "And what you hint at, and the implications of what I might do with that, are something the CCP would not sanction or tolerate."

"It is a fine line, to be sure. Just as your government walks a fine line. They don't stop your efforts and those of other Sunnis from undermining the West. Still, they don't want you to be too effective and destabilize their situation. The royal family walks an unsteady path."

Rashid raised his eyebrows as if to ask, 'so what'?

"You must keep your best efforts secret from your own government, even while they know about your financial support of various jihadist groups. Groups that fight both directly and politically."

"And you are operating in the same manner? I find that hard to believe."

Now Zhōu smiled. "I can protect myself with many layers, just like my superiors. When our two generals were killed, it greatly changed our strategic plans. It set them back. There has been a subtle change in perception and a subtle change in appetite for more direct action. Suitably disguised, of course."

Chapter 5

Rashid observed Zhōu. The man seemed to be ready to come to the point of his visit. Zhōu leaned forward.

"I can help you acquire this compound, the same as what was lost to you in the Caspian."

Rashid's face did not reflect any emotion. *Now we are getting somewhere.* "We are talking about anthrax, to be specific. You can do this? Without your government knowing? Or do they know and approve? It strikes me as odd that your superiors would risk getting their hands dirty with such dealings."

Zhōu smiled. "Yes, anthrax. And my government won't know. They look the other way while I ensure I cover my tracks which, in turn, covers any tracks leading to them. Everyone has deniability."

"But these pathogens all have markers indicating where they come from. You cannot supply any from your labs. That would be discovered, and your country would be declared a terrorist state."

"Maybe or maybe not. China is large and has much economic influence in the world. To declare us a terrorist state would mean not doing business with us. The world can't afford to do that." Zhōu took a sip of his coffee. "But my plan does not involve any pathogens from my country."

"Where will you get them?"

"That is my problem...and my business. That is what I can offer you. Sources from labs around the world. They can be traced to those labs but no further."

"You'll steal them? You have access?"

Zhōu shrugged. "I will acquire them. It is best you don't know or worry about where or how."

"Ah, but the links are important. If they can be traced back to a, shall we say, theft? And that theft can be linked back to you."

Zhōu now looked at him with a hard expression in his eyes. "As I said before, this is what I do. My business. I don't assume to tell you your business, you should not tell me mine."

Rashid watched him for a long moment, then nodded. He would take his own steps to insulate himself from Zhōu if that ever became necessary. There was an awkward moment of silence.

"I need the material in an aerosol form," Rashid said.

"Not all of it will be ready for such use. Some of the anthrax will have to be milled or micronized so it can be used in an aerosol."

"You can do this?"

Zhōu shook his head. "You will need to take care of that part of the process. My service will be to procure the powder for you."

The discussion continued for two more hours, during which Zhōu presented a figure of twenty million U.S. dollars for his services. It was a large sum, but not beyond what Rashid could pay.

"You will be able to retire after you get payment for this job."

Zhōu smiled, looking out the window. "Maybe. It is like insurance against any complications I run into after this project."

"Your masters may turn on you?"

Zhōu shrugged. "It is an experiment outside our normal procedures. Therefore, it comes with some danger, both to the government and certainly to myself. One can never know exactly how this will work out."

"Yet you're willing to try. Is it the money?"

"Not just that. It was hinted from above that I should help you. If it all works out, not only will I reap the financial reward, but I will be able to retire in my country with honor and safety for me and my family."

"Securing your future in more ways than one."

Zhōu nodded.

† † †

Anthrax is a naturally occurring bacterium, *bacillus anthracis*. It is spread through the bacterium's spores. Cutaneous anthrax is caused by the spores entering the body through the skin. This form of infection is rarely fatal. The problem lies with inhalation infection. Symptoms develop after a few days to a week and are hard to distinguish initially from a cold or flu infection. Once inhaled, the spores travel in the blood and collect in the lymph nodes. They produce toxins that kill the host. There is a forty-five to seventy-five percent fatality rate from inhalation anthrax.

To be an effective aerosol weapon, the spores need to be collected and then micronized or milled. There are currently no antibiotics for this infection. A single kilogram of micronized anthrax spores released in a city of ten million people could result in 100,000 deaths. With a long shelf life, it is an easy bio-weapon for a terrorist organization to use.

Rashid had earlier decided that he wanted to deliver a massive blow to multiple American cities. The most effective method would be a biological attack. The number of deaths would be overwhelming, and the economic fallout from such an attack would bring the U.S. to its knees. A large number of agents would have to be smuggled into the country, and they couldn't come through customs. He wanted no record of them, unlike the 9/11 terrorists. These agents would connect with sleeper cells in the country whose men could fit in better than his smuggled recruits.

† † †

The National Biosafety Laboratory, Nemzeti Biztonsági Laboratórium, a Level 4 lab, was located on the south side of Budapest, near the Danube River. It was just north of the massive train yard and near the sprawling, close-in suburbs with neat, orderly houses built on small lots along a strict grid of streets. It had been in operation since 2007 and was connected to the National Public Health Center. No one seemed to recognize the irony of joining such a lab to the public health system. It really wasn't, but the name served to gloss over its darker function of exploring the dangerous and deadly world of bio-pathogens and gain-of-function experiments on deadly diseases, in effect, weaponizing them.

Like all Level 4 labs, this one was essentially a building within a building operated at negative air pressure, so all air movement would be inward, not outward. Multiple HEPA filters treated the air that had to be let loose into the atmosphere. Counter to the recommendations that Level 4 labs be located away from dense population centers, this one was established in the capital city of Hungary.

Bela Mihok was a mid-level technician with four years of experience at the laboratory. It was a good job. It paid well, and he was liked by his superiors. He was twenty-seven and had a small apartment in the city. Life was good; he had a solid income, friends, and respect. He also had a Chinese girlfriend, Wang Li Xiu. She was an exchange student studying at the Budapest University of Technology and Economics. She and Bela had met two years earlier at a pub. She caught Bela's eye and then seemed almost too shy to respond when he approached her. However, he was able to buy her a drink, and since she could speak English, which Bela spoke, they had a common language from which to start. She was studying biotech and how the discoveries in this field could be applied to products. She was also learning to speak Hungarian, which Bela admired. He offered to help, and that formed the basis for the beginning of their relationship.

Within months they were sleeping together. Bela was overjoyed at being able to attract such an exotic beauty. His friends and fellow workers were suitably impressed, if not jealous. For her part, Wang Li Xiu seemed to enjoy Bela's company, especially the conversations about his lab work. She appeared impressed by his position and the responsibilities it entailed.

"You have permission to enter the lab independently, without a supervisor?"

Bela nodded. "When I'm working on a project, they expect me to do what is necessary to get my work done. We're all trained in the proper procedures, so it is quite safe."

Wang nodded with an admiring look on her face. "It sounds so exciting."

"It's not really. It's just work. Sometimes it's a bit boring."

"But you handle important material. Important but also dangerous. You have to be very careful."

"We are."

"Can anyone in the lab get into the dangerous areas?"

"No, no. There are levels. Special clearance is needed to work with the deadliest pathogens. Others, like those in the administration area, do not have access to the inner building."

"How are they kept out?"

"Well, their ID cards indicate what areas they can enter, plus we have a double ID requirement for the most secure areas. You need the proper card to swipe and then a handprint scan." He smiled at her interest in his work. It always flattered him. "It's pretty foolproof. Stealing a card won't get you in."

Wang nodded, her eyes glowing with admiration. Bela felt a familiar warmth grow inside of him. It came from her adoring looks and how she always seemed to affirm his importance through his work.

That night their lovemaking was especially robust and satisfying.

Chapter 6

The woman in St. Mark's Plaza looked Dan up and down. Her obsidian eyes shone with an intensity that seemed to bore through him. She was one of a group Dan had come to call Watchers. He had discovered them on his first mission, and as improbable as it seemed, they had turned out to be a hidden asset, allies in his fight against the terrorists or agents of darkness, according to the Watchers. They saw Dan's missions as part of a larger struggle of good against evil, darkness against light.

"You suffered much in your last mission. I can see the wounds you endured. You were severely tested this time."

"I survived."

"Yes. We saw a tear in the darkness. You removed one of the stronger evils and crippled the Arab's ambitions. Yet there is no peace for those who fight back against the darkness. Just as there is no peace for those who keep watch. The evil never rests. It is always trying to move forward, to spread over our world, blot out the good."

Dan looked at her. This small woman who still radiated intense energy. Like him, she never rested in her fight against the darkness. He took a deep breath with some dread at what would come next.

"You have some information for me?"

She fixed him with her intense gaze. "The man you contend with, from the heart of the darkness. The man whose assassin you killed. We sense he plots to take his vengeance on your country. There is a connection between him and a Chinese man. We do not know who. Also, a very dark figure. He knows someone killed the generals. And now he wants to help the Saudi."

"What will they attempt?"

She shook her head. "We don't know the details. But something in the U.S. Something deadly for many people. It might be what you prevented before."

"I will need to go to the U.S.?"

The woman nodded.

"I'm not supposed to operate at home. Jane can't bring me back to do that."

"She will have no other option. We sense the danger is too great. Wait for her call, but prepare yourself. There are many enemies, even among your own people."

She turned back to her scarves.

"Is there more?"

She turned again to face Dan. "Not now. The plans are too vague, and I only can see bits of them."

Dan walked away as the gypsy woman opened her kiosk and readied it for the day's business. He would get no more. Watchers provided help, but it was often vague and shadowed. Still, they could give him a path, however unclear, to follow.

He took a deep breath. *Looks like vacation is over*.

† † †

Congressman James Greely was a rising star. He had some big investors behind him and many business connections, including extensive overseas money, which he brought into the country through donations to "think tanks" to support his campaigns. His fundraising abilities gave him considerable clout in his party. The business ties he had forged with China were extensive and, on the surface, legitimate. The truth, when one dug deeper, was that many of the companies he had connections with through his and his family's investments were connected to the CCP.

"Have you come up with any further info on the CIA's black ops?"

Greely posed the question to his top aide, George Randall. George had been with Greely since he began his political career. He was an adroit fixer, making scandals disappear and putting a positive spin on bad news. He was also adept at handling relationships with less upright actors to do any dirty work that needed to be done to further the congressman's career. George could talk the language of the underworld as well as the political class. Although to him, the differences sometimes seemed quite small.

"Nothing beyond what Gardiner gave at the hearings."

"And that wasn't much. I'm going to need more if I'm going to shut down these covert operations."

William Gardiner was the Director of the CIA. He could trace his lineage back to the Mayflower and was a member of the east coast elite. He grew up in Massachusetts, attended the Phillips Academy in Andover, graduated from Harvard, and attended Yale Law School. His father was a career diplomat, and William had an automatic entry into the high-level ranks of the government. He chose a career in the administration side, not wanting to get into the down and dirty of the political arena. He preferred to do his politicking at the more gentile level of clubs and expensive restaurants.

"I know," Randall said. "I'm working with an FBI contact. The man doesn't like him. He's willing to help...working with his connections, but he says Gardiner is pretty much out of bounds. He thinks Easton, the DDO, might be able to be taken down. He's convinced Garrett is turning a blind eye to some rather nasty, dark ops, allowing them to run pretty much unchecked."

Garrett Easton was second to Gardiner in the CIA hierarchy. He was also part of the eastern elite, and the two men shared similar backgrounds and world viewpoints. They got along well.

"This FBI agent, he have any hard info?" Greely asked.

"No. Just some suspicions. We have to move carefully. Easton also has a lot of friends in high places. I'm thinking it's best if we go after the next level below Garrett. Then we won't have to take on Garrett and all his allies."

Greely smiled. George was, again, working all the angles. He would soon bring down the covert operations. He would clean house and gain much political clout in the process.

"Remember, you have that meeting with the Chinese minister, Zhōu Ming. It's right after lunch."

Greely nodded and returned to the papers on his desk, dismissing Randall.

Chapter 7

Greely met Zhōu at a small, out-of-the-way restaurant in Chinatown. No politicians went there, and neither did the power brokers in their lobbying efforts. In fact, no one in the establishment spoke any English. This was not a problem for Zhōu, and Greely made do with Zhōu ordering for both of them. The establishment had one thing to recommend it. It was far enough off the beaten path that there was no way for the meeting to be noticed or recorded.

"I have another $200,000 coming this week," Zhōu announced. "It will go into your Asian-American Center for Global Development. Of course, you can direct it as you wish once the funds arrive."

Greely tipped his drink to Zhōu. "I appreciate the donation. We're making progress on improving Sino-American relationships and restoring some of the trust that was lost since COVID hit."

Zhōu smiled. He didn't need the cover story. He knew he was buying influence. Now he waited for Greely to ask what he could do for him. It was always better to wait for the other party to ask, especially when they felt indebted.

As if on cue, Greely continued, "So what can I do for you? You didn't ask me here just to announce your donation."

"No. You have been helpful in working to keep relations between our two countries on good terms. Now I need something different. I need you to push the administration to get pressure off the border."

Zhōu had been developing his relationship with Greely for three years and over two million dollars. Greely had helped to block some of the more egregious anti-China legislation under the umbrella of engagement and global prosperity. Now Zhōu was leading Greely into different territory. He needed the southern border to remain porous. There was much money to be made with the cartels and fentanyl. His country supplied it, and the cartels smuggled it in. It was working to hollow out a generation of Americans, which Zhōu knew would pay off in the long run.

"The administration already has a lax policy. They're in favor of keeping the influx of migrants flowing. You know, it helps on many levels, business as well as politics."

"Yes, but there is a growing segment in congress that is raising opposition."

James nodded. "That's true. You know it's probably temporary due to the recent news about migrant deaths. It will pass."

"You must help it to pass more quickly. I have confidence in your abilities. And there is a piece of legislation coming forward to toughen the stance and send more migrants back to their home countries."

"I'm aware of it."

"Make sure it doesn't come to the floor for a vote."

Both Zhōu and Greely knew that a vote could not pass but could embarrass his party and erode some of his colleague's chances for re-election. Zhōu smiled.

Greely knew he was on the spot to deliver. There were always things to do for Zhōu to keep the money train chugging along. Thankfully, they were things he could feel reasonably good about. What harm was it to benefit from maintaining close relationships between such massive business partners? That collaboration was only going to increase, no matter what conservatives squawked about with their protestations about fair trade. And as far as the border was concerned? Almost everyone tacitly understood and agreed that a healthy supply of migrants was good for business, helpful in suppressing wages, and beneficial to his party in the upcoming elections.

† † †

Half a world away, the call came to Wang Li Xiu. Tonight was the night. She was ready. She had been prepared for days. She knew the layout of the lab, where the checkpoints were, where the minimal night staff was located, and how to loop the cameras on the security system. She would create a ten-minute loop from her laptop that would replay repeatedly. She wasn't worried about it being noticed since nothing went on. The cameras only showed empty halls and closed doors night after night. The security staff had long ago stopped studying the monitors, now only giving them a cursory glance every so often. If they showed the same picture, it raised no flags but only reinforced the belief that things were normal—dull and quiet.

After dinner at Bela's apartment, they got cozy on his couch. Wang felt she owed it to Bela. He was, after all, a nice guy and, if she were honest, a good sex partner. He always looked to please her. It was something she found most Chinese men didn't bother doing.

After an exceptional steamy round of lovemaking, Bela rolled back on the bed. "Li, you are wonderful. I can't get enough of you. Girls have it better than guys. They can have orgasm after orgasm. All night long, it seems. We guys are usually done after two. Tonight, I made it to three orgasms, thanks to you."

He leaned up on his elbow and looked over at Li. She had a trim body with lovely proportions. He touched her cheek tenderly.

"Do you think you could settle down with me?"

Li looked at him and smiled at his hopeful expression. "That is a complicated question. You see, after my degree, I'm supposed to go back to China. My funds come from the government, and they want me back to work for them."

She stroked his cheek in return.

"Do you think you'd be happy going to China?"

Bela's expression clouded over. "I don't know. I have such a good job here. They are not easy to get. I couldn't speak the language, so how could I earn a living? Here, at least, I can support you. And with your skills and language, you could easily find work. Maybe we should lobby your government to see if you could extend your stay."

Li Xiu patted his cheek. "We'll see. For now, I'm tired, and I'll bet you are. You wore me out."

Bela lay back on the bed; a smile crept over his face. *I wore her out*. Not many guys could claim that. Soon, a blissful sleep crept over him. He was satisfied, drained, and madly in love with the girl of his dreams lying beside him.

When his breathing became deep and regular, Li crept out of bed. She crossed the room to retrieve her backpack. In it were zip ties. She brought them back and gently secured Bela's wrists without waking him. Then she took a cord, pulled his arms up to the top of the headboard rail, and tied it off. Bela now began to waken.

He looked at her questioningly.

"I don't think I can do more tonight, even if it's kinky."

Li Xiu smiled and put her finger to her lips.

"Don't talk. Let me have some fun."

Bela lay there secured and watched his lover. He could almost get satisfaction just watching her body move.

She took another length of rope and tied it around one ankle. She threw the cord under the bed and pulled it out from the other side to secure his other ankle.

"Are you comfortable?"

Bela nodded. He wasn't into bondage and hadn't realized Li Xiu was. But she was so beautiful, he was happy to not protest and just go along with her. When she was done, she stood up and examined her work.

"Can you move? Get free?"

Bela gave a half-hearted attempt and said he couldn't.

"Try harder. Let me see you really try."

Bela sighed. He was not going to get to go back to sleep, it seemed. After a few moments of real struggle, he gave up.

"You really have me secured. What now?"

Li Xiu smiled at him as if proud of her handiwork. "Did you enjoy this evening?"

Bela nodded.

"Was it the best one so far?"

"Yes. I can't believe how sexy you are. You inspire me."

"You inspire me as well. I just want you to know that these past two years have been great fun for me. More than I imagined when I met you."

"And the years to come. At least until you graduate and have to go back, will be even greater."

"That's the problem. They won't be. I must go tonight. This must be our last night together. I'm glad it was such fun for you. As much fun as it was for me."

"But why?" Bela's look changed, and his body tensed.

"I have been called back."

"That's not fair!" Bela's face now showed a rising panic. "And why tie me up? You're going to leave tonight?"

Without answering, Li went back to her backpack and pulled something out. Bela could not see what it was.

"Don't worry. I'll untie you after we've had one last round. A last round for my sake, if not for yours."

"Oh, Li Xiu. I don't want to lose you!"

Without answering, she mounted Bela and moved her body up closer to his face. He felt her grab his head and pull it up towards her. Did she want him to pleasure her orally? They had done that before, but he wasn't a fan. He couldn't see her right hand as it came around and jabbed a needle into his neck.

Li pushed the plunger, and then the needle was ripped out as Bela jerked his head back.

"What the hell? What did you do?" Bela was now thrashing around, but, as he had tested earlier, Li's restraints were working.

Li smiled at him and touched his cheek tenderly as she climbed off him. "Something to relax you. For your final journey."

"My final journey? What the hell are you talking about?"

"I have to go, so you have to go."

"Are you going to kidnap me? Take me to China?"

Li shook her head slowly. "No, my love. You are going on a different journey."

Bela's thrashing began to diminish as the sedative took hold. Li picked up a pillow from the bed, climbed back up on top of Bela, and placed it over his head. His thrashing didn't increase. The panicked desire for oxygen that his brain signaled was diminished by the sedative that betrayed his body in its most dire moment of need. Within minutes Bela relaxed in death. His bladder emptied on the bed. Li was glad his dinner had not progressed far enough to be let out as his involuntary muscles stopped responding.

She climbed off and quickly undid his bindings. She then dragged his body into the living room and laid it on the rug. She pulled the coffee table to one side. With Bela on the rug, Li proceeded to cut through his right wrist with her tactical knife, which was scalpel sharp. Still, she had to bear down to sever the joints of the wrist.

When she was done, she placed the hand in a plastic bag, put it in her coat pocket, and made a call. After she hung up, she rolled the body into the rug. Soon two men would arrive. They would not know who had been in the room with Bela. They would not see her. Their instructions were only to take the rolled-up rug with a body inside and ensure it was never found.

With her task done, Li Xiu looked around the room. It had been a pleasant experience, and she felt that she had sent Bela off in a reasonably gentle manner. After picking up Bela's ID card, she opened the door, stepped out into the hallway, and down to the street.

Chapter 8

Rashid flew into Mazatlán. His public purpose was to talk with officials about growing the port facilities with expanded docks and cargo handling equipment. A rail line to a distribution terminal farther inland would also be discussed. It would use cheaper land, not suitable for tourism, to set up warehousing and logistic operations, which would expand Mazatlán's value as a port of entry for Mexico and Central America. While there, Rashid would also make time to meet with Alejandro Mendoza.

After a respectful but careful wanding of his clothes, he was ushered into Alejandro's suite on the top floor of a modern office building.

"Welcome to my new home city. It is quieter than Mexico City, and the air is cleaner, but I sometimes miss the bustle of the capital."

"It is good to finally meet you. Congratulations on taking your uncle's position of leadership. I enjoyed working with him. He had vision. I am guessing you, like him, see the need to expand your business, to branch out into new areas."

"My people are always investing my money into what I refer to as clean enterprises. This diversification helps protect my overall position. My uncle lost much when he was assassinated. He had not moved far enough forward, and in the aftermath of his death, his lieutenant was also killed. With many other cartel leaders shot as well, the industry turned on itself. It was a bloody time, and one had to be ruthless to survive, let alone grow. When I came to power, I vowed to create more stability for myself and my family."

"But you also diversify into areas less clean, as you say. In every respect, you seem to have done well."

Rashid sat down on the comfortable couch and took the coffee offered.

"You are here about the port expansion business. And you also know that we are involved. We must be coordinated in our efforts because I need to have my people on the inside of the operations as much product for our business comes through here."

"Imports from China...fentanyl?"

Alejandro nodded. "It is going to fill the gap in income that is developing from marijuana legalization in the U.S. It may become our most profitable product."

"It seems to be hollowing out America from the inside."

Alejandro shrugged. To Rashid, his expression seemed to be one of disinterest.

"You have an ideological framework, from your faith, that you see everything through. I am Catholic and still hold strong to my faith. You are Muslim and hold to certain radical ideas. In this we differ, yet we can do business together." He leaned forward in his chair across from the couch. "America is a market. The richest country on earth with many of its people wanting to be drugged." He leaned back with a smile. "It is my *cajero automático gigantesco*, my gigantic ATM. You, however, want to only bring about the destruction of the country you see as the enemy of Islam." He shrugged again and took a sip of his glass of tequila. "For me, it is about getting rich off of them."

"We have differences, as you say, yet we can work together. That is enough."

A wry smile spread across the younger man's face. "Perhaps I should *not* help you. You want to destroy my ATM."

"Yet you do. You know I pay you well for your help bringing my agents across the border."

"Maybe I don't believe you will be successful, and helping smuggle your men into the U.S. only helps me expand and control this growing industry." He stood up to refresh his drink. "Do you know that smuggling illegals into the U.S. is the fastest growing segment of our business next to fentanyl? I sometimes wonder how ones so stupid can hold power in the U.S., but I'm happy to take advantage of their blindness."

"It is a blindness caused by their ideology. For both of us, they are what Lenin called useful idiots."

Their conversation went on in a relaxed manner. Alejandro would ensure Rashid's agents were safely smuggled across the border. Alejandro promised to have his best lieutenant involved to make sure there would be no mistakes. There would be two box vans waiting to carry them far into the interior of the country.

Rashid had purchased a small farm near the southern tip of Illinois where the men would modify the trucks so they could disperse the pathogen. During this time, they would finalize the plans for their attacks. He did not want to rush. The attacks had to be done precisely to be most effective. Zhōu's last communication indicated that some of the material would have to be milled, and Rashid decided he would have that done at the Illinois farm. There was a risk, but he wanted the anthrax to be in the country and not have to move it around to an outside lab.

The farm was under one of his company's names. It was hinted to all involved in the purchase that the property would be used as a retreat center for training new executives away from the bustle of the usual resort areas. It was located just to the west of a small town called Dongola. The farm nestled up against the Shawnee National Forest at the end of a long, private, gravel road. There were forty cleared acres that now grew hay, and the rest was woodland running into the forest. There was a creek that fed a small lake on the cleared side of the property. It was to the north of the main house with a small, wood pier jutting out from the shore. To the south and east were three outbuildings; a barn, workshop, and multi-use structure that could house trucks, autos, or farm equipment.

Chapter 9

Jabbar Badawi was a distant nephew of Rashid. He had Bedouin blood in him, as did Rashid's mother. Rashid had carefully brought him into his jihadi network as the boy grew up and became more radicalized. Under Rashid's guidance and the teachings of some militant imams, the young man developed an enmity for the west that mirrored his own. He was pleased to see that Jabbar could be relied upon. He was clever and subtle. He had an education from Great Britain and could easily move among westerners. Many of the men Rashid used in his struggle stood out and caused more suspicion due to their lack of western mannerisms and the often-obvious chips on their shoulders regarding the customs of the world of the west.

Rashid had set Jabbar up as the leader of his ten-man strike group. Some of the men, unknown to Rashid, quietly resented the young man's position. They were older, more experienced jihadists and felt their experience should take precedence over Jabbar's westernized mannerisms. Nevertheless, they quietly went along. It was neither prudent nor appropriate to stand against their master when he had made a decision.

Still, the resentment remained. This mission would be the grand attack. The one that would bring America to its knees, and Jabbar would have his name attached to it, if not in public, then in the houses of Islam and coffee shops throughout the middle-east.

Prior to the insertion of the jihadists, Rashid sent his nephew to meet with Zhōu in Madrid; Zhōu's visit was ostensibly to talk contracts with the Spanish officials for a high-speed rail line connecting the Iberian Peninsula and Jabbar to seek investments in some port facilities for his uncle.

"Your uncle was smart to choose you to lead the team," Zhōu said after they had purchased drinks from the small coffee shop located in the Parque de El Retiro.

It was a large green space of around 310 acres located in the heart of the city. A few roads ran through it, and it contained a small, artificial lake. The two walked along one of the many crisscrossing paths through the thousands of trees in the park. Away from prying ears and eyes, they sat on a bench.

"He wants us to be subtle. Right up to the end."

"Subtly is good. Something not always practiced by the faithful."

"Many are hardened warriors whose experience is confronting other warriors for the apostate sects. It is a matter of force against force." He turned to the Chinese spy, "This attack must be carried out with sophistication and stealth. If we do it correctly, no one will know anything except what we decide to reveal."

"I have arranged to send the powder to the mosque in Richardson, Texas, as directed by your uncle. You must deal with bringing it up to the level of readiness yourself."

"It is not hard. I have read up on it."

Zhōu nodded. He understood this young man's confidence. He had not yet experienced how plans could go wrong in so many ways. It all looked straightforward to him. To Zhōu, it looked convoluted and fraught with danger, with many opportunities for the plot to be uncovered and defeated. Still, there was a decent chance for success. His backup was the fentanyl connection which he continued to pursue with Alejandro independent of Rashid.

And there was the 20 million, which would put him on another level within the CCP. He would be careful to not let his masters know the total amount. Much of it would be stored off-shore in bank accounts set up in Malta, the Cayman Islands, and Belize. His superiors would only see a fraction of the total. That amount would be brought back to China, through Singapore and Hong Kong, via circuitous routes. They would see him use it to bolster domestic investments, making him a stronger player in the government hierarchy.

"Your uncle made arrangements with Alejandro Mendoza to smuggle your men into the U.S."

"He told me about those arrangements."

"There is more."

Zhōu thought for a moment. How much information should he give to this young man? He wanted him to be successful, but a part of him doubted he could accomplish this task. Zhōu decided to let Jabbar know there were other forces at play.

"Both your uncle and I are interested in two things, an open border with Mexico and crippling the CIA."

"Your interests coincide in these areas?"

Jabbar was surprised. He could not understand the connection.

Zhōu nodded. "Yes. An open border helps us smuggle agents and drugs into the country. We both work with Alejandro to that end. Alejandro sees the U.S. as just a market. And in this, he is correct. But your uncle and I see the drugs as a way to hollow out our adversary." He leaned towards the young man. "Now, whether you are successful or not, you should make sure you get away safely. You are important to your uncle's plans." Zhōu sat back and gazed across the groomed grass and trees. "The others may die in the effort, but do not sacrifice yourself. There are more avenues for attacking the U.S., and most of them require the subtly you possess. The fighters you have with you are crude weapons of your jihad. Unfortunately, they are expendable. You," he looked over at Jabbar again, "less so."

Jabbar listened without a word. Zhōu knew what he said would sound harsh to his ears. He knew Jabbar understood he was different, being educated, being a nephew, however distant, to Rashid, but the young man probably never had heard the differences between him and the others expressed so clearly and brutally.

"And the other thing?"

Zhōu smiled. Jabbar stayed on point.

"We both have been hurt by the CIA. Or, to be more exact, by someone in the CIA. Someone who is part of a deep, black operation. An assassin. He killed two of our generals and many of your uncle's fighters, including his most deadly assassin."

"The man many called Scorpion."

"Yes."

Zhōu again stopped to consider how much to tell this young man. His uncle knew of his own efforts but not the full extent. Jabbar needed to understand the other activities going on to undermine the U.S. so he would not feel this mission was do-or-die for him. Zhōu wanted this Oxford-educated young Arab, related to a billionaire, and radicalized to pursue jihad against the U.S., to understand that he could play a part in the multifaceted campaign that was continuing to attack America. He wanted to not have Rashid's asset lost to a mission that Zhōu had doubts could be pulled off without many involved dying.

"I am working to infiltrate the government officials in the U.S. That is all I can say. My work already bears fruit by helping to keep the southern border open. Something that will make it easy to get your fighters into the country. It is also helping to put pressure on the CIA."

He put his hand on Jabbar's shoulder.

"You may play a part in these operations going forward, no matter how this mission ends."

Jabbar nodded to the man.

"If we succeed, your work will not be necessary. We will bring the Great Satan to its knees."

Zhōu smiled an almost sad smile. Sometimes information was received but not processed. Sometimes zeal clouded judgment. He could offer no more. He may have provided too much as it was, but this young man, Jabbar, was an asset that should not be readily sacrificed.

"You must overcome the older fighters' natural dislike of being led by someone younger and less experienced. They may harbor resentment. However, once they see your plan working, they will begin to accept your leadership."

"They will accept my leading them because my uncle decreed it. He is the one ultimately in charge."

Zhōu smiled and said nothing. He had given his warning. There was nothing more to do but hope they would succeed.

Chapter 10

The men flew into Mexico in pairs, landing in Monterrey, Guadalajara, and Mexico City. From each point, they traveled by cars purchased for them to rendezvous at a small town named Nueva Rosita. The Sinaloa cartel had a safe house there for the men. The town was two hours south of Piedras Negras, the border town just across from Eagle Pass, Texas. This was a hot spot for illegals to cross. They often overwhelmed the Border Patrol, which was the cartel's technique to keep the officials occupied while their mules smuggled in fentanyl, and other drugs.

The cartel made money off the illegals, charging them from $2,500 to $8,000 depending on how far they had to bring them to reach the border. Once there, the fee for crossing the Rio Grande ran about $1,500. Many illegals could not pay the full price, so the cartel "loaned" them the money in exchange for doing work for them once in the U.S. This work usually involved transporting drugs around the country. For Rashid's men, there would be no loans. He was paying for a concierge-level of service, which included trucks waiting for them on the other side.

Sergio, one of Alejandro's lieutenants, supervised the operation.

"We have many migrants waiting on this side. Our plan is to move them across in one group. It will be big news in the U.S. and cause quite a disruption. That will make it easier to move your men across and avoid the Border Patrol. The other illegals don't mind getting caught. They know what to say to claim asylum, and with catch and release, they will be let go to travel to their final destination."

"The authorities, let them go free?" Omar asked Jabbar when he heard the plan. "America lets hundreds of people just stream into their country?"

Omar was an older jihadist and often acted as a peacekeeper between the younger Jabbar and Taimoor, an experienced fighter, who resented Jabbar's leadership.

"Not just hundreds, thousands," Jabbar said.

"They are fools, and we will take them down."

Jabbar noted the disdain in his voice. It seemed that the more, the older jihadist learned about America, the more he felt it was rotten and ready to fall.

"Yes, but we still must not underestimate them," Jabbar said.

Taimoor, who was listening, shook his head as if to dismiss Jabbar's caution.

The next day the cartel began to release the hordes waiting to cross. By late afternoon and evening, they had piled up a thousand strong on the U.S. side of the border, all waiting to be processed by the agents and let into the county. That night, while the Border Patrol was busy with the migrants, Sergio relocated Jabbar and his men.

They moved north, past the chaos they had created, and Sergio led them across the river. He had a line fastened to the shore on the far side that the men could hold on to in order to balance against the current. The water was waist-high and, in some spots, generated a strong pull. The men didn't know how to swim, so getting swept away could mean drowning.

Once on the U.S. side, Sergio led them through the wire fence that presented only a semblance of a barrier. It was a dark night with a new moon. The men hiked, single file, through the sand and brush with an occasional crouching to hide as a helicopter flew overhead or a patrol jeep went by. Soon, they were miles from the border, deep into the Texas desert. The barbed wire enclosing various fields was cut by the cartel to avoid long detours. When they encountered them, they skirted the few farmhouses. Near the houses, there was more substantial wire and vigilant dogs in an attempt to deter the illegals from venturing too close. When they reached Highway 277, two box trucks were waiting for them.

Jabbar shook hands with Sergio, and the four senior men piled into the cabs, with the others getting into the boxes. Jabbar drove one of the trucks while Omar, the older jihadist, drove the other. Taimoor was relegated to the passenger seat, much to his discontent. Dawn found the trucks three hundred miles north, near Dallas.

They drove down I 635 on the north side of downtown Dallas and got off at the Richardson exit, a suburban city making up part of the continuous sprawl of the greater Dallas area. There was a Muslim cultural center located in the town. Jabbar would not go there but headed to a small mosque in the community. It had been picked because the Imam was sympathetic to Rashid's ambitions. He was a strong proponent of jihad, often preaching it in a subtly disguised manner so he would not draw the attention of the authorities to himself. It was not hard to remain off the radar of both local and federal authorities, considering the government's sensitivity to accusations of anti-Muslim discrimination.

"We will get a good halal meal here," Taimoor said. He approved of the stop.

The men unloaded into the mosque and were taken to rooms in the basement. These were off-limits to anyone but the Imam.

"Enjoy it," Jabbar said. "It may be our last. Once we leave here, we will be on our own."

Taimoor gave the younger man an angry look but said nothing.

Waiting for them in the rooms were two crates of weapons. Taimoor and the others enjoyed opening them and checking out the AK47s and semi-automatic pistols. Additionally, a thousand rounds of ammunition for the rifles and pistols were in the crates.

Also waiting for them were five ballistic cases containing the sealed tubes of anthrax. They had been delivered by courier from Mexico two days earlier. The courier had come across illegally. It was a safer route than trying to hide the cases in a vehicle and cross at the usual border checkpoint.

Chapter 11

Jane was in her office when Fred Burke knocked on the door. The room was not much to look at, just a small square space located on the lower levels of the CIA headquarters at Langley, Virginia. It was windowless and had walls painted in an institutional cream color which did little to elevate the sense of tightness and confinement. Jane had made a half-hearted attempt to relieve the cramped feeling with some photo prints of dramatic landscapes.

Fred was an integral part of her small team. His passion was pouring through all the intelligence feeds as well as public news feeds, looking for links that might lead to threats not readily perceived by others.

Warren Thomas was the other half of Jane's technical team. He was the programming wizard who could hack into databases around the world. His skills coordinated well with Fred's, and between them, they could uncover connections that most other people would miss. The two young men worked in a larger room divided into two spaces just outside Jane's office. Neither of them complained. They felt they were on a mission, and events of recent years had substantiated that feeling. The group was supervised by Henry Mason, an old-school warrior, who set up their covert operations to create an effective unit to fight the ever-growing threat from terrorists, both religious and political.

"What's up?" Jane asked after telling Fred to come in.

"I've found an anomaly that I think deserves some attention."

"Sit down." Jane pointed to one of the two office chairs in front of her modest desk.

Fred took a seat. Jane waited for him to begin. He was shy and nervous in front of her, even after the years they had worked together. He took a deep breath.

"Over the last three weeks, there have been attacks on some Level 4 bio-labs around the world."

Jane didn't say anything but waited for him to continue.

"I know there are occasional attempts to break into these labs from time to time, but this seems odd to me. The number and the close timing in occurrence."

"What are we talking about?"

"Specifically, four labs over a period of three weeks." He paused for a moment. "That has never happened before as long as I have been monitoring these events."

"Do you think they're related?"

"I can only guess. I just know it's an anomaly and wanted to bring it to your attention."

"I'm aware of the thefts. That intelligence comes across my desk. You know that. It seems that they all have separate issues relating to them."

"I understand. The one in India might be the work of the CPI. It seems they planted a bomb at the nearby prison, which resulted in the escape of around forty prisoners. The authorities think that was a diversion. While the escape was going on, the lab was attacked. The guards were killed, and a bio-hazard was stolen."

"Anthrax."

Fred nodded.

"From what we know," Jane said, "it was not weaponized."

Again, Fred nodded. "But it is an odd coincidence."

"Go on."

"Then there is a lab in Gabon. It appears that a disgruntled employee with credentials, a mid-level technician at least, entered the lab after hours and removed a container of anthrax."

"Do the authorities know who this is?"

"They have a suspect. One of the technicians has disappeared. His family has no idea where he's gone…or why. I looked into all the reports, and the wife is perplexed. According to her he is a good husband and father."

"This anthrax was also not weaponized as I understand it."

"Correct. But there are two more, as you probably know. The theft from the Budapest lab and the one from Saskatoon in Canada."

Jane nodded. "The anthrax from the Budapest lab had been micronized as I understand it."

"That's correct. The authorities link a tech's entry after hours to the theft. The lab has a dual level of security requiring a proper level ID badge as well as a handprint to gain entry. This tech has since disappeared." He looked down at the floor for a moment before continuing. "He apparently had a Chinese girlfriend, a student at the university. She's also disappeared."

Jane gave him a sharp look. "You're sure of this?"

Fred nodded. "He was very open about it, according to friends. She was quite the catch, and they were all a bit jealous, it seems. Now they are both missing."

"What would they want with anthrax? It seems quite a reach that they stole it and then fled to China. The authorities would not want to be associated with such a situation."

"That's just it. No trail of them can be found. I looked through all the travel logs and reservations. Did a running search for them under multiple keywords. Nothing has turned up. They've just disappeared."

"And the Canada lab? The authorities think it's the work of white supremacists, although I didn't think they were much of a force up there."

"They're not. At least judging from their presence on the internet. Just a few small groups that hate the French and don't like how the government bends over backward to accommodate the indigenous population."

"This anthrax wasn't weaponized," Jane said.

"Right. The lab worked with it to find vaccines to protect the beef industry from outbreaks."

Jane leaned back in her chair. "And you think they're related?"

"Right now, only in the timing of their occurrence and the fact that it's the same pathogen." Fred leaned forward towards Jane's desk. "But it is unprecedented from what I can tell."

"Okay. I'll go with unprecedented. How do we make any more of a connection?"

"I asked Warren to contact the NSA, so I can review phone and email traffic to see if anything pops up with some reference to Level 4 labs or anthrax."

Jane looked across the room. "If these are connected, we may be facing an extraordinary level of threat. Right now, everyone is noting these events individually but not putting them together." She turned back to Fred. "I don't think I can sell Henry or his boss on the connection without more evidence. It's possible, but a bit too much of a stretch at this point."

"I don't disagree," Fred said. "But I can't dismiss how unusual this is."

"Keep working on it, and let me know the minute you find something more substantial, something to connect them. Meanwhile, I'll brief Henry."

Fred nodded and got up. He had his orders. This was what he loved. Digging through massive amounts of data, using his computer skills to sift and sort the data until a pattern emerged that otherwise would have remained hidden. It was work that could only be done with the help of high-speed computing but also needed a thoughtful, guiding hand. Fred had his gut feeling about certain situations and, over the years, had found it to be a good guide. It was talking to him now. He would find the connection.

Chapter 12

When the men got to the Illinois farm, they pulled the trucks into the shed. Inside there was a Suburban SUV waiting for them. They carefully unloaded the ballistic cases with the anthrax, placed them in a larger metal container that had been purchased, and put them in the far corner of the shed. The space would be divided between parking for the trucks and an inner room that would be sealed off. There, the men, under Jabbar's leadership, would mill the anthrax into a micronized powder that could easily be sprayed throughout an urban area.

The process was not complicated and didn't require exotic equipment. The Jet company in New Jersey made and marketed a product they called the Rapid Jet Mill. The mill came in various sizes, from small units with a two to four-inch intake used for small batch processing in research to larger ones with intakes up to twelve inches which could process more commercial-sized quantities. There was a healthy market for the mills in the pharmaceutical industry and with the makers of various supplements. Micronizing the product meant it readily blended with other ingredients and could more easily be dissolved in liquids for consumption. The four-inch unit that was ordered easily fit on a tabletop. The challenge was to contain the product so that it didn't infect and kill the ones processing it.

"Now we wait?" Taimoor asked, speaking in Arabic. He was the most senior member of the group.

"Until the processing mill arrives," said Jabbar. "The powder is not in a form we can use. The mill has been ordered. We must ready the space. It is not hard to process, but hard to keep contained."

"Why wasn't this done before we received the anthrax? We should not spend more time than necessary here. We need to strike quickly and then disappear."

"My uncle wanted the anthrax here as quickly as possible. He knows it is not hard to process and that I know how to do it."

Taimoor smiled, but it did not soften the look of disdain on his face; something Jabbar noticed. "And you have done this before?"

Jabbar shook his head. "I have studied the process. As I said. It is not hard. What is difficult is that we must ensure it remains contained, sealed off from the rest of the shed and that we don't contaminate ourselves."

Taimoor shook his head. "All the more reason to have had someone else do this work."

"Taimoor, let us not argue about this. You know my uncle. When he decides something, it is decided." Jabbar paused and looked hard at the older man. "You may contact him if you disagree."

Taimoor's eyes flashed in anger. "You know that's not possible. We can have no contact with our *zaeim*. That is a silly suggestion."

"Then let us do the job we have been sent to do...without discord."

Jabbar tried to soften his voice. He knew he needed Taimoor. The man had the respect of the rest of the team and was needed to carry out the attacks. Jabbar knew his contribution was to carefully plan and coordinate the operation and have an exit plan in place after execution. The country would be in turmoil after three to five days as the cases multiplied and panic set in. They needed to be back across the southern border by then. The irony to Jabbar was that it was easier to enter than to exit the country. But once in Mexico, his uncle's connections to the cartel would provide them with cover and a secure passage back to the Middle-east.

The men spilled out of the shed and went into the house to unpack and claim beds in the four bedrooms. There were enough beds to hold eight people, so two men had to sleep on the floor or on the couch. Jabbar, in the interest of winning favor, chose the couch. Another, Ehsaan, the most junior member, was relegated to a pad on the floor in one of the bedrooms. He also took on the role of the cook.

Two coolers packed with dry ice were brought in. They contained lamb and other meats that would make up the meals. Jabbar wanted to interact as little as possible with the nearby town. He knew their eating habits would draw attention in the Midwest. They could purchase chicken, the western version of yogurt, and goat cheese, along with rice and vegetables. Still, some of their eating habits might raise eyebrows. It was better to be seen as little as possible.

Once unpacked, the men laid out their prayer rugs for Asr, the later afternoon prayer. One of them spent some time orienting towards Mecca. After the prayers, Ehsaan immediately went to work to make up an *Omani Shuwa*, a slow-cooked dish of marinated lamb, along with rice and a large bowl of hummus. The ever-present pita bread was also served.

"Ehsaan," one of the men said with a smile as he dug into the food, "you will make someone a great wife with your cooking."

"Shame on you for speaking such to our companion," another said. "We are blessed that he has the ability and the desire to keep us strong with good food,"

"I just hope we can keep to our diet while we are here," Taimoor said. He turned to Jabbar. "How long will you take to do this work?"

"The mill should arrive within a week. That gives us time to prepare the space. The milling will only take one or two days. But much care must be taken with such a dangerous substance."

"The more dangerous, the better," Taimoor said. "It will kill many *kafir*."

"Death to the infidel," another man said.

After dinner and the evening prayers, the men headed to the rooms to sleep. Jabbar went outside to sit on the porch. He was joined by the older jihadist, Omar. The two men sat in silence, listening to the din of the crickets in the trees. Their clacking came in waves of sound, flowing through the trees as the insects competed for mates. The air was filled with dragonflies performing their amazing feats of aerobatics as they pursued the insects that flew in the gathering dusk. The smell of the hay in the fields blended with the wet from the lake. It was a rich combination of odors, exotic to those accustomed to the sparser aromas of the desert.

"This is a fat land, is it not?" Omar said.

"Yes. Fat and soft."

"Our attack will take them down?"

"My uncle thinks so. I have studied the literature. We can cause nearly half a million casualties and completely disrupt the economy. No one can imagine such an attack. It will go down in history."

Omar sat quietly for a moment as if to contemplate the scene.

"And then we can take over this fat land?"

"And make it our own. We will convert those who remain. Convert them or kill them."

"It is a fair choice. One our prophet often applied in his jihad." He turned to Jabbar. "You must be careful with Taimoor. He has much pride and is unhappy with not being the leader."

"I know. But it is what my uncle insisted."

"I understand. You know the ways of the west. Taimoor does not. He wants to attack outright. He is not a subtle man. Strong, fearless, loyal, but not subtle."

"We must add subtleness as part of our strength. That is how we can do more damage."

"I think I understand. But it is hard for those who fight with the gun and bomb. This seems less ferocious, less a battle."

"But with more casualties."

"Let us hope so."

The two men, one younger and in charge, the other older, wiser, but only able to advise, sat in silence as the evening darkened.

Chapter 13

Fred knocked loudly on Jane's door.

"Come in already, don't break it down," Jane said.

He burst in and rushed to her desk. "You wanted me to connect the dots, the attacks on the lab. I think I've done it."

"Sit down and tell me."

Fred sat down and laid out some papers, one of which held a diagram of sorts, hastily drawn. "The anthrax was stolen from the labs in a three-week span." He pointed to the four marks on his chart. "That occurrence is unusual, but you said you needed more."

Jane nodded.

"Remember the Hungarian tech? He had the Chinese girlfriend. It seemed odd that they would disappear and odder that they would be involved in such a theft. Why would China want to involve itself in that? They have their own labs with quantities of anthrax. Were these two rogue agents trying to sell it on the black market?"

"The authorities think so."

"But we've not gotten any hint of that."

"Agreed."

"Now, I found another connection. Our rich Saudi, Rashid al Din Said, traveled to Beijing a month before these thefts began."

“He is working with the Chinese on their Belt and Road projects. We know that.”

“Yes, but he usually sends his top lieutenants to Beijing to do the negotiating. It seems unusual for him to go personally, especially when no contracts seemed to have been signed.”

“Go on.”

“Then, ten days later, a Chinese official named Zhōu Ming traveled to Saudi Arabia. We think to meet with Rashid, but I can’t confirm that. Zhōu’s quite a murky figure. Connected high up but kept at a distance. He seems to be someone who moves between the central bureaucracy and the outright spy work. More than just a low-level agent.”

“I’ve heard of him. But he’s not someone we keep a close eye on.”

“It was shortly after that meeting that the thefts started to occur.” Fred paused, then added. “And remember, the girlfriend is Chinese.”

Jane gazed at the wall. “They often plant spies in western universities.” She paused for a moment to think while Fred sat upright, eager for her to agree with his conclusions. “It’s still a bit tenuous, but if they’re related and if they’re connected to Rashid, we’ve got a major threat on our hands.”

Fred nodded. “That’s what I feel.”

Jane looked over at him. “Clean up your diagram and get it back to me right away. I’ll take it to Henry.”

Before Jane could meet with Henry, her secure phone rang.

“Jane here,” she said after answering.

“Hello, Jane.” The voice was so familiar.

“Dan. Nice of you to call and not at 3am in the morning.”

"I thought I'd go easy on you this time."

"I assume this is not an emergency since you waited until morning east coast time. Where are you?"

"I'm at home, enjoying a cup of coffee after my lunch. I did my morning bike ride, showered, had breakfast, did some work around the house, and felt bored, so I thought I'd call you. Actually, there is something that has come up that I want to run by you. It may be nothing, but my source is pretty damn good."

"I'm all ears."

"I ran into the old woman in St. Mark's Plaza last week—"

"The Watcher?"

"Yeah. She said something about an attack close to home in the U.S. It involves Rashid and, get this, a Chinese operative. She also said it would involve a deadly pestilence."

There was silence on the line.

"Jane, you there?"

"Of my God! She really said that? You may have just connected the dots on our end."

"What did you uncover?"

"Fred found an anomaly. Four thefts of anthrax from bio-labs around the globe. All within three weeks of each other. He's also uncovered a rather murky Chinese official who visited Saudi Arabia recently."

"That's too many coincidences."

"Agreed. But I needed more to go to Henry and get him to take action. You may have given me the part of the puzzle I need."

"Except that Henry really doesn't know about the Watchers. And I'm not sure he'd put much credence in them or their effect."

"It's tricky, I know. I'd have to bring him up to speed on their history of helping and then convince him they're not just a group of whackos."

"A worldwide group of whackos who seem to get no financial return from their wackiness, seek no publicity, and yet provide important information that proves true when my life is on the line."

"I know. It should be easy to show him. And maybe it will be. But remember, he's old-school. This is something quite different. From the perspective of the Watchers, we're operating on more than a geopolitical level. For them, it's a level of good versus evil on a scale beyond human ambition. I get a sense of a grand struggle that involves reality itself."

Dan was quiet for a moment. "I don't think I'd go that far when you talk with Henry. Just say I have connected with some people who seem to have better-than-normal insights into things going on. They're linked to my connection to Tlayolotl, the Mexican shaman. He knows about him, although he doesn't place much value in him beyond saving me from dying in the desert."

"He might buy into that…enough to not write off your addition to the connections we're finding." Jane paused for a moment. "Did she say anything else?"

"You'll love this. She said I would need to go back to disrupt whatever plot is going on."

"You know we can't do that."

"I told her. She said you would not have any choice."

Jane thought for a moment. "Let me take this into Henry. I'll see if he can't move it up the ladder, and then we'll see what plays out. It wouldn't be unprecedented, but it's dangerous, especially at this time. We're under quite an intense scrutiny. Everyone is trying to lie low, especially our small section."

"You want me to come back?"

"You miss me?"

"Well, there's that, but I want to be available if you need me."

"No, stay where you are. Rest and be ready. You can get here quickly if we need you."

"Okay. Good luck with Henry, and take care of yourself while the hounds are sniffing around the house."

The line went dead. Jane sat in her office for a long time. The Watchers were really never wrong. Sometimes she or Dan misinterpreted what they might say. Sometimes a threat was masked, and they couldn't see it clearly. Then what they had to offer was vague and difficult to work with. But this information gave strength to what Fred had uncovered. Henry needed to be convinced.

She put pen to paper and wrote down Dan's information. She would add it to the diagram Fred had created

.

Chapter 14

It was late on a Thursday evening when George Randall pulled into the dark parking lot just north of Union Station. The lot fronted on First Street, NE. He waited as another car pulled in next to him. A door opened, beckoning George to get in. He sat down in the back seat. Carlos Becerra was sitting next to him. Carlos was a top lieutenant to Alejandro Mendoza. He was the voice of his commander, especially communicating with U.S. nationals regarding Mendoza's business dealings.

This was not Becerra's first visit to the congressman's aide. Carlos and George were the faces of the relationship created between Mendoza and Congressman Greely. They were the surrogates to insulate Greely from any connections to underworld characters.

"We are concerned about the growing negative news surrounding the southern border," Carlos said. "I'm here to learn what your boss is doing to tamp this down."

George was always a bit nervous when meeting with Carlos. The man was smooth, but there was always an undercurrent of potential violence lurking. It was not mitigated by the men that surrounded him. They were clearly dangerous. George always suspected they would kill him at a moment's notice from Carlos. Yet he enjoyed the sense of danger, the rush it brought.

"We're working on this. It's just a passing storm due to recent events."

"You talking about the truck?"

George nodded. The truck was a recent discovery of thirty-four dead bodies in an abandoned tractor-trailer truck, illegals who had crossed the Texas border. For an unknown reason, the driver had abandoned the truck and disappeared with the illegals still locked inside. The Texas heat had done the rest. Conservatives had raised a hue and cry about how inhumane the open border was, allowing the smugglers to mistreat those they were bringing into the country, even after collecting hefty fees from them.

"That was not us. We're trying to eliminate some of those coyotes. It's better run under our control. You know that."

"I do...or at least, I think I do. But this doesn't help. We need to just wait out the storm. My boss has not changed his position. But events like this don't help. You need to get that part under control."

"You are making much money from our efforts. Remember that."

"I do. But it's not worth my political suicide or that of my boss."

"You received a sizeable check last week, did you not?"

"I did."

"That one is for you alone. You get to line your own pocket separate from your boss. For that, I expect you to control him and have him keep the border open."

"Believe me, I'm trying hard. We're working on this." George pointed his finger at the man. "We both need to do our part for this to work. Let your boss know that the sooner he gets his side of the border under control, but smoother things will go on this side."

George risked an escalation. It was better to put the other party on the defensive. That was his instinct.

"And that girl you sent me last week. She was terrible. She was not compliant or clean."

Not only did Carlos pay cartel funds to George, but he also provided the aide with young women. Girls, really, who had been kidnapped by the cartel while being helped across the border. They were put into sex work, ostensibly to pay off their debt, something which never happened. Carlos loaned some of them to George. He understood the man had twisted tastes and indulged them with the women he was given. Carlos had seen the results of George's actions.

"You should be thankful that I offer you this bonus on the side," Carlos said. He indicated he would not be intimidated."

"And another thing," George said. He acted like he had not heard Carlos. "The climate in D.C. is getting more heated. It requires more effort to continue to keep the border open. I think you need to increase my fees for making sure everything goes smoothly on the legislative side."

Carlos looked at him coldly. George worked at not wilting under his dead-eyed stare.

"You think you deserve more money? While we see pushback and more cries to close the border?"

"Those cries are not our fault. And they will die down."

"My friend. You don't get to milk us for larger amounts of money without doing more for us. It doesn't work that way."

"I'm asking because the environment has gotten more difficult. It makes my work, Congressman Greely's work, more dangerous."

"I give you the girls. On top of that, I give you drugs to sell on your own to increase your income. If you want to receive more, you must do more. This talk about things getting hotter doesn't carry any weight. Did you think you would simply collect money from us for a few favors and no risk? It is why we pay you. For the favors and the risk involved."

Carlos gave him a cold smile. "If you want more, then I want more." He stopped and stared at George.

"What do you want?" George asked. He risked opening a can of worms with the question, but it had to be asked.

"I want you to put pressure on the congressman who is attacking the open border using this issue of the dead illegals. I want you to shut him down."

"How do I do that? He's on the other side of the aisle. He won't listen to me."

"That is your problem. You have friends locally, I assume. Friends who can exert pressure. Some well-placed threats could soften his opposition. Work through his aide. You tell me how you can control Greely. Then get to that aide and make sure he understands the need to get his boss to back off."

Carlos indicated the discussion was over.

"I expect to see some change in the talk within a week. Get busy."

George got out, and Carlos drove off. George always felt relief after these conversations. Now he was on the spot, though. He thought about Greely's conversation with Zhōu. It was along the same lines, and that wasn't a coincidence. While George worked the cartel, his boss worked Zhōu, who represented the CCP. They both desired open borders for not only drugs but agents. This desire dovetailed with the administration's policies but was cloaked under the banner of migrant rights and humanitarian principles.

The pressure had increased. George could see where it could get ugly if he and his boss couldn't tamp things down and let the normal, in this case, steady illegal migration over the border, get back in place. Maybe increasing the crackdown on the CIA could be a distraction. Nothing like a spy scandal to turn the public's attention. The press would also love it and be quite helpful in promoting such a distraction. And the congressman Carlos had mentioned? George wondered why Carlos didn't just threaten him himself. *Probably wants to stay off his radar.* He would have to figure out how to do it on his own. He had some local contacts, unsavory men who would do things for him. It would cost him. But if he got this done, he could extract more payouts from Carlos.

† † †

Jane entered Henry's office and sat down.

"You look tired," Henry said. "Getting enough sleep?"

"Not what I would call sound sleep, but enough. It's the pressure of this spotlight we're under. I don't know exactly what to do."

"Like I said, keep your head down."

"But there are challenges, threats. That's why I'm here."

Henry closed the file he had been reading and put it aside. Jane gave him the diagram and proceeded to outline what Fred had uncovered. She emphasized the unprecedented nature of the coincidences.

"That's interesting, but not quite enough to generate action. I'm not sure, in this climate, I can get Roger to act on it."

"There's more. You remember the Mexican shaman?"

Henry nodded.

"He was more than you think he was." Jane went on to chronicle how Dan's connection with Tlayolotl had led to others who had insight into Dan's various missions. Henry listened without comment.

"You believe all this?" He asked after she was done.

"I've seen it in action. How the insights have proven to be correct. How they have helped Dan, even saved his life at times."

"Jane, even if I could swallow this, which is a lot to ask. How in the hell could I get Roger to go for this? To add this to Fred's coincidences and say it's solid intel. We don't do intel on pronouncements of mystics or psychics."

"But you know me. You trust me, don't you?"

"You know I do. That's why I put you in charge of this group."

"Well, I've been operating under the assumption that what these people are saying is accurate, or as accurate as they can be. I haven't been misled yet. And you see the results. They speak for themselves. Dan has terrorists staying awake nights worried about running into this phantom that no one can identify but who can quickly end their life. He's eliminated Rashid's most deadly assassin as well. All without calling any attention to us and the organization. That success has been partly aided by these rather special people."

Henry shook his head. "I might have to consider your estimation of these people to be accurate. But I know Roger won't. Believe me. He's one step further away from the action than I am, and that makes him many steps more skeptical."

Jane gave Henry a sly smile. "Maybe that's why we operate in the black, off the record. Maybe we do that now."

"You're not suggesting—"

"A domestic operation? Heaven forbid! Just that you give me the green light to look into this. You know, even if you could convince Roger, it would be dangerous to turn this over to the FBI. Think of the panic that would ensue if the public got wind of a potential plot to attack multiple sites, probably urban centers, with anthrax.

Henry," she leaned forward over his desk, "the FBI can't keep secrets, you know that. There're too many agents that love to talk to the press, then sit back and watch the shit show that erupts. We have to start the process ourselves, clandestinely."

"You ask a lot. This could cost me my job."

"As much as any of the other of our operations could have."

"But there's more pressure now, more oversight."

"I'll be more careful. You know I can do that."

Henry looked out of his window for a long moment, sighed, and finally nodded. "Go ahead. But keep your head down in the process. And don't let our man, Dan, bust out of the corral and create a shit storm of his own. We don't need that."

Jane beamed Henry a bright smile and stood up. "Will do, boss. You can count on me."

† † †

"How's my favorite boss?" Dan said when he picked up his phone.

"Always looking out for you," Jane replied. "Pack your gear. I'm sending a plane for you."

"You want me back in the states? I don't think I want to go back, even if the Watcher said I would have to. You said yourself it's best to stay away for now."

"I did. But things change, and I need you here."

"Okay, boss. But don't send the plane here to Venice. Send it to Milan. I'll drive there and meet it.

"Always the careful one."

"Always the discreet one. I'll live longer that way."

"I'll schedule the plane to touch down tomorrow late afternoon. And Dan, bring your gear...all of it."

"Are you—"

"We'll talk when you get here."

Jane hung up, and Dan sat back to ponder the many ramifications of their brief conversation. He didn't like any of the conclusions he came to.

Chapter 15

After Wang Li Xiu left Bela's apartment, she walked two blocks and called a cab. The driver took her to the train station. After getting dropped off, she headed to the parking lot, where a Fiat Panda awaited her. She got in and drove to the lab. It was late at night, and the facility was closed. However, Bela's ID card got her into the building. From their pillow talk, Wang Li Xiu had learned the route to follow to successfully navigate the building. The print from his severed hand allowed her to enter when she reached the door to the inner section that housed the dangerous pathogens. Inside, she quickly located the canister containing the anthrax. Carefully removing it from its storage bin, she placed it in a cushioned case with a bulletproof shell and left the building.

From there, she set out for Istanbul. It was a long drive, but she was energized by the night's activities. The morning was breaking when she arrived at the Istanbul International

The airport was located to the northeast of the city, near the Black Sea. She parked in the long-term lot and left the keys under the floor mat with the doors unlocked. Within a week, the car would be stolen.

Next, with a wig and under a different name and identity, she purchased a ticket to New Delhi. From the ticket counter, Wang went to a row of lockers and put the ballistic case in one of them. She would mail the key to a contact in Istanbul when she arrived in India. Once on the plane, she relaxed unsuccessfully as she tried to sleep for the six-hour flight. After landing in India, she changed wigs, took out a different identity, and purchased a direct flight to Beijing. This would be a more extended flight so she could get more rest.

Once aboard, Wang Li Xiu ordered a double whiskey and allowed herself to think about Bela. She smiled, remembering his naiveté as well as his attentiveness. *He did have a good last night*, she thought as she drifted off to sleep. On her arrival in Beijing, she was met by a black car as she exited the terminal. With her inside, the car drove off to a secret location.

Wang Li Xiu would remain unseen until she was needed again. She would spend her time waiting and training, like a sophisticated tool that is kept ready but only brought out to deal with particular problems. When she emerged again, she would be effective; her handlers had no doubt.

† † †

After a long week's wait, which the men used to prepare the milling room, the milling machine finally showed up. It was packed in a large, wooden shipping carton labeled machine repair parts. The men unloaded the carton and took it inside the shed's inner room.

"Now we can get about our business," Taimoor said. "Sitting around is no good. We are warriors for Allah."

His mood only slightly improved with the arrival of the milling machine. He had chafed under the week of waiting and being unable to leave the farm. Jabbar had insisted they not go into the nearby town of Dongola. Part of the way through the week, Jabbar allowed Ehsaan, who had become the cook for the group, to drive into the town for some supplies.

He had gone with a small list of rice, beans, fruit juices, coffee, and tea. His interaction with the clerk in the grocery store was uneventful, but the clerk had much to say when he sat down in the bar with his friends after work. He told them about the exotic Arab living somewhere outside of town and his rather strange grocery list. It was not a great story, but worthy of a free beer for him.

Later one of the men in the bar would mention the new residents to the sheriff, who would mention them to his deputies. The next day the sheriff went over to the real estate office to get the full story on the new residents.

"Far as I know, a corporation purchased the property. They want to use it for corporate retreats." The agent paused for a moment. "You say some Arabs are living out there?"

"At least one. Probably more," the sheriff replied. "Calvin said he purchased more food than one person would consume."

"Beats me. Last time I checked, it wasn't illegal for a corporation to own land in Illinois."

"Hank, don't be smart. Don't you think it's odd to put a corporate retreat way out here? No golf? No fancy restaurants? No nearby airport?"

The agent shrugged his shoulders. "Hell, with all the corporate navel-gazing going on, maybe that's just what they want to get away from. I'll bet within a few months we get an application to put in a private runway so they can fly their people in."

"Ain't enough room to land a jet there."

"Maybe not, but a turboprop could get in and out. It wouldn't surprise me at all."

The inner room inside the shed was insulated behind the aluminum siding that formed the outside wall. Over the insulation, heavy-duty plastic was taped and glued to the studs to create a final inner seal. There was a strong metal door with double seals on the jam. The structure was not up to certifiable bio-hazard safety levels in any measure, but Jabbar was satisfied it would work for their purposes.

They had four Level 4 positive pressure protective suits. These were completely sealed from the outside once a worker was in them. They could be hooked to a compressed air line and operated under positive pressure, regulated by the wearer. There was a one-way valve that vented the suit's air into the room.

The men had built an anteroom where they could get in and out of the suits. From that room, which was also positively pressured and vented into the inner work room, they could exit into the main part of the shed. Before starting the milling process, Jabbar went over the procedures repeatedly for the next two days.

"Jabbar, you waste time," Taimoor said. His voice evidenced his disapproval. "Are you afraid to begin? We could just distribute the anthrax as it is if you are afraid to mill it." Taimoor gave him a vicious smile. "But how will we explain that to your uncle?"

"This mission could go all wrong if we don't follow the proper safety procedures. Do you think they are for children? This material can kill even someone as tough as you." Jabbar always tried to throw Taimoor a compliment, but they didn't seem to help.

"All I know is that we waste time. The longer we are here, the greater chance we can be discovered."

"Relax. No one knows we are here. And if they do, they think we are part of an advance team evaluating the site for a retreat center."

"Some in town know we are here. Ehsaan went shopping. Do you think they don't recognize he's an Arab? Do they think he's from this country? Don't be foolish."

As the two men talked, a sheriff's car pulled up in front of the house.

"Quick," Jabbar said. "Everyone up the stairs. Make sure to take your weapons."

The men quickly exited the main floor, careful not to be seen from the windows. Taimoor stayed behind. Jabbar looked at him.

"If there is trouble, I will end it."

Jabbar shook his head. It was better to not argue at this moment. "Just stay out of sight and don't speak. Let me do the talking."

Jabbar was dressed in western jeans and a T-shirt with running shoes on his feet. Taimoor disapproved of the T-shirt since Saudi dress codes do not allow men to wear short sleeves.

They had argued about this repeatedly, with Jabbar insisting that his form of dress should be considered a disguise rather than a violation of the dress codes. Taimoor was dressed in traditional loose pants hemmed at the ankle with a long-sleeve shirt covering his waist. He wore sandals. The net effect was to telegraph that this person was from the middle-east and somewhat traditional.

Jabbar stepped out with Taimoor, against his orders, immediately following. At this point, with the person getting out of his car, Jabbar could not say anything. He gritted his teeth and gave the visitor a bright smile.

Frank Kline was the county sheriff with his office in Dongola. His work in the county involved little drama, the occasional vandalism, teenage mischief, and rare auto accident. There were a few incidences of drunkenness and wives or girlfriends getting beat up. Usually, the repentant perpetrator reconciled with his female partner after sobering up and promising to stay on the straight and narrow. Thankfully, few of them were serial abusers that had to be dealt with more severely. Frank liked it that way.

What concerned him were new things, new issues that might present new problems that he and his community had never faced before. The farm purchase and rumors about the plans for the one hundred acres were just such a thing. Better to drive out and meet the people so he could better evaluate the potential for problems, and put the more colorful rumors that he knew would emerge to rest.

He stepped out of his three-year-old Explorer and adjusted his equipment belt. Two men emerged from the front door and stood on the porch. He had caught a glimpse of others going up the stairs, past the hall window. The first man was dressed in regular mid-west country clothes and had a large smile on his face. The other man seemed more oddly dressed, foreign, maybe middle-eastern. His face was screwed up in a scowl that had "not welcome" spread all over it.

"Hello, officer," the first man said as Frank approached the porch.

"Howdy. My name's Frank Kline. I'm the sheriff of Union County. I wanted to come by and introduce myself to you and welcome you to our area."

"That's very nice of you, Sheriff," the first man said.

The second just stood there with the scowl still on his face. His eyes bore into Frank with a hint of restrained aggression.

"I understand that a company called Evergreen purchased the property. Do you work for them?"

It looked for a moment as if the second man was going to speak, but the first one put his hand on the man's arm.

"We do. We're here to create a contextual plan for how to develop the property."

"The word is that you're going to set up a corporate retreat. That correct?"

"The rumors are true. However, we don't want to alarm the local residents, so we're keeping a low profile. This is only the first stage of planning."

Frank chuckled. "Yeah, they get easily alarmed. Most often, it's by new things. You should have seen the uproar when the state widened the main road in and out of town. You would have thought it was going to bring an invasion of tourists." He looked around the fields. "Not sure what tourists would see here in our county. More likely, the few people interested in Southern Illinois visit Cape Girardeau or Cairo. Both of them are on the river and offer tourist activities."

"That's one of the side possibilities we considered. But the main point is to make this a true retreat with few distractions."

"Well, you can certainly get that here. How long are *you* here for? I assume you're just visiting since you said you were the early planning team."

"We have a week or two if we need it. Then you'll find the farm mostly idle with no visitors until the planning advances."

Frank nodded.

"So, is there a problem with us being here? Being outsiders?"

The man with the scowl finally spoke up. Frank noticed the first man turn with a shocked and angry look but said nothing.

"No. We don't have problems with outsiders, although, as I said, it can upset some people too set in their ways."

"So, do you stop by to say hello and check out every new arrival? Or is it just people who might look different?"

"Don't pay any attention to my friend here. He is still smarting from some insults he received before we got here." The first man stared hard at his partner. "I have told him not all Americans are like that."

"We certainly aren't."

Frank paused, then added, "And I'm not here to check you out. More to welcome you."

"We appreciate that gesture," the first man said.

"And where are you from, I might ask, since you indicated your friend got insulted."

"Actually, Evergreen is a truly international company. Many of us are from the U.S., others from Europe, and some from the Middle East and the far east. We have a large contingent of employees from India. It's a very good labor market."

Frank nodded. "Well, I'm glad to hear you employ Americans as well."

He looked around for a moment, noticing the outbuildings. There seemed to be new construction around the vehicle shed, but Frank figured that with the attitude of the second man, he didn't want to make any comments.

"I guess I'll be going. What is your name, if I might ask?"

"Joseph Smith," Jabbar said using his alias.

"Just like the founder of the Mormons. That's a famous name in the U.S. You all have a good day. It's nice to meet you."

He turned and climbed back into his SUV. As he drove down the long drive, he could see the first man, Joseph, talking in an animated manner to the second man. They seemed to be arguing.

Joseph Smith. An alias if I ever heard one.

He got back to his office and immediately went on the internet. His secretary, Mary, poked her head into the room to announce she was leaving for lunch.

"Before you head home, would you go next door and get me a burger and fries?"

"You too busy to go?"

"I've got something to look up, and I want to stay at it. Be a dear, would you? He reached into his pocket and pulled out a ten-dollar bill."

Mary sighed. "Okay." She grabbed the money and left.

"Let's see what we can find out about Evergreen," Frank said to himself.

Chapter 16

Dan's plane landed at Dulles Airport's general aviation terminal. An SUV was waiting for him as he disembarked. The driver helped carry a rectangular hard case. A piece of luggage containing his favorite weapons, all broken down and carefully packed away.

As per Jane's instructions, he was driven to the Rosslyn section of Arlington in Virginia, just across the Potomac River from Washington, D.C. where Jane had an apartment. Even with Henry's reluctant approval, Jane knew it was best to keep everyone above her in the dark from this point forward.

An hour after Dan arrived, he had showered and was dozing following a sandwich and beer when he heard the door open. His instincts immediately kicked in, and he went from sleeping to high alert as he stood, ready for action, and watched the door. Jane came through and carefully locked it behind her.

"You look ready to attack," she said as she turned to him.

"Habit. Helps keep me alive."

He walked over to her, and they embraced.

"It is so good to see you again," Jane said as she nuzzled against him. "Especially not banged up or injured."

"Take a good look. This is the best you'll see. It may be all downhill from here."

She stepped back from his embrace and slapped his chest.

"I doubt that, big boy. I expect many more years of seeing your best."

Dan shook his head. "You set a high bar...but I'll try to live up to it."

They walked into the living room and sat on the couch.

"Now, why did you call me back? And why did I have to come so quickly?"

Jane got up and went into the kitchen. The apartment was an open floor plan, so the kitchen was one end of the living room, separated by a dining table. She poured two glasses of wine and came back to the couch.

"Long story?" Dan asked as he took the glass from her.

Jane went over the events starting with Fred's anomalies and what Warren had found out about Rashid's visit to Beijing and Zhōu's visit to Saudi Arabia. When she was done, Dan didn't speak. He stared across the room as if thinking hard.

"Your thoughts?" Jane asked. "Tell me if you think I'm being paranoid or heading off on a dead end."

Dan shook his head. "I don't think either of those things. We've operated on less than this, even though it's circumstantial." He paused for a moment. "How do you see me fitting in? This is more investigative at this point."

"With a possible need for extraordinary speed and action. If a multiple-city attack is in the offing, we don't know how soon it will take place."

"Agreed. But we need more info in order to know where to start. The terrorists could be anywhere, and we can't wait until they attack. It'll be too late. If the anthrax is weaponized—micronized, it will probably be released as an aerosol. That could be done in so many ways. Hell, they could have a sacrificial jihadist just sit in an airline terminal next to an HVAC vent and slowly let it drift out of a container. No one would notice, and hundreds would get infected, some of them to fly off to, who knows where?"

Jane repeated the alarming statistics from Homeland Defense. A kilogram of anthrax released in a big city could kill a hundred thousand people. Multiply that by four or five cities, and you have a significant breakdown in the economy. The devastation would go way beyond the actual casualties, although those would be horrendous.

"I get it," Dan said. "But we still need to know more."

He got up and began to pace the room while Jane watched and waited. She had brought him back to the U.S. in order to make use of his tactical knowledge as well as his investigative abilities. Dan had come to her attention years ago when he was seeking revenge on the mafia for the killing of his pregnant wife in Brooklyn. He had shown himself to be not only an effective sniper and assassin, but someone able to ferret out the mob's operations and disrupt them. He had not only wanted to take down the ones directly responsible for Rita's death but cause severe disruption to the mob's income stream. For them, it was all about the money, after all.

"Have Fred and Warren find out everything they can about Zhōu, starting with anyone he might meet with here in the U.S.? You say some of the stolen anthrax was not yet weaponized, so it will have to be processed."

"Right. They'll need to mill it in order to micronize it."

"Check all the operations capable of doing that, starting in the U.S."

"They could have had that done overseas."

"True, but we'll start here. Could they do it themselves?"

"Yes. The procedure's not hard. It doesn't take any highly specialized equipment. It's just they would need to create a safe environment. If any of the anthrax got loose, something quite possible, it would kill those working with it."

"We have to assume they might try. Have the guys check all the sources for that kind of equipment and if any was sold recently."

"With a small amount, they wouldn't need a large production mill."

"That'll help narrow down the search."

Jane got up and made the two phone calls. The two talked further into the evening when Jane finally suggested they take a break for something to eat. They walked three blocks to Sfoglina, an Italian restaurant where they both had a seafood special with mussels, calamari, lobster sauce, and squid ink pasta. They finished the meal with tiramisu and coffee. On the walk back, Jane slipped her hand into Dan's.

He gently closed his grip. It was nice to have someone to hold hands with. Still, he could not relax. His eyes kept up a constant scan for threats. He could feel her relax as they walked along, bumping against him with gentle pressure as they swayed. He enjoyed the sense of security she expressed with him, her sense of closeness. He realized that, even though he liked the sensation, his world experience had so infused his life that he could not stop looking out for possible danger points. It had become second nature. Jane seemed to have lost some of that instinct in the years since she had retired from fieldwork. Dan hoped she understood that those same instincts still were present in him in a powerful way.

He smiled. She would understand. She knew his world. That was what gave their relationship a chance, unlike the others.

When they were back at the apartment, the two sat on the couch. Jane cradled a cup of herb tea while Dan helped himself to a large glass of water.

"Why not have the FBI work on this problem?" he asked.

"Too many leaks come from them. Someone over there will think of the political angles and leak the threat to the New York Times. If it helps the current administration, you can bet there'll be people on the inside looking to leak anything."

"They've become that political?"

Jane nodded. "Even Henry agrees that we can't risk setting off a panic. That's how I got him to let you come back.

"He actually said that?"

Jane hesitated for a moment. "No, but he didn't tell me not to." She continued, "Our small group is going to dig into this and find out what's going on. I think Henry plans to bring the FBI in when we know more."

"If we find out in time."

"That's the danger. But that's the same even if the FBI were in on the investigation."

"Except that they bring more resources into play."

"I have a lot of faith in Fred and Warren."

Dan thought for a moment. "What about Roland and Marcus. Can we bring them into this if needed?"

Roland and Marcus were two ex-Delta Force soldiers that Jane had recruited. They had worked with Dan on previous missions all over the globe, and a special warrior bond had developed between the three men.

"Do you think you'll need them?"

Dan shrugged. "Who knows? But if it's multiple cities, that means a lot of people, and we may need more than me...one guy."

"One very effective guy."

"Flattery will get you everywhere, my dear." Dan raised his glass to her. "Let's table this for the night. I think we have some other things to catch up on."

Jane gave him a sly smile. “I was hoping you would get around to that. A girl likes to be asked, not always doing the asking.

Chapter 17

As Frank drove away, Jabbar turned to Taimoor and jammed a finger into his chest. "You just can't keep quiet!" He spoke with a barely controlled fury. "That is all I asked of you. Yet you had to say something. You had to try to poke the man in the eye. Now he is thinking about us rather than dismissing us."

"He is a kafir. Not worth us worrying about."

"A kafir who can unravel our plans. We still have to grind and secure the spores before we set out. And we want to use this farm as our base in between the attacks. You may have jeopardized that part of the plan."

Taimoor turned to go inside. Jabbar followed, still angry. He caught up with him when they were inside and grabbed the older man, pulling him around.

"Do not turn from me while I am talking to you."

Taimoor gave him a furious look and shoved him backward. "Do not touch me. I am not one of your young, impressionable followers."

Jabbar came at him swinging his right arm to smack him in the face. Taimoor caught his arm with his left hand and, with his right, drove a blow into Jabbar's side. Jabbar stumbled back in shock as the other men descended on the two. They grabbed each of them and kept them apart.

"You are disobedient! You do not follow my directions and endanger the mission," Jabbar shouted.

"You are foolish and too accommodating. I am a seasoned warrior for Allah. Remember that. I have been tested many times in the field of battle. You do not value my experience, and *that* puts us in danger."

Omar, the most senior of the jihadists, came between the two men. "We must not fight. That is what the enemy would wish. We need both of your skills. But sometimes, one must hold sway over the other. Make peace with one another. We have a common enemy."

Jabbar looked at Taimoor, who scowled and turned away.

Work on the room continued as the men tested the milling machine with benign powders. They also began working on the two box trucks, modifying them so the micronized powder could be released by someone inside and flow out of the top. They tested the room by releasing some chili powder that they had ground into a fine dust. It was not micronized, but it was the best they could do. Jabbar didn't want to contaminate the mill with a spice that might contaminate the anthrax, allowing it to be discovered when it was released. He pronounced the test a success as they sniffed the air exiting the HEPA filters that vented the positively pressured room. There was no discernable scent of the sharp spice.

† † †

Back at his office, Frank had finished his lunch and sat back from the computer monitor. He had found the Evergreen company. It had a website, but as he worked his way around it, he could not, for the life of him, figure out what exactly they did. They didn't manufacture anything but seemed to perform some vaguely described consulting for various companies, most of which Frank didn't recognize. He couldn't tell how many employees they had, and he couldn't tell exactly where the main offices were located; they seemed to be all over.

He did get an email address and sent them a message asking if they were putting in a retreat center in the U.S. There was no phone number. He finally closed off the search with an unsatisfied feeling. Something didn't add up. Maybe he could come up with another reason to go out there and inquire how to reach the home office. He'd have to be careful. With the attitude of the other man he had encountered, he didn't want to get everyone's skivvies in a bunch.

† † †

Two days after being assigned their task, Fred and Warren entered Jane's office.

"Got something for you," Fred announced with an air of importance. "Seems like five small mills were purchased in the last two months. All from a company called Jet Grinding Technologies in New Jersey. We're tracking them down as we speak." He smiled like someone who had correctly guessed the number of candy balls in the glass jar.

"Only one source?" Jane asked.

Fred nodded. "There're others, but they mostly make production-sized machines. None of them have sold anything small like the terrorists would use in the time frame I'm searching."

"Can you find out where they were sent? I can't send an agent around to question the company. We're not supposed to be doing any sleuthing, and you know we have to leave the FBI out of it."

"We'll work on that." Fred looked over at his partner. "If Warren can hack into their system."

"I'll have the info for you this evening. Just let me have the dates."

"They're only approximate."

"Better than nothing."

Fred looked at his boss. "What are you going to do when we find out where these mills went? Do you think they're really going to grind the spores here in the U.S.?"

"I'm not sure of anything. But we need a thread to start pulling to see what might unravel. My sense is we don't have much time."

That evening, Warren sent Jane a text with the addresses of the five mill purchasers. Three of them were universities, and two were private research firms. They needed to be checked out first. One of the two was in California, the other in Illinois.

The firm in California, Pharma Testing Lab, had contracts with Eli Lilly. The other firm, Micronized Technologies, was associated with a company named Evergreen.

"Check this out," Jane said to Dan as they relaxed on her couch. "We tracked down companies that purchased small milling machines. The ones that can micronize powders—or spores, in this case. Three went to universities, so they're at the bottom of the priority list. Of the other two, one is contracted to Lilly, the pharmaceutical company. The other is connected to a company called Evergreen. I don't know who this is, but we need to check it out. It could be a front."

"You know all this sleuthing doesn't really involve me. Fred and Warren are quite adequate for this work. I'm getting bored already. We're worried about an impending catastrophic attack, and all I can do is sit here. What the hell are you expecting me to do?"

Jane gave him a slightly exasperated look. She could feel it on her face. "You being here makes it easier to put you into action. Once we find who the terrorists are, you go take them out and stop this."

Dan gave her a wry smile. "I'm the gun in your holster."

Jane thought about that for a moment. "That's about right."

Dan got up to grab a beer from the fridge. "Well, at least I know where I stand."

When he came back to the couch, he had a serious look on his face.

"I just want to get something straight. I work alone or with a small team. The point is deniability. I get that. But here, in the U.S., that's going to be the plan in spades, is it not? If the shit hits the fan, everyone, and I mean you, Henry, and the others, will have no knowledge of me." He paused for a moment as Jane gave him a wary look. "And I'll have to leave no trace of communication back about this operation. It'll be radio silence all the way. I'll be totally on my own. Have I got that correct?"

"You make it sound worse than it is. You always work with a degree of separation."

"Not here. Not to the level I think is going to be happening." He sat down. "I don't resent this. It's just that I need to know the ground rules for the game at hand. I'll live longer that way. If I'm to be a shadow, non-existent, with no backup, then I need to know that ahead of time."

Jane sighed. Her face looked sad. "I think you have things about right. But I want you to know that I will stand up for you no matter what happens."

"Jane, don't be foolish. If things go sideways, you can't help me. You can only help bring down Henry and the others. And that will include Roland and Marcus as well as Fred and Warren." Dan shook his head. "No, you have to think about denying all knowledge. Otherwise, everyone goes down. You would provide a link to them, and you can't do that.

"Oh, Dan," she sighed, "I *don't* want to put you in this situation."

"But you did. Too much is on the line. I get that. It's okay. I can take care of myself."

He grabbed her hand and led her into the bedroom, hoping they could shut out the world and its complications for the night.

Chapter 18

After some digging, Warren found that the Jet mill sold to Evergreen had been delivered to a courier company in New Jersey. He forwarded the address to Jane, who then left her office to meet Dan.

"I've got the first hard lead for you to follow," Jane told Dan when she returned to the apartment.

"Good. I don't think I can sit around here much longer. Even going over Key Bridge and running on the canal towpath doesn't relieve the boredom when I spend the rest of the day couped up here."

"Well, now you can head out." She gave Dan the address where the mill was sent. "Go there, and find out where they delivered it. That might lead us to the terrorists."

"Assuming they bought the mill." Dan thought for a moment. "I won't have any authority to force them to give me any information."

"I know that. Warren tried to find out, but there seems to be no link to the routes of the couriers and what's delivered. The company seems to have that part of their system offline in a different repository, either manual or a stand-alone computer."

"The safest kind. No connection to the internet. Non-hackable, especially when it's shut off. So, I'll operate as I see fit. Henry won't mind if feathers are ruffled?"

Jane smiled. “I promised you wouldn’t do too much upsetting of things, but this won’t register or be linked back to you or us.”

“I’ll pack some gear and head out.”

“Are you going to attempt a break-in?”

“Probably talk to some of the staff first. See if I can persuade them to give me some information.”

They ate an early dinner together. After, Dan and Jane embraced. He had rented a car under his Victor James alias. Leaving Jane’s apartment in Rosslyn, Dan took the Metro out to Reston, Virginia, to the end of the line that would eventually extend to Dulles Airport. From Reston, he ordered an Uber ride to the airport. After getting dropped off at the terminal, instead of going inside, Dan, with his gear bag, took a shuttle to the rental car facilities. There he picked up one he had earlier reserved from his burner phone. That phone was now retired and another put in place to be used in the very rare exception that he needed to contact Jane. Contact with her wouldn’t be done if things got out of control, but only if he found information that she needed or if he needed more from Fred or Warren. In the case of extraordinary action, Dan would be on his own.

Once in the car, he settled in for the five-hour drive up the I95 corridor. He had rented an electronic pass device that charged the tolls to his rental account. When he reached Metuchen, where the courier service was based, Dan found a motel and shut down for the night.

The next day, he set out early to reconnoiter the operation. He was in place with a view of the main office entrance at 7 am. The company was run out of a block and metal building in an industrial park. There was an office up front and roll doors along one side, one at loading dock height, the rest at ground height. Two box trucks were parked along the side of the building. Drivers started arriving soon after Dan. They went around to the side where the trucks were parked and gathered to talk and drink their coffee while waiting for the doors to open. Around 8 am, office workers began arriving. Dan watched where they parked, assuming the more senior staff would be parking closer to the entrance. There was always a pecking order to such things.

A man, probably in his mid-forties, arrived around 8:30 and parked up close. He was the only male that wore a tie along with his dress shirt. *Probably a supervisor.* Dan noted his car. He would pay him a visit after work today. After keeping watch for another hour, Dan drove away to find a suitable place to intercept the employee. He shared Jane's concern that they didn't have much time, so he couldn't invest in another day to surveil the man's home and talk to him there. Besides, that could involve a family, and Dan didn't need that complication. Better to grab him near work, convince him to help, get the address, and get the hell out of there.

It was 6:30 in the evening when the man Dan had targeted walked out of the building. He had put in a long day. Dan pulled out and drove down the street. He would pull his car away from the curb to block the road. He had picked a spot where a tractor-trailer truck was parked. On the other side of the road were some parked cars, essentially creating a nearly single-file passage through the gap.

Dan sat in his car, watching his side mirror. When the car came into view, he pulled out at the last minute as if making an unsuccessful U-turn. The driver stopped with a squeal of the tires. He honked his horn.

Dan got out and walked quickly to the man's car. The angry look on the driver's face turned to one more wary as

Dan strode up to the driver's door. The man pressed the lock button and looked up at Dan. Without a word, Dan pulled his Sig Sauer from its holster in the small of his back. He pointed it at the man and motioned for him to open the window.

"I didn't mean to upset you by honking. I'm sorry," the man said after cracking the window open. Dan could see the fear on his face and hear it in his voice.

"I'm not going to hurt you if you do as I say. Pull your car over to the curb."

The man hesitated.

"Now!" Dan's voice carried a threat along with his command.

The man backed up and pulled to the curb.

"Now get out and walk over to my car."

The two walked to Dan's car. With the man inside, Dan backed it up and parked it along the curb. Then he motioned for the man to get out, and they walked back to his car. Dan got in and had the man drive off. The whole incident took two minutes, leaving behind an anonymous vehicle parked in front of the tractor-trailer truck.

"What do you want?" the man asked.

Dan didn't answer but directed him to turn left. He had already picked out a dead-end road that led to a warehouse construction project that had been abandoned, probably due to the developer running out of money. There was a For Sale sign now posted in front of the property. Dan directed the man to drive around to the back of the building, where they were out of sight and alone.

"I haven't done anything," the man said in a timorous voice. "I don't owe anyone money. What did you grab me for?"

"What's your name?"

"Tom."

“Tom, I need some information from you.”

“I don’t know you. What information do I have that you could want?”

“Your courier service. You delivered a milling machine. It came from Jet Grinding Technologies. I need to know where you delivered it.”

“That’s confidential information. I can’t reveal that.”

Dan almost smiled. Here the man was, unarmed, with a gun-wielding stranger who might, for all he knew, kill him on the spot. And he claimed confidentiality.

“I don’t have much time to convince you, so let me say this. We are going to go back to your office. You will find the delivery records. I know they’re kept offline, but they’ll be in the office somewhere. You’ll get me that address, and that will be the end of it. Your breaking confidentiality will never come to light. The people who ordered that equipment will never do business with your company again. Whether or not you give me the address.”

Dan paused for a moment.

“I’m making it simple for you, Tom. The address. This evening. And you can go home. You’ll never see me again. Try to refuse, and I’ll hurt you...really bad. There is too much at stake to worry about how you feel. You *will* tell me in the end.”

He stared at Tom as the man digested what he had just said.

“What if I can’t find it?”

“That will be bad for you. But I think you’ll be able to do it.”

“There’re people in the building. Even after hours. We do business twenty-four hours a day.”

“I understand. We’ll just walk in together. I’m guessing you don’t have to answer to the night shift about your coming and going.”

They drove back to the building.

Chapter 19

It took the manager a half hour to find the record for the milling machine. It showed a delivery to a second courier company in St. Louis. Dan almost ground his teeth in frustration. It would take another day or two to track down where the mill went from that point. It was looking more and more certain that this piece of equipment was going to be involved in a terrorist operation.

The two men left the offices and got into the manager's car.

"Now we're done, and you'll never see me again." Dan paused for a moment. "Unless you talk to this other courier company, or unless you talk to the police. Then you'll see me, and it won't be good for you. Do you understand?"

The man nodded.

"Say it."

"I understand."

"Good. Now drive me to my car and go home."

When he was back at the rental car, Dan immediately departed. It would be a long drive to St. Louis, and he didn't have much time to waste. After getting on I 287 north and safe from any possible police pursuit, Dan called Marcus.

"What's up, *amigo*?" Marcus asked when he picked up the call.

"I've got a mission assigned to me. I can't contact Jane, and I can use your help. You and Roland."

"Going around Jane's back, are you? That's no way to start off a relationship."

"Never mind my relationship. I don't remember you being a paragon of human relations."

Marcus chuckled. "And you need both of us?"

"You never know. Not sure exactly what I'm up against."

"Okay, where do we fly? And can we get one of the company's private jets? I really like that way of traveling. When I hit the lottery, that's the first thing I'm gonna do, lease a private jet."

"Don't hold your breath. And, no, you're going to have to go commercial. Call Jane. We have a safe house in St. Louis. Tell her to ship what you need to it and give you the address. Don't tell her you're with me. She needs to be left in the dark."

"Jesus. Are you operating domestically?"

"Something like that."

"Jane knows?"

"Yes, but no one else. And I have to keep her at arm's length throughout the op."

"We're on our own, then...completely."

"That's about it, *compadre*. We've been there, but never this close to home."

"When do you want us there?"

"As soon as possible. I'm on my way by car. I'll drive straight through if I can."

† † †

It was the fifth day of testimony for the hearings into CIA activities by the House Permanent Select Committee on Intelligence. Today, Roger Abrams, the man below Garrett Easton, would be the major figure testifying. There were other minor players, some retired CIA agents who hinted at dark things and then invoked their confidentiality agreements with their former employer in order to not have to say much. They were and would continue to be a frustration for Congressman Greely. But Abrams...Greely felt that a lot of pressure could be put on him, and he guessed Roger was closer to the action. However, Roger proved to be an adroit witness, able to not let himself be pinned down.

"Are you running any so-called black operations? Activities that are hidden and buried inside your budgets to avoid congressional oversight?" Greely tried to bore straight into the heart of the matter after the committee's opening statements and Roger's dancing around some softer questions by other committee members.

"We run various levels of operations. In my section, we do what is called PSYOPS, where we send out confusing information to our adversaries to keep them off balance. Most of our work, though, is to uncover threats to our country."

"So, you *do* run active operations, not just what I would call 'defensive' operations, looking for threats."

"As I said. There are certain circumstances where we see threats emerge in third-party countries. Where other, more powerful countries are trying to subvert our influence or gain influence over another country; to turn them away from us. It's a bit like a chess match."

"And it involves action on your part."

"It often involves spreading certain information around that undermines the ones trying to turn opinion against the U.S."

"Do you ever authorize the use of deadly force? Do you ever authorize strikes against perceived enemies?"

"Do you mean like drone strikes against terrorists? That's authorized by the military and the president. We only provide the information when needed to make such decisions."

And so it went, back and forth; for the next hour until breaking for lunch. All Greely's fellow politicians, the ones from his party, took their shot at Abrams, but they couldn't shake him. At the end of the session, Greely finally got Abrams to state that he had no direct knowledge of any group that engaged in direct, lethal action against the country's enemies. It was short of an under-oath, direct denial, but it was the best he could do.

Back at headquarters, Roger tried to relax. Garrett came by to inquire about how it went. Roger could see Garrett wanted to know but didn't want to spend much time around him. He understood. Even a physical association could come back to haunt him. He was "unclean".

When Garrett left, Roger headed down to Henry's office. It was not in the basement, not hidden away like Jane's. Still, it was not as well located or plush as Roger's. There was a definite pecking order to office size and location at CIA headquarters.

"How did it go? Was it a rough day?" Henry asked when Roger poked his head in.

"Yeah, but it's over. Greely couldn't hook his claws into anything solid. I gave him soft mush. Things that the media can't do much with to stir up the public. If the media can't get the public baying for our hides, we'll weather the storm. We should probably stay away from each other. We don't want them to dig into this link. I just wanted to let you know. We've gotten through the first part of this in pretty good shape. Without any hard data emerging, I don't know how much longer Greely can keep this going."

"Pretty soon, voices will come out hinting he should quit the investigation," Henry said.

"And if he doesn't have anything solid, the media will stop pounding the issue, and the public will have moved on."

"Time is on our side?"

"We hope."

Roger left, and Henry sat there thinking about the permission he had given Jane. He would not inquire about it and didn't want it brought up. *I hope Dan doesn't turn this job into a shit show and give Greely something to re-energize his attack*. He wondered, again, why he had given Jane the green light. And then he remembered the stakes...they were too high to not take action, even if it was only precautionary, which is what he hoped.

Chapter 20

Frank Kline sat back and thought about his situation. The facts didn't look like they added up to an innocent story, but he didn't know what else it could be. The men weren't Americans or even Westerners. Even the guy who spoke to him. He was glib, easy to talk to, with an engaging smile, but he used an obvious alias, one no American would select. The other guy, the one with a chip on his shoulder? He was definitely middle-eastern. And he definitely didn't like Americans. And the Evergreen company? It was a mushy wall of corporate speak with nothing solid to it. Yet, what else could be going on?

Southwest Illinois was not the place to set up a smuggling operation or any criminal enterprise. Too many people set in their ways, inquisitive, and wary of strangers. No, strangers stood out. Strangers like these, which is why Frank paid them a visit. He smiled at the irony. In one sense, the angry man was correct. It was because they were different that Frank paid them a visit. Had it been someone like the rest of the people in this part of the country, no one would have talked about it, and Frank wouldn't have felt the need to go out there.

But he did. And things didn't look any better to him after that. He scratched his head. *What could be going on*?

His sixth sense told him it was important for him to find out.

Out at the farm, the tests had gone as well as hoped. Whether or not they indicated the system they set up in the shed was safe remained to be seen. Jabbar knew they were operating in an imperfect environment. And imperfection meant the possibility of contamination and death to some of his team if the micronized spores got loose while being milled.

He ordered the men to start modifying the box trucks. They were to install a roof vent with a fan to disperse the powder. The powder would be held in a bag upstream of the fan. The whole structure would be sealed from the rest of the cargo box with a pair of gloved hand inserts so the operator could reach inside and open the container of micronized anthrax powder. The powder would be poured into a pan. Once poured out, the fan would be turned on to suck the powder out through the roof vent. An air intake with a one-way valve provided airflow into the system. It was simple and, Jabbar hoped, effective at both dispersing the powder and keeping the men inside the truck's cargo area safe.

Taimoor called for starting the milling process. He saw Jabbar's delay as a sign of weakness and insecurity. Taimoor didn't worry whether any fighters got killed in the process of milling the spores; that was part of the price to pay in the fight. What concerned him was any delay that could compromise the plans.

"We cannot continue to wait. It is time. If there is a problem, so be it. It is the will of Allah. But we must not delay. The powder must be ready when the trucks are ready."

Jabbar had to acquiesce to his demands. Two men had been chosen to do the milling. They had practiced with the machine using flour and cornmeal. Now the equipment was cleaned and waiting in the sealed room.

When the test day came, the men assembled in the shed. Work on the trucks stopped as everyone wanted to watch the test. While they were assembled, the men heard the sound of a tractor in a nearby field. They all looked to Jabbar.

"That is too close. It must be in one of our fields," Taimoor said.

Without a word, Jabbar went to the shed door and looked out. In the field to the right of the long gravel drive, he saw a man driving a tractor with a rotary mower attached. He was cutting the tall grass in straight rows from end to end.

"What is that *kafir* doing in our fields?" Taimoor asked as he stepped out behind Jabbar.

Jabbar turned and motioned for the other men to stay inside. At this point, no one knew how many men were at the farm, and Jabbar wanted to maintain that concealment for as long as possible.

"I do not know. I will go down to talk to him." He turned to Taimoor. "You stay here."

"No. If there is trouble, I need to be there to end it."

"Taimoor," Jabbar said, turning to the older man, "you are the cause of trouble. I can handle this without you."

"And if there is trouble? How will I explain myself to your uncle?"

Jabbar shook his head. Taimoor was stubborn and not going to relent. The man would not let him or anyone confront the intruder alone.

"Just please hold your tongue. Let me speak. This is what I'm here to do. Talk smoothly and misdirect these unbelievers."

Taimoor stared back at Jabbar and barely gave him a nod.

They walked out to speak with the man, waiting for him to come back to them as he mowed the grass in neat rows. When he was abreast of the two men, Jabbar waved at him to stop.

The man idled the tractor and opened the cab.

"What can I do for you?"

"Why are you working in our fields?" Jabbar asked.

"I'm cutting the grass to make hay."

"You can't do that without our permission."

"The owner gave me permission."

"We represent the owners. They recently purchased the farm. And we are going to use it for something other than farming."

"That's fine. But I have an agreement with the previous owner. I paid for the seed, planted it, and now I'm preparing it. I cut it, ted it, rake it, and then bale it. After that, we can discuss whether or not my agreement is valid."

"No, that won't work," Jabbar said.

The man looked down from his tractor and smiled. "I appreciate you may not want to continue with the agreement, but it's valid, and I made an investment in these fields. Both money and time. It don't work for me to be cut off from recouping that investment."

Jabbar shook his head. "You must stop. We can talk about this later, but you have to stop now and leave."

"That ain't right. I'm trying to explain. You may be the new owners, but you're stuck with my contract. And that runs through the baling and me transporting the hay back to my farm."

Taimoor stepped forward. He gave the farmer an angry look and opened his shirt to show him his pistol stuck in his pants.

"You will obey my friend here. We can talk about this later, but you go now. Do not make things worse for you."

The man looked startled at the presence of the weapon. “The grass can’t wait. It has to be cut and then tedded at the right time to have the proper nutrients.”

“You go now, or there will be big trouble for you,” Taimoor said.

“We can pay you for your investment and trouble,” Jabbar added, trying to soften Taimoor’s threat. “We can do that later.”

“Go. Now,” Taimoor said again, stepping forward.

The farmer looked at both men. “Can I finish cutting at least?”

“No!” Taimoor said in a loud voice before Jabbar could suggest any compromise.

The man looked at Jabbar, who didn’t offer any help. With a muffled obscenity, he closed the tractor door, turned the machine around, and trundled off through the field to the gate and down the drive.

“You must be firm, my young friend. That is the only way to deal with these unbelievers.”

Jabbar looked at the older man with a mixture of anger and incredulity on his face. “You may have stirred up the hornet’s nest this time. I am afraid he will take his tale to the authorities. They may be coming to visit us.”

“Then let us not wait, but get back to the milling.”

The two men turned to go back to the shed.

When they returned to the shed, Jabbar motioned to Amir and Yakub, the two men chosen to do the milling. They entered the anti-chamber and put on their hazmat suits. There were coiled air hoses attached to the suits. After they entered the milling space, the hoses were plugged into a compressed air socket built into the interior wall. A compressor outside the structure was plumbed into the wall socket to provide positive air pressure inside the suits. A regulator on the compressor ensured that not too much pressure was sent to the suits.

Once in the interior room and plugged in, Yakub retrieved a canister from its holding case and took it over to the mill.

The pressure inside the mill was created by compressed nitrogen fed into the venturi chamber at supersonic speeds, creating a spiral movement of particles where they would collide with one another, each collision reducing their size. Centrifugal force directed the large, heavier particles outward to continue being smashed against each other, while the smaller, micronized particles migrated to the center, where they exited with the exhaust gas from the compressed nitrogen. After the particles had been separated from this gas, it was carefully filtered before being released.

The end product was collected in a reinforced, flexible plastic bag. It was impenetrable. Nothing could seep into or out of the material. The opening at the top, where it connected to the machine, had a sealed cap that would be installed after disengaging the bag from the mill.

The five canisters would all be milled since the men could not distinguish between the micronized and non-micronized powders. After milling, the powder would be put into two separate bags, which would be secured inside the delivery chamber in the trucks. These would be used to attack the four cities selected by Rashid: Washington, D.C., New York, Chicago, and Los Angeles. Each truck would travel to two of the cities once they left the farm.

A microscope on the table would allow Amir to examine the first test of the actual spores to see if they had achieved a proper level of micronization. The two men had worked with the flour samples, so the feed rate and pressure were set to the levels Jabbar guessed would be correct. A final check would determine if this was accurate.

Yakub appeared nervous as they entered the space. After he retrieved one of the canisters, Amir started the mill. Yakub opened the canister with an unsteady hand and poured some of the powder into the hopper. He poured only a small sample and quickly put the lid back on the canister after a struggle.

When the sample was collected, Amir shut down the mill. He took the tiny powder sample and put it under the microscope. The test would only determine whether or not the pressure inside the milling chamber was correct. The feed rate, done manually by Yakub, was the other variable that could not be accurately tested from the sample. The men would have to just rely on remembering how fast they introduced the anthrax into the mill and try to replicate that same feed rate.

Amir looked up from the microscope and gave Jabbar a "thumbs up" sign. Jabbar waved back at him with a smile. Yakub stood nervously at the feed hopper next to the now-closed canister resting on the metal-topped table. Amir came over to the mill and started it again. He nodded to Yakub to start pouring in the powder.

Yakub picked up the canister and unscrewed the lid. The gloves made his hands clumsy, and the top dropped on the table with a bang. The sound was muffled to the men inside their suits. Amir gave his partner a sharp look and gestured for him to start pouring the powder. Yakub tipped the canister over the hopper, and a large surge of the anthrax rushed out. It flooded the hopper and then the milling chamber.

Amir shouted something no one could understand and motioned for Yakub to put the canister on the table. He adjusted the pressure on the nitrogen feed upward and waited for the overload of powder to work its way to the inside of the cyclone in the chamber and into the collection bag.

Yakub screwed the cap back on the canister and stumbled to the anti-chamber. Amir shouted after him but stayed at the mill to complete the milling of what had been dropped into the machine. Without disconnecting the collection bag, he shut down the mill and followed his partner into the anti-chamber.

Yakub had turned on the fan to blow particles back into the inner room and was just starting to remove his hood. He stopped when Amir came into the room. They both put out their arms and turned around to let the air flow clean the suits of any possible contamination. Once done, Yakub quickly removed his hood and suit and unlocked the exit door.

"Why did you stop?" Jabbar asked as he left the anti-chamber.

"I'm sorry, Jabbar. I panicked. It is too tight inside the suit for me. I felt I couldn't breathe."

"Why did you leave?" Amir asked as he came out. "You were clumsy, and then you left. I can't run the mill alone." He turned to Jabbar. "I think I was able to properly grind the load by raising the pressure, but I can't know for sure." Turning back to Yakub, "You must do it like we practiced."

"I'm sorry. I can't. I feel too closed up in the suit."

"You did just fine while we practiced," Jabbar said.

"Yes. But with the anthrax, I feel death all around me. It is different. I can't go back in there."

"You are a coward. Not worthy of jihad," Taimoor said as he stepped forward. "I don't know why Jabbar picked you. I would not have."

"Quiet, Taimoor," Jabbar said. "We don't need you to tell us how you would have decided better."

Chapter 21

Frank looked up from his desk as Joe Harris stormed into his office.

"What's up, Joe?"

"I'll tell you what's up. I just got kicked off the Baker farm by the new owners. They said I couldn't mow my hay. They want to void my contract with Baker. We did it before he sold the place. I paid for the haying rights, invested in the seed, and done the work. Now they won't let me harvest it."

"I'm sure we can work something out. I'll have a talk with them. Do you have a copy of the contract?"

"You bet I do. But, Frank, they turned me away at gunpoint."

"What?"

"You heard me. One of them opened his shirt and let me see his gun, a big semi-auto pistol. He made me believe that if I didn't leave, he might use it."

"He say that?"

"Not in so many words. But he had this look."

Frank thought for a moment. "He middle-eastern looking? Have a beard and thick hands? Wear loose pants and shirt?"

"Sounds like the guy. You know him?"

"He had an angry look about him? All the time?"

"Yeah. That's the look."

"I think I met him. He doesn't like westerners. His partner, a much more amiable guy, said he had been insulted by some Americans and is holding a grudge. That isn't a crime, but brandishing a weapon may be." Frank sighed. "I'll go out there and talk to them."

"You want me to go along?"

"No, you go back to your place. If I make any progress, I'll stop by and let you know."

"Don't wait too long, sheriff. That grass needs to be cut and worked now, not a week from now."

"I understand. I'll get back to you in a day or two. No more than that."

It was late afternoon. Frank decided to wait until the next day to go out to the farm. He didn't relish stirring things up, but Joe's accusations needed to be addressed. As much as Frank didn't want problems, it seems the purchase of this farm by some obscure corporation had planted trouble right in his lap.

† † †

Jabbar sensed their time was limited. That farmer was not going to drop the issue, especially since Taimoor showed him his weapon. He'd probably report the incident to the sheriff, who would come back to talk to them. He could not be allowed into the shed. *Maybe an apology would work.* Jabbar wasn't sure, and it probably would have to be accompanied by letting the farmer back onto the fields to mow his hay. If he could keep Taimoor out of the discussions, that would help. There was no reason for the farmer to come to the house or outbuildings. He probably would want to stay as far away as possible in any case.

He made a decision. Jabbar pointed to another man, an older jihadist. "You will take Yakub's place. He can tell you what to do. We must work on the powder through the evening. I expect we will get a visit from the sheriff since Taimoor here was incautious and allowed the farmer to see his weapon."

Taimoor started to speak up, but Jabbar grabbed his arm.

"You don't need to defend yourself. What's done is done. The man, though, will report this to the sheriff, who will visit us again."

He turned to the others. "I work to protect you from the infidel while we must remain under cover. This is not an open battle but a stealthy one. I want to kill many *kafir*, as do you." With that, he pointed at Taimoor. "But I know we must be careful to not be uncovered before our attack. Otherwise, all is lost."

Farid, the man chosen to replace Yakub, was uneasy. He was not afraid to be in the suit but worried that he would not do well and cause the milling process to fail.

"You are a warrior. You are tested," Amir said. "You will do well. Just listen to me."

Farid nodded.

The men entered the inner room again after putting on their gear. Amir waited for Farid to get accustomed to being in the pressurized suit. He went over again how to pour the powder into the hopper and how to be careful to not catch his suit on any part of the mill. There was a very good chance of spores being released as the powder was poured into the hopper. Further possible points of release would be when removing the collection bag and sealing it, as well as cleaning the inside of the mill after the grinding was completed. They would not worry about that last situation as Jabbar had said they would simply abandon the mill in place and depart. There was no time to spend a day doing an exacting cleanup that would ensure the mill could be safely removed and transported.

† † †

It was a fourteen-hour drive to St. Louis via I 80 west to Akron, Ohio, then I 76 down to Columbus, where he picked up I 70, which would take him to his destination. It was an exhausting journey, made more so by the flat terrain from Columbus west. Once past Pennsylvania's mountainous and hilly terrain, the land became flat as he entered the mid-west. From Columbus through Indianapolis, the scenery was mostly flat, open fields with long horizons. This was part of the great farm belt stretching to the west that fed much of the country. From Indianapolis to St. Louis, the straight road was relieved only sporadically by occasional hills that produced gentle curves in the broad interstate.

Dan pulled over near the courier business to catch a few precious hours of sleep before it opened. He would note who came early and who left late. He would select one of the late departures and hope for the best; that the man could get him into the building and to the records he needed.

The early sun woke Dan with a start as it flashed off the rear-view mirror into his eyes. He sat up and flexed his stiff joints before getting out of the car to relieve himself. *I'm getting too old for this crap*. He didn't mind the physical work or the stress, but sleeping in the car left him yearning for an easier way to do his work. *If only I could farm this part out*. Unfortunately, that was wishful thinking.

An hour later, the early birds started arriving. He picked out someone dressed less casually than the others and, like before, who parked up close. *There's my man.* Dan hoped he was right. He had one shot at this without giving himself away. Once he had targeted his mark, Dan drove off to get something to eat. He'd be back in the afternoon to pick out his ambush spot and wait for the man to come out. He hoped he would work late like the other one did.

While at the diner, his phone rang.

"Dan here."

"We've landed in St. Louis, boss," Marcus said. "What's next?"

"Let's meet up. Get your gear at the safe house. I'll send you the address. I have to grab someone who can show me where we go next."

"A bad guy?"

"No, a civilian, actually. But he may have the key to where we go to stop a pending terrorist attack."

"So, we can't be too rough on him? Just asking."

"Right. But we still need the info. Serious threat posture should do the trick. And keep his mouth shut after we're gone."

'How do you want to play it?"

"We'll talk when you get here. I'll fill you in on everything."

"Copy that. Send the address."

Dan knew that Marcus and Roland would memorize the address, check it on a map, and turn off their phones so no tracking could be done through them. They were burner phones, but none of the men wanted to be careless. They were all cognizant of how good some hackers were. Warren was proof of that.

Three hours later, the two men drove up and parked behind Dan. They were on a side street just off the road that went past the courier company. Marcus and Roland got out and loaded themselves into Dan's car. The two men filled the back seat, with Roland having to duck his head slightly.

"You want to fill us in now?" Marcus asked.

"Hope it's important," Roland said. "You took me away from some relaxing downtime with one of my ladies."

"It's always 'one of your ladies'. I wonder if you make these things up." Dan said.

"You wish you could come along to witness my skills with the fairer sex." Roland leaned forward to whisper in Dan's ear. "But you're probably too old."

Dan just smiled at the friendly barb. He began to fill the two men in on the suspected attack.

"Jesus," Marcus said in a soft voice. "That's putting together a lot of thin evidence."

"Agreed, but think of the consequences if we're right."

"But we don't know who they are, where they are, how many they are, and what cities they'll attack," Roland said. "Boss, I don't see how we'll be able to intercept them before they pounce. Maybe afterwards, but not before."

"I get it. The odds aren't good. But afterwards is too late."

"So, the only thing we can do is to follow this trail, which will hopefully lead us to these guys before they head out. If there are enough of them and they split up, we'll never stop all the attacks." Marcus paused for a moment, then continued. "Maybe the FBI should be called in. They can alert all the probable target cities. Keeping this under wraps like Jane and Henry want to do may be the wrong move."

"They think it'll get leaked, and there'll be a nationwide panic. That could be as bad as the attack itself," Dan said.

"Less a couple of hundred thousand casualties."

"Let's just nail down something firm. Then we can give it to Jane and let her and Henry decide from there. No one can do anything until we get firm corroboration of what's going on."

"I'm good with that," Roland said. "But time is of the essence, as you say."

Chapter 22

After Warren had found the sales information on the small mill, Fred asked him to see what he could find about Zhōu and his finances.

"Follow the money," Fred said. "Isn't that what Jane always preaches?"

Warren nodded. "But that's sometimes easier said than done."

"True for most hackers, but not for you."

Warren smiled and turned to his desk with multiple monitors on it. This was what he enjoyed more than anything else. It was one of the great loves of his life. Within an hour, he was on a trail like a bloodhound picking up a scent. His fingers flew over the keyboard, and his eyes scanned the myriad of screen images showing data tracks and long lists of accounts to dig into.

Hours later, after Fred had gone home, he closed in on one trail that he felt he could follow to the end. He drilled through the proxy accounts, going further down along what, for many, would be an impenetrable maze of false leads. Most of the time, he could sense going off the path and so avoided long trails leading to dead ends. By midnight, he had found two banks in the Cayman Islands, one in Belize, and two in Malta with accounts that looked promising. Warren picked one, and for the next hour, he stripped away the layers of protection. He inserted himself carefully into the system so as to not trigger a response by their security software. Warren moved almost delicately; there was a touch of artistry and sensitivity to his work. The result was he could get into and roam around protected systems, taking his time to find the information he needed, copy it, and exit without the system knowing he was there. His digital trail was erased as he backed himself out of the bank's servers. With one done, he moved on to the next. By morning, Warren had the complete picture.

"You've been here all night?" Fred asked when coming into the office they shared.

Warren nodded with a grin on his face.

"I found them." Fatigue sounded in his voice, along with a sense of victory and pride.

"What do you have?"

"Five accounts in five different banks. He used banks in Malta, Belize, and the Cayman Islands."

"Very cosmopolitan of him."

Warren shoved a piece of paper across his desk.

"Fifteen million dollars. In five different accounts. All within a short time frame. He'll probably break it down more, but I can easily follow the trail from where I left off."

Fred whistled. "A lot of dough."

"Let's go see Jane," Warren said. He stood up, went over to the side counter, and poured himself a cup of hours-old coffee from his all-night probe through digital land.

"What do you have?" Jane asked when her two researchers came into her office.

Warren told her about Zhōu's finances.

"Fifteen million dollars is a lot. With the timing as well, this has to be connected to the anthrax. It seems to confirm that he was responsible for all the thefts." She paused for a moment to think. "Warren, see if you can follow his movements since the thefts."

"That'll take a bit of time. I worked all night on this."

"I understand. Take a break, if you're too tired, but get on it as soon as you can. We need to push down every trail we can to find out more about this threat."

Warren gave her a salute. "Something to eat and more coffee and I should be good to go."

† † †

Dan, Roland, and Marcus waited through the long afternoon. After 5 pm, some employees began to leave. Dan's target, thankfully, remained in the building. But before all the office staff had gone, the man came out and got into his car.

"I'll pull out and block the road," Dan said. "Marcus, you jump out and get control over the driver. Have him pull over to the curb. I'll park and we'll go back in his car."

"Got it," Marcus said.

The ambush went as expected. Dan blocked the road. The driver stopped abruptly and honked his horn. Marcus got out and sprinted up to the driver's window, showing the man his pistol.

"Pull over to the side of the road, slowly, if you don't want to get shot."

The man obeyed. Dan parked, and he and Roland went over to the car. The four men then drove back to the courier company.

"You have a key to the door?" Dan asked.

The man nodded.

"Keep going," Dan said, as the parking lot still had cars in it. "I want to wait until the office is empty. Then we'll go in. You're going to find a delivery address for me, and then we'll be on our way."

When the last of the office staff left, they returned to the parking lot. Dan explained what he needed.

"I don't know if I can find the record," the man said.

"That will be too bad for you," Dan replied. "You'll have to come up with it...or else."

"I have a family. Please don't hurt me."

"Then find the address."

Without another word, the man went to work. "You know I can get in a lot of trouble for doing this."

"You'll get into more trouble if you don't," Marcus said. "And we aren't going to tell anyone."

Finally, the man found the delivery document and showed it to Dan with a smile and a flourish.

"Where in the hell is Dongola, Ill?" Dan asked as he read the document.

"It's in southern Illinois, just north of Cairo. Here," the man fired up a computer. "It's pretty small so not many have heard of it. Here's the map."

"Shit," Roland said. "That's not far. We can be there this evening." He clapped the courier employee on the back, nearly dropping him to the floor. "You did a good job."

The man turned to Dan. "So, you'll let me go now?"

"Let me have your driver's license." Dan held out his hand. The man looked at him questioningly but produced the document from his wallet. Dan read the address aloud.

"I'll let you go, but understand one thing and don't forget it. Each one of us is capable of killing you without a second thought. We all just heard your address. We don't forget important things we hear. If we learn of any police on our trail, one of us will pay you a visit and kill you and maybe your family, depending on how much trouble you caused us."

He grabbed the man's shoulder, who now turned deathly pale.

"Do you understand me?"

The man nodded.

"We are working undercover to stop a massive terror attack. You must keep your mouth shut. Tell you wife you had to work late. No one will know you helped us. No one will know we paid you a visit. And you'll never see us again. Got it?"

The man nodded again.

"Say it."

"I got it."

"Good."

Dan wrote down the address, and the four men left the building. After dropping Dan and the others off, the courier employee drove home with his hands trembling on the steering wheel.

"Let's get going, boss," Roland said after the employee left. "Now we got an address; maybe we can stop all this crap from happening."

† † †

Amir and Farid were in the middle of the milling when Farid stumbled and fell against the mill. He was carrying another canister of anthrax. It fell against the table and to the ground. Farid's face mask raked across one of the clamps on the mill, and it tore open. The lid of the canister on the ground had fallen open. No visible spores had spilled out, but that didn't mean they weren't in the air.

"Ahh no!" Farid shouted. "Amir, help me."

Amir stared at the fallen canister, the mill now forgotten. He pushed Farid back away from the deadly tube and carefully put the lid back on it, screwing it down tight.

Farid was panting in a panic, breathing heavily. The men watched in horror from outside the room.

"Get out of there!" shouted Jabbar.

Amir ran for the anti-chamber. Farid started to follow when Amir closed the door and locked it.

"No, no!" shouted Farid. Let me in.

Amir just stood at the door, not speaking, not answering. Then he turned on the purge valve to forcefully stream air across his suit and into the inner chamber, where it would eventually pass through the HEPA filter to the outside.

Once he was confident that he was uncontaminated, he exited the anti-chamber into the shed. Farid kept pounding on the inner door; his shouts could be heard by those watching from the shed.

Amir looked at Jabbar, who stared back at him with a look of disbelief on his face. Taimoor didn't say a word but went over to the air tanks and switched the air over to pure nitrogen. He started pumping the air into the inner chamber, replacing the oxygenated air with nitrogen. Jabbar ran over to him and tried to grab the tanks. Taimoor hit him with a solid blow to the side of his head. Jabbar went down, and Taimoor dropped on top of him to rain blows down on him until the man was unconscious.

"What are you doing?" The older Omar grabbed Taimoor and wrestled him off of Jabbar.

"What has to be done. Do you want to stand in my way?" Taimoor stood up to confront the older man. "He wants to let him out, but Farid is a dead man. We wait for days for him to die and he infects us as well, or we let him die quickly and he doesn't infect us. He is dead either way."

"You kill him? Cut off his oxygen?"

"It is Allah's will. He made a mistake. We must not let it destroy our mission."

Farid began to feel the lack of oxygen. His shouting and panting only accelerated the process. Soon he dropped to his knees, whimpering, staring at the men outside. No one could hear him, but they could see him trying to speak. Then he fell over to the ground. Taimoor kept the nitrogen flow going strong for another ten minutes before shutting it off.

"What about Jabbar? You almost killed him," Omar said.

"He is soft. He would have let Farid out and risked killing all of us. I am taking over leadership of the mission. We don't need to mix with the infidel any more, we don't need to pretend. We will finish the milling when the room is safe and leave. Tonight, if necessary."

"We can't leave Jabbar. And you can't kill him. He is the nephew of our *zaeim*. He will not be pleased that you have usurped his nephew."

"And you will tell him that?" Taimoor gave Omar a dangerous look. "He will heal. And if we prevail, our *zaeim w*ill be pleased, even though his nephew was wounded."

Just then, they heard the sound of a truck coming up the long drive. The men froze.

Chapter 23

"Quick, put Jabbar behind the trucks so he can't be seen," Taimoor said. "Tend to his wounds. He'll recover, but keep him quiet."

Taimoor peeked out from the shed door. "It's that damn sheriff," he said, almost to himself. He turned to the men. "Omar, you come with me. You will be calm and soothe the sheriff. He must not suspect us. We need time to finish and leave. Even if he comes back tomorrow, we will be gone."

The two men stepped out and walked towards the oncoming SUV.

Frank noticed the men as he approached the buildings. One was the unfriendly guy from before; the other was a new face. The smooth talker wasn't with them. He pulled to a stop about fifteen yards from the waiting men and got out of his vehicle. He adjusted his hat and belt and walked up to them.

"Howdy," Frank said. He wanted to try to keep things on a friendly level as long as possible.

The two men nodded in greeting.

"I remember talking with you the other day. Where's the other man that was with you?"

"He's not here right now. I'm in charge while he's gone. What do you want?"

Frank let out a small sigh. He would have to deal with the unpleasant one. That was going to make things harder.

"The two of you had an encounter with Joe Harris. He's the farmer who was cutting hay in your fields. He came to see me. He says you ran him off. Rather forcefully according to him."

"We didn't use force. We just insisted that he stop and leave. It is our property so we have that right. Or do we not?"

Frank smiled. The man almost seemed to be trying to goad him.

"Yes, you have the right. Except that Joe has a contract which indicates he has the right to harvest the hay. That right remains even if the property is sold."

"I don't see how that is possible. We did not agree to that. He should take his issue up with the man who sold the farm. This is not our problem."

"Well, Frank has invested time and money in the haying. He bought the seed, planted it, and now he needs to harvest it. After that his contract is finished and he won't come around."

"Mr. Sheriff, we don't want him coming around. We are working on planning the development of the property. He is a distraction and a noisy one."

Can't be that noisy, Frank thought. Nevertheless, he conceded the point. "That may be, but there is the issue of the contract." Frank pulled out a bandanna and wiped his forehead. "There's another issue as well. Joe says you threatened him with a pistol. I'm going to need to see your FOID card."

Taimoor gave him a look that told Frank the man didn't know what he was talking about.

"FOID card. Your Firearm Owners ID. You get it from the State Police. You need it to own a handgun in this state. I need to see it."

"I was never told about such a card."

"That doesn't matter. It's your duty to know the laws of the state you're in."

The second man, older, spoke up.

"Perhaps," Omar said, "Taimoor doesn't know about the card because he doesn't have a weapon. I think your friend Joe is incorrect. Maybe he was excited and thought Taimoor's phone case was a weapon."

Frank smiled at the older man. He now had a name for the tough guy, even though it might not be of much help.

"Joe knows firearms. He's not the type to mistake a cell phone for a gun." Frank turned back to Taimoor. "I'm going to have to check for weapons since I'm out here. If you have none, then I'll go back to Joe and talk with him, but if you do...well, we have a problem. In any case, you're going to have to honor Joe's contract, at least through this year's haying."

"Maybe," Omar said, "we let this Joe continue with his hay making. It is not what we prefer, but we don't want to create more problems. When he finishes, that can be the end of it."

"That works. But I still have the issue of the weapon."

"Can we just assume Joe was mistaken? We don't have any weapons," Omar said.

"I'd like to believe that, but Joe is a reliable guy. It would be better for me to confirm that you don't. Then the issue is put to rest with no question."

"You will need a warrant to search us or the property. That is what your laws state, do they not?" Taimoor now spoke up.

"There are exceptions to the rule. If I think evidence might be destroyed, the gun hidden or removed, for example, I can conduct a search right now. Since Joe felt threatened, I could state that my safety is at stake and I could search you."

He eyed Taimoor directly with this last statement.

"You risk having our company sue you, if you continue. I have done nothing to threaten you. It seems like you give yourself reasons to not follow your own laws. I think you should go now."

Frank took off his hat and wiped his forehead again. The situation was getting more tense. He didn't want to escalate things, but he didn't believe for a moment that the man did not have a weapon. And he certainly did not have an FOID card. But if he got a search warrant and returned the next day, there would be nothing to find.

As Frank was considering his move, the shed door opened, and out stepped a man Frank barely recognized. His face was battered, with one eye closed shut, scrapes on his cheeks and forehead, and lips swollen. However disfigured, he could see it was the easy-going man from the day before. He braced himself against the door and shouted to the men something in a language Frank didn't understand. The two men turned in surprise.

"Go back in the shed, you are not well," Taimoor shouted back in Arabic. Frank didn't understand a word of either man.

"No, you go back into the shed. I will handle this man. You will only make things worse," Jabbar said. His words were slurred by his battered face.

Taimoor turned back to Frank. His eyes flashed in anger. "You must go now. My friend has hurt himself and needs my attention. Tell your farmer we will let him continue, but when he is done, that is all. I don't want him back on our property."

"There's still the weapon issue." Frank started past the two men towards the shed. "And there may be an issue with what has happened to your friend. It looks like he was beaten by someone or some group. How many men are there here?"

"Sheriff, stop. You have no right to trespass on our property," Taimoor said.

Frank turned to him, "I have every right. There is an injured man who looks like he was attacked. I'm going to investigate."

"Do you want to start an international issue?" The second man spoke up in a quiet voice. "This man had an accident. He was not beaten. And we assure you there is no gun. Your farmer was mistaken. We have given in to what he wants, now let the rest go...or you will hear from our lawyers and there will be a large disturbance, all laid at your feet. This is especially true if you force the issue now, against our rights and your laws."

Frank stopped. "That's not going to work for me. I have to talk to this man. He turned back to the shed.

Jabbar stepped outside and closed the door. Frank heard it latch from the inside. He walked up to the man and looked him over carefully. At that moment, the two he had been talking to came up.

"Tell me what happened to you," Frank said.

"I fell off the upper floor. One of the rails broke."

Frank looked at Jabbar closely. "No broken leg or arm? What is your name?"

"Jabber."

"Well, Jabbar, I wasn't born yesterday and I've been around. I deal with drunks and people who get into bar fights. I also deal with domestic violence, so I know when someone has suffered a beating. And that is what I'm seeing. Please don't lie to me."

"He is not lying to you. Now please go," Taimoor said as he came up to Frank.

Frank turned to him. “You, keep quiet. I’m talking to this man. And stand over there,” Frank pointed to his right side, “where I can see you.”

Taimoor didn’t move.

“I told you to stand over there, not behind me. Now do it.”

Frank’s voice now slipped into his official, police mode. The one he used when dealing with unruly drunks and bullies.

Taimoor still didn’t move.

“All right.” Frank now turned directly towards Taimoor. “If you don’t do what I say, I’m going to put cuffs on you for your safety and mine until I get to the bottom of this mess.”

Jabbar now said something in Arabic, as did the other man, Omar. Taimoor moved over to one side as Frank had directed.

Frank turned back to Jabbar. He put Taimoor’s non-compliance aside for the moment. “Let’s go inside,” Frank said to him. “I want to see where you fell.”

Jabbar shook his head. “There is nothing to see. I was not beat up. I fell and that is all there is to it.”

Frank stared at the man. His face looked painful. His words were garbled and almost not understandable. So many women he had dealt with over the years, women who suffered from their mate’s violence, exhibited the same behavior. They didn’t want to admit it or take any action that could change their situation.

He knew there were more people inside. From the initial two men, he now was dealing with at least four.

“How many people are there here? How many are inside this shed? I know there’s at least one because I heard the door latch shut.”

“It is none of your business,” Taimoor said.

Frank turned to him, now getting angry. He was being played, and he didn't like it. The more the situation continued, the more he was sure something odd was going on here. Maybe in this very shed.

"I didn't ask you. You keep quiet until I talk to you or I'll haul in right now for not obeying an order." He turned back to Jabber. "We're going inside and you'll show me where you fell. If you still maintain the story, I can't help you, but I'm going to see what's inside. See where you were hurt."

Frank pointed to the door. "Let's go," he said to Jabbar.

The man didn't move. Just then, Taimoor pulled his pistol from behind his back and pointed it at Frank. "Enough with your orders and insults, *kafir*. You do not see inside."

Frank looked at the man in disbelief. Jabbar and Omar also stood transfixed. "Easy now. No need to get violent." He put his hands out, palms down in a smoothing gesture. "We don't want this to escalate any further."

A smile crossed Taimoor's face. It didn't look friendly to Frank.

"No. It is too late for you. You will go to hell like the rest of the unbelievers in your country."

"Don't make things worse—"

A blast from Taimoor's pistol interrupted Frank in mid-sentence. He staggered back with a surprised look on his face as his brain registered the fact that a bullet had torn into his chest. His legs began to give out, his breath came in shocked, wet gasps. As he sank down, another blast came from Taimoor's gun, and Frank toppled over backwards to the ground. Darkness closed over him, wiping away his surprise and all consciousness.

Chapter 24

"What have you done? You fool! Now we cannot stay here. We will have to go tonight," Jabbar shouted.

"Get back inside and shut up. If you had not come out, we could have handled the sheriff. He's dead because of you. He was not going to leave without seeing inside. There was no other possibility except for me to kill him."

Taimoor shoved Jabbar through the now-open door.

"I am in charge now." He yelled at the other men. "You will follow my orders, not Jabbar's. He is soft and would let these infidels tell us what to do. We do not submit to them. We are warriors for Allah and take our fight to them tonight."

He shoved Jabbar to one side and stepped forward.

"Gather up the powder and let's begin loading the trucks. Someone drag that body inside and stuff it in a corner."

Taimoor turned to Jabbar as the men began to get busy. "You have done enough. You will now follow my orders, or I will beat you some more. I will take this fight to the Americans. And don't threaten me with your uncle's name. He knows my history. When we are successful, he will understand that I had to take over. You may yet become a warrior, but you will have to shed your western ways in order to lead experienced fighters."

Jabbar looked at him through one good eye but didn't say a word.

"Amir, you go back in and retrieve the bag of milled powder. Load it back into its cannister and repack all the others. We'll take them as they are and go. There is no more time to wait."

Amir nodded. He turned the air back on and entered the anti-chamber to suit up. After putting on the hazmat gear, he tested the air coming into his suit. When he was satisfied it was adequate, he entered the inner room. It took an hour to pack the milled powder back into its canister. Amir was careful, not wanting to cause a spill and perhaps suffer Yakub's fate. As he worked, he studiously avoided Yakub's dead body lying on the floor.

While Amir was in the room packing, another jihadist came up to Taimoor. "We are not finished with the roof vents. They need to be completed so that we can safely disperse the powder."

Taimoor gave the man a harsh look. "Get busy and finish it. We must leave, if not tonight, by first light."

The man nodded. "It may take most of the night to complete, but we will finish the vents."

† † †

Dan and his two companions drove quickly in the gathering dusk. They knew they were fighting an unknown deadline and that with every hour that passed, their chances of catching the men decreased. When they arrived at the small town of Dongola, it was dark, and most of the shops were closed.

"Let's try the bar," Marcus said. "They may know where this farm is."

"What do we ask? Can you tell us where the property the terrorists bought is?" Roland said.

"No, dumbass. We ask where the farm is that the Arabs bought."

Dan pulled to the curb without a word and got out. His two ex-Delta Force companions followed.

They stepped into the building. Country western music was blaring. It smelled of sweat, peanuts, and beer. Few people turned to look as they went up to the bar. Those who did paused at the sight of the three large men, all of whom looked quite dangerous.

"What can I get you?" the bartender asked as he came over.

"Three beers," Dan said. "Whatever's on tap. And some information."

"Beer now, information later, if I can help."

The man went to the taps and pulled three glasses of frothy beer. He brought them back to the men and put his hands on the edge of the bar. "Now, what do you want to know? But I got to tell you, ain't much going on in our little town."

"We're looking for a farm. It probably was sold or rented recently. Probably to some Arabs. You heard of it?"

The bartender smiled. "Like I said, not much goes on here, so, yes, I heard of it. Most everyone has. What's your interest?"

Dan ignored the question. "Can you tell us how to get there?"

"I ain't sure of all the roads and turns. Been a while since I've been out in that direction."

"Anyone here can tell us?"

The bartender looked over the crowd. Most were mechanics, farmers, and people who worked in Cape Girardeau at one of the Southeast Missouri State University facilities or local industries. Some were unemployed and had lots of time on their hands. He shook his head.

"Don't think this crowd can help. There is one farmer, Joe Harris. He's doing some haying out at the farm I think you're asking about. Ran into some Arab types and they weren't all that friendly. Word is, he reported it to Sheriff Kline, but I don't know that he's done anything about it. Got Joe pretty pissed off, though."

"Sounds like the people we're looking for. Where can we find Joe?"

The bartender shook his head. "I don't know the man personally. He doesn't much come in here. I live in town, so I'm not very familiar with the farms."

Dan kept his frustration from showing. The man was not very helpful and not as informed as he hoped a local bartender would be. "Can you point us in the right direction at least?"

"Yeah. You go south on I87 a few miles. Take the first exit going west. The way I understand it, the farm is located up against the Shawnee National Forest."

The three men looked at each other.

"It's a start," Marcus said. He turned back to the bartender. "You know where this sheriff lives? We may want to talk to him."

The bartender smiled as if glad he could give some exact information. "He lives on Jackson Street. It's a house with a wrap-around porch. Painted yellow, about half way down the street. You can't miss it. What's so important about these Arabs, 'sides that they're not from here? They do something to you? Break some laws?"

"Just need to talk to them, that's all," Dan said. He drained his beer and stood up. "Let's go."

Dan put a twenty on the bar, and the men turned to the door. Once outside, Dan spoke. "I don't think we want to visit this sheriff. If he's got a complaint and then we show up asking questions, he'll have a bunch for us."

"Yeah," Marcus said. "I just wanted to know in case we decided to call on him."

"Why don't we?" Roland asked. "We can say we're FBI undercover, so we don't have badges. We can fake that. He's just a small-town sheriff. What does he know?"

"He might want to check up on us," Dan said.

"Got to wait until morning to do that. We'll be gone by then. Hell, while we're running around in the dark, looking for this farm, the jihadists could be gone as well. The delivery address didn't come with directions."

"I get that. And my phone doesn't give me a location from that rural route number," Dan said.

"My cell coverage is getting spotty as well," Roland said. "Don't think it'll be any better at the Shawnee forest."

"Let's do it," Marcus said. "Two to one is the vote. We have to push boundaries if we're going to get anywhere."

"Okay. On to Jackson Street," Dan said.

Chapter 25

Frank's wife answered the door when the men knocked. The house, as the bartender described it, was easy to spot on the street.

"He said he was going out to the farm to talk about Joe's complaint. He hasn't come back yet." She looked at her watch with a worried face. "I don't know what's keeping him. Cell reception is not good over by the national forest, so he probably can't call. He usually is good about that if he's going to be late."

"Can you tell us where the farm is? We'll drive out there."

"That would be great. I don't know exactly, but you go south on I 57...no...no wait. It's better to just head west out of town and take Route 3 off to the right. Follow that until you get to county road 352." From there, Frank's wife gave the men a series of county roads to follow, which they all put to memory.

"Can you remember all of that?"

"I think so, ma'am," Dan said. "We better go now. It's getting late."

The men drove back towards the I 57 interchange, where there was a gas station, and bought some sandwiches and sodas. Then they headed out in the direction Frank's wife told them to go.

"We going to find this place before morning?" Roland asked.

"Who the hell knows?" Dan said.

"When we get closer, we'll stop again and ask. The sheriff's wife was getting more vague as she got farther away from town."

"People around here aren't big on exact directions," Marcus said.

† † †

Amir finished getting the containers ready for transport while the work went on to finish the venting system.

The night was waning. "Put your efforts on one vent for now. Get one finished," Taimoor said.

"But we need both of them," one of the men responded.

"We are going to split up after we leave. The plans have changed."

He called all the men over to talk to them. Jabbar was brought to the edge of the group. He had his hands bound with Ehsaan, the cook, looking after him. Taimoor had told him he was not to speak unless he wanted another beating. Taimoor divided up the men. He directed Ehsaan to watch Jabbar and told him they would come with him to D.C. and New York.

"The truck with the finished vent will go to Chicago. The other one will head for Washington, D.C. We will find a place to stop and finish the vent. We will take four of the canisters, and we will hit both the capital and New York. After you spread the powder in Chicago, head back to Texas and the mosque. They will take care of the truck and hide you until we catch up with you. If we haven't come in three days, make arrangements to go to Mexico. The cartel that brought us over will take you back. The mosque knows how to contact them.

"It is getting light. We must depart and complete our work later. Others will be looking for the sheriff because he didn't come home last night. We must not be here when they come."

The men looked doubtful due to the dramatic change of plans. From a safe, anonymous location where they could prepare without haste, they were now thrown into a more desperate situation of having to depart without being fully prepared. Most of them understood the chances of discovery had now increased.

When the work on the one truck was finished, the men packed up and prepared to depart.

"We will set fire to the shed. It will destroy the evidence and burn up the sheriff's body."

"Are we going to take Yakub with us?" one of the men asked.

"No," Taimoor said. "We must bury him here, on the battle field where he died in jihad."

He directed three men to go out behind the shed and dig a grave for the dead man.

By the time they had finished and had a brief ceremony before covering Yakub, the sun was starting to come up.

"It is time to go," Taimoor said.

He made sure the fire was set to the shed, and the men got into the two trucks and headed down the drive.

† † †

Joe Harris was driving to the farm, contract in hand, intent on exerting his rights to harvest the hay. On his way down the road that led to the farm, a box truck passed him heading towards the interstate. It almost forced him off the road. He noted the license plate as it went by at a high rate of speed. It was a Texas commercial plate starting with the letters LCH followed by the number 8. He couldn't get the rest of the numbers before it disappeared. A second truck came out of the gravel drive leading to the farm just before he arrived. It turned towards the interstate. This time Joe was careful to note the license plate, also from Texas. It read CLM with the numbers 375 and one other digit that Joe couldn't make out.

He turned into the drive, and as he approached, he noticed smoke coming from the shed. He parked his pickup and ran towards the building. The door was locked. Joe ran around back and found Sheriff Kline's SUV. He tried to call but couldn't make a connection. Next, he went to a window and broke it open. Heat flashed out at him, followed by smoke.

Joe stepped back. He could not go in, and if he did, he could do nothing to put out the fire. He ran back to his truck. The only option was to drive out to find cell reception and make a call to the fire department. He got in and started down the gravel drive.

Half of the way down the drive, he saw another car approaching. He slowed and waved his arm out of the window. The car stopped. It had three men in it.

"There's a fire at the farm, can you call the fire department?" Joe yelled to them.

The driver pulled out his phone and tried to make the call.

"What's the address?" he asked. "I've got a few bars."

"Tell them it's the Baker farm. They'll know where it is."

The man made the call. Then he looked over at Joe.

"Who are you and what are you doing here?"

"I'm harvesting the hay under contract. The new owners, Arabs, tried to force me away. Sheriff Kline came out to talk to them. His SUV is around behind the building that's on fire. I think something bad has happened."

"Anyone still there?"

Joe shook his head. "Two trucks left as I was approaching."

"Shit."

Joe heard one of the men in the back seat curse.

"You get a description?"

"Yep. Got partial license numbers on both trucks. They're Texas licensed. Probably rentals."

"Damn. We're too late," Marcus said.

"What are the partials?" Dan asked.

Joe repeated what he had seen while one of the men wrote down the letters and numbers.

"We're going up to see if we can do anything," Dan said.

"I'll go with you," Joe said. "Who are you guys, anyway?"

"Undercover investigators," Dan said.

The two vehicles drove back to the farm. By that point, the building was fully ablaze.

"We can't do anything here," Roland said. "Let's get after the trucks.

Dan took Joe aside to talk to him.

"The men who you encountered, the ones who just left, are very dangerous. They're terrorists. I can't keep you from reporting their plates to the authorities, but you must inform them that these men should not be approached. If they are stopped, the police should cordon off a large area around the truck. A quarter of a mile at least and wait them out."

"Whoa. Do they have bombs?"

Dan nodded. "Very powerful bombs. Emphasize that no one should approach them."

"Aren't you going to tell them yourself?"

Dan shook his head. "We don't have time to get into it with the local police. We're going after these guys. We're not far behind and may be able to stop them." He put his hand on Joe's shoulder. "They threatened you. They may have killed your sheriff and they're aiming to kill more people. Make sure the authorities listen to you. Otherwise, a lot of people could get killed."

Joe stared wide-eyed at Dan, who turned back to Roland and Marcus. "Let's go. We have a chance with the tag numbers."

Chapter 26

As soon as they were back on the road heading for the interstate with Marcus driving, Dan called Fred.

"Jane said we weren't supposed to communicate with you."

"This is important, but don't tell Jane. She has to be insulated from what I'm doing."

"Why?"

"Don't ask questions, just do as I say. I have two Texas plates for you to run. Commercial, truck plates. Probably for rentals. Get Warren to find out everything he can and then figure out how to locate them. They'll probably be on I 57 in Illinois. You need to locate and track them so we can intercept."

"I'll do my best."

"Make it fast. They're on the move."

"Can Warren do it?" Marcus asked

"We're screwed if he can't."

"They're probably headed for Chicago," Roland said. "Why don't we call the state police and have them put up a road block?"

"That's a possibility and it'll happen after that farmer talks with the police. But it risks killing a lot of people depending on where they stop the trucks." He looked out of the window at the passing scenery. They were approaching Dongola again to get on the interstate. "And it will take some time for the message to get through, be treated seriously, and a plan put into action. We're already in action."

Ten minutes later, Fred called back. "The trucks were rented in a suburb of Dallas. Someone with an Arab name."

"They probably had help from the community there before they headed north. Can you locate them?"

"Warren hacked into the highway cams and found two white box trucks heading north. They're about an hour ahead of you, not speeding, staying with the traffic flow."

"Where?"

"Near Marion. There're cameras at most of the interchanges."

"Great. You two keep updating us. We'll try to close the gap. And, remember, don't tell Jane."

"What do we do if she wants us to do something else?"

"Tell her anything. Make up some bullshit, but make it dazzle. You can't leave this. Without you two we're blind."

Less than an hour later, Fred called. "They passed Benton. The second truck exited going east. Warren says he probably can't follow them. There aren't traffic cams on the secondary roads."

"Damn." Dan said. "Can he use any cameras in the towns?"

"If they have them. That's why I'm doing the talking. Warren's working like a demon on hacking the cameras. But it'll take some time to hack into a town's system, so it's best to know ahead of time which towns to target."

"We'll lay out a route east for you to work on. I'll get back in touch."

"Looking pretty sketchy," Marcus said.

"The truck that stayed on the interstate must be going to Chicago. You can bet on that," Roland said. "The other? One can only guess."

"East. If they're going east, that means D.C. or New York. Those are the only two worthwhile targets."

"Lots of cities along the way," Roland said.

"None with the symbolic value of those two. You can bet on that."

The men lapsed into silence as Marcus pushed the rental car to its limits while trying to not make a spectacle on the highway. He worked his way up to over ninety, slowing only to make smooth passing maneuvers, then accelerating again until he reached another cluster of cars. Traffic on the interstate tended to move along in waves of closely grouped vehicles, separated by empty spaces. Marcus made good use of the spaces to gain speed and close in on the trucks.

Dan worked out a possible route east figuring the truck would want to stay off the interstate roads where the chances of getting stopped were greater. He phoned Fred and gave him a list of towns along what he hoped would be the route. If Warren got a hit, that would serve to solidify the route. A couple of hits would make things even more certain.

"What if they stop somewhere?" Roland asked. "We won't know where and we'll drive right past them."

"This is like playing chess blindfolded. We don't know the other's moves and barely see our own," Marcus said.

"If Warren doesn't get a hit for some of the towns when we should expect it, I'll have him check alternate towns. If he gets nothing, we can assume they've stopped and we'll start backtracking."

"That ain't a lot to go on," Roland said.

"I know, but it's the best we can do."

Just then, Fred called. "The trucks have a GPS transmitter. I checked with the rental company. It's not online, but transmits to them in bursts every four hours. It goes straight into their computer which is separated from the online business operations."

"Meaning what?" Dan asked.

"Meaning, Warren can't hack it."

There was silence on the phone.

"But I can call them and make up a story and see if I can get an update on where the truck is."

"Try that," Dan said. "If they're passing through the towns I listed for you, we'll just keep moving in on them. If they stop, we'll need to know where in order to close in."

"Got it."

Fred hung up.

"That gives us a chance," Marcus said.

"Let's hope Fred is persuasive," Dan replied.

† † †

"Where can we find a place to hide out and finish the vent?" Omar asked.

"Have one of the men look in their phone maps," Taimoor said. "Maybe some place near a forest reserve. This country has a lot of area left undeveloped. We can find a place to hide there."

After a few minutes, one of the men said, "I have it. We can stop at the Hoosier National Forest. It is very large and has few houses."

"But where will we stop?" Omar asked. "We need a shed to hide our work."

Taimoor thought about the problem for a moment. "We will find an isolated farm, take it over and use it. We will hold the people hostage. They will cover for us. They will think cooperating with us will save them, but we can kill them when we're done. No one will know what has gone on and we'll be far away by the time they are discovered."

He smiled at how well events were beginning to play out. They had one truck on its way to Chicago to kill thousands. They were on their way east and would find a safe place to hide and complete their work. Then they would strike a second and third blow before heading back to Texas.

Chapter 27

James Greely was frustrated. Roger Abrams, head of SAD, had proven unflappable. He wasn't getting much out of the CIA's top brass. Still, the heat was causing them some discomfort. He could take heart in that. It was a soft, early fall day in Washington, D.C. He was meeting with his top aide, George Randall, his go-to man for getting things done. Especially things that might be a bit sketchy and require anonymity and deniability.

"Zhōu Ming wants to meet with me tomorrow," Greely said.

"About the hearing?"

Greely shrugged his shoulders. "I'm sure. He was hoping we could cut the CIA off at the knees. God knows they have done enough to warrant it, but they're slippery, hard to pin down."

"He's afraid they're getting too interested in China and their influence here?"

"You got it. Shit, everyone's involved with China. The whole world. Why should we be any different? If we stand apart, we just miss out on the gravy train."

"And they're still going to commit industrial espionage. That can't be stopped. I'm not sure the government should even have a role in that arena. That's the responsibility of industry."

"And *they're* all in bed with the Chinese. You see how our tech and social media companies submit to their demands in order to do business over there. Hell, they submit to their demands when it comes to actions over here as well."

Greely's statements were not so much a complaint as a justification for his close working with Zhōu, who he suspected was more than just a lobbyist for certain Chinese industries.

"What's interesting is that Zhōu is also concerned about us not closing the southern border," George said.

"They've got interests in that, for sure. It's not something we've talked about and I'm not sure I want to go there."

"You stay away from that topic. I'll get you any information on it, if you think that's necessary."

"That's what you do," Greely said. "But it's still interesting that he brings up that issue."

"The open border is not something that we have to worry about. The administration is happy with the status quo. We've got thousands coming over, filling up our cities, needing our services. Who do you think they'll support when it comes time to vote?"

Greely gave his aide a wry smile. "But George, they're not supposed to vote."

"Oh, right. I guess they'll just ask their relatives here to vote instead. In any case, we should be able to give our party permanent control over the government in a few more years, despite the growing clamor. Let's let the executive branch handle that issue. We just have to deliver the votes when they need them."

"And get the CIA to stop running black ops and lay off China."

The next day Congressman Greely sat with Zhōu Ming in 1789, an exclusive restaurant frequented by high-level politicians. The high prices kept out most of the "unwashed" and paparazzi, allowing the ruling elite to experience the perks of their exalted status untroubled.

The meal was exorbitantly priced, but Greely didn't mind. Zhōu was paying with his government most likely picking up the bill.

After the meal, over coffee and a brandy, Zhōu talked about his interests.

"You did not get much out of the hearings yesterday. I hope you can uncover some of the more egregious examples of CIA operations that go against your own laws. You know we don't want to interfere, but we worry about that organization harassing our own citizens within your country. Many come here to get the benefit of your universities and to foster closer relationships among our people. My government worries about their safety and security."

"Domestic operations are the domain of the FBI," Greely said. "And if your citizens are not breaking the laws, then they'll be left alone."

"The FBI seems to be sensitive to the issue, but we worry about the CIA, not just intimidating our citizens, but planting incriminating evidence to cause the FBI to act. The spy agency could work behind the scenes to cause trouble. That is why I'm supportive of your hearings."

"They are hard to pin down, as you well know."

"Indeed. You have not uncovered much substance."

"No, but we've introduced allegations and hints. We've created questions and doubts among the press. They'll run with it. They love a scandal, especially one involving spies."

"Maybe I can help with that," Zhōu said.

Greely gave him a quizzical look.

"I can find some hints. I can possibly find someone who could indicate they were intimidated by a covert agent.

Maybe someone caught someone else trying to plant incriminating items in their rooms."

"You have such evidence? And you didn't tell me about it?"

Zhōu shook his head. "Since you seem to need it, I may be able to find something that will help. Leave it at that."

Zhōu went on to outline another business venture that he could let Greely's brother in on. His brother was a minor investor in various Chinese companies. The money that flowed from doing deals in China was carefully spread around the family, with James getting a major cut. He was the rainmaker, after all. His position as a congressman opened the doors for his brother, father, and father-in-law.

† † †

He met her two months earlier in Chef Geoff's, a bar and restaurant located near American University. It was frequented by students as well as various levels of politicians. George Randall often went there to pick up impressionable coeds who were wowed by his close connection to a powerful congressman. Dropping a few names, offering hints of inside information, could lead to a night's tryst in bed followed by him generally having to disengage over the next week as gently as he could.

This girl was different. She was Chinese to start, attending AU on a scholarship. She majored in political science (an odd term to George's ear). She could engage him on a much more sophisticated level than he had experienced with other young females. Her name was Wang Li Xiu, and he was smitten. She didn't go home with him the first night he met her but agreed to exchange phone numbers.

The next day he texted her about dinner together. She was busy but offered to meet the following day. He took her up on it, and they had an expensive and enjoyable meal at Le Diplomate. George chose it for its exclusivity, which came from its price range. Still, the meal lived up to expectations. That night, he was able to bed this beauty from the far east.

In the morning, he woke to find her dressed and leaving.

"You going already? I thought we could have coffee, maybe breakfast together," George said.

She turned from gathering her things. "I must attend a lecture this morning. You don't expect me to give up my classes do you?"

"No, of course not. I just wanted you to stay around a bit longer."

She smiled. When she did so, her eyes lit up and dazzled George.

"Call me later. Maybe we can meet for coffee this afternoon." She gave him a serious look. "I am not just one of your conquests? A one-night stand, as you say here in the U.S.?"

George smiled back at her. "No, you are definitely not a one-night stand. There's something special about you. You have substance."

"I fascinate you?" She smiled again as if satisfied with the compliment.

"More than that. I want to get to know you better." He got up and walked over to her. "I want to spend more time with you."

He reached out and took her in his arms. She didn't resist, and he kissed her. When he released her, she smiled up at him.

"Text me later. Maybe we can get together this weekend. I don't have classes after Friday noon."

With that, Wang turned and let herself out. George went to the kitchen and made himself a cup of coffee. He thought about the encounter. She had been an enticing combination of shyness and excitement in bed. He wondered how experienced she was but couldn't be sure. She moved adroitly to increase not only his pleasure but her own. Still, he wasn't sure if that was due to past encounters or her instinct. She remained shy and innocent-like during his foreplay, and that sense remained throughout the evening even as she more fully engaged with him. Ultimately, he concluded that she was an intoxicating mix of innocence and vixen, wherever that came from.

Chapter 28

The man studying the map on his phone looked up and announced he knew where they should stop.

"I found a small farm at the end of a long, dirt road. It is next to the forest. There are no other houses near it. It should be a good place to hide and finish our modifications."

"Excellent," Taimoor said. "How far is it?"

"I can't be sure. Maybe two more hours."

The men drove on through the day. Taimoor silently willing the trip to go fast and smooth. If they could get to a place to hide, he would have time to finish the vent, plan the rest of their mission, and prove Jabbar wrong. He would be successful, and no one would worry about the beating he had inflicted on Rashid's distant nephew. More importantly, Taimoor would be seen as the leader, and it would be his name that would be elevated. His future among jihadists would be secured. He even began to imagine a position of authority close to Rashid.

† † †

Fred called in to report that he had seen the truck in a traffic camera in the town of Vincennes, along the Illinois and Indiana border. Dan instructed Marcus on how to adjust their route to follow. Marcus kept hammering the rental car along the secondary roads when clear of towns, now being less cautious about police interception.

"We're still on the right track," Dan said.

"And they're staying off the interstates," Roland said. "If they were making a run for D.C., they could have used I 64 to the south and run that right into Virginia."

"They're worried about being stopped. Which means that they think there'll be reports of them using trucks when the mess at the farm is discovered," Dan said.

"They'd right about that," Marcus said.

"Let's catch the sons of bitches and send them to paradise, minus the seventy virgins," Roland said.

"That's seventy-two," Marcus replied.

"What the fuck. Who cares? Seventy, seventy-two. The point is to kill them. And the way you're driving you just might kill us or land us in a local jail."

"Okay, wise guy. What'll it be? Hurry and catch them? Or don't hurry because we risk getting a speeding ticket?"

"Give it a rest, you guys," Dan said.

"I'm just pulling his chain," Marcus said. "It's part of the fun."

"Fuck you," Roland said. "Just don't run us off the road."

The men drove on in silence, with Marcus not moderating his speed except for going through small villages. Once past the houses and shops, he sped up to the maximum the road and the rental car would allow.

No more calls were coming from Fred, so Dan called him.

"I got a hit just outside of Elnora where Route 1500, a pretty small road, goes under I 69. That was over an hour ago. Nothing since."

"They stop?"

"There's a Naval Surface Warfare installation nearby. They may be trying to avoid it and any cameras associated with it. There's more development in the area from the installation and the Hoosier National Forest. It's probably a big draw."

"They're thinking about traffic cameras on the back roads?" Dan asked, almost to himself.

"Who knows? They probably won't go north to Bloomington. I'll check all the smaller towns east of the Naval facility. I'll monitor the ones with cameras and let you know."

"Copy that." Dan hung up the phone.

† † †

The man guided the group around the naval center, and Taimoor instructed the driver to take a back road to avoid the town of Bedford. An hour later, they turned off the paved road onto a gravel one. From there, they turned onto a narrow gravel drive. At the end of it was the farmhouse where they would hide and finish preparing for their attack on D.C. and New York.

"Omar, you and I will go up to the house. You will explain to whoever comes out that we are lost," Taimoor said.

He turned to the man with the map. "Find a nearby place that we can say we're looking for. Omar, you keep the person talking and I'll find a way to get control over them."

"You will kill him?"

Taimoor shook his head. "No, we keep him alive. If anyone calls while we are here, they can cover for us. Whoever is here will cooperate. They will think this will let them live. After we are done, we will kill them."

He smiled.

"We only need to fool them long enough to overpower them. It should be easy."

They slowed as they approached the buildings. The house was a modest wood-sided, two-story structure with a large barn next to it. The grounds around the house and barn were mowed grass. Beyond, the fields were filled with corn and hay ready to be cut. Behind the house, the hills rose steeply, with a dense cover of trees. It was the national forest against which the home was nestled. Omar drove up to the house and stopped at the grass.

"You will go to the back and open the door so our men can get out," Taimoor said to the man who had the map. "Tell them what is going to happen. Omar and I will overpower whoever comes out, then you must rush the house to find anyone else before they can call for help."

He and Omar stepped out and started for the house. The door opened, and an older man came out and stood on the porch. He watched the two men approach. Omar put on his brightest smile, as did Taimoor.

"What can I do for you?" the man asked.

"We are lost," Omar said. "We're trying to find Great Oak Lodge. We are to meet some friends there."

"Did you come up from Kurtz? You should have gotten directions there. You're headed in the wrong direction."

"I guess we didn't understand the directions. Then we come up this road and it ends at your home," Omar said.

"Well, you have to go back the way you came." The man thought for a moment. "I'll have to write out the turns and local route numbers for you. Otherwise, you'll just get lost again. Wait here, I'll get some paper and pencil."

He turned to go. As he did so, Taimoor sprang forward and grabbed him.

"What the hell—?"

The man cried out as Taimoor's left hand closed over his neck.

"Do not fight me or you will die."

With his other hand, Taimoor pressed his pistol against the man's head.

"Who's inside?"

"No one. There's nothing of value. What are you doing?"

"We need to use your house and shed for a little while. Cooperate and you will live. Don't and you will die."

At that point, the rest of the men clattered up on the porch and rushed inside to check the house. Taimoor led the man through the door after the others had gone in.

Inside, they found the man's wife. Both were in their late sixties, retired farmers living off their meager savings and social security.

After the house was searched, the two were seated on the couch in the living room. Around them stood ten strangers, all dressed in clothes that indicated they were not westerners. Taimoor spoke Arabic to the others, and they dispersed to make sure the house and outbuilding were secured.

"Do you live alone?" Taimoor asked in English.

The two nodded.

"No one will be coming here later?"

They shook their heads.

"Do not lie to me. If you do, we will kill whoever comes, along with you."

"No one is coming," the man said. "What do you want? We have nothing."

"We need to stay here to work on our truck. Then we will leave and you will never see us again." Taimoor pointed to the woman, "You will make us something to eat. One of my men will watch you. We will work and will be gone by tomorrow."

"You won't hurt us?"

Taimoor shook his head. “Just do as I say. If someone calls you, we will listen in. If you warn them or ask for help, you will die and we will be gone. Before anyone can get here.” He leaned over the two who cowered on the couch. “Warning others will not help or save you.”

Chapter 29

"I don't see t hem."

"What do you mean?" Dan asked. He was taking a call from Fred.

"They haven't shown up on any cameras. There's plenty around the naval installation and Bedford."

"They probably avoided those, like you said."

"Yeah, but there are two other towns, further east. They have cameras and Warren says nothing has shown up. If he's right, they should have gone through one of those by now."

"Are you sure?"

"No. But if they're heading to D.C. and they don't want to be on the interstate, they'd skirt the national forest. Going between it and the interstate. Warren checked the towns in the area and they haven't been through them."

Dan turned to Marcus. "Pull over. Fred thinks they've stopped. Somewhere up ahead. Did you check about getting the rental GPS data?"

"No. I've been helping Warren with the traffic cameras."

"Got it. Call them now and see what you can come up with. Be persuasive."

"What do I tell them?"

"Tell them you're with the investigative arm of the U.S. Marshalls office. It'll be hard to corroborate that right away. You suspect a wanted fugitive is traveling in that truck and you need to locate it."

Dan hung up.

"Boy, you make up some whoppers," Roland said.

"Got to be creative."

"So now we wait?" Marcus asked.

"Now we wait...and hope Fred can get us the information."

"Why would they stop?" Marcus asked. "It makes more sense to get to D.C. and mount the attack. They're on borrowed time and they've got to know it."

"Maybe they had to leave before they were ready," Dan said. "We saw some equipment in the shed that was burning. Maybe they had to finish processing the anthrax."

"But they left the equipment. Burned it," Roland said.

"There could be other issues. Hell, I don't know. I'm just hoping they've stopped. If Fred can find them, then we can take them out."

"And if he doesn't? Where does that leave us?" Marcus asked.

"Fucked." Roland said.

"Maybe not," Dan said. "Warren will have to keep monitoring the towns until he gets a hit. Then we get on the move again."

"Jane's going to have to be brought into this at some point. Fred and Warren can't just monitor traffic cams for the next twelve hours or more."

"I'll deal with that later. One problem at a time."

"If we locate them, you got a plan this time?" Roland asked.

"Do I ever?"

"Sometimes. But never an exit plan. Seems like you always want to improvise."

"More like I have to improvise." Dan smiled at Roland. "And you guys are getting better at it. Encouraging for dumb Delta Force pukes."

"Watch your mouth, sniper guy." Roland said. "Remember we're the ones always pulling your ass out of the fire."

The men lapsed into silence as they waited for Fred's call.

It was three hours later when he called back.

"Thought we'd never hear from you," Dan said.

"It wasn't easy. I had to go up the ladder to the manager, and he was out. When he came back, he told me I had to get his area supervisor to approve my request. I kept stressing the time factor. That this was a bad guy who needed to be brought in, and if they took too long, we might lose him. It didn't help.

"The area supervisor asked me some difficult questions. Like who was my boss, where my office was, what kind of warrant was out for this guy, and his name. Good thing I boned up on some of the details before I called. I got the area office right, but told him I worked out of another district, so I wasn't on their list of marshals. We sometimes travel a long way in pursuit of our quarry."

"Sounds like you had a good time with it."

"It was stressful. I couldn't have done it in person."

"You get what we needed?"

"Yep," Fred said. Dan could tell he was proud of his undercover work. "I asked the supervisor to call the manager and tell him to get me the location. I told him I was running out of time and afraid they would do some harm before we caught them. He agreed to make the call."

Fred took a deep breath.

"After I hung up, I waited a few minutes and called the manager back. He had gotten the message and had checked his GPS feedback bursts. This is a onetime thing as my cover will be blown if the supervisor checks with the area office."

"That's okay. Did you get a location? We're wasting time here."

"Thirty-eight degrees, nineteen minutes, fourteen point two seconds by eighty-six degrees, thirty-two minutes and zero point six two seconds."

"I like that precision," Dan said. He read them back to Fred as Marcus noted them down.

"Now close up, so Jane doesn't see anything, but stay by your computer."

"After hours?"

"You got a hot date or something?" Dan asked.

"No, no. But Jane will wonder why I'm working late."

"Damn it, Fred. Make up a story. You're getting pretty good at it. And make sure Warren stays as well."

"Okay." Fred's voice now sounded hurt as well as intimidated.

"And, Fred...thanks. This is good work."

"Okay, boss. I'll be standing by," a more chipper-sounding Fred replied.

"Gonna be dark in an hour," Marcus said.

"Yep. That'll work to our benefit. Let's find this place without getting noticed. After that we can plan our attack. I'm betting they're at some abandoned farmhouse. They got to be out of sight and need some shelter. That's why they're stopping."

"Hopefully it'll be abandoned. But we could have a hostage situation on our hands," Marcus said.

"Let's find out," Dan said.

They drove off, with Dan trying to figure out which roads led them to the coordinates they were given.

Chapter 30

The three men finally got on a gravel road that closed in on the coordinates. As they drove, Dan could see that they needed to be a little further to the north or le ft of their direction of travel.

"They're in that direction, a half-mile or so ahead." He pointed towards the driver's side windshield.

"I don't see this road going left anywhere," Marcus replied.

"If you do, we don't want to drive down it and run into them. Be careful," Dan said.

They drove on slowly. There were no street lamps on the back road. Their headlights illuminated the narrow lane out of the blackness of the night out in the country. A narrow gravel road appeared to their left, the headlights almost missing it. There was a mailbox at the edge where the drive intersected the road they were on. Further up what seemed to be a driveway, they could make out the glow of a farmyard light.

"Don't stop," Dan said. His voice was low, even though there was no need to whisper. "Just drive by. We'll go far enough to make sure no one can see us, then douse the headlights and find a place to pull over."

"Easier said than done on this narrow lane," Marcus said.

"Up there, on the right," Dan said. "There's an entrance to a field."

A culvert had been put into the ditch, and dirt filled in over it to allow tractors to cross the ditch and get into the field with their equipment for plowing and harvesting. Marcus pulled the car off the road and onto the dirt. He killed the lights while stopping. The men lowered the windows and sat silently in the car listening for any sound of a vehicle starting up. If they heard anything, they would drive away and work their way back later. For now, only silence came to them. Silence and the hum of cicadas making a last effort to mate for the season.

"Let's do some reconnoitering," Dan said.

They got out, opened the trunk, and put on their tactical vests. Besides their sidearms, they took M4s fitted with suppressors. Dan left his M110A2, a lighter model than the original he had used in Mexico. It was equipped with a suppressor and had an NVD night vision device fitted to the end of the scope. The rifle was powerful and accurate but too large for close-quarters work such as they were going to do. After checking his M4, Dan put three extra magazines into his pockets.

Roland and Marcus grabbed their M4 carbines along with extra mags. Their rifles were also fitted with suppressors. These devices would not make the weapons silent but allow them to fire without instantly notifying others, making it harder to locate where the shot came from.

"Let's head out," Dan said after the men had assembled and checked their gear.

"Through the fields?" Roland asked.

"Yep. I like the one with the silage corn. It will give us cover."

"Got to be careful, though. We could make a racket walking through those dried stalks," Marcus said.

"Copy that."

† † †

After the men had eaten, Taimoor sent the handiest of them outside. They moved the truck into the barn, turned on some lights, and got to work. Taimoor took the still-manacled Jabbar aside. He gave him a careful look.

"You will recover. Broken nose, split lips, maybe a cracked cheek bone and rib. Nothing a warrior can't deal with. This is the pain those of us experience when we operate on the front lines, where one can lose one's life. We don't fight at meetings, or undercover, or with words. We fight with violence. I hope you are beginning to understand."

Jabbar glared at him. "I understand you have revolted against my authority and put our mission in great danger."

Taimoor almost smiled at him. "We have one truck going to Chicago to strike. Maybe as soon as tomorrow. We are safe from discovery here and can finish our vent. Then we will go to Washington and lay waste to that city. While they are recovering, we will drive to New York and do the same to them."

"You are a fool, Taimoor. I would have gotten us there with no one looking for us. Now everyone will be on the alert for white box trucks."

"Do not worry. We are going to paint this one. While we finish the vent." He paused for a moment as if to think. "You, however, will have to remain shackled since you seem to not recognize my authority. I will not have another challenge. Our path is set and it will produce victory."

He got up and walked over to the farmer.

"I need some paint for our truck."

"I only have barn paint...for wood."

"That will do. What color is it?"

"I have some green and some red."

"You and I will walk to the barn and you will gather the paint. We will use whichever you have most of."

"I don't have any spray gun."

"We will use brushes. It does not have to be pretty."

They got up and walked outside. It turned out that there was more red, so Taimoor got two men busy painting the sides of the box and the cab in red. Up close, it did not look good, but Taimoor felt from a distance, and at speed, it would not look that unusual.

Back inside, three men were sitting around. Jabbar remained in the corner with his wrists cuffed.

"Two of you go outside and keep watch. You," he pointed to the remaining man, "rest. You will relieve one of them in three hours."

"Is there need?" one of the men asked. "We are so far out in the country."

Taimoor gave him a stern look. The man didn't say anything more but went outside to stand watch. The two men had their AK47s with them, along with their sidearms.

† † †

After ten minutes of careful walking through the corn with the men cringing at each crunch from an errant step punctuating the still night, Dan put up his hand. He motioned for Marcus to head towards the drive to see how close they were. Marcus slowly crossed the rows. It was harder than moving along a row, and he had to slowly part the stalks to not make a sound or cause a waving at the top that could be noticed.

Ten minutes later, he was back. "About two hundred yards to go," he whispered. "The pole light shows a house and barn. There's a car in front of the house and lights on in the barn. I don't see the truck. We sure this is the right place?"

Dan consulted his hand-held GPS. "We're within seconds of the coordinates. You see any other farm or clear space around?"

Marcus shook his head. "The corn field ends about twenty yards or so from the grass in front of the house. We should be able to get that close."

"Let's go, then. We'll see better if our guys are here when we're closer."

Chapter 31

Joe Harris remained at the farm after calling in the fire. A deputy from the county sheriff's office arrived. Joe explained that a body might be inside the burning shed and that Frank Kline's official SUV was out back. The connection didn't look good.

The deputy put a call into his local office. Soon he had two more officers on their way to the farm. Joe told the deputy about the two box trucks that had left the farm. After hearing his story, the deputy called the state police and told them to be on the lookout for the trucks. He was able to give them a description and partial license plate numbers.

By the time the fire department finally extinguished the blaze, the shed had collapsed. Now the men sifted through the ruins, looking for a body. In searching, they found odd pieces of metal, melted and twisted. No one could figure out what they were, but the metal didn't look like farm equipment.

Out back, the men excavated a fresh mound of dirt and discovered a body wrapped in a white sheet. It was an Arab-looking man. Shortly thereafter a burned corpse was found. By this time, a forensic team was on its way from Cape Girardeau.

The state highway patrol units working the I 57 corridor were on high alert. The partials on the plates quickly led to the exact license numbers.

"You've got to stop them, but keep your distance," Joe said. He kept repeating himself multiple times since he wasn't sure his message was being transmitted to the patrols.

"And you say this because some unknown civilian-types told you? They said they were special investigators trailing these men?"

"They're terrorists. The man was clear about that. And I don't doubt him. Look at what they did here? That's probably Frank's body burned beyond recognition. And they killed one of their own for some reason." Joe's voice was filled with anger. "You can do what you like, but seems to me that the prudent thing would be to play it safe."

His entreatments finally got through to the officer, and he called back to his supervisor to pass along the recommendation to not approach the trucks if they were stopped.

Hours later, a patrol car radioed to the District 10 area supervisor in Pesotum that he was following a single white box truck with the noted license plate. The patrol car was on the interstate south of Champaign at that time. The supervisor got on the phone with the District 21 office in Ashkum. Between them, they decided to set up a roadblock south of Paxton, a small town beyond Champaign and just north of Rantoul. They could stop all southbound traffic and shunt it onto Route 45. Meanwhile, a car would stop the northbound truck before the town's exit. Additional patrol cars would direct all northbound traffic to use an emergency turnaround and head back to Rantoul to get on Route 45 to continue north.

When the southbound traffic was finally blocked, the patrol car turned on its lights and siren and pulled in behind the truck. The patrolman followed the truck for a quarter mile as it began to slow.

"What is going on?" Farid asked. "We are traveling the speed limit. We're not breaking any rules. Why are they pulling us over?"

"I don't know," said Nasir, who was driving. "Since we haven't done anything wrong, I'm going to stop."

"Is that wise?"

"What else can we do? We can't outrun them the rest of the way to Chicago. We must act like Jabbar. Be smooth and innocent. Then we can go on our way."

He braked and pulled onto the edge of the highway. The patrol car stopped thirty yards behind him with its lights on. No one got out.

"Why is he not coming up to us?"

"Maybe he's checking our license plate. Making sure the truck is not stolen."

Nasir shook his head but didn't say anything.

Once the truck had been stopped, the District 10 office contacted state police headquarters in Springfield. This call triggered a state-wide alert and sent a bomb squad unit along with an armored personnel carrier on its way to the roadblock.

"What do you want me to do?" the patrolman radioed.

"Just sit tight."

"Something's got to give, they'll either get out to approach me or drive off. We can't just sit here for an hour or more."

"We got resources on the way. Keep them in the truck."

As the words were said, the driver's door opened, and Nasir stepped out.

"Get back in your vehicle," the trooper said over his loudspeaker.

Nasir stopped and looked at the patrol car. “What do you want?” he shouted. “I have to get on with my schedule.”

“Get back in your vehicle. I’ll be up there shortly.” The trooper knew this was a lie. They all had been given strict instructions to not approach the truck. Everyone was worried there might be a bomb inside.

“I have to meet my brother to help him move. He has to get his belongings out today and put them in the truck. You are making me late.” Nasir stood his ground. “I was not speeding. Why did you stop me?”

“Get back in your vehicle, sir. I’ll talk with you shortly.”

It was all the trooper could do. Two more patrol cars showed up. Now traffic had stopped coming past them as other officers had set up a roadblock a mile behind and began to turn traffic around.

“Do you notice something strange?” Farid asked. “There is no traffic coming from the north. Where did it go?”

Nasir looked in his rearview mirror. “There is nothing coming from the south either.”

“They are setting up road blocks,” Farid said. “They know we are carrying something dangerous.” His eyes were wide with panic. “We will not get to Chicago. Taimoor was right. We cannot complete our mission trying to be subtle or nice.”

Nasir gave him a questioning look.

“We must go. Now. The police cars cannot stop us. Soon they will send more equipment, heavy trucks to block our way.”

“They will shoot us down before we get to Chicago,” Nasir said.

“Maybe we go to the next town and release the powder. Maybe we release it right now.”

"Here?" Nasir asked. He waved his arms around the cab's windows, indicating the flat farm fields. "There are no people here. We will only infect crops and animals."

Farid slammed his fist on the dash. "We must try. Allah will provide something. If we cannot get to Chicago, any town is better than fields."

He picked up his phone and called one of the men in the back of the truck.

"Get ready to release the powder. We have been stopped. We will not get to Chicago. Open the rear door when we go. There are police cars behind us. If they come forward or try to shoot, fire on them."

He turned to Nasir. "You go now."

Chapter 32

When they reached the end of the cornfield, the men crouched down, still under cover, and watched. They saw two men standing on the porch with carbines slung over their shoulders. The men were talking with one of them looking around occasionally. They didn't seem too alert or interested in maintaining a strict watch.

The east side of the house had no yard light since it looked out on the fields. The side towards the outbuildings had a light that partly illuminated the deep dark of the night out in the countryside.

"Any doubts about this being the right place?"

Marcus shook his head. "We have a complication, though. The car tells me we've got some civilians inside. Hostages now. We have to figure out how to not get them killed."

"Yeah," Roland said. "No blitzkrieg charge on the house. That's always fun, but probably not good for any hostages inside."

"More reconnoitering. I'll sneak up to the back of the house. These jokers don't seem too interested in keeping a sharp watch. They should be patrolling the perimeter or even walking the wrap-around porch. I'll try to locate where any people are inside. Then we can figure out how to separate the civilians from the others."

"Go do your super sniper sneaking," Roland said.

"How long did it take you to think that up?" Dan asked.

"Just came to me in a flash of inspiration."

Dan smiled, but Roland couldn't see it in the dark. "I'm gonna go towards the side a bit before leaving the cornfield. I've got to get across the grass without being seen."

"And without a ghillie suit," Marcus whispered.

"If it looks like I'm spotted, take out the snipers and get up to the house. We'll have to storm it fast before anyone inside can react and kill the hostages…or use them as shields."

"Copy that," Marcus said.

"It'll take some time. If nothing changes, just be patient. I'll be back so we can discuss a plan."

"If you're not seen," Roland added.

Dan slipped away to the right to put distance between himself and the men on the porch. When he had gone about fifty yards, he unslung his rifle and lay down at the edge of the cornfield. After a long look over at the now barely visible figures on the porch, Dan began to crawl onto the grass, cradling his rifle in front of him. He moved slowly. The point was to not hurry but to stay silent. He crawled a few feet, stopped and watched, then crawled a few more feet. He could barely see the figures as he kept his head on the ground, turning sideways to look. He didn't raise his head, fearing it would stick up above the sight line of the flat grass and alert anyone looking in his direction. *Patience*. He kept repeating the mantra in his head.

Twenty minutes of careful crawling brought Dan to the side of the house, back at the rear corner. From this point, he could not see the figures on the porch. Neither could they see him. He peeked into the window on the side but only saw the kitchen. He could see the opening into another room, but from his angle, little was showing. He turned and crept to the corner, peered around, and then stepped to the rear of the house.

The window at the back showed the kitchen and, through the opening beyond it, the dining room. No one was visible. Dan kept moving across the back of the house. When he reached the back door, he tested it. He slowly tried the screen door. If he felt any resistance, he would stop to avoid a squeal or screech. It opened smoothly. Dan tried the knob on the back door without opening it. It turned. *A way in.* He moved on.

The next window revealed a small washroom that seemed to serve as a mud room for boots and clothes. Dan kept going. He reached the corner, and crouching down, peered around it with his head near the ground. Anyone watching would be less likely to notice him at that elevation. The side was clear. The porch stopped at the front corner, wrapping around only on the other side, facing the cornfield.

He moved beyond the washroom window. At the next window, he looked in. There were people inside. Sitting on a couch was an older couple. Standing in the room were two men, both armed with AK47 carbines. Another jihadist was sitting on the floor with his hands tied.

What the hell is that? Dan wondered.

He watched. One of the men was talking and pacing. His gestures indicated he was lecturing the other man. He seemed to be the one in charge. After some back-and-forth discussion, the other one went out the front door. *Shit. Hope that doesn't trigger Marcus and Roland.* Dan readied himself in case the two men charged the house. He'd take out the jihadist before he could harm the civilians.

Instead of gunfire and charging men, one of the sentries came inside. He sat down in a chair and put his carbine on the floor. The leader spoke to him and then sat down himself. The room went quiet. The farmer said something to the leader, who gave him a short reply. Then there was more silence.

Dan sat back from the window. *Two jihadists to take out in the living room. The one tied up won't be a problem, at least initially. How many more are there in the barn?* He turned his attention to the building across from the house. He could hear sounds of work going on but could not discern how many men were involved. *What are they doing?*

Dan decided he needed to know more about what was going on in the shed before they attacked. He turned back to the rear of the house. He'd cross over the open yard as far from the front as possible. The new sentry might be more interested in keeping watch than the previous one was. It was better to take some time to ensure he was not seen. It looked like the terrorists were not going anywhere soon. He began to crawl across the grass.

When he reached the barn, Dan's problem was to find a way to see inside. There were no windows on the side, which he couldn't use anyway due to the risk of being seen from the house porch. He stepped around to the rear. Hopefully, there was a working rear door that he could get open.

Dan found a door. It looked like it hadn't been used for quite a long time. He lifted the latch and gave it a gentle pull. Nothing. *Damn!* Dan tried again. Again, nothing. He knelt down and dug into the dirt with his hands, pulling it away from the bottom of the door. It was slow going. He pulled out his tactical knife and used the blade to dig into the hard ground.

Once he had some clearance to allow the door to swing, Dan sheathed the knife and tried the door again. This time it moved with a creak from the rusty hinges. Dan froze. The door had opened about two inches. He peered inside, trying to determine if anyone had heard the sound. He could see part of the truck and hear the men talking and working. The rhythm of their activity didn't change.

He breathed a sigh of relief and waited for more noise. When he heard the sound of a drill working on metal, he gently pulled again. The creak came as before, but the door moved; this time, a foot farther open. Dan pulled out his 9mm and watched. There was no change in activity. No one inside had heard over the noise of their work.

Now Dan could see more clearly inside. Two men were painting the truck with brushes. Others were working on the truck, something involving metal fabrication. One man was on the roof with a drill, and the rest were inside the box.

What are they doing? Dan thought about the work as he watched. The weapon was anthrax. It had been micronized from all the evidence they could gather. To attack the cities, they needed a way to distribute it. *That's it. They're going to blow it out of a roof vent.*

Dan gently pushed the door back but didn't latch it. He turned and headed to the house. From there, he crawled back to the cornfield and then to the two men waiting for him.

"Finally," Roland whispered when Dan reappeared. "We thought you forgot about us. They changed guards, but that didn't raise the level of competence."

"Yeah, I know. I got a look inside. There's an older couple held hostage in the living room. Three men inside, one of them, oddly is tied up. The leader is in the house. There's more in the barn. They're modifying the truck. Making a roof vent to blow out the powder. Looks like they'll be at it most of the night."

"They aren't going to leave that couple alive when they go," Marcus said.

“Probably not,” Dan replied. “We’ll have to split up and take the house and barn simultaneously.”

They began to plan their attack as the jihadists kept their lazy watch.

Chapter 33

Nasir started the engine. A small cloud of smoke came from the tailpipe as the motor caught.

"They're on the move," shouted the trooper into his mic.

He hit his siren again and pulled his car forward. The van pulled out and the rear door lifted. The trooper accelerated, and a burst of automatic fire hit the front of his car. Bullets flew through the windshield, smashing into his face and chest, killing him instantly. His car swerved to the right as his body jerked back against the seat and pulled the steering wheel in his death throes. The following police car swerved to the left and shot forward, only to receive more gunfire. The trooper ducked as bullets flew through the windshield and the front of the vehicle. The truck accelerated away, gaining distance from the second patrol car. The car did not respond but limped along. Damage to the engine computer most likely shutting down the throttle, allowing the machine to only idle forward.

A mile ahead, two more state police cars were parked facing each other to block the northbound lanes. Nasir saw them and turned to Farid.

"What do we do?"

"Go faster. We can push them aside. Don't hit them head on. Use the shoulder and hit one in the rear. It will spin and you will only damage our fender."

The state troopers were outside of and behind their cars. They had their carbines leveled at the oncoming truck.

"Aim at the car and duck. They are going to fire."

The two men up front ducked as the police opened fire. Nasir kept the throttle floored. They braced for the impact as the truck slammed into the rear of the right-hand car. It spun backwards, as Farid guessed, and the truck slewed past the blockade partly on and off the highway. Once past, the men in the back opened fire, and the two state troopers fell before they could aim at the departing truck.

The truck raced north, skipping the exit for Paxton, which was guarded. The state police abandoned the blockade and set out in pursuit. The men in the back of the truck closed their doors on Farid's orders. When Nasir saw the pursuing police cars closing in, he told Farid, who ordered the back door opened again. The men began to fire at the vehicles, which caused one to crash and the other to drop back.

"We need some heavy-duty equipment to block the road ahead. Lay out some spike strips," one of the troopers radioed into his supervisor, who was coordinating the men.

"How far north?" came the reply.

"They've passed Loda and it looks like they'll go past Buckley. Anywhere north of Buckley," the trooper replied.

More vehicles and spike strips were positioned just south of the exit at Onarga. The men saw the blockade, this time with more vehicles, and Farid noticed the spike strips.

"Exit here. We won't get through. Go on the shoulder, they have spikes set out to puncture our tires."

Nasir nodded as he wrestled the wheel. They were going eighty-five, bumping up against ninety miles per hour. The truck would do no more.

"I don't know if I can control it on the shoulder."

"You must try. We will go to the right and head into the small town. I'll tell the men to get ready to release the powder. We'll turn north and hopefully get to the next town before we're stopped."

Nasir started to slow as he approached the barricade.

"No!" shouted Farid. "You must go full speed. That is the only way."

Nasir pushed his foot to the floorboard, and the truck began to build speed again.

"Get low, but try to see enough so you can stay on the shoulder."

Both men crouched down, Nasir peeking over the dash and Farid fully undercover.

Nasir aimed the truck to the side. The troopers opened fire. One of the troopers started to run into the road to move the spike strip, but another stopped him as he would be in the line of fire. The truck roared past, gravel flying as it slewed to one side and the other. The troopers continued to fire at the truck as it sped past. They peppered the sides with holes and blew out a left tire.

Nasir slammed on the brakes to slow for the turn at the end of the ramp. The truck slid wide and went into the oncoming lane. There was no traffic due to the roadblocks, so he could recover control. The van swerved as it went down the road, not wanting to go in a straight line.

"Something is wrong with the steering."

"Maybe they shot out a tire," Farid said. "Keep going. Turn left at the light."

He called back to the men in the box to ready the anthrax for release. They hooked the bag to the nozzle and started up the blower. Thoughts of safety were now discarded. They knew Farid and Nasir would not let them be caught without spreading the anthrax. They also knew they would not be stopped until they were killed.

Nasir slowed after he turned left, and the men began to release the spores. After five blocks, the buildings ended and Nasir sped up. Farid told the men to stop the blower. Two more miles up the road was another small town, Gilman. Again, Nasir slowed, and Farid told the men to start the blower. After ten blocks, the town gave way to farm fields, and Nasir sped up. The pursuit had now caught up with them, and more shots were fired.

"Only a few more miles and there is another small town. This is the best we can do," Farid said.

Nasir nodded.

The secondary road on which they were traveling had deep ditches on either side. Up ahead, the two jihadists could see a large fire truck blocking the entire width of the road. Behind it were multiple police cruisers from state and local authorities. Men ranged across the back side of the fire truck with rifles aimed. Behind the truck, more police cars followed with their lights blazing and sirens wailing.

"Stop the truck," Farid ordered.

Nasir looked at him.

"There is no way around. We cannot push through such a heavy truck."

'But why stop?"

"To release the rest of the anthrax and shoot as many infidels as possible. If the wind blows the right way, those at the barricade will be infected."

He called back to the men and told them to start the release again. Nasir stopped. The pursuit stopped fifty yards behind them. The wind was blowing out of the south, directly towards the blockade.

No one could see the micronized powder from a distance. The wind dispersed it too quickly to remain in a cloud and be seen. The deadly toxin drifted on the breeze over the unsuspecting police manning the barricade.

"We are out of the powder," came the report from the back of the truck."

"Put fresh magazines in your rifles," Farid said. "On my order, jump out and charge the police behind us. Nasir and I will charge those in front.

After a short minute came the reply, "We are ready."

"Then go. *Allahu akbar!*" shouted Farid. He and Nasir jumped out of the cab and ran forward with their AKs firing on automatic. Both went down as a hail of gunfire riddled their bodies. The men in the back did the same. They fanned out from the truck with their AKs firing as they ran towards the police. Three officers were hit, but the return fire from the police was more accurate. The rounds tore through the terrorists as they charged. In a few short moments, it was over. All the jihadists lay dead on the road.

Chapter 34

Marcus, you and Roland deal with the ones in the shed. I'll take care of the ones in the house, hopefully without injuring the farmer and his wife."

"How are you going to keep the civilians from getting killed?" Roland asked Dan.

"Not sure. You and Marcus have a problem as well. You have to avoid getting exposed to the anthrax while you take out jihadists."

"Shoot from a distance," Roland said. "At least that's the way to start."

"Looks like we're both going to be improvising," Dan said.

The three headed out, following Dan's route to the house. From there they would split up, with Marcus and Roland going to the back side of the barn and Dan going to the rear door leading to the mud room.

"We'll have to wait until we're both in position. When one group attacks, the other will be alerted," Dan said.

"Give us time to get to the rear of the barn. We'll wait until we hear your shots, then we'll attack. The civilians in the house are safer if you're a complete surprise to the bad guys," Marcus said.

"Roger that."

The men crawled onto the grass and began their slow, painstaking traverse of the lawn where they had the greatest chance of being seen. Part of the way across the open space, an owl hooted in the trees behind the house. The three froze, flattening themselves to the ground. One of the lookouts walked to the side of the porch and peered towards the rear of the house. Dan and the others were strung out along the grass in single file. From his prone position, face turned sideways to the ground, he had a view of the porch, even though somewhat distorted and unclear. He could just make out a figure staring back in their direction. His breath came in shallow draughts, quiet and not causing his torso to rise up and down. No movement could be allowed to catch the lookout's eye.

They waited for two minutes which seemed like an hour. The sentry finally turned back and walked to the front of the porch. The men could hear the two conversing in Arabic. Dan began to crawl forward again.

When they reached the back of the house, Dan pointed to the dark behind the barn. "I've cleared some of the dirt that blocks the door," he whispered. "You'll have to clear more to get it open enough for you to get inside. The hinges will squeal, so try to time moving the door to when they are cutting or drilling metal. They won't hear you then."

"We hope," Marcus said.

"Best we can do in the circumstances. I should be able to see you when you get to the door. I'll give you five minutes to clear the dirt, then I'm going in."

"We'll start in and be ready to fire when you shoot," Marcus said.

He and Roland set out for the back of the barn. Dan unhooked the spring on the screen door and carefully opened it. He tested the door knob; still unlocked. When he could see the two men at the back of the barn, Dan checked his watch.

Five minutes later, he slowly turned the door knob. When it hit the stop, he began to push in. The door opened without a sound. Thankfully, it was used regularly by the couple. Dan stepped inside and stopped, carbine at ready, and listened. There was no sound except for an occasional few words of Arabic spoken.

Probably talking about keeping an eye on their captives. Dan had no expectations that the jihadists would leave the man and woman alive when they departed. He wondered why they hadn't yet killed them. *Maybe keeping them alive to answer the phone if there's a call. Fortunate for them.* Dan meant to continue keeping them alive...somehow.

He walked forward, keeping to the walls to avoid any floorboards creaking under his steps. He turned and went into the mud room. He stopped again to listen. To get to the living room, Dan had to go back out into the hall. The living room was off to his right, where the rear hallway ended. Ahead was the stairway enclosure that separated the living to his right and the kitchen and dining room to his left.

He went forward, testing each step as he slowly set his weight on it. If he felt or suspected a floorboard moving, he withdrew and put his foot in another spot. At that rate, it took five minutes to get to the end of the hall. *If they have to take a piss or want to get something from the kitchen, they'll see me.* Dan wanted to surprise the terrorists in the living room, taking out the two before they could react. Then dealing with the sentries, which he expected would rush back inside. The one tied up would, conveniently, remain so.

The two men found the door at the back of the barn, as Dan described. They immediately began digging and scraping the dirt away, widening the door's swing. Once done, they sat back.

"So how do we do this?" Roland whispered to Marcus. "Don't relish catching anthrax."

"Me either. I don't have any plan other than to go in and see where everyone is. At least we don't have civilians to deal with. We can kill everything that moves."

"Let's hope you're right."

"I doubt they would have bothered to take a hostage into the barn. That would just slow them down. The two in the house are probably all there are."

"There'll be some men inside the truck and some outside."

Marcus gave his friend a wicked smile. "We start from the outside and work our way in."

Roland returned the smile. "Shooting fish in a barrel."

"Only more satisfying."

They slowly pulled the door open, waiting until the sounds of construction increased. With the delays, it took a few more minutes to open it fully. Marcus slipped inside, with Roland following. Both large men moved silently. Once inside, they crouched behind the wall of an animal stall and observed the activity under the lights in the main, open area of the barn. Two men were painting the truck. There was a man on top, working with others inside where they could hear more banging. The truck was facing them, so they couldn't see how many were on the inside, nor would they be able to see them when they got out.

With gestures and a few words whispered close to each other's ears, the men planned their attack. Now they waited, listening for Dan's shots.

Chapter 35

"The jihadists are in Illinois!" Fred said, bursting into Jane's office.

"How do you know?"

"I just do. I'm told you need deniability. But believe me, they're there. I just confirmed state and local police stopped a truck in a blockade and shoot out. The men look Arabic. The truck's been cordoned off under suspicion of having a bomb or something else inside."

Jane sat still. Had Dan been talking with Fred? How would Fred know all this?

"Where's the truck?"

Fred told her.

"Where's Dan?"

Fred gave her a panicked look. "I...I...actually don't know."

"But you've been in touch with him."

Fred nodded without speaking.

"And he told you not to tell me anything? That it?"

Again, Fred nodded.

"I'll deal with that later." She gave him a stern look. "Where is Dan? You have to know something."

"What does it matter? He's handling it."

"So, he's in Illinois? With the police?"

"I doubt it."

“Is this the only truck? Is the threat neutralized?” Jane stared hard at Fred. “I can’t believe their only target was Chicago. That may be where this truck was headed. But too much anthrax was stolen for just one target.”

Fred took a deep breath. “There’s a second truck.”

“Alright, where is it?”

“Illinois. Dan’s following it. I tracked it to a farm house.” He held up his arms. “That’s all I know.”

“Okay. But no more secrets. If Dan calls you, or you need to tell him something, you tell me about it. Understand?”

Fred nodded.

“Now give me the details about this first truck. Where it’s stopped.”

After Fred gave Jane the location, she motioned for him to exit and picked up her phone.

“Henry,” she said as her boss answered. “I have to see you right away.”

A few minutes later, she was in his office.

“There’s a truck stopped at a blockade in Illinois. It’s somewhere north of Onarga and south of Kankakee. Seems it was headed to Chicago. Driven by terrorists. I think they were all killed. The troopers have been warned of a possible bomb inside and aren’t approaching the truck. Probably waiting for a bomb squad. It’s not a bomb, however. The truck has the stolen anthrax inside. It’ll be contaminated. You should call the state police and advise them to bring in a hazmat team. And clear the area.”

“Our friend’s work?”

“In a way.”

“He there?”

“No. He’s dealing with a second truck.”

“Jesus.” Henry rubbed his hand through his thinning hair. “How many more trucks?”

"These are the only two we know about. Our friend has the second truck under surveillance. My guess is he's waiting for a safe way to neutralize it."

"And no one knows he's involved?"

Jane shook her head. "I don't have the details. I'm being kept out of the loop. But if anyone knows there's someone else involved, they don't have any idea who it is."

Henry's face was grave as he looked at her. "Let's hope you're right. How long before we know about the fate of this second truck."

Jane raised her hands. "Who knows? I told you we're out of the loop."

Henry's expression indicated his displeasure with that situation but also his resignation of its necessity. "Let me know when you find anything."

"You want in the loop?"

"Not the details, just let me know the outcome."

"Will do." Jane turned and left. The less time spent around Henry, the better for both of them. Now Fred was another issue. She needed to restore her command over that situation. As much as she cared for Dan, as much as she had told him he was on his own, she couldn't let him give orders to her staff. On her way back to her basement office, she began to smile as she parsed through the ramifications of Dan's actions. Without Fred and Warren, he probably wouldn't have been able to track down the trucks. His only chance was to find them while they were stopped. Once he had missed that opportunity, he would have had to use the boys. Jane was glad he did, even though she would never let Fred or Warren know.

† † †

Back at the roadblock, a call came through to the on-site commander. The message said that there likely was a deadly pathogen inside the truck, not a bomb. Orders went out to evacuate all people in a mile radius and wait for a hazmat team. He could see inside the box and, amid personal packs, which could have housed explosives, there was a bag attached to a blower attached to the roof vent. The light bulb went on in his head. He grimaced as his binoculars showed the bag seemingly empty. What had it contained? Had it already been dispersed?

The commander got on the phone with the state headquarters in Springfield.

"I think they may have already dispersed the pathogen, whatever it is. We have to assume an area from our first encounter, Onarga, to Ashkum is exposed. Do we know what it is?"

"Anthrax," came the reply.

"Oh, my God."

"I'm calling the governor to send out the National Guard."

"I recommend we isolate those towns and expand our radius. We don't know if those people have been infected and with what. It may be very contagious."

"It is."

"What about the troopers who stopped the truck? Some of them may have been downstream of the anthrax."

"I'll have them report to a local hospital. They can start treatment."

"If there is any."

Within an hour, the call went out to the 44th Chemical Battalion and the 33rd Military Police Battalion, both part of the 404th Maneuver Enhancement Brigade, to deploy to the truck and the surrounding, possibly infected towns. The governor was in close communication with the Director of the State Police along with the Deputy Commanding General of Operations for the state national guard.

Chapter 36

Dan started down the hall. As he was going forward towards the living room, a loose floorboard finally caught him out. There was a loud squeak. He paused, frozen. The conversation in the other room stopped. *Time's up.*

He took two quick steps and burst around the corner of the living room, eyes searching for targets. A jihadist standing near the one tied up swung his carbine towards Dan and opened fire. Dan dropped to the floor as the rounds went screaming over his head. He rolled to one side to get his carbine into action. The man tracked towards him, and Dan fired a burst from his M4. The jihadist's carbine tilted up as the man staggered back from the rounds and his shots flew into the ceiling. He fell back to the ground, his AK dropping to one side.

"Get down!" Dan yelled to the shocked couple on the couch as he dove for the stuffed chair in the corner The barrel of an AK swung around from behind the couch, and a burst of fire sprayed through the air where Dan had been crouching. Had he not moved, he would have been hit multiple times.

He swung his rifle around the chair and fired a burst through the back of the couch. The two civilians had thrown themselves off the couch and onto the floor.

Just then the two sentries charged through the front door. He turned and fired two short bursts from his carbine, dropping both men before they could target him. Another burst of automatic fire slammed through the couch, the bullets screaming just over his body.

Dan swung back to the couch, and glimpsed a figure disappearing into the dining room. Dan fired, but he had lost the target. He heard the back door slam as the leader exited the building. At that moment, shots rang out from the barn.

There was no further discussion. When Marcus and Roland heard the burst of automatic gunfire coming from the house, not the muffled sounds of Dan's M4, they fired on the two men finishing their painting. Both men were flung to the ground with multiple rounds hitting them center mass. The man on the top of the truck jumped to the ground at the rear. Marcus and Roland quickly spread out, waiting for the other men to come out from the van. There was silence in the barn for a moment.

Then a man dashed out from the back of the truck, his AK firing on full auto. The rounds were not aimed; he was just spraying the area ahead, hoping to hit something and hoping to suppress return fire. As he came into Marcus's field of fire. Marcus loosed a short, accurate burst, and the man spun to the floor, his AK flying to one side. There were other two men behind the van. Seeing their fellow jihadist's fate, they ran straight back from the truck to find cover in the recesses of the barn.

Silence inside. With hand signals, Marcus indicated he would go to the left, and Roland should work his way to the right. They could pin down whoever else had been in the truck while keeping themselves from being outflanked. Not knowing how many they faced was a worry to both men.

Dan checked the two civilians to make sure they were unharmed.

"Gather the weapons. Do you know how to use one of these?" Dan held up an AK carbine.

The man shook his head. His eyes were wide with fright, but Dan could see his determination.

"You have a gun? A rifle?"

The man nodded. "Upstairs."

"Get it. Take these weapons up there as well. Hurry."

Dan fairly shook with the need to go after the missing jihadist or, at least, help Marcus and Roland out.

The farmer did as he was told. And in less than a minute, he returned with a 30-06 bolt action hunting rifle.

Now Dan turned to the jihadist who was tied up.

"I need more rope."

"Don't have any here," the farmer said. "It's all in the barn."

"Got a belt?"

"Yep."

The man stripped off his belt and handed it to Dan. He took it and went over to the jihadist, who glared at him with unconcealed hatred. Dan looped the belt around the man's wrist ties and then to a steam heat pipe coming out from the wall.

"Any tape?"

"In the kitchen." The wife had found her voice, which was surprisingly steady.

She got up and ran into the kitchen, returning with a roll of duct tape. Dan used it to tape the man's hands so he could not manipulate the knots or belt. Next, he strapped the man's ankles together along with some wraps around his knees.

"Guard him. I'd like to interrogate him after I find the other one. If he tries to get out though, shoot him. I don't care where. He will kill you if he can, so don't waste a moment of pity on him. These men were going to kill you after they worked on their truck." Dan started for the front door. "I'll be back shortly."

After a quick look around for the missing jihadist, he ran off the porch towards the barn. Dan guessed the man had fled into the fields. When he got to the front sliding doors, he dropped to the ground and crawled to the opening. He scanned the interior. The space was well-lit around the truck but dark along the periphery.

Hope the guys don't shoot me. The momentary thought passed. He was confident the two men could distinguish between the unsuppressed 7.62 round used in the AK47 and the suppressed 5.56 round used in the M4.

From his vantage point, Dan noticed one of his men working towards him to his right. He turned his focus back to the rear of the truck and the darker regions of the barn behind it. *They got to be somewhere in that direction.* Dan assumed that his other man was making the same move on the far side of the truck.

Dan's vantage point at the door gave him a better view of the rear of the truck. He concentrated on that area, looking for telltale motion. Many combatants gave in to impatience and moved too soon or with too much noise, thereby giving away their position, often to their own demise.

Soon enough, a shadow, almost indistinguishable from the other shadows near the barn's wall, moved. *Shadows don't move. Living things move.* Dan focused, sometimes looking slightly away, so he could bring the more light-sensitive receptors around the edge of his retina into play.

When he had a firm positioning of the shadow, Dan slid his carbine forward and sighted into the dark. He took his time. If the shadow moved again, he'd see it and could reset. He wanted one shot, one kill. He didn't want the shadow to disappear and his cover to be blown. If there were any other jihadists in those shadows, he would be an easy target for them. He'd have to shoot and then roll away from the door.

With the shadow firmly in his sights, Dan squeezed off a short burst. The M4 uttered a staccato of muffled explosions. The shadow lurched upward and back, disappearing to the floor. Dan rolled to his left, away from possible return fire.

Roland was moving around to the truck's right, away from the barn's large sliding door. However many jihadists that had emerged from the truck were back in the shadows, minus one. As he cleared the side of the truck, he stopped. He could not proceed into the dark without locating the enemy. He understood patience. Wait for movement.

While he was waiting, a short burst of a muffled 5.56 carbine came from the barn door. *Dan!* Roland saw a dark shadow lurch up and then to the floor. *Another one down*. He waited. If there were more, they would quickly panic and try to move.

Sure enough, a shadow closer to him began to move along the floor. The man was crawling. Crawling towards him. He hadn't seen Roland moving into his position. Roland smiled. Almost too easy. Then stilled the thought. Being involved in a deadly dual was never too easy. He preferred unfair advantages whenever he could give himself one.

With his thoughts put aside, Roland sighted the movement, and when he was certain of his shot, gently squeezed the trigger. His M4 uttered a similar staccato of sound, and the shadow collapsed.

Silence. No movement. It stayed that way for three long minutes before Marcus called out.

“Dan, you there?” Marcus called.

“Here,” came the reply from somewhere out front.

“Roland?”

“Roger. Holding position.”

The men waited another three minutes.

“Moving,” Marcus said. Neither Dan nor Roland needed to be told that meant towards the area behind the truck.

“Copy that. The same,” Roland said.

“Holding,” Dan called out.

Two minutes later, Marcus yelled, “Clear.”

Dan crept through the open door and worked his way over to where Marcus and Roland were standing.

“Looks like there were only five men in here. Two painting and three in the back of the truck.”

“Leave the truck untouched. It’s too dangerous,” Dan said.

“We’ve got a captive and a runner from the house.”

“You’ve been a busy boy,” Roland said.

“Yeah, and we have some tracking to do.”

After checking the men to make sure they were dead, the three carefully made their way back to the farmhouse.

Chapter 37

Zhōu met with Congressman Greely a second time after the hearings. This time they were at Bullfeathers on Capitol Hill. It was an expensive bar and pub with great sandwiches and a good selection of beer and whiskeys. Zhōu ordered a Salmon BLT, and Greely ordered a Cuban, a sandwich of roasted pork, ham, and Swiss cheese, with pickles and mustard mayo.

"We have established a trail of links from Garrett Easton to the killing of the Syrian diplomat two years ago."

"The one killed in Aleppo?"

Zhōu nodded.

"Was he involved? No one ever admitted to the killing. It was never attributed to anyone."

"It was a sloppy job. Innocents were killed including some children."

"How do you know this? Do you have evidence?"

Zhōu nodded again.

"And you can link the DDO directly to this?" Greely thought this could be the connection he had longed to find. Still, he wondered if it was real. How could Zhōu come up with this?

"I have sources you don't know about. If you leak this, the press will run with it. They love a scandal and won't look too closely at the links."

"So, more innuendo than reality? Is that what you're saying?"

"What have you come up with so far? Your speaker is getting tired of your show. You need something else."

James Greely leaned forward, his face intense, and stared at Zhōu. He wanted to uncover bad actors he knew were operating in the CIA. Ones that were antagonizing our partners in the Middle-east with their violent actions. Jihadists had to be tolerated to a certain extent. Keep them over in Europe was his approach. Don't antagonize them and their masters, and they would leave us alone. Powerful business interests on both sides did not want to upset the status quo too much. But this; if it wasn't real, how could he run with it?

"What do you suggest?" he finally asked.

"I will get the connections to your aide, Randall. He can leak them to the press as an anonymous source. You can then express your outrage and the need to get the agency under control. It will give new impetus to your crusade. It will put the CIA on the defensive and, with your party's majority, legislation could be advanced for reining it in. Putting it under greater oversight."

Zhōu used all the right words. Greely recognized that fact. Still, they excited his imagination.

"Go ahead. But I want to see what Randall gets before he leaks it."

Zhōu shook his head. "Not a good idea. You have to be separated from the source of any leak. If Randall is uncovered, he's an aide who got it wrong. Got out of control. The blowback might stain you, but not damage you. There will still be the leak and the press's desire to run with it."

The two men finished their lunch and walked out into the afternoon sun.

"Why do you want to see me rein in the CIA so badly?"

Greely had his suspicions but couldn't help asking.

"They do damage to the relationship between our two countries. We do a lot of business with Americans. You experience that. You get the opportunity to make lots of money from our joint ventures. We get your help with legislation to further our businesses. It is good for both parties. We both must think globally. Borders, trade restrictions, corporate espionage, making judgements on how we do business in China, all these are not productive to our mutual profits. We have our ways and don't criticize the U.S. for its ways. Smooth relations allow all of us to prosper."

Zhōu had made this pitch before but understood that Greely sometimes needed a reminder when his zeal seemed to fade. A reminder of the reality of making money, lots of it, served to shore up any weaknesses in Greely's zealousness.

† † †

Wang Li Xiu quickly became a regular part of George Randall's life. Unlike the other short-term affairs and one-night stands, she captured his attention and didn't bore him. She was deep, a bit mysterious, and an amazing lover. Had he finally found a long-term partner? He didn't want to speculate but preferred to enjoy the relationship while it flourished. Who knew what the future would bring?

They were together one night when Li Xiu looked at him with a serious expression on her face.

"What's up, my bird?"

He liked calling her his bird.

"I have a problem."

"Tell me. Maybe I can help."

"It's about you."

"Are you having second thoughts about our relationship?"

George's heart gave a hitch. He never had a worry about such things before. Now he was concerned about their affair ending.

"No, my love." Li Xiu snuggled close to him and kissed him tenderly.

"That's a relief." George couldn't keep himself from saying what he was feeling, even if that left him uncharacteristically vulnerable.

Li Xiu looked down with a coy expression on her face. "It is about us, in a way, though."

George waited for her to proceed.

She took a deep breath.

"You see, for we Chinese to get permission to study here, really to go abroad for most any reason, but especially as a student, we are required to help out when the authorities need us to do so."

"What does that mean?"

"It can mean most anything. I've heard stories of hard things being asked. Mostly it is just information. Like how to contact certain people we might know, or what their interests are."

"Spying." George paused for a moment. "Are you spying on me?" He feared the answer but couldn't help but ask the question.

Li Xiu shook her head vigorously. "No. You are important enough, the authorities know who you are."

"What is it then? Get it off your mind."

She looked up at him. Again, with eyes that would melt ice. "I've been asked to give you some information. I don't know where it came from. I only know I'm to give it to you."

"Okay. What is it?"

Li Xiu got up, went over to the side table, and reached into her purse. She took out a USB stick and handed it to Randall. “They said you would know what to do with this.”

“Do you know what’s on this?”

She shook her head. “I was told to just give it to you. I…I…don’t really want to know. I like being around you, being close to important things going on, but I’m just a student in the end. I don’t want to be involved with politics and intrigue.”

George smiled. She was more than just a student. He hoped he had let her know that. But he understood that whatever was on the stick might get her dragged into affairs that she’d prefer to only view from a distance.

What a mix of innocence and mystery. He marveled again at his good fortune in hooking up with this woman/girl.

The next day, in his office, Randall inserted the USB stick into his computer. He sat back and listened to a recording of Garrett Easton’s voice. A voice authorizing the Aleppo raid. He smiled. This was the smoking gun. How had it been recorded? Who had made it? He knew that fakes existed. If one had enough recordings of someone, they could put together almost any speech using their own words. Experts, though, could tell such a recording was fake. The background noises wouldn’t fit, or the inflection might be wrong. There were multiple places where a fake could be exposed.

Nothing in what Randall heard indicated a fake, but he was no expert, and the recording begged the question of who had made it? Who at the CIA would risk their career, maybe their lives, by recording the DDO authorizing a raid that now could hang him?

Randall decided the recording could not see the light of day. What could be made public, though, was the transcript of the recording. And that could be leaked to a favorite journalist at the New York Times, who could be relied upon to expose it with as much drama as possible.

He smiled. *Gotcha*. Garrett Easton was shortly going to have a lot of trouble on his hands, and his boss was going to have a new platform from which to attack.

Chapter 38

Inside the farmhouse, the three men found the farmer and his wife sitting on the couch. The man held his hunting rifle on his lap with the barrel pointed at Jabbar, who remained tied to the heating pipe with a scowl on his face. Dan walked up to the man.

"Your friend deserted you…and the rest of your crew. He's run off."

Jabbar's look didn't change. He didn't speak.

"Nothing to say?" Dan crouched down in front of the man. "Your truck that was headed for Chicago has been stopped. All the men in it have been killed. The authorities know there's a pathogen inside, so a hazmat team will handle the vehicle. No one is getting killed.

"This truck," Dan pointed towards the barn, "is now neutralized. All the men killed. The anthrax will remain inside the truck until the authorities get here with another hazmat team."

He paused for a moment. "It looks like a complete failure to me. How about we talk it over. Maybe you can convince me that I should let you live." Dan leaned forward and whispered to Jabbar. "You see, we're not regular authorities, in case you hadn't noticed. We're ready to kill you, or, maybe take you away never to be seen again. Torture you until you give up all your secrets."

He leaned back.

"Now, if you give us something useful, we can leave you for the authorities. You'll go to jail, but, since you were held captive, you can plead that you had second thoughts. Maybe tell them you tried to stop the others. Your bruises and the testimony from these people will corroborate your story. You could get a lenient sentence. Certainly not the death penalty. You could spend your life in prison, converting other inmates to Islam."

Dan smiled at Jabbar. "Not too bad for a failed mission, don't you think?"

Jabbar only scowled back at him.

"Tough guy. Who is the one that ran away?"

Jabbar still didn't say a word.

Dan stood up. "Okay. We'll just take you with us. I'm sure the police will pick up your compatriot soon enough."

He walked back to the couch.

"What now?" Marcus asked.

"We can't track the one who ran in the dark. We'll have to wait until daylight. Not sure we'll be able to follow then. It's been dry."

"We want to spend time on that?" Roland asked.

Dan shook his head. I don't think so. The cops will pick him up. They'll be a full-on manhunt started for him as soon as they get here." Dan nodded towards Jabbar. "We'll take him with us. He's got info to share, I'm sure."

Dan walked over to the man and his wife. The farmer had put his rifle aside after Dan and the other two came into the house.

"We're with a special anti-terrorist team. We'll take this man with us. Our team needs to question him further. The other man is probably long gone. He's figured out that all his men are dead. There's nothing left for him to do but to run, try to escape.

"When we leave, call 911. Tell them you have the second truck with the pathogen in it. Tell them the terrorists were killed. Tell them about the one that got away. You can mention us, but understand that we're undercover and can't be exposed. You'll never see us again after we leave. And, remember who saved your life. Help us out by not providing details, including that fact that we're taking this guy with us."

Dan looked at the man and his wife. "Got it?"

Both of them nodded, their eyes wide again.

"You understand? You're okay with what I said?"

The two nodded again.

"Okay." He turned to Marcus and Roland. "Let's go. Roland, you take the prisoner. Marcus and I will fan out and take point. The other guy may be dumb enough to stick around. Don't want to get shot by him after all this."

Roland and Marcus nodded and moved towards the door. Dan cut the tape from Jabbar's legs and yanked him upright. The four men exited as the farmer went to the telephone to make the call.

Taimoor fled out of the door. He didn't stop until he reached the cornfield. There, under cover of the stalks, he turned towards the back door. If the intruder came out, he would shoot him. The door didn't open. He thought he saw a figure going to the barn, but not clearly enough to take a shot and give away his position. He had heard muffled shots coming from the barn as he ran. There were enemy combatants inside, engaging his men. How many? His mind raced. How had they found him? The Americans seemed to have almost magical abilities. Was there nowhere to hide from them?

The shooting stopped. All was quiet. Then shots rang out. Not from his men. They were muffled reports from the enemy. There was a long pause, then another short burst, also muffled. Finally, he heard voices. Three men emerged from the barn and slipped into the shadows before he could engage them.

Three. *They killed all my men?* Taimoor was caught between disbelief and awe. *They have Jabbar.* That thought triggered his decision. He would ambush the attackers. He expected them to depart. They were not part of the regular authorities. They didn't act like it. If it had been the police, they would not have attacked but waited for reinforcements. Then they would have called out for surrender, giving Taimoor time to organize a counterattack. These men operated like jihadists themselves.

He had to intervene. Jabbar must be killed. He would give away too much, including his uncle. Taimoor had no doubts that these men could and would torture him into talking. He was not hardened and would crumble in fear and cowardness. Taimoor would make sure he ended his life before Jabbar could do any more damage.

The men would not be here when the authorities came. He watched and waited. He would get a chance when they made their move. They had to have a vehicle somewhere. He would find it and wait there. If they took Jabbar, which Taimoor felt was a certainty, they would be encumbered by their prisoner, giving him an advantage.

Chapter 39

Dan and the others trudged down the dirt drive, their feet softly crunching on the scattered gravel. They were spaced out so someone shooting could not hit all of them in one burst. Roland walked with Jabbar, who shuffled along out of pace with the three men.

"I don't like this, Roland said in a quiet voice. "We'll be sitting ducks when we get to the car."

"You hear something I don't?" Dan asked, turning his head back towards Roland.

"No. Just my sixth sense. That guy's out there. He could run off through the fields with no sense of where he's going. On foot, so the cops can surround and catch him. Or, he could figure we got here in a vehicle and it'd be easier to kill us and take it."

"Good point," Dan said after a moment. "Not much we can do, though."

"Let's not just walk up to the car. Let's approach with some caution," Roland said.

"Two of us could do a reconnoiter before we approach," Marcus said. "If he's out there, he'll have to be close enough to see us. We scout the area and clear it if necessary."

"He's a seasoned fighter. You will not see him," Jabbar said. It was the first time he had spoken since Dan took control over him.

"He speaks," Roland said. "And he speaks good English. Where'd you learn to talk like that?"

"England," came the reply.

"Well, my English friend," Roland continued, "we're also experienced and I'll bet on my team any day over your ragtag group. We just eliminated all of them. The ones in the other truck are also dead, just to remind you."

"Don't waste time rubbing it in," Marcus said. "And we might want to keep him from making any noise to alert this guy. Although why he'd want to help the ones who beat him so badly, I can't imagine."

Dan reached into his vest pocket. "I brought along the duct tape. Figured we'd need it when we got to the car."

He walked back to Jabbar. "I know this won't be comfortable, but to be honest, I don't give a crap."

He pulled off a strip and taped Jabbar's mouth closed. Two more strips ensured the man could only make hum-like sounds.

"That'll help," Marcus said, having come up to inspect Dan's work.

They continued in silence.

Fifty to sixty yards from the road, Dan raised his hands, and the group stopped. They crouched down along the side of the drive. Dan brought their heads close together.

"I'll go through the field on our left, Marcus, you continue and cross the road to check the far field. He had time to get to the other side."

"Roger that."

"We each work our way to the road and the car in a back-and-forth pattern. It'll take time. We have to go quietly. If we're clear, we'll load our guy and leave. If you come across anyone, shoot first. There're no civilians out in these fields tonight."

Marcus nodded. "On my way."

He got up, stepped onto the grass and weeds alongside the gravel, and silently made his way towards the road. Crossing would be the most dangerous, made less so only because the car was a couple of hundred yards down the road. If there was an ambush planned, it would be there.

"Keep our guest quiet here," Dan said. "I'll check this side of the road."

"Roger that, boss."

Roland pushed Jabbar down on the side of the drive and crouched just out of reach in case the man tried to lunge at him, even tied up.

"Try to make a move, alert your buddy, and I'll pop you in the leg. I won't kill you. I'll save that for later...and do it slowly."

Jabbar looked at Roland's hard expression. When he looked away, Roland turned his attention to the cornfield. He knew the enemy was there, somewhere in those stalks, waiting.

Dan entered the cornfield. After a few steps, he stopped to listen. It would now be a stalking game. One he had played before. But the field created so many opportunities to slip up. To crunch a dried stalk and give away his position. It was as bad as navigating the woods in the fall. He'd have to be extra careful.

With his M4 in the low-ready position, he moved slowly forward. He carefully placed each step so he wouldn't snap a dried stalk. Going across the rows was the hardest, but it was what he had to do to sweep the field up to where the car was parked. After a few steps, he stopped to listen. He needed to go slowly, but his problem was that they didn't have all night. The cops were probably on their way. They needed to be in the car and gone before they arrived.

The urge to hurry was balanced with the need to not get shot. Roland was correct. The escaped fighter most likely would seek out their vehicle and try for an ambush rather than set out on his own, cross-country, to an unknown destination. With no hope of instigating a terror attack, would he try to escape or decide to die in the fight? Die in one last attempt to kill some Americans? The fanatical mindset of a jihadist who truly believed in dying for the faith was something not to casually dismiss.

Ten minutes later, Dan guessed he was far enough into the field to begin heading towards the road and the parked car. He stopped and crouched in a row. Following it towards the road would be quieter going and allow him to move more easily and safely.

There was a soft crunch to his left, towards the road ahead. Dan smiled. That was probably not a deer. You rarely heard a deer walking through the woods or fields. Their delicate hooves seemed to be soundless, even as they bounded away from you, their white tails flashing like a "follow me" sign.

Dan went to the ground and crawled forward, avoiding the dried leaves so they wouldn't rustle. The night was still and cool. A half-moon was up in the east. It would increase the light, which could be a blessing or curse to either party in this deadly game.

After crawling for twenty yards, he stopped to listen. No sound came back to him. Whoever made it was now being more careful. An experienced fighter would understand that a few of those mistakes could mean death. Going to have to do this the hard way. There would probably be no telltale giveaway of his foe's position. He'd have to find him on his own.

Chapter 40

His progress continued. Ten yards. Stop and listen. Then repeat. In the soft, growing light of the moon, Dan scanned the rows ahead and to his side. The last sound had come from his left, so he concentrated there. He was pretty sure the enemy had not crossed over the row on which he was advancing. Still, there was a lot of cover to search in dim light.

He may not know I'm in here, looking for him. He's probably worked his way closer to the road so he can attack. *Three quick shots, and he's got us.* Dan smiled. His advantage was he was unexpected, therefore, unwatched. He began to move forward more quickly.

I'll be coming in from behind. He won't be watching his six. It was a reasonable assumption, but a little voice in his head warned him to not be too confident. A wary attitude was useful for survival.

As he closed in on the road, he heard a soft rustle again. Closer this time and still to his left, only now slightly. *He's just ahead. We're near the road.* Dan now inched his way forward. He needed to get eyes on the man, even his shadow before he suspected Dan was close.

Then he heard some movement from further away. From across the road. *Is Marcus going to break cover?* The thought accelerated Dan's heart rate. He hoped Marcus knew better than to expose himself before Dan finished his sweep. They would have to get eyes on one another before shouting an "all clear". Marcus was probably right at the edge, so he could see across the road and into the corn.

But if Marcus could see into the corn, his enemy could see Marcus. Dan moved forward. He had to intercept the shooter before he killed Marcus. *He just might not wait for the rest of us to arrive.*

Dan began to move. Suddenly there was a rush of sound, stalks crunching or being brushed aside. Dan dropped flat to the ground. He saw the shadow now. The shooter had turned back towards the corn. Dan saw his gun barrel wave as he scanned behind him in a sweep. *He saw Marcus and knows we're sweeping the field!* It made sense. *If we scouted across the road, we'd scout on this side.*

Dan slid his carbine forward. He couldn't help but create movement in whatever shadow he made. The barrel snapped back towards his position. Dan rolled to one side as a burst from the AK splattered the ground where he had lain. Dan shoved his carbine forward and fired a short burst, immediately rolling sideways again. More answering rounds spit out from the AK, spraying bullets right where Dan had been. This time, Dan could see the light flashes from the other muzzle and swept the spot with an automatic burst. He pushed off with his legs and dove farther to one side, increasing his lateral distance from his flash signature. There was a grunt from the other shooter, but, again, a round of return fire, this time sweeping not only at where Dan had shot but to one side. His lurch forward saved his life.

Now Dan lay still. His M4 pointed in the direction of his last shot. The shadow was not visible. Was that because the man was also lying flat, waiting for Dan to move? Or was it because he had been shot and was badly wounded?

Waiting seemed like the best option.

"Coming over!" Dan heard Marcus shout.

Marcus knew that Dan was very likely in his line of fire. He guessed Marcus was moving in order to spook the ambusher. Cause him to bolt from a pincer movement. Dan didn't answer. The shooter was only about ten yards into the field. He'd have to deal with Marcus right away to not get hit from behind. Marcus was forcing him into action.

There was a rustling sound, and Dan saw a shadow move. The man was turning towards this new threat. Dan raised his carbine to his shoulder. The man was to his right now. But where was Marcus? He didn't want to overshoot and hit his man.

This time he got up to a kneeling position. It exposed him, but he was betting the shooter was looking away from him, and Dan wanted his shot to go downward. If he didn't hit anything, he wanted the bullet to hit the dirt. He centered on the shadow and squeezed the trigger.

His shot rang out just as another muffled shot came from the road. The shadow collapsed. Without a pause, Dan dove forward and to his left. Again, clearing away from the flash of his rifle.

"I think we got him," Marcus yelled. "I heard you shoot."

"Approach cautiously. I'm just to your right, so you won't hit me, if you have to shoot again. I'll go to the road and then over to you."

"Roger that. Going forward."

After a few tense moments, Dan heard Marcus call out.

"I've got him. Come on in."

Dan got up and walked towards Marcus' voice. When he arrived, Marcus stood over Taimoor, whose breath came in shallow, bubbly pants.

"Three shots it looks like. One to the lungs, one to the shoulder and one to the leg. He won't last long."

Dan looked at the jihadist, who stared back at him with a look of unmitigated hatred. Dan had seen it before. Usually, just before he had dispatched a warrior to whatever hell or paradise awaited him.

"All clear," he shouted towards Roland. "Come on in."

"Copy that," came the reply.

"We try to get any info out of him?" Marcus asked.

Dan shook his head. "No. This one's hard core. But I'll use him to impress the other one."

In a minute, Roland came up dragging Jabbar who stumbled along behind him.

"He still alive?" Roland asked. "We can't hang around. Remember the cops are coming."

"Pull our captive forward," Dan said.

Roland jerked Jabbar in front of him. "Here's your buddy. He the one who beat you up?"

Taimoor's eyes now fastened on Jabbar. He tried to speak, but frothy bubbles of blood only came out of his mouth.

Dan grabbed Jabbar's head and turned it to him. "This man cannot tell us anything. He is near death. See what I do with him. I will do that and more to you if you are of no use to me." He released his head. "Take the tape off of his mouth and make him watch," Dan said.

Roland grabbed Jabbar's head and made him look at Taimoor. Dan took out his pistol. He shot Taimoor in the foot. He waited for the pain to fully register, then shot him in the other foot. Taimoor cried out with a gurgling sound, blood and saliva coming from his mouth in a pink froth. Dan then put a bullet in each calf, again waiting between each shot for the pain to register. His next shots were into the man's legs, above his knees. Taimoor was now gurgling out loud in excruciating pain beyond the pain from his initial wounds. Dan paused and turned to Jabbar.

"You see?" Dan asked. "Death can come slowly, so slowly you beg for relief. I can continue up his arms and then leave him here to lie in pain for an hour while he bleeds out. Or, if you cooperate, I can send him on his way. To his virgins, with my next shot." Dan paused as Jabbar looked at him with terrified eyes. "What will it be? If you don't decide, that is a decision. A decision for me to finish shooting him and then leave him here in pain."

"No." Jabbar's voice was weak.

"No, what?"

Jabbar swallowed. "Don't leave him in pain," he whispered.

Without a word, Dan aimed his pistol at Taimoor's head and fired a shot. The man's eyes went blank, and his body went limp, the tension of his pain now gone in oblivion.

"Let's get out of here," Roland said.

Without another word, the four hustled back to the car. Dan taped Jabbar's mouth, and the men lifted him into the trunk. They put some cloth under his head and curled him up to make him as comfortable as possible. Then they got in and drove off as fast as they could into the waning night.

Chapter 41

Garrett Easton sat in William Gardiner's massive office on the top floor of the CIA. Gardiner, the Director, had called his DDO into his office that morning after seeing the Times article. It purported to have the transcript of a recording of his DDO ordering the drone strike in Aleppo. The strike that not only killed a suspected jihadist but a high-ranking Syrian official and six children. It had been a scandal. Many argued that the deaths were not real but set up for the press. Their voices, however, were drowned out by the outrage over innocent children being killed by the brutal tactics of the U.S.

"What the hell is going on here?" Gardiner asked, waving a copy of the paper in the air.

"Beats me, Bill. You know I didn't put anything on tape. You also know that I was not directly involved in ordering that strike. That has to be a manufactured recording. If it even exists."

"They're claiming it does exist and they just are printing the transcript." He leaned over his desk. "How do you propose we get ahead of this? Greely will use it to his advantage. He's been tilting at windmills, finding nothing. Yet he continues to smear with innuendo. Now he's got some red meat to run with. We're going to have pressure from the rest of congress to rein in our clandestine operations."

Garrett shook his head. "I know it's bad. I think we should demand the actual recording. We can send it through our analytic team and prove it's manufactured. The tech is good, but not so good as to be indistinguishable from the real."

Gardiner looked at his watch. "I'm going to get a call from the President soon, you can bet on that. And all I've got to tell him is that this is a fake? That everyone just needs to believe you?"

"I know it isn't very strong. But we need to get our hands on the tape."

"The public will never buy it. Us analyzing a recording that impugns our integrity. They'll want independent experts reviewing it—"

"And who knows what they'll find."

"Precisely." Gardiner paused for a moment. "Do we have a mole inside?"

"That's always possible, you know that. But in this case? No. Because I never said what was in the transcript."

"Who ordered the hit?"

"It came from SAD."

"So, Roger?"

Garrett nodded.

"Go talk with him. Find out what the hell went on. How it was authorized, who was present, who knew about it. I want to know everything Roger knows ASAP. I'll be called on to comment and I need some background to know how to shape our reply."

Garrett got up and left to find Roger. He knew his boss would be hearing from the President shortly and would be called on to enlighten him about this disastrous turn of events.

"I didn't directly authorize the strike," Roger said. "You know I'm not pushing the drones for just the reason that this one became such a toxic item. They're a blunt weapon. Effective, but blunt. Even if there is no collateral damage, it can be made to look like there is. Then we are fighting an uphill battle of denial, which we don't do all that well."

"If you didn't, who?"

"Look, you know this was to be a low-key operation. A minor jihadist official messing around in Syria. We tracked him and had a chance to take him out. It didn't rise to your level, the Director or, God knows, the President. This was supposed to be a small action in the middle of a civil war. I left it to the station chief to make the call. He used the local air assets we have nearby."

"Why not have him ambushed by an assassin?"

"We didn't have an asset in the area that could pull it off. It could have been farmed out to locals, but that comes with its own set of problems. Our man decided that a small drone strike was the cleanest way to proceed."

"And look at how that got fucked up."

Roger didn't say anything. Every op could backfire; he knew that from painful experience. This one more than others, but it wasn't the worst. Bay of Pigs ranked up there as one of the bad ones. This was more a manufactured crisis, with manufactured outrage. That, however, didn't slow down the press, who liked outrage, manufactured or real.

"I can't give the press the whole story. I'm going to have to just stick to denial." Garrett got up. "I've got to get back to Bill. He's going to be called up to the President's office. I expect rather shortly. He'll need to be able to give him the full story."

"Not to say I told you so, but this is why I wanted to create the op you let me set up. We've had some blowups, but nothing that could come back on us like this."

"Point taken. Meanwhile help me figure out how we go forward, and for God's sake, don't let your team get exposed. Lie low. Now more than ever."

He slammed the door. Roger heard his footsteps echoing down the hall.

† † †

George Randall drove up to Baltimore. He got off I 95 on Russell Street, which went past the football and baseball stadiums. He drove west, away from the University of Maryland Medical Center, towards the Hollins Market neighborhood. He parked just down the street from the Neopol Savory Smokery and walked up to the restaurant. The area had a rough edge to it, and he was nervous about being there at night. Still, it was the only place the man he needed to see would meet with him.

George entered and located the man, Mario, in a corner booth. He was accompanied by an enormous man. Probably his bodyguard. George walked over and sat down opposite his contact.

"How you doin'?" Mario asked after George sat down.

"Doing okay," he replied.

"This here is Tiny," Mario said, referring to his enormous friend.

The man said nothing and just stared at George. His hands were large and meaty. They would make a fist, thought George, that could smash your face with one blow.

"So, what do you want?"

"I need you to talk to a congressman's aide. Get him to convince his boss to back off on an issue."

"What's the issue and why me? Why don't you talk to him yourself?"

"It's complicated."

Mario snorted. The waitress came over.

"You want something? A beer?" Mario asked.

George shook his head.

"Don't be a cheapskate. The gal has to earn a living and we're taking up a booth."

"Okay," George said. "I'll have a draft, whatever's on tap."

Mario smiled and turned to the waitress. "I'll have a Makers and coke. He's got the tab." He pointed to George.

Mario leaned back. "Now tell me your story."

George went through the issues surrounding the southern border and why Mario and his boss should care about that. He told him about the recent furor regarding the deaths in the trailer.

"Sounds like that'll die down on its own. Why do you need me?"

"I'm thinking we can play this for a longer-term gain. You could let the aide know the downsides to not convincing his boss. You could also let him know the upsides for doing so."

"And what would that be?"

"If he works it right, he could find himself on the receiving end of a steady payout for supporting our side. The case can be made that it's good for business in general, but it could pay off in a direct way to him."

"Yeah, and just who's gonna deliver that payoff. My boss ain't paying no congressman's aide. He's got his own pay list here in Baltimore. Why would he need to spend money in D.C.?"

"Maybe he wouldn't have to. I may be able to get someone I know to pass through some funds. There's enough to go around."

"Maybe for you. My boss don't see it like that. And if I'm going to do this. And I ain't saying I am. That's for my boss to decide. You'll need to pay me for my efforts. After all, he could blow the whistle and cause a big scandal, bring the heat down on us."

"Just let me know if you can do this and how much. When you're done, I'll follow up with this guy and make sure he doesn't cause an uproar."

"I thought you wanted to stay out of this."

"I do. But I can manufacture a reason to talk about his encounter...and offer some advice."

Mario shrugged. "Up to you. I wouldn't go near the subject if I were you."

The waitress brought the drinks. The booth lapsed into silence.

"Why do they call you 'Tiny'?" George asked.

"It's a joke," the man replied in a deep bass voice. "When I was a kid. Just stuck."

"It shocks a lot of people when I mention getting a visit from Tiny and he shows up," Mario said. "That's usually all it takes to get people back in line."

"You'll send Tiny?" George asked.

"Maybe."

Mario finished his whisky and stood up. "I'll be in touch."

He and Tiny left the booth, and George searched for the waitress so he could pay the bill. He didn't relish staying longer than necessary.

Chapter 42

Jane called both Warren and Fred into her office. She had a stern look on her face. Fred had announced earlier that Dan and his two companions had found and neutralized the second truck. And no, neither Fred nor Warren knew where the three were now.

When the two came in, Jane pointed to two chairs she had set up across from her desk. "You both will sit down and debrief me on what you know. I," she thumped her chest, "am your boss, not Dan. So, whatever he told you does not prevail contrary to my orders." She paused. "Got it?"

Both men nodded, almost like schoolboys brought into the principal's office.

Jane pointed to Fred. "Start from the beginning and tell me what transpired."

Fred recounted the events and how he had to bring Warren in to scour various computer systems and databases to find the connections, however tenuous, so Dan could pursue them. Jane listened patiently as Warren took over the narrative, recounting how he had to hack multiple towns' traffic cameras to catch the trail of the second truck. Fred told how he was able to bluff his way to get the rental company to divulge the GPS location of the truck. After that, they had no further contact with Dan except a brief, cryptic call saying mission accomplished.

"Where are they now?"

Both men shrugged. "Dan hasn't communicated with us since that last message," Fred said. "That's been six hours ago."

Jane exhaled in frustration. "You carried out a dangerous op without my knowledge or permission. If the shit had hit the fan, I would have been left looking stupid or incompetent, or both."

"With all due respect," Fred said, "it would have given you deniability. That was something Dan said you wanted."

"I wanted to protect the department, not myself. I wanted Henry and Roger protected. The rest of us are expendable."

"But if the trail led to you, it would lead to Henry. It would be the string that would unravel the knitting, way up the ladder," Warren said. "There would be no way to have it stop at you."

Jane gave Warren an angry look. He was right, of course. She knew that, but she was left feeling out of control and with her authority challenged. Still, these two men had accomplished almost the impossible. Dan, as effective as he was, and had been on this mission, would never have been able to catch up with the terrorists without Warren and Fred working in the background. She realized, again, what a resource these two shy men were, both to her and Dan.

"Okay. You make a point. With the threat neutralized, there will be lots of inquiry and speculation about 'unknown special agents'," her fingers formed air quotes, "both at the first farm and the second one. Fingers are going to be pointed at us."

"It might take some wind out of this latest leak involving our DDO," Fred said.

"Maybe we can help to make that happen," Jane replied.

† † †

"So, what do we do now?" Marcus asked.

They had been driving for three hours, and the sun was coming up. They were well away from the farm and the crime scene it most likely had become. The state police and, by now, the FBI were crawling all over the area. They would have taken the farmer and his wife off to a safe place to get detailed statements from them. The couple would recount how some unknown men, special operators, had killed the terrorist and saved their lives. The descriptions would be vague, not only because they wanted to honor Dan's request but also because one's memory, in such high-tension situations, was not all that accurate and reliable.

"We have to find a place to stash our man and interrogate him," Dan said. "Not sure where that is at the moment."

The men lapsed into silence.

Suddenly, Roland spoke up. "I've got a hunting cabin in West Virginia, near Cabwaylingo State Forest. It's south of Charleston, outside of Logan. Very isolated. I like it that way."

"Let's head there," Marcus said. "The threat is neutralized. We can take our time getting whatever this guy knows out of him."

"Plot the course," Dan said.

Eight hours later, they were deep into West Virginia, having gone south from Bloomington to Louisville and then east on I64. Now they were on the serpentine state and county roads that wound around the hills and through the hollows. The further they went, the narrower and less well-paved the roads became. Finally, Roland indicated a gravel side road that worked its way up one side of a mountain hill, around it, and back into a steeply sided valley with a stream at the bottom. Dan would have enjoyed the wild scenery if not for the passenger in their trunk.

They had stopped twice in remote areas to let the man out to relieve himself and give him some water. Now they were near the end of their journey, but another challenge lay before them. They had to get information from this youthful jihadi, hopefully without damaging him too much. Dan intended to turn him over to Jane after they were done if that were possible.

A badly graded dirt road now turned off the gravel one. It was pocketed with potholes, some still filled with water. There was a "No Trespassing" sign at the entrance. Branches hung low over the roadway indicating little use. The rental sedan struggled up the hill. Dan was careful to not let its lack of ground clearance hang up the car and strand them. In his rearview mirror, he could see no sign of the gravel road they had turned off of. *Good. No one can see us either.*

"You don't maintain much of a driveway," Marcus said as they bounced and crawled up the drive.

"Haven't had much time to put in here. Maybe this fall, if Dan can stay out of trouble. Besides, it discourages visitors."

"Good thing that," said Dan as he sawed away at the steering wheel.

Finally, the drive flattened out in a clearing near the top of a hill. At the far end was a log cabin with a porch on the front. It had a chimney, and a supply of wood was stacked under the porch roof. An outbuilding to one side held an additional pile of split wood under its extended roof.

"I splurged last year and bought three cords, cut, split, and dried. All I have to do is burn it."

The men got out and stretched. Dan unlocked the trunk, and they helped Jabbar out. His bonds were cut, and the tape taken off his mouth.

"Walk around. Loosen up. If you try to run, I'll shoot you in the leg," Dan said.

Jabbar gave him a sidelong glance and cautiously started walking around in circles. He swung his arms as he went, trying to get circulation back into them.

"Any food here?" Dan asked.

Roland nodded. "Fully stocked for hunting. If you like Dinty Moore beef stew, you'll love the cooking. There's a pump in the kitchen as well as in the side yard. Outhouse is out back where the crap can slowly work its way through the soil and down the slope."

"All the comforts of home," Marcus said. "I take it you don't bring too many ladies here."

"It might surprise you, but no. Only a few have ventured out with me."

He smiled as if remembering.

"But those few...wow. They were something special."

"I don't want to know," Marcus said.

"Let's get inside," Dan said, "and make our guest comfortable."

When they got inside, Dan had Jabbar strapped, this time more gently, to a chair. The other two went into the two bedrooms to make up the beds. The rooms were small, with just enough space for two single beds and one dresser. Folded linens were neatly stored in a cedar chest.

"You're quite the homemaker," Marcus said as they made the beds.

"Momma raised me right," was all Roland would say.

Dan started the wood stove. When the others came out, they began to heat up some of the cans of stew. Besides the canned stew were different kinds of canned meats, including Spam, along with vegetables. Not the best diet, but one that would keep you healthy and well-fed.

Once the stove got going, Roland banked the flames and put a separation ring on the burner to lower the heat.

"Let's go outside," Dan suggested.

The three exited the front door, leaving Jabbar alone. No one had acknowledged his presence other than to tie him to the chair.

"What do you want to do now, boss?" Roland asked. He usually used the phrase "boss" when there was a difficult decision to be made, one which he was happy not to be responsible for. "He's not going to just give up what he knows without coercion. He's one of the true believers, especially to be sent on this mission."

"So, we torture him?" Marcus asked.

Dan gave him a painful look. "I don't know. We're not under any time pressure to prevent a disaster, the anthrax attack has been stopped." He paused for a moment. "And, being here, in the U.S. It doesn't feel quite right to me."

"Copy that," Roland said. "I've been wrestling with the same thought."

He kicked the dirt.

"Shit, here we are," Roland said, "after killing multiple jihadists, standing around with our hands in our pockets, wondering how to treat this piece of shit. Aren't we the badasses?"

Marcus gave out a short, cynical-sounding laugh.

There was a silence among the men.

"I got an idea," Marcus finally said. The others looked at him. "Let's water board him. We know it works. Had it done to us in training. Scares the shit out of the victims and doesn't injure them. We have time to work him up to it to intensify the psychological aspects. Anticipation lets one's imagination go to work. You already freaked him out by the way you killed that other jihadist. He knows he could suffer that fate. If we tell him what's in store for him, and the possibility of drowning—"

"But that's just it. Done properly they don't drown," Roland said.

"He doesn't know that."

"I like it," Dan said. "We'll be nice tonight with a few hints at what's coming, then we let him sleep on it and start tomorrow. I'll be the bad cop. Marcus, you be the good cop and Roland you be kind of neutral, his jailer so to speak."

"Plan," said Roland. "Let's get something to eat. I'm starving."

Chapter 43

Hank Russell was a senior aide to Robert Hanson. Hanson was the opposition congressman that Greely wanted to bring over to his side. George Randall had dug up some facts about Hanson. His financial situation was not the greatest, having made some bad real estate investments. Along with that, his top aide, Hank, looked to be dabbling in insider trading on information he could glean from Hanson's briefings. Both men were vulnerable and ripe for the picking. Zhōu and Carlos would be able to keep their hands clean, and George would increase his value to them and, hence, his payout.

Like most aides, Hank Russell often worked late. It was dark when he left the capitol offices. The short walk to his townhouse on Capitol Hill was a good time to clear his head. As he walked along, a car pulled up, and the driver lowered the window.

"Can you help me?" he said with a smile. "I'm trying to get back to Georgetown."

"You're pretty much turned around in the wrong direction," Hank said. He thought for a moment. "I can direct you to M Street. That'll take you into the heart of Georgetown. Don't you have a GPS on your phone?"

"Never figured out how to work the damn thing."

"Okay." Hank looked down at his phone. "I'll get you started and then you can ask someone else." He looked down at his phone.

"That'd be great."

The back door of the car opened. It had tinted glass which made it impossible to see inside. As he heard the door open and someone step out, Hank looked up, but it was too late. A massive hulk of a man grabbed him, lifted him up off his feet, and clamped a meaty hand around his mouth, stifling any attempt to shout. In a moment, he was thrown into the back seat, and a hood was pulled over his head. The car drove off. The whole incident took less than a minute.

"Who are you? What's going on? What do you want?" His arms were pinned to his side by the two men sitting next to him.

The questions were always the same, thought Mario. And the answers never came...at first.

Hank was jammed between two men. The giant who threw him into the car put a thick finger to his lips and shushed him. No one spoke as Mario drove to an abandoned warehouse next to the Anacostia River. He parked in the back of it, facing the river, well away from prying eyes.

"If it's money you want. I have a couple of hundred on me and I can go to an ATM and get more."

Mario turned around and smiled. "We don't want your money. We want to talk, that's all."

"You're not going to hurt me?" Hank's muffled voice still reflected his mounting fear.

"We know a lot about you...and your boss. With that info, we thought we could make you an offer you can't refuse."

Mario's smile broadened. He couldn't help himself from using that line. It was so classic.

"Your congressman is a loud voice promoting tightening up the southern border. There're many people who are not so happy about that. We are in a position to reward you for getting Hanson to, shall we say, take a less loud stand. Maybe shut up for a while and let things settle down. The deaths in that trailer will soon fade, and the public won't pay it much attention anymore. He's trying to keep things stirred up, which don't help.

"Now, you could be rewarded for getting him to lower the heat. You, along with the congressman. Or," Mario now paused for effect, "we know where you live and where your family lives. We also know about the D.C. girlfriend you keep on the side.

"Play ball with us, and you get wealthier. Don't, and you get ruined, or hurt. That goes for your family as well."

Hank just sat there without answering.

"I know. It's a lot to take in. But like I said, there's no upside to your decision to not play ball with us. Better to take the money. Most everyone else in Washington is on the take in some fashion."

"Not me," came the whispered reply. "And not Congressman Hanson."

Mario thought about that for a moment before replying. "So, you want a medal for being a good Boy Scout? You didn't get that I'm serious about the consequences?"

"Don't bring my family into this. They haven't done anything."

"It's up to you. I get you're a clean guy. You aren't on the take. But now you got to make a choice. Take the money and do what I'm asking or things get ugly. Fuck, give the money to charity if it'll make you feel better. But do right by your family. It ain't so hard, is it?"

After a long silence, Hank shook his head.

"All right. Good choice. See, I told you it was an offer you couldn't refuse. So, here's how this is going to work. You'll get Hanson to stop with his interviews on the news. He'll say he's busy. He doesn't want to comment on ongoing legislation. You make up whatever bullshit you want, but he doesn't go out there spouting off about the border. We expect to see that happen before the week's out.

"If you talk to anyone, go to the police, we'll know about it and then you're going to get a visit. Both you and your family. You try to move them, hide them, we'll act. And, believe me, you don't want us to act."

"Are you the mafia?" Hank's voice sounded shaky, filled with fear.

Mario laughed. "Just concerned citizens. We like open borders, like most businessmen. Cheap wages. Just like your family hires back in Missouri."

Mario patted Hank's head. The two men on each side of him had a tight hold on his arms.

"We good? You understand?"

Hank nodded.

"Say it."

"We...we're...good."

"Great. You get me the results, there'll be an envelope in your mail box with some money you'll enjoy. Now we'll get you back on the street so you can finish your walk home."

Chapter 44

The three men walked back inside the cabin. Roland went to tend the stove. The day was quickly waning, and a chill began to seep into the cabin. The warm air rising met the cooler night air descending, and a mist began to form in the valley and creep up the slope.

No one spoke to Jabbar. He was ignored as the men prepped the meal. The three men ate at the table, leaving Jabbar tied to the chair. When they were done, Roland brought him a small plate of food along with some bread and water.

"Eat. You'll need to keep up your strength."

Jabber didn't answer and just stared at the plate as Roland unbound one of his wrists. His waist and legs were still tied down. He was given no eating utensils, so he would have to use his fingers.

"May I wash my hands first?"

No one answered him. Marcus cleaned up the dishes while Roland made a fire in the fireplace. Dan just stared out of the window.

Finally, Jabbar began to sop up the stew with his bread and pick up chunks of beef with his hands. Soon the plate was empty.

Roland took the plate and brought it to Marcus. Dan walked over to the man and stared at him for a long time. Jabbar worked to return his gaze.

"What's your name?"

Jabbar shook his head and kept his mouth shut.

"Tough guy, huh? You saw what I did to your buddy back at the farm. He was of no use to me. I can do the same to you if you're no use." Dan leaned over Jabbar, "And I can take more time to do it.

"You were setting out to kill thousands of innocent people, civilians. You, or your partner would have killed that farmer and his wife when you were done. So, I don't have any sympathy for you and no reason to be civilized in how I treat you. If you don't cooperate, you'll suffer and disappear. Help us, you don't suffer. You may never be free, but you can spend your life studying Islam in some federal penitentiary. Not a bad outcome considering."

"Jabbar."

"That's better. I'm Dan. I'm the one to watch out for. I don't like jihadists. I kill them whenever I find them." He pointed to Roland. "The large guy is Roland. He's your jailer. The other guy is Marcus. He's inclined to be more lenient than I am. But I wouldn't test him too far."

After he spoke, Dan pulled the hood back over Jabbar.

"Your interrogation will begin tomorrow. If you don't cooperate, I can start by cutting off your fingers, one by one. I'll cauterize the wounds, so you won't bleed too much. It's quite painful as other terrorists could testify…if they were still alive. Think long and hard about how you want this to play out."

Roland lifted Jabbar, chair and all, and took him into the second bedroom. One of the beds was brought out so Roland could sleep on it. Jabbar would remain hooded until morning.

After putting Jabbar into the room, the three men put on their jackets, and with a bottle of Blood Oath's Pact No. 7 bourbon and three glasses, they went out to the porch.

Roland poured each of them a couple of fingers, and they sat back on some wooden porch chairs.

"That's quite a name," Marcus said, examining the bottle. The bourbon had a deep copper color.

"Yeah. That's what first attracted me. But it's a good bourbon."

He tipped his glass to the other two and took a sip.

"That's got quite a mellow finish," said Dan.

"It's finished in sauterne wine casks from Bordeaux. I think that gives it that slightly sweet end to the taste."

"My compliments," Dan said. He raised his glass to take another sip.

"I had help picking it out, believe me."

"I believe you," Marcus said.

"Fuck you," Roland replied with a grin on his face.

"So, how do we play this tomorrow?" Marcus asked. "How far do you intend to go with this guy? You going to start cutting off fingers?"

"No. That was just something to kick start his anxiety. But you know I'm capable of going far as I need to, to get him to talk. But we'll go with the plan. Cutting off fingers just doesn't seem quite right. Out in the field, without the luxury of time, the quick and brutal approach seems to work best. Here...I don't know."

"Remember," Marcus said, "these guys consider it a badge of honor to resist interrogation. From what we know about the rendition sites, they have to be brought to a point where they feel they've done enough and there is no shame in capitulating." He paused for a moment. "The challenge is to get there while the subject is still intact."

"Not drowned, you mean," Dan said.

"If we go with water boarding, we should tell him that." Roland said, "That we're not experts and we hope we don't really drown him. That should raise his anxiety level."

"Good point," Dan said.

The men lapsed into silence as the night grew darker. An owl hooted in a nearby tree. A coyote howled out on a distant ridge; down in the valley, they could hear frogs croaking.

In the morning, Marcus explained to Jabbar that they didn't expect him to just roll over. No jihadist they had encountered had ever done that. He said they were going to waterboard him. Jabbar's eyes opened wider at the mention of the technique.

"Our problem is that we're not experts at it. If it's not done properly the subject can drown. I'm trying to keep Dan from cutting off your fingers and toes. It's something he's done before and gets results. I'll try to make sure you don't drown as well."

He stood up and looked at Jabbar, still tied to his chair from the previous night.

"But I can't make you any promises. I'd settle things with Allah before we begin."

"Can I get a prayer rug?"

Marcus looked sad and shook his head. "I can give you some time in here alone. That's the best I can do."

He turned and left the bedroom, closing the door behind him. Dan and Roland were building the board, nailing planks onto a frame that would put the victim's head below his feet. It was a posture that increased the terror but also helped ensure water would not go down the tortured man's lungs. The men knew the sound of the hammers and saw would only serve to heighten Jabbar's fear of what was to come.

"Kind of like hearing them put up the gallows before you would be taken out to be hanged," Roland said in a whisper.

"Something like that," Dan replied. "Let's hope it works."

Chapter 45

Despite the CIA's denial, the furor of Zhōu's transcript of the recording evidencing Garrett Easton's direct involvement in the Aleppo drone strike kept growing in intensity. The agency maintained it was a manufactured fake and demanded to know the source. The reporter refused and claimed the lofty privilege of protecting his sources. His refusal statement dripped with his sense of moral superiority.

"This is not going to be easy to contain," said Gardiner.

"We just have to keep driving the narrative that this is disinformation, manufactured by a foreign agency. It helps that it's the truth," Garrett replied.

"The public isn't buying it. This is adding fuel to the hearings. There'll be demands to cut our funding. To set up closer oversight on the agency and our operations."

"We can still keep the truly black ops hidden."

"But we can't avoid the funding cuts if things go far enough."

The two men were conversing in Gardiner's office. The mood at headquarters was bleak. Everyone was discouraged by the bad press and intense scrutiny. It didn't help that the opposition party was not coming to their defense. This latest revelation had given many politicians cold feet and a desire to not be seen supporting what was looking like a rogue agency that needed reining in.

† † †

Dan and the others slept well that night in the hunting cabin. Jabbar sat, tied to his chair with his hood on. The blackness in front of his face was impenetrable and disorienting. His mind raced over the thoughts of what would take place tomorrow. He did not swim; he didn't like the water. Repeatedly over the night, he had to push hard against a panic that threatened to overwhelm him. In the evening, the sound of his captors making some sort of torture device that he would be placed on in the morning caused his stomach to turn and the bile to rise in his throat.

Dawn came subtly in the forest, the light slowly easing back the dark, slowly unveiling the details of the trees and brush from the dense cover of nighttime. Jabbar was jerked out of a fitful sleep by the sounds of the men in the other room. There was more banging and thumping, which Jabbar tried to imagine. He could not envision exactly what was being constructed, and he had exhausted himself over the night trying. His body started to shake. He knew they would come for him soon.

The door opened. The larger man, Roland, entered. He yanked off Jabbar's hood and began to untie his arms and legs. He seemed unconcerned that Jabbar might try to run. There was the challenge of getting past this large man, then getting past his compatriots in order to gain some fleeting freedom in a forest that he did not know or understand. He had been raised in the lush countryside of England and its urban centers, with brief sojourns in the desert to visit his home and family. These North American forests were foreign to him.

He felt his legs start to buckle. Roland could see him sag. He reached out to prop him up with his arms but didn't say a word. Jabbar's thoughts turned to the reality that he was not cut out for this. *This is what Taimoor meant*. He was more of a manipulator, a deceiver. He was not a front-line fighter able to match up with hard men.

Roland led him out of the room. In front of Jabbar was an inclined board with tie-down points to which he would be strapped—pinned. He paled at the sight of it. There was a table to one side with a large bucket of water on it.

"It's time," Marcus said. "I don't guess you want to tell us everything. We'll try not to drown you, but, as I said, we haven't done this before."

"Enough talk," Dan said in a gruff voice. "Time to dish out some pain."

Almost as if his voice had a mind of its own, Jabbar heard himself mumbling, "No...please...I don't want this."

If they heard, no one indicated. They went about strapping him to the bench. When he was immobilized, a towel was placed over his face.

"No!" Jabbar said reflexively.

Then the water hit him. He gasped, which was the wrong thing to do, as water entered his mouth and cut off his breath. His body shook against the restraints. He tried to shake his head and turn away from the water pouring over and into him, but his head was locked tight. His body jerked against the restraints without control. When he thought he was gone, the towel was removed, and he coughed and spit up water until he could breathe clearly.

No questions were asked of him. As he began to recover his breath, the towel was placed over his face again. Before he could cry out, the water poured down over him. Again, the sensation of drowning surged through his body. Just when he thought he would die, the towel was removed. He got a quick gasp of breath back into his lungs, and the towel was placed over him for a third time. The water flowed over him, choking his breath. His torso spasmed, his back arched off the board. The restraints cut into his wrists. The towel was removed and he gasped and coughed as the precious air flowed into his lungs. This time, after removing the towel, the board was lifted to a more upright position.

"Are you ready to talk?" Marcus asked. "Dan here wants to continue and to make each session longer. That could be fatal for you. Most warriors I know of can only last three sessions, which you have done. The others bet you wouldn't last two before you would be crying your eyes out like a baby. I told them you were made of stronger stuff." He leaned closer to Jabbar. "But everyone talks in the end. You have done well for yourself."

Jabbar looked up at him with a wide-eyed expression. Almost like a child being told something wondrous. Marcus smiled at him.

"I didn't cry," he said.

"No, you didn't. And for that, you can be proud. You withstood as much as some of the hardest warriors I have seen." Marcus looked at his companions. "I think they're impressed, although they don't want to say it." He bent back down to Jabbar. "It's time to come clean. You've done your part and acquitted yourself well. Will you tell us about this mission?"

Jabbar stared at him. Marcus smiled back. *I did my part. If Taimoor hadn't been so foolish, we'd have been successful. This is all his fault. I can do no more.*

He nodded, his face grave and serious.

Chapter 46

Over the next two days, the furor over the transcript of the recording kept gaining momentum. The President, Charles Rosser, had called Gardiner into his office to meet with him and his Chief of Staff, no one else. Rosser was a tested member of his party. He had fought his way up through state-level politics to become the party's nominee for the presidency. Surprisingly, he won the election and, with his brawler's style, took hold of the party. He liked the open borders for political reasons, thinking they would create a generational majority for his party. His donors, the captains of industry, old and new, also liked open borders, so their interests aligned closely.

His Chief of Staff, John Franklin, was also considered a brawler, even more willing to get down and dirty for his boss to ensure his continued seat in power. His presence as the only other person was not a good sign in Gardiner's eyes. The President had made it very clear that Gardiner would take the fall if he could not deflect. Simply denying the transcript's authenticity was not going to satisfy the media mob howling for his head. Daily messages of outrage kept coming from the mainstream media. They got their talking points from the more fringe elements, whose reach was not that great. But with their ability to set the storyline, the extreme got its message out to the majority of the public in a way countervailing viewpoints could not.

"So, all you've got is that you are sure the tape is a fake and you can prove it once you get your hands on it," the President said.

"That's correct, sir."

"But how do you propose to not only get the tape, but convince the public your analysis is not phony?"

"We're willing to have the forensics done by a joint group. Our guys, maybe the NSA, and any other experts the New York Times wants to bring in."

"That would be a media shit show for sure," Franklin said. "Boss, we need to consider that having this crisis going on is taking all the focus off the border. No one's shouting about that right now."

"All well and good," replied Rosser, "but I don't like getting rid of one crisis by igniting another one that can reflect on me. That's too self-destructive."

"Greely's running with this, isn't he?" Gardiner asked. "Maybe lean on him."

The President smiled. "He can be leaned on, to some extent. But as you see with his hearings, he has his own agenda and has a lot of power to work it. We'll have to be careful with him."

"Still, it wouldn't hurt," Gardiner replied.

He made his way back to headquarters in a funk. He still had nothing. His only hope was to get hold of the tape.

"Maybe you can put some pressure on the FBI to get their hands on the tape," Easton said.

"No way Murphy wants to dig that out for you. He's being all sanctimonious about upholding the freedom of the press. Not only will they not touch it, I'm not even sure that someone in the FBI didn't leak the transcript to the media. It wouldn't be the first time. I proposed that the source could remain anonymous. But the veracity of the tape had to be tested. That fell on deaf ears. Murphy was going to stay at arm's length from the blowup."

Both men stared out of the window as if looking for relief.

That same day, the full account of the foiled terrorist attack in Illinois and Indiana broke. There were statements by the state police and FBI. The press was trying to locate some witnesses to get a clearer picture of what had happened. The official sources gave a frustratingly sanitized recitation of events.

There was an interview with a farmer who came upon the scene and talked with three men who said they were special undercover operatives. They indicated that they would pursue the trucks that had fled the scene.

Another witness, the farmer, and his wife, held captive by the second group of terrorists, told of a similar group of three men who had killed all the terrorists and saved their lives. They were grateful that the government had such capable men protecting the country. They were adamant that when the terrorists had finished modifying their truck to disperse the poison, they would have killed both of them.

William Gardiner got the call to come to the White House immediately. He grabbed his notes and left to meet the President. On arrival, he was led into the Roosevelt Room. Inside was the President; his Chief of Staff, John Franklin; DHS Secretary, Evan Roseman; Ed Winslow, the Attorney General; and Paul Murphy, the FBI Director.

Everyone looked as Gardiner entered as if they had been waiting for him. Franklin pointed him to a seat.

"I want to hear from each of you. Anyone have more information than what we're getting from the media?"

No one spoke up.

"Paul," the President said, turning to his FBI Director, "your men are on site. What do you know?"

"Not much at this point. We're just assembling the reports from the local and state police along with the witnesses. We've got a hazmat team working with the state police in both states. So far we have determined that this white powder is most likely anthrax. We haven't told the media that yet."

"Did it get loose?"

"It seems so with one of the trucks. The one stopped in Illinois. It had an empty bag connected to a roof vent with a blower attached. We're canvassing the nearby towns that the truck passed through. We want to round up everyone who might have been exposed and have them examined. The state troopers who stopped the truck were in danger of exposure. We're having them checked."

He shifted in his chair in a nervous gesture.

"The truck in Indiana had a similar venting mechanism, not completed, along with a full bag of the powder. It looks like they had stopped to finish the dispersal mechanism. We're going to test the couple who were held hostage."

"What about these supposed undercover agents? Seems like they did quite a job on the terrorists. Killed them all?" He turned to Gardiner, "You know anything about this?"

"No sir. You know we're not allowed to operate domestically. We don't have any agents chasing terrorists here in the U.S. If we had information on any domestic terror operations, we'd turn it over to Paul to pursue. We were caught off guard, like Paul here."

Gardiner made sure to add that last comments. If anyone was going to take the heat for not knowing about a domestic attack, he would make sure it was Paul. The man couldn't avoid shouldering this fuck-up.

"You didn't have any hint of this from your overseas surveillance?"

Gardiner took a breath. *Stay calm. This is not on you.*

"We had separate reports of thefts of anthrax from around the globe. There was nothing to link them. NSA passed on the information. It was put in the PDB. The thefts, were widely separated by continents, North America, Europe, Africa, and India. Attempts like this occur occasionally and are rarely successful."

"But these were?"

Gardiner nodded. "Still, we didn't find a common thread to tie them together."

"Except for this attack," said Franklin, the Chief of Staff.

The President turned to Paul Murphy again. "Can you estimate how much anthrax was involved? You have the full amount in one of the trucks. Assume that the other held the same amount. How much is that?"

Paul Murphy paused for a moment. "The early estimates are that it could be as much as five or more kilograms."

The President looked over at his Chief.

"That translates into a hell of a lot of powder. More than eleven pounds of it."

"Jesus, Joseph, and Mary," the President said. "How the hell did they get that into the country? How many people could that kill?"

Evan Roseman, the DHS Secretary, now spoke up, seeming to want to be a part of the conversation, not just an observer. "Studies indicate that released in an urban center, a kilo could kill up to 100,000 people."

"Holy shit," Rosser exclaimed. "How many people do you think have been affected by the powder that was released?" This question was directed to Paul Murphy again.

"We don't know yet. They traveled through three small towns. Thankfully, the terrorists were stopped in a rural area."

"Headed for Chicago?"

"That's what we think, sir."

"And where was the other one headed?"

"East, probably to D.C. or New York...or both."

President Rosser pondered that answer for a moment. "We dodged a massive bullet here." He turned to Gardiner, "So who were these mystery agents? Who's responsible for them?"

No one answered.

"Come on. These were not good Samaritans. They were trained, from the reports Murphy gave me. And, they had some very good intel to be able to track down these trucks when none of my agency heads knew there was anything going on." He looked around at each of the men. "You know how bad this looks for each of you? My top agencies, CIA, FBI, DHS, NSA, were all blind to this threat. You guys knew nothing?" He rose out of his seat, now starting to vent his anger. "And some unknown trio, somehow knows of the threat and can find it, even when the attackers are on the move. Then three of them take out multiple terrorists, save two civilians, and disappear into the night."

He pounded his right fist into his left hand. "I want to know who these guys are." The President paused. "Is it Mossad? Would they operate here without coordinating through you?" He directed this last to Gardiner.

"Highly unlikely, sir. But I'll get on the horn with my counterpart and find out."

"If he'll tell you anything. Jesus!" His voice raised again. "What a bunch of incompetent fuck-ups you all are."

"Sir?" Franklin, the Chief of Staff, spoke up. "For now, maybe we should play this as the FBI being responsible for the take downs. This is a big enough win for the accolades to go around to everyone. The NSA can say they intercepted emails that indicated a possible attack. The CIA followed up and identified some terrorists that came into the U.S. with fake documentation—"

"Not over the Mexican border, please. We're getting enough crap about that," the President said.

"Okay. They came in legally. The CIA then alerts the FBI who works in coordination with DHS to locate, track and bring down the terrorists. The FBI used a special swat team, the three guys, to complete the take down and limit the spread of the powder."

The President continued to pace around the room.

"I like it. We may as well get the kudos for doing this."

"It will take the heat off the border issue and Greely's hearings. Without having to confront him. He can't object to us protecting the people and the press will run with this story. It'll take the wind out of his hearings."

"Rehabilitate the CIA?"

"In a way, Mr. President."

"All right. But," he turned to look at each of his top men in national security and law enforcement, "I want to know who those three men are. Find them. One of you has them on staff. They're not military. They belong to one of you."

He turned and stomped out of the room, leaving Franklin to work out the details to coordinate the press release and follow-up information.

Chapter 47

Both Fred and Warren burst into Jane's office with excited looks on their faces.

"What, no knocking now?" Jane looked up with a cross expression on her face.

"We got some info from Dan. They captured one of the terrorists and got him to talk."

"Sit down. Tell me everything."

Fred proceeded to recount the information that Dan had gotten from Jabbar. Warren chimed in with details along the way.

When they were done, Jane leaned back in her chair.

"So, we know Rashid bankrolled it. It was his men involved. And Zhōu arranged to steal the anthrax. They worked through Mendoza to get their men and the anthrax into the country. They stop at a mosque in Dallas and then go on to the farm in Illinois. She summed up the rest of the story to ensure she had the details correct. It was an amazingly complete tale of intrigue with no elements left out.

"He must have been very persuasive to get such a complete story. And this Jabbar knew quite a lot."

"Remember, he's Rashid's nephew, at least in a distant way," said Fred.

"And he says Zhōu has infiltrated some of our politicians?"

Fred nodded.

"Follow the money. There has to be a money trail. Zhōu didn't do this on direct orders from his superiors. They may have allowed it, turning a blind eye to what he was doing, but I'm betting their hand prints are nowhere to be found. The money if the key. If any flowed to Zhōu, find it. How much and where it went."

Warren nodded and began to write something down.

"No notes. Keep it in your head," Jane said.

"And if he's got some politicians in his pocket, that takes money as well. Start with Greely. It's as good a place as any. Also check his senior aide…I can't remember his name, but you can find it."

Warren nodded again. "Just to be clear, you want us to spy on a sitting congressman?"

Jane gave him a sarcastic smile.

"Are you worried about that transgression? With all the others we've just committed?"

Warren and Fred looked at each other briefly and shook their heads.

"Okay. Get to work. And if Dan calls, tell him to update me now that the action is over."

The two stood up.

"And boys," they stopped at the door, "that was great work. Congratulations."

The two smiled and left the office.

† † †

Wang Li Xiu kept collecting tidbits of information from the after-sex pillow talk she and George Randall engaged in. His guard was always down after an orgasm, and Wang made sure he had amazing orgasms. She was always interested in his important job, so close to the centers of power; his boss being Chairman of the House Permanent

Select Committee on Intelligence. The tidbits helped paint a picture of where the U.S. was in their thinking regarding intelligence issues; areas of concern, the ones that struck them as important, needing to be addressed, and the suspicions that arose in the community, especially regarding China.

All this, Wang knew, would be helpful to her bosses. She understood Randall had a large enough ego to not wonder at her interest or worry that his teasers would be collected and analyzed by anyone. Wang also understood that Randall couldn't help thinking of her as a decoration or an amusement. Yes, he was smitten; she had made sure of that. But he could not put aside his disdain for younger women, so he could not think of her as warranting caution about sensitive matters of state. Besides, his bits of inside information only seemed to turn her on, which made their lovemaking even hotter.

† † †

Robert Hanson had quieted down regarding his constant outrage at the open southern border while the events unfolding in Illinois and Indiana had taken center stage. The official story was a glowing testimony about how the country's security agencies had worked closely together, properly handing off intel to each one as events warranted, culminating in the FBI and DHS takedown of the terrorists. The word was that the men came to the U.S. with proper, albeit false, documentation, not across the southern border. There was no definitive explanation of how the large amount of anthrax had gotten into the country. Most assumed it was smuggled in a shipping container. The word was this part of the plot was still being investigated.

In short, Hanson had no axe he could grind about the open border in this set of events. He also had spoken to his aide, Hank Russell, who advised him to lower his rhetoric regarding the open border. Hank spoke about being pragmatic. They needed to keep money flowing for re-election campaigns which occurred every two years. The one he had coming would involve a serious challenge. It would not be a slam dunk. Russell advised the congressman that if he wasn't so strident, he could attract a wider pool of donors who would help finance his campaign. After all, getting re-elected was what it was all about, wasn't it? If he lost the upcoming election, what good could he do? Better to soften his stance, so he could gain another two years. After that, he could step up the heat.

The message was distasteful but not entirely without merit. There would be another day. Perhaps now was the time to soften his rhetoric. He had established his credentials and could properly defend his actions. Now was the time to start courting the bigger money. To get his campaign chest full again.

Chapter 48

Dan sat on the porch of the hunting cabin. Jabbar had been a wealth of information. It was one day after Jabbar had broken and told them all he knew. Dan had called Fred and told him the story. He knew the two men would go to Jane and fill her in. He told the two researchers he wanted to know about any money trail they could pick up on Zhōu and the congressman Jabbar mentioned. Dan knew Jane would also be pursuing that track as well.

Marcus came out of the door with a coffee in his hand. "What do we do now?"

"Good question. Fred and Warren are working on the money trail. Both Zhōu and the guy, Greely."

"You know Jane's going in that direction as well. Do we head in and turn this guy over to her?"

"Not sure. I'm thinking it might be best to keep him hid out here for now. Until we see how this all plays out in D.C. There're so many conflicting currents at the moment. Anyone of which could turn on the CIA and Jane in particular."

"And you can't be seen. You can't exist."

"Neither can you...or Roland, for that matter. At least for right now."

The two were silent for a moment.

"I don't like it. Hanging out here, doing nothing," Marcus said.

"Neither do I." Dan stood up. "I'm going to call our tech boys again."

"Maybe talk to Jane about our guy."

"We'll see."

"Go up to the top of the hill, there's a rock outcropping where you can get some reception."

† † †

Jane turned the key in her lock and let herself into her apartment in Rosslyn. It was a section of Arlington County located just over Key Bridge from Georgetown in the District of Columbia. The CIA headquarters where she worked was a short drive upstream along the Potomac River on the George Washington Parkway, which went from Mt. Vernon to the south of the district, past Reagan National Airport, past D.C., following the river, until it terminated at the Washington Beltway. The entrance had been marked in the seventies by a humorous sign with the words "Alaska Highway Research Bureau". Everyone, of course, knew what it was. Now the road sign more accurately said "George Bush Center for Intelligence".

She entered and noticed a light on farther into her apartment. Jane stepped forward, wondering if she had left it on that morning. Entering the living room, she saw Dan sitting in a chair with a glass of bourbon in his hand.

She sucked in her breath.

He raised his glass to her in a salute. "Glad to see you're hard at work."

"What are you doing here?" Jane asked after she recovered from the shock. She put her coat on the back of a chair and went into the kitchen to pour herself a glass of wine. “I thought you wanted to stay away from D.C.,” she called out.

“Mission over. Mission successful. I’m just reporting in. It was only two weeks ago you sent me out on a wild goose chase with little chance of success. And here I am. Back after saving the nation.”

“You, Fred, and Warren. I know how you highjacked them into helping. Without my knowledge or approval.”

“Marcus and Roland also. We work well as a team.”

Jane sat down across from him.

“No hug? No welcoming kiss? I feel disrespected.”

Jane smiled. “Time for all that later.”

“Right.” Dan hunched forward in his chair. “What’s the fallout? Anyone own up to saving the nation?”

“You’ll be pleased to know the President got everyone in on the act. Us, NSA, FBI, and DHS. There’re accolades enough to go all around.”

“Does anyone know what really happened?”

“Not a clue. Although the President told all his agency heads he wanted the identities of the three mystery agents who it seems were instrumental in saving the country.”

“I’ll bet he does.”

“It’s also come to light that there was one more terrorist. One who was taken by the rescuers.”

“That’s unfortunate.”

“And you have him.”

“That’s how we got the info for you. Marcus and Roland are babysitting him. He’s out of the way, safe in the woods.”

Jane scowled.

“Don’t worry. No one will find him.”

“Okay. Let’s leave him there for now.

I wonder what the President would do if he had all the information?”

“I don’t want to find out.”

“We’re the main suspect, though,” Dan said. “The only ones with black op guys that could pull this off.”

“Thankfully, that will never be disclosed. That’s why it’s called black ops.”

Jane took a large sip of her wine.

“Are you going back to Italy?” she asked. “Do you need a plane? I’ll have to come up with a reason to travel in order to smuggle you over there.”

“Are you anxious to get rid of me?”

Jane looked at him with a grave expression on her face. It was a mixture of close familiarity and concern, affection, and anxiety. “It’s just that you don’t like D.C., and it isn’t a good idea for you to hang around. Remember, you can’t be seen.”

“Let’s talk about that later. Right now, if I’m allowed to stay, let’s order in, have it delivered and spend the night being quiet and cozy.”

Jane smiled and began to relax. Her affection for this rather untamed, dangerous man welled up inside her. This was not the time to be his boss. This evening could be a timeout. She certainly needed it, and she suspected Dan did as well. It was something to her that he chose to show up in her apartment and not call her from someplace else, like Montana, where his sister lived. She was his first stop coming in from the cold. She liked that.

Dinner consisted of veal parmigiana along with a salad. Jane’s wine cabinet offered up a nice light red that went well with the dinner. A lemon sorbet from her fridge was a light finish to the meal.

Afterward, they sprawled on the couch in each other’s arms. Jane wanted to know everything that had happened. She said she was past worrying about deniability since all the other agencies had taken ownership of the mission.

"It sounds like the true heroes of the story are Fred and Warren," she said after Dan had recounted their pursuit and take-down of the terrorists.

"Pretty much," Dan said. "Even if we had stopped the first truck, we'd have never caught the second one. That one would have wound up here. If it got no farther, it would have been bad enough. Imagine 100,000 people or more killed in the capital."

Jane shuddered and pushed up close to Dan.

"What do you do about this guy Zhōu?" Dan asked.

"We'll follow the money and try to neutralize him. Sooner or later."

"And the congressman?" Dan knew of the connection from Jabbar.

"We're working on that. Warren is infiltrating his computers. If we find evidence of his complicity, we'll get the FBI on him."

"You think that will do any good? They're going to follow the lead of the President. And it doesn't seem like Rosser wants to kill off one of his party members. Greely may have gone after the CIA, but he's solidly on the open border side of things." He paused. "And his CIA pogrom is pretty well shut down."

"A good side effect of the aborted attack. But the search is on for you and the others."

"They'll never find us, as you said." Dan leaned back and looked into Jane's eyes. "But Greely gets away? You go through the FBI and that's what happens. You know that."

Jane shrugged. "We can't do this ourselves. It's enough that we're spying on him electronically. We know someone at the FBI would alert him if they knew we were looking into his possible involvement with Zhōu." She sighed. "We may have to be satisfied with stopping a disaster."

Dan didn't answer but pulled her close. "Okay, timeout now. No more shop talk."

"I like the sound of that."

Chapter 49

The news reports spread around the world. It was only hours after the takedown of the terrorists that Rashid learned about the failed attempt. He was in his office suite on the top floor of his Riyadh high-rise. He paced the room. His secretary and aides left him alone. No one knew how he might lash out in his fury. They didn't understand what had triggered their boss, but no one wanted to inquire to find out. Better to wait for him to summon an unlucky fellow who might bear the brunt of his wrath.

Rashid picked up his cell phone and made a call.

"Zhōu," he said when the Chinese spymaster picked up, "have you heard what happened?"

Zhōu paused for a moment before answering. He wanted to remain calm in the face of what he knew would be furious anger. It had to be directed someplace, and Rashid was unlikely, at least at this point, to direct it towards himself.

"I have." He filled his voice with as much calm as he could muster.

"Do you know anything about this? You have contacts at high levels in the government."

"I am pursuing this course of action. So far, no one knows. This interception of your team came as a complete surprise. My sources so far have told me they knew nothing about it."

"But you haven't polled all of them?"

"Correct. But I expect to hear the same story."

"Are they covering for themselves?"

"Perhaps. It is always possible. They wouldn't want to be seen as knowing important intel and keeping it from me. It would jeopardize their relationship with me and the money that brings."

"How is this possible? No one on my end knew of this except my closest aide and the men I sent out." Rashid paused for a moment. "Mendoza knew. He smuggled the men and anthrax in. But he has a vested interest in continuing business with me. He would not cross me."

"Maybe not. But he did not express much hope for your success. Perhaps he knew something in advance?"

Zhōu did not want to engage in speculation, nor did he want to cast a cloud over Mendoza. He needed his help, but it was a possibility that should not be overlooked as Rashid cast around for leaks. At least he had not questioned Zhōu's part in the mission.

"Find out if there were any survivors, any men captured. One report said all the men were killed."

Zhōu was quiet for a moment. "Your nephew."

"Yes." Rashid's voice was softer now. His anger displaced by familial concern about his nephew's welfare.

It was a disaster that the mission failed so completely, but to lose Jabbar as well only made a bad outcome worse. Still, to have him captured would not be good either, even if it meant he remained alive. Would he be jailed like other criminals and dealt with by the courts? Or would he be taken away, disappeared? To some black site to be interrogated, tortured? Jabbar knew much that could be detrimental to Rashid's plans.

"See what you can find out. If anyone of them is alive, I want to know where they are," Rashid said.

"I will do my best. And my condolences for this failure and the loss of your nephew."

Rashid clicked off the phone. His anger was not quelled, but he had to start plans to hide his operations from what might be uncovered if Jabbar was captured. Until he knew his fate, his network was in danger.

Zhōu thought about the situation. He was in Paris at the moment. He didn't relish the idea but felt he ought to travel to D.C. He had to impress on a certain congressman the need to find out everything about this operation.

† † †

Dan woke early the following morning. Jane looked over at him, still sleepy-eyed from their vigorous night together.

"Where are you going so early?"

"I can't hang around D.C., as you pointed out."

"So…you're leaving? Where are you going?"

"I don't know. As much as I love being with you, I can't just hang around your apartment all day. I'll go crazy."

Jane gave him a questioning look.

"I might go out to my sister's place. Hang out there for a while."

"You don't want to go back to your place in Venice?"

"Seems premature. There're still loose ends."

"Dan." Jane's look turned serious. "If you're thinking what I think you are, don't. You have to leave this alone. Even if some people get away. I can't have you messing around D.C., going after Chinese spies or worse, congressmen."

"Don't worry. I'm not about to run off and kidnap a congressman and waterboard him."

"Promise me. And don't think about doing anything else."

Dan stepped over to the bed and reached down to give her a kiss. "I'll take care of myself. Be discreet. Not get into trouble. Don't worry. I just want to see how this plays out…and not from a distance."

"Dan—"

"I gotta go. I'll be in touch." He turned to her at the bedroom door and smiled. "And, thank you for last night. For loving me and caring for me. Especially when I feel hollowed out and not so good about myself, from all the things I have to do." He paused for a moment looking for the right words. "I guess I'm trying to say, in my own way, I love you. You heal my soul."

He turned and closed the door. Jane heard him leave the apartment while she sat in bed pondering the words he had just spoken to her. It was more than she ever expected.

Once on the street, Dan felt a weight lift from him. He had a mission. It was clear-cut. It didn't involve tiptoeing around politicians and power brokers. It involved action. It was what animated him. He would deal with this Congressman Greely. How, he wasn't sure at this point, but it would be something that would change Greely's life. He was sure of that. Zhōu? Others? That remained to be seen. He got into his rental car and headed to Baltimore. The first stop was a theater costume shop where he could get facial makeup that would change his appearance.

Chapter 50

What do you know?" Zhōu presented the question to Congressman Greely without any lead-in dialogue. It was important to get to the heart of the events that had taken place in the Midwest.

"The Illinois State Police got a call from a local cop about an incident on a farm and the subsequent departure of two trucks."

Greely went on to explain in detail what had happened. Zhōu listened without comment. When Greely came to the part about three undercover agents that had been at the scene and then left to pursue the trucks, his interest perked up. These men had inside information. They had told the local farmer to let the state police know the trucks were carrying dangerous materials and should not be approached, but cordoned off to protect the surrounding area.

He also listened carefully to Greely's recounting of the incident on the Indiana farm that indicated these men, if they were the same group as in Illinois, were very capable and very deadly. The type of men one would hire to track down and kill jihadists. The type of men capable of killing Rashid's most lethal and experienced assassin, Scorpion. These were also the type of men who could have assassinated his two generals.

But how did they get wind of the plot? That question still was left unanswered. As much as he led Rashid to examine his network, Zhōu did not think there was any leak there.

"Do you have any idea of how this undercover group got wind of the plot?"

Greely shook his head. "No one knows. Publicly, the word is that it was an FBI swat team, but we hear the president has called on all his agencies to find out who was involved. He is convinced it's agents from one of our defense departments."

Zhōu sat in amazement. This great country kept secrets from itself, from its leader. How could it maintain leadership in the world without strict top-down management? The seeming conflicts in the American system never failed to cause him wonder.

"You are working to find out who these men are? Where they came from? You, after all are the leader of the intelligence committee."

"I'm working on it. Partly out front as chairman and partly behind the scenes through other contacts."

"Good. I will remain here in the city for a few days. I hope I can hear back from you."

"Why, may I ask, are you so interested in this? It was a victory for our intelligence to thwart such a potential deadly attack. It has nothing to do with you. I'm betting none of the anthrax came from China."

"Such an event causes more paranoia in your country. This affects police agencies. We Chinese are often the targets of such paranoia. It is therefore a concern to me. Our people might suffer from the general mistrust that grows when such incidents occur."

"So, it's all about mutual friendly relations?"

Zhōu smiled. "That is what helps the wheels of commerce and trade turn smoothly. We all benefit from that. Terrorists who want to take down the U.S. do not have anyone's interests at heart but their own. They want to ruin our mutual profitability."

"I understand that point, but you want to know who found this out and took these men down…why?"

"So I can know which agencies are your most effective. We want to maintain especially good relationships with them."

He could see Greely digesting this statement. He could tell the congressman wanted to believe there was nothing nefarious in his interest. His greed caused him to hunt for a rationalization, an explanation that would quiet the inner voice of concern. Zhōu understood a lingering element of patriotism and duty still inhabited Greely. He needed to keep supplying the congressman with rationalizations to quiet that small voice. That, and adequate financial recompense.

† † †

After purchasing his make-up kit, Dan drove to an empty parking lot at an abandoned building in Baltimore. Using a mirror he had purchased, he applied a prosthetic nose, inserted colored contact lenses, added a black wig with longer, disheveled hair, and put on a pair of fake glasses. The result was a rather frumpy-looking person staring back at him from the mirror. His clothes were suitably innocuous and didn't conflict with his new look. He could fit the persona of a traveling salesman, one not too successful in his field.

He drove to the west of D.C. and rented a room in a cheap motel. It catered to traveling tradesmen and salesmen who would stay a week, finish their assignments, and then move on. They worked as independent contractors for regional or national companies offering repair or remodeling work to homeowners. Some were storm chasers, following significant storms involving high winds, lots of rain, and, sometimes, if they were lucky, large hail stones. They came and went. Always anonymous. They were generally a quiet bunch, preferring to sit down with a six-pack and the TV after a long day of manual labor. There was little partying except for the occasional visiting hooker or girlfriend.

It was the kind of place where Dan would not stick out. He could come and go without worry. The only threat to his anonymity would be if he stayed too long and put himself outside of the established pattern.

"Warren here," came the voice on the phone.

"I want to know what you've found out," Dan said. "About Zhōu and that congressman."

"Jane said you might be calling. Are you in town? She tried your sister, but you haven't shown up there."

"It would be too soon to get all the way out to Montana. Don't worry about me."

"I'm not supposed to divulge any information to you."

Dan thought for a moment. "You and Fred acted outside of Jane's approval and we saved thousands of people from dying. Now it's time to act again. To save others from dying and some from corrupting our government."

"I don't know. This is different. There's no immediate threat."

"But a threat nonetheless. Jane doesn't trust the FBI. That's why she had me going out to operate domestically, against all rules. And I brought you in. You and Fred were instrumental in intercepting these guys. You were knee deep in operating outside the rule book and look at what we accomplished. Without you two I'd have been flogging around with no clue and the attacks would have occurred.

And if you had asked Jane, she would not have let you go forward."

He paused for a moment.

"And right now, she's asking you to operate illegally, by electronically spying on a congressman. That could get you jail time. Now I'm telling you that what you uncover doesn't do us any good unless we can use it as leverage. And, Warren, I'm the guy to apply the leverage."

"Jane's going to kill me."

"But she won't fire you. And, remember, you don't want me on your bad side."

"Crap. You always come back to that."

"You know what I am. Don't fuck with me. I'm your best friend...or, your worst enemy."

He waited for that to sink in.

"Now what's it gonna be?"

"I'll let you know what I find. But don't tell Jane."

"Don't worry. I'll cover for you. Now that we're on the same side."

Chapter 51

With his make-up on to disguise his looks, Dan traveled to D.C. to begin his surveillance of Congressman Greely. He parked in a garage near M Street in Georgetown and started walking towards the neighborhood where Greely lived.

Greely's townhouse was located in Georgetown, east of Wisconsin Avenue. It was an upscale neighborhood with tree-lined streets. The buildings were all three-story brick homes. A few had the addition of a short driveway, enough to pull a car off the road, ending in a garage rarely used to house a vehicle. Greely's home had second-floor balconies in front of French-style doors, each one opening to a different room.

On his way, Dan noticed someone following him. His senses, always alert to the slightest anomaly that could represent danger, noticed the man. In the neighborhoods above M Street, there was far less pedestrian traffic, making it harder for a stalker to conceal their actions. Dan turned the corner, now, not heading towards his goal. The man followed. After another turn, Dan was certain he was being tailed and not by anyone with much skill.

He made a last turn and then stepped into the bushes to wait for his tail to follow. The man turned the corner, and Dan stepped out and seized him from behind with his left arm around the man's neck, his right free to counter any defensive action.

"Don't hurt me. I'm not a threat," the man said. His voice was thin due to Dan's pressure on his neck.

"Why are you following me?"

"I need to talk to you."

"You don't know me, why would you say that?"

"I *do* know you. We all do."

It was an odd statement. So bizarre, Dan released the pressure on the man's neck and turned him around so he could look at him directly. He looked to be about fifty years old. He was dressed in khaki slacks with a plaid shirt on, along with a partially zipped-up dark brown jacket. The colors didn't quite match, and the effect was somewhat frumpy. But there were the eyes. They had that intensity he had only found in Watchers.

"Are you—?"

The man nodded. "Yes. I knew you had arrived in the U.S., but you went off so quickly on your chase that we couldn't help guide you. Of course, your assistants sufficed to enable you to intercept the threat and avoid a catastrophe."

"The mission is over. What do you need to talk to me about?"

The man gestured to a small bench at a bus stop. "Let's sit down. The bus doesn't come for a half hour and usually no one is waiting for it anyway."

They walked to the bench and sat down.

"You don't look like the typical Watcher to me, although you have the eyes, the stare."

"We come from all walks of life. Here, in the U.S., we're often called from the middle class ranks as well as the working or lower economic class."

"Have you had this gift all your life?" Dan was always curious to know more about this strange community of people with these extraordinary skills.

The man smiled and nodded as if to himself. "I did. But during my youth, I didn't recognize it for what it was. No one in my family before me had the gift. When I got older, I met others who initiated me, so to speak, in the fraternity."

"What do you do for a living?"

"I'm a retired college professor."

Dan thought about that for a moment. He knew that professors could and would teach long into their old age.

"Retired so young?"

The man smiled again and nodded. He looked at Dan with his intense stare. "My gift got in the way. I could see that too many of my students were becoming possessed. Not by demons, but by ideology. They were caught up in the liberal group-think that is now so pervasive. But, with my gift, I could see there was a darkness behind it. It was the perfect way to possess the young. Give them a narrative of oppression and a role in being saviors of the oppressed, the planet, society. It was attractive but enslaving. Their minds were closing down and rationality, an examination of opposing viewpoints, was fading from their consciousness."

"But with your gift, you were positioned to fight against this, were you not?"

The man shrugged. "You might think so. But how would I explain to these young minds that I could see the darkness behind the ideology? I would not only be ridiculed, but driven out."

He shook his head vigorously.

"No. I decided to retire, drop out. I could fight like the rest of us, helping those who were battling on the front against the darkness."

He paused for a moment.

"Of course, I still maintain some ties with my former students. I follow them in their careers. The ones who are not totally sold out, often respond to my comments and thoughts now that they have experienced the real world beyond college. In that world, not everything conforms to the ideology, or gives evidence of its veracity."

Dan thought for a moment. It was an interesting story. His conversations with Watchers over the years rarely went beyond the crisis of the moment. But a crisis still existed. Dan sensed it. He felt driven to approach and wrestle with it even though he worried about the lines he might have to cross.

"It would be nice to talk more about your story, but you didn't follow me to tell me about yourself."

"No, I did not. You sense more to do. I'm here to tell you that your intuition is correct. The congressman on who you are focused is, indeed, a pawn of the darkness we fight against. But he is not part of the darkness—not an evil man. He came to Washington with a crusader's heart. His enthusiasm has been misplaced by his lack of understanding that evil does exist and must be confronted. He thinks weeding out corruption, however he defines it, is enough, and people will do good. You should find a way to stop him. But a non-lethal way.

"His aide, however, is a different story. This is the man who you must deal with. He is the one who is enveloped in darkness. He embraces it, profits from it, satiates his desires from it. We can't see the details, but the darkness that hides him from us, also marks him as the agent of the enemy."

"What should I do with him?"

The man shook his head. "It is not for me...us to say. You must decide. We just point the way."

He stood up.

"I am not important. Just a Watcher, one who sees, however dimly and can point the way. You, however, are the warrior, just as Tlayolotl said. You are the one to act."

Dan stood up, and the man shook his hand. Then, without a further word, he turned and walked off towards M Street.

Chapter 52

Dan continued on his way to scout the congressman's house. It would be important to get familiar with the man's habits. He most certainly had habits. Everyone did. And that made them easy targets for those who wanted to harm them. He took a tour of the capitol building to locate Greely's office. He spent time watching and was able to see Greely arrive. He had a driver who probably doubled as a bodyguard.

Along with learning the man's itinerary, he noted the terrain around the house. There was a narrow alleyway between his building and the one to the left. It probably led to an enclosed backyard with no other way in or out. It might be a point of entry, should he need it.

Three days of monitoring Greely confirmed his routine. The congressman left home early, around 7 am. He often had his driver stop for coffee and a bagel. From that point, each day could vary quite a lot. But Dan could bank on the details of an early departure for the capitol, his car parked on the street, and the driver's car arriving at 6:30 each morning from wherever that man lived, probably over Key Bridge in Rosslyn, Virginia.

On the fourth day, Warren called.

"I've got Fred on the phone with me," he said when Dan picked up.

"What do you have?"

"Our congressman has got quite an intricate tangle of companies that he and his family are involved in. There's one, called NewGen Investments. This is run by his brother, but the congressman owns shares in it. He's not the majority owner. It seems he keeps all his investments below the level where he would have to make detailed disclosures."

"What does NewGen do?"

"A bit of everything," it was now Fred who spoke up. "But it's all connected to China. A real estate development project in Beijing, port development in Shanghai and Hangzhou. It appears he's gotten the opportunity to make other investments beyond this company. Some companies, invested in by his wife and son, have acquired shares in some of the major investment firms in China. Ones that dwarf NewGen. Not many outsiders have access to such investments."

"The bottom line?"

"He makes a ton of money in China, from the Chinese business community and the fact that he's allowed to play a part in its Wild West style capital investment projects. It's a bit like the Chinese princes, family members of the old guard, that are given special access to be involved in these investments."

"Where's the money go?"

"Mostly to overseas banks. Off shore accounts. A reasonable amount of money is repatriated and taxes paid to keep everything looking on the up and up. But you can be sure a decent fortune is sitting outside the U.S."

"Here's an interesting tweak," Warren said. "Greely's senior aide, George Randall, is hiding a sizeable amount of funds of his own off-shore. He's got quite an elaborate system of washing the money through various accounts to make it hard to trace. It took me a while, but I could finally follow it. He's not part of any of the investment ploys his boss is running."

"Or you could say, his boss's family," Fred said.

"Right," Warren said. "But he's definitely receiving payments from somewhere. Money is flowing into these accounts to run through a maze of transactions. I'm working on the sources, but I'm guessing one of them may be Zhōu. Though I don't know why he'd pay this guy Randall."

"Good work, guys," Dan said. He thought about what the Watcher had said. Randall must be the one he was referring to.

"What are you going to do?" Fred asked.

"Don't you worry about that. Just get me the rest of the information, especially on this aide and where he lives."

Dan kept watch on Greely until he was thoroughly versed in his routine and the layout of his house. Warren helped in acquiring access to the floor plan. Dan also knew where the driver and Randall, Greely's aide, lived.

Meanwhile, the accolades continued to come in regarding the interception of the terror plot. President Rosser made good use of the positive publicity to strengthen his re-election position. Nothing seemed to have been done about the intimacy between Greely and the Chinese via Zhōu. Dan was not surprised. During this time, he remained out of communication with Jane. Fred and Warren fed him information as they uncovered it. Jane finally decided that Dan had gone underground to nurse his anger. She was sad but could only be patient and wait for him to emerge and contact her.

Dan turned his attention to George Randall, Greely's aide. He decided that whatever action he took would start lower than Greely. His reconnaissance of Randall uncovered an interesting item. The man had a Chinese girlfriend. She was quite good-looking and seemed to be a student at George Washington University. *Could this be the same girl that dated Bela Mihok?* Dan thought it highly unlikely, but the odd coincidence stared him in the face.

† † †

After a night out at a fancy restaurant, George took Wang Li Xiu back to her apartment and drove off. Dan pulled from the curb and followed. Randall went through the city to the Anacostia River waterfront. He pulled into the entrance of an abandoned warehouse and drove around to the back, out of Dan's sight.

Dan parked a half block down the street and got out of his car. He was dressed in dark pants and jacket with a black watch cap over his head. He had his suppressed 9mm Sig Sauer P320 in his pocket, along with extra magazines. Just then, another car came down the road. Dan stepped back into the shadows as the car turned into the same lot as Randall. When it had passed, he followed.

At the end of the drive, the pavement opened up to a larger parking lot. Most of the overhead lamps were out, leaving many areas in deep shadows. Dan edged around the building, keeping close to the wall and in the darkness. Out in the parking lot, the two cars had stopped near each other under one of the working lamps. Dan watched as the driver of the second car got out and opened the back door. Dan could not see inside, but even from a distance and in the limited light, he could tell that the driver was most likely Hispanic.

Randall got out of his car and entered the rear of the other one. *A late-night conference. Something not good is going on.* Dan watched for a while. When the rear door opened, he slipped back around the building and sprinted down the road to his car. *Want to see where this car goes.*

The second car came out of the driveway and turned left. Before Randall's car emerged, Dan pulled out and switched on his lights after the car ahead made a right turn. Soon they were in traffic, and Dan could follow without fear of being noticed. The car got on the South East Boulevard, which merged onto I 695. The highway became I 395 when it crossed over the Potomac. After crossing the river, the vehicle exited on Route 1, going south. Just past the Reagan National Airport, it turned right towards the Del Ray area just south of Four Mile Run, a creek that empties into the Potomac. Dan followed more carefully now in the local traffic. The car turned into a shopping center with two restaurants in it, one Mexican and one offering Peruvian chicken. Dan followed and parked far enough away to not be noticed. He took a small pair of binoculars out to get a better look at the car's passenger under the better light.

He was a Latino. In the light, Dan could tell his driver was the muscle. The look was similar to gang members he had encountered in Brooklyn, only Hispanic instead of Italian. *Need to find out where this guy stays*. He was important because Greely's top aide came to meet with him and sit in his car. An indication of the relative status of the two men.

A long hour later, around midnight, the two left as the Mexican restaurant closed. Dan followed them to a small house in an anonymous neighborhood. There were four cars parked both in the driveway and on the street. It spoke of a group house, something not unusual in immigrant neighborhoods where large groups lived together to cut down on expenses.

Dan stayed near the end of the block long enough to conclude this was the last stop for the duo. He noted the address and headed back to his motel room.

Chapter 53

The next day Fred called. "This guy George Randall. He's getting his money from Mexico. It's from a company that handles port activities on the west coast. Mazatlan and Guaymas. They're pretty regular and don't go directly to Randall, but to off-shore accounts. We only know they're for Randall because Warren was able to untangle the subsequent deposits to their final accounts in his name. He's got one in Switzerland and one in the Caymans."

"Money from Mexico," Dan said. "From who?"

"Checked that. Warren said the company is owned by Mendoza. He's moving money regularly from the drug business into private companies. And this is one of them. They generate so much illicit cash, they are almost overwhelmed by it. Mendoza is apparently putting in a lot of effort to not just warehouse the cash, but get it into the legitimate economy."

"Then he can live off of it," Dan said. "Establishing assets for the future, for his family. Maybe he learned something from his uncle."

"While keeping enough cash around for bribing the government."

"Apparently that doesn't take the majority of the money they rake in. I wonder if his boss knows Randall's collecting on the side?"

"And what is he doing for these payouts?" Fred asked. "Guiding his boss to keep pushing open borders? That would only help Mendoza's business."

Dan's subsequent trailing of Randall didn't lead to any further meetings with the mysterious Mexican. Warren checked the Alexandria address and found it was owned by a Mexican investment company that rented it out to one Carlos Becerra. A search for this name through the internet led to the discovery of his employ at a company named Tecnologías de Seguridad Portuario, or Port Security Technologies.

Why would someone working for that company spend time in the D.C. area? The question rattled around for a short time in Dan's brain, but he knew the answer. *He's working for Mendoza.*

Two days after Randall's meeting with Carlos Becerra, Dan followed Randall to Baltimore. He observed the man meeting with some underworld types in a restaurant in the Hollins Market area. Dan had followed Randall into the restaurant and sat at the counter where he could surreptitiously watch as Randall talked to two men. One of them was in charge; the other, a huge fellow, was obviously the muscle. Randall passed a package to the smaller guy who opened it. He took out a pill and examined it. Then put it back in the package and slipped it into his jacket pocket. He took an envelope out and passed it over to Randall, who started to open it. The man reached over to stop him, looking around the restaurant to see if anyone was watching.

Dan lowered his eyes as the man's gaze swept past him. He couldn't tell if he noticed him. When Dan looked up, Randall was stuffing some bills back into the envelope and putting it inside his coat. He reached over to shake the man's hand and then got up to leave. Dan stayed where he was and worked on the beer and nacho plate he had ordered. Randall left, followed by the other two men.

There would be no following Randall, but it didn't matter. He was probably headed back to his townhouse. Dan had discovered enough. It looked like he was dealing pills to a drug dealer. Was it fentanyl? Was he getting money *and* drugs as a payoff? The drugs would be less costly for the cartel, so they would be happy to pay part of however much Randall was worth to them that way. Randall could then leverage this payoff to increase his net take.

Dan gave the men five minutes, then put a twenty on the counter and left the restaurant. He was on his way to his car when the two men approached him. He saw them come out from the shadow of the building; one very large figure accompanied by a regular-sized man. Dan stopped at the car and turned to the approaching figures.

"Can I help you?" he asked while preparing himself for combat. His Sig Sauer sat in its holster under his arm. With the suppressor attached, it would not come out quickly. He might have to deal with the giant by hand, not something Dan looked forward to attempting.

"You seemed to be very interested in my conversation with my friend back there in the restaurant. I just wonder why."

The giant stood silently. He didn't speak. Dan knew he wouldn't go into action without a provocation from him or some sign from his boss. Dan watched the smaller man carefully.

"I was taken by how big your partner is. I've rarely seen guys that large." He turned to the big man. "Did you play football? You'd be a terror on the field."

The large man didn't respond.

"That it? It seems a bit convenient. You came in just after the other guy. Then you leave just after we leave. It looks like you were there just for us."

"That's just coincidence."

"You from around here? You don't sound like you are."

"I'm from Brooklyn." The man gave him a quizzical look. "Not the Brooklyn here in Baltimore, the one up north, in New York."

"Don't sound much like it."

"I've been away for a while."

"You a cop? Undercover?"

Dan shook his head.

"Maybe we check to see. If you're a cop, you'll have a badge and a gun. Undercover, you'll still have a gun."

This was the moment. Dan was ready. The talker would make a signal, then the big guy would step forward, not expecting any significant resistance. Trusting in his overwhelming size. He would expect his target to shrink back in an instinctively defensive move.

The little guy nodded. The big man reached out with his right arm. Dan offered his left as if to block him and stepped forward. Dan's right hand shot out and upward, skimming the big man's chest and slamming into his throat. He hit the throat with his fist flattened, allowing his knuckles to crash into the man's larynx. At that same moment, Dan's right leg came forward, ramming his knee into the man's crotch.

There was a shocked gurgle from the giant, and he bent over in pain as his testicles were nearly smashed. His hold on Dan's left arm released as he struggled to breathe and stay upright. The smaller guy reached inside his jacket and pulled out his weapon. He fired it as Dan turned towards him. The bullet ripped past Dan's left arm as he swung his right through the air to land on the man's neck. Without giving the smaller man time to redirect his aim, Dan leaped on him following his blow and grabbed his right wrist. The gun fired again, but harmlessly in the air as the two crashed to the ground.

Dan landed on top, and the force knocked the air out of the smaller man. Dan drove his knee into his chest as he slammed his right hand to the pavement dislodging the gun from his hand. He grabbed the weapon and jumped to his feet. The man recovered his breath and looked up at him with a mixture of anger and amazement on his face.

"Now I've got a couple of questions for you since you were so concerned about me watching your conversation. Your friend here," Dan nodded to his giant partner on the ground, struggling for breath, "has a partially crushed larynx. He's only got a few minutes before he passes out and possibly dies. You need to get him help right away.

"Now tell me what did George Randall give you? Fentanyl?"

The man glared at Dan.

"Your friend here is on borrowed time."

"Yeah," he said. "You're a cop, right?"

Dan shook his head. "You're in luck, I'm not a cop. But I'm still going to take your fentanyl and dump it. That might save a few lives. But I'm not going to turn you in. He do this often? Randall?"

The man didn't answer.

"Remember, you only have a few minutes to save your friend."

"About twice a month."

"How much do you pay him?"

"Thirty grand a package." He glanced at his companion, whose eyes were growing larger as he struggled to breathe.

"Almost done. What's it worth on the street?"

"Seventy, eighty grand."

"How long has this been going on?"

"Almost two years. Who the hell are you?"

"All you need to know is I'm *not* a cop, so this is your lucky day in a way. Hand it over and I'll be going...with the package and your gun."

The man took out the pills and gave them to Dan. Dan grabbed the package.

"Call 911 and get the medics here pronto. No time to lose." He backed into his car, leaving the smaller man making a call on his phone as he drove off.

Chapter 54

Dan sat in his motel room sipping a bourbon. It was not of the same pedigree as he had drunk at the hunting cabin. *Wonder what those two pukes are doing? If Jane keeps them out there babysitting, they're gonna be pissed.*

He went over what he knew. Greely and his family were deeply involved with China and were most likely beholden to Zhōu. Greely's trespass in Dan's eyes would be to promote or slant legislation to favor China. He would be counted upon by his Chinese benefactors to help maintain a positive attitude towards a county that was dedicated to our downfall. He was, thought Dan, probably not the only legislator in such a position. Just one of the more important ones.

Randall, his aide, was more down and dirty. He might be on the take from Zhōu; Dan didn't know. But he had proof, thanks to Warren and Fred, that he was on the take from Mendoza. On top of that, he was dealing in his own right. It seemed his payoffs were not enough; he liked leveraging them into more money. *Probably gets an additional ten to fifteen k hit from the exchange. And probably enjoys the excitement, dealing with the underworld.*

Okay. Two issues to deal with. Where do I start, and do I add the Mendoza guy into the mix? Dan took another sip and thought through the issues at hand. *Don't want to tip off Greely or Randall. Better to start with the Mendoza guy?* He continued to work through his options; what to do to end this transgression and how to avoid a trail that could lead back to Jane. What to do about Zhōu. And did he need to go after the nephew of Mendoza? That one would be hard. The younger man would have learned from his uncle's demise, and it would be difficult to get close to him. He wasn't worried about himself. He was a ghost and would remain one. By early morning he had his plan.

† † †

"Jane here," she said as she picked up her phone.

"Just your loyal servants checking in," came the reply.

"Marcus? That you?"

"Bingo. How long do you want us to stay out in never-never land with the package? It's getting pretty boring."

"You shouldn't be calling in."

"Got a burner phone. Don't worry. Just answer my question."

"A little while longer. No one above me knows about you guys and your part. I need to keep it that way right now."

"You mean until the public interest dies down."

Jane was silent on the other end.

"You know you could put the package in your own storage area. Then we could go on with our own lives."

"That's the plan, but it involves other people, so I've got to wait. Where's Dan. Have you heard from him?"

"Not since he left to go to D.C. Didn't you talk with him?"

"I did, but he's left and I don't know where he's gone."

"Probably back home."

"No. I checked. Did he say anything about taking some action here...in town?"

"No. But I can tell you, he wasn't happy to listen to our guy's tale of high levels of corruption."

"That's what worries me."

"Can't help you there. Just get us the hell out of this babysitting detail. Roland may commit a transgression on your prized package if this goes on for too long."

Jane hung up the phone. There was no good answer for Marcus at this point. As each day went by, she got more and more nervous about whether Dan might be planning some sort of action.

† † †

Rashid got a call late one night. It was from Zhōu.

"Are you still in D.C.?"

"Yes. I've been digging. I got access to the police reports in Indiana and learned that one of the attackers was taken away. The farm couple who were held hostage, finally, after multiple rounds of interviews, let slip that the three men who killed the other jihadists left taking one with them. A body was found in the cornfield, next to the road. The couple were sure, when they were asked to identify it, that it was the man who organized the attack."

"Jabbar?"

"No. It was an older man. The couple finally came out and said a younger man had been tied up by the older leader. He was held in their living room along with them. When the rescuers attacked, the older man, the leader, fled. The three men took the younger man, still tied, with them when they left. He's not been found."

"Jabbar may be alive."

"That is what I am thinking. I am also thinking that may not be good...for either of us. You had me meet with him to fill him in. Now that information is with our enemies."

"Maybe not. He is a strong person."

Zhōu let out a short laugh. One empty of humor. "He is not a warrior. You and I know that. He will not last long in the hands of our enemy. They will easily break him and he will tell all."

"What will you do?"

Rashid already knew the CIA was aware of him. His main assassin had been killed by one of their operatives. His protection came from his status in Saudi Arabia. They could not get to him through the government. He was safe in his country. So long as he acted through agents, he could continue to operate, even if that meant being less effective.

"I'm going to round up my assets," Zhōu said, "and have them quietly depart. We will do it slowly so we don't alert anyone who's watching."

Chapter 55

Warren called Dan late one night. "Do you remember that I said George Randall had a Chinese girlfriend?"

"Yeah, what about that?"

"Well, I got a picture of her off a surveillance camera at the university. I decided to search for a picture of the Chinese girlfriend of that guy in Hungary—"

"You can find that?"

"Once you know what you're searching for, it's just a matter of time and knowing where to look. There's lots of CCTV in Hungary. Just like here in the U.S. It's hard to be anonymous today."

"You found something?"

"Yep." Warren seemed to shift from the side track he had started down and returned to the subject of his call.

"I'm going to send you both photos. I've cleaned them up, but they were pretty good to start with. The results are interesting."

"You're becoming quite a tease. Send them right away."

"I just want you to make your own impression."

Warren ended the call, and Dan's phone lit up a moment later with an incoming message.

He sat in the chair in his room and studied the photos. It was the same woman. After coming to that conclusion from a general once-over, Dan proceeded to note details;

the shape of the nose, positioning of the eyes, chin, and lips; it all matched. The photo from D.C. showed evidence of more stress, perhaps. *Was she happier in Budapest?*

Bela Mihok had disappeared. It was now clear this woman, his girlfriend, hadn't. What had happened to Bela? Had she killed him? Left him to be killed by others? There was no doubt in Dan's mind; poor Bela was dead. And this woman, who posed as a college student, had something to do with it. His handprint had been used to gain access to the lab. Dan understood the ramifications of that fact.

Now she's the girlfriend of a congressional aide. Zhōu was probably behind her activities. If that was so, maybe he was still here in D.C.? That could be helpful. Dan smiled at the thought of getting hold of Zhōu. It would not be easy. He probably stayed at the Chinese embassy or close to it. If he went out, it would be with bodyguards. Taking him would cause an uproar that could send Jane into a tailspin. Maybe fracture their relationship. *Stick with smaller fish for now.*

Dan called Warren.

"I need you to backdoor a computer for me. I need all its activities monitored and the hard drive dumped."

"Sounds like you want me to install a keylogger, maybe an infostealer."

"Yeah. I'll have to rely on you for choosing what's needed."

"If you can log into it and start it, I can do something with software."

"I don't have the password."

"That presents its own set of problems. In that case, the best way is for you to install a physical backdoor inside the computer. Is it a laptop?"

"Probably not. A home computer. Most likely a desktop."

"You don't know?"

"Not yet, but count on it being a desktop."

"That's easier. Larger case."

"It won't be found?"

"If you open the case. But how many times do you open your desktop case?"

"Point taken."

"Whose computer am I hacking?"

"That's not important. But I want to know everything that's going on with it. I also want a dump of the hard drive. I need email history as well."

"I can do all of that once I'm in."

"Great. Now, can you set me up with an audio bug...or bugs for a home?"

"Easy peasy. Sounds like you're doing a full-on surveillance."

"That I am."

"This wouldn't be for a certain congressman and I'm gonna go to jail for ten years when it's discovered?"

"No. Not a congressman. And it won't be discovered."

"When things blow up, this stuff gets discovered."

"In that case, don't let it get tracked back to you."

There was a pause in the conversation. "You keep sucking me further into your world. I told you once before, in Switzerland, that I like playing on the periphery. I'm a bit player."

"I remember. And just like back there, your skills are necessary in today's world. You be the anonymous computer geek. I'll be the front-line soldier...and, in this case, the installer."

Warren sighed. "You want video feed or audio only?"

"You can get me both?"

"Of course. But video is going to be more difficult to install. Got to hide the camera, but still allow it to see things."

Dan thought for a moment.

"Let's go for all of it. I'll figure out where to put them."

George Randall lived just off Capitol Hill. In a two-story townhouse just north of Lincoln Park. It was a long-time gentrified neighborhood. His unit was an end cap with an alley bordering it. There was a small backyard with a stockade fence. The townhouse was not imposing, and one would only give it little consideration except for its location, which gave it a premium price tag.

On a gray, late fall day, after George had left for the Capitol, Dan stopped near his townhouse. There were more open parking places now that residents had left for work. He was dressed in tan pants and a jacket. It was reversible with a dark blue color when turned inside out. Dan carried a soft briefcase. He had a dress shirt under his jacket but no tie. The look was professional but casual. It didn't stand out in this neighborhood.

When he got to the townhouse, he walked up to the door. There was a security camera out front which was recording him. He took out his lock picks and made short work of the deadbolt. Once he got Warren's hardware installed, the video of his entry could be erased. If Randall checked his feed assiduously, he would notice the missing time. Still, Dan was betting that his monitoring was irregular at best. The sign out front of a professional security installation and the obvious camera probably gave Randall a false sense of deterrence.

In his briefcase, Dan had an assortment of video cameras. The most useful ones were the smoke detectors with a camera and mic inside of them. The camera gave a wide-view look at any room in which it was installed. There were three smoke detectors in the townhouse. One in the kitchen, one in the living room, and one in the upper hallway that connected the bedrooms and the bathroom.

After putting these detectors in place, Dan took down a framed print on the bedroom wall. He used a small pick to puncture a pinhole in the upper corner of the print. Behind the hole, he mounted a tiny pinhole camera that was motion activated to save battery life. From the front, it would take a careful examination of the print to find the pinhole. If one took the image down, the camera would immediately be seen on the back. But without any suspicion, no one would give the print such a close look.

When he was done, Dan found the desktop computer and installed the device Warren told him to purchase. With that completed, he called Warren, who tested each device and pronounced them successfully installed.

Chapter 56

Dan gathered data for a week, reviewing the mass of information that Warren sent him from the hacked computer's hard drive. The emails showed a steady flow of communication between Randall and Carlos. Most likely the man who Randall had met with in D.C. From what Dan could glean, Carlos' boss was none other than Alejandro Mendoza.

The emails also showed Randall regularly involved with a minor gang outside of the cartel's territory in Baltimore. These communications confirmed what Dan had observed. Randall sold them fentanyl, and they distributed it or used it to mix with other drugs.

There was a disturbing sequence of emails from younger female college students. They were a couple of years old but evidenced Randall's manipulations with the younger women, including demands that they perform certain sex acts with him or face an embarrassing disclosure of compromising pictures. The man seemed to have toned down his actions more recently. Still, Dan concluded that George Randall was a thoroughly disreputable person, even before you got to his open borders stance.

† † †

Jane sat in Henry's office. Henry was feeling conflicted. Jane had accomplished the near impossible. He was sure that Dan was behind it and that it violated all the CIA's rules against domestic operations. Still, he had given her broad hints that she could proceed, and she had delivered. It was now incumbent on both of them to make sure nothing of the operation leaked out.

"Tell me who knows about what went on besides you."

Jane paused for a moment. "Do you really want to know?"

"I'm beyond any deniability. I need to understand the full picture to help ensure this story never gets out."

"Henry. I need your assurances that nothing will happen to the ones I name. That they don't' disappear in the name of mission anonymity."

Henry gave her a sharp look. "We're not Russia for God's sake."

"It has happened. I'm not naive."

"But never under my watch. I choose my people so that I don't have to worry about anyone going rogue. I chose you with that in mind and I assume you chose your people with the same concern."

"So, I can count on your assurance that these people will not be disappeared?"

"Damn it! I told you I don't do that."

"Tell me specifically. Tell me regarding these people."

"You don't trust me? What the hell has gotten into you?"

"Henry, I trust you. But the more you don't give me a direct assurance, the more worried I become."

Henry sighed. "I never thought I'd hear this talk from you. Okay, nothing will happen to your team. The one's you tell me about. I just need to know how many people are in on this (his fingers made air quotes) secret mission. Is that good enough?"

Jane smiled. “That will do. Thank you.”

“Now to the point. Who else is in on the secret.”

“Dan, of course. He’s the main actor.”

She paused for a moment, then continued.

“My two researchers, Fred and Warren. They’ve been in on almost every mission. They’re the tech team. We’re blind without them.”

“Anyone else?”

“My two backups for Dan, Marcus and Roland.”

“The two ex-military types?”

Jane nodded. “Ex Delta Force.”

There was a pause.

“That all?”

Jane nodded. “Some of Warren’s old acquaintances at NSA have been asked to provide some data, but they don’t have any idea what it’s in connection to.”

“Well, that’s better than I hoped.”

“We’re a tight unit. But we get a lot done.”

“Indeed. You’ve accomplished the impossible. Have you wrapped things up? It’s time to cover this up, wipe away the fingerprints and move on. There’ll be enough speculation and most of it centered on the CIA. We’re the only ones who could have done this. The president will know that, but we have to remain silent.”

“Even from the president?”

“That’s up to Gardiner. If he wants to own up to it, so be it. But he doesn’t know about us. He would have to give Garrett the order, who would pass it down to my boss, Roger, who would tell me and any other clandestine groups to disclose anything we’re involved with. I can keep you and your staff secret, but the project would be exposed.”

“No chance to keep things from drilling all the way down?”

“Possible. If the president just accepts that it’s a clandestine op and leaves it at that. A good argument can be made to him that such would be the best course of action. He needs some protection, even if it's one of his own party putting the heat on us."

"Maybe this can get Greely to stop."

"If the president wanted to press the matter. But he seems reluctant to force Greely. I think he likes keeping us under a bit of pressure and doesn't want to risk a split in his party."

† † †

Dan had followed Randall and the Chinese girl to a restaurant in Georgetown called Apéro. It was on P Street near the P Street Bridge, going over Rock Creek Park. Dan knew it was an intimate place with a well-known French recipe and an award-winning wine and champagne list.

Perfect restaurant for lovers. The two would be safely ensconced there for at least three hours. He headed back to Capitol Hill and Randall's townhouse.

Dan drove through the neighborhood. Parking was at a premium, with the street-side parking being limited to residents with stickers on their cars. He headed towards Lincoln Park, where more curb-side spaces became available. It would be three blocks from his target, but that was okay.

After leaving his car near the park, Dan started walking back. It was 8:30 in the evening. He could be assured that the two love birds would not show up until at least 10:30 or 11 pm. He had plenty of time.

He walked back to the townhouse, dressed in dark pants and jacket. Under his jacket, he wore a dark blue hooded sweatshirt. He left the hood down as that gave too menacing a look for the area. His facial disguise, renewed every day, would suffice to throw anyone off his trail. Under his jacket, Dan carried a suppressed .22 LR semi-automatic pistol. It was whisper quiet and, up close, if carefully aimed, delivered a lethal hit.

† † †

Dinner was proceeding as George Randall expected. Wang Li Xiu was suitably enthralled at the romantic restaurant. She was getting tipsy from the wine he plied her with. George was getting more excited with anticipation of an aroused evening. One where he hoped get some great photos of this Chinese beauty performing all manner of lewd acts on him. It would not only be enjoyable but useful for future leverage if she decided that she no longer wanted to enjoy his company. But for the moment, they would have a thoroughly wanton evening of which this intimate dinner was only the beginning.

By 11 pm, they were ready to leave. Wang Li Xiu leaned on George's arm as his car was brought around. It was a Porsche Cayenne SUV. It never went off-road but had all the necessary capabilities to do so. It gave George a commanding view of the road and was suitably filled with luxury to satisfy his vanity.

Chapter 57

It was just past midnight when George found a space a block from his townhouse. He parked, and the two walked arm in arm to George's residence. Along the way, there were whispered expressions of desire, along with a few giggles. George unlocked the front door, and the two went inside.

They left their coats in the hall closet and headed for the living room. George liked to start there with a nightcap and then proceed to the bedroom for the real action. As they entered, a light flicked on with the shade opened to point straight at the couple.

Both stopped in shock. They could not see behind the light. But they both could see the pistol the intruder allowed to be shown.

"Go over to the couch and sit down, nice and slow. Don't do anything foolish or you'll get shot."

"Who are you? What do you want? I have some money in my wallet if you're here to rob me. But I don't have a safe in the house."

The gun waved towards the couch. There was no answer.

After the two sat down, Dan spoke.

"This is a silenced gun. No one next door will hear it. If you want to stay alive, you will do as I say. If not, I'll shoot you. Somewhere it will hurt like hell. That's before I kill you."

"What do you want?" George asked again. His voice was thin with fear.

Wang Li Xiu said nothing but kept her eye on the gun in Dan's lap. George looked around to see that the curtains had been drawn. No one outside would notice anything except a soft light in one of his rooms.

"I've been reading up on you, George. You're a piece of shit in my book and I'd just as soon put a bullet in your head as talk to you. But others would like me to be a bit more generous—"

"You're CIA?"

Dan didn't answer.

"I knew you guys were up to no good. It's against the law to do what you're doing. I'm connected to an important congressman. There'll be hell to raise when he hears about this."

"Shut up. None of your bullshit is going to work here. You need to listen if you want to keep on living."

George stopped the rant he was just beginning. Wang Li Xiu said nothing, alternately shifting her gaze from the gun to trying to see Dan's face.

"Dealing drugs in Baltimore is illegal and could sink your beloved congressman. I also know you are getting quite a lot of cash from a Mexican cartel and you're cozy with a certain Chinese source. Speaking of Chinese sources..."

Dan shifted his attention to Wang. "Whatever happened to Bela? You two were quite an item in Budapest, especially among his friends. You both disappeared after the anthrax was stolen. And now you reappear here, as a college student in D.C. And you're dating this guy. Do you know what became of Bela?"

Wang didn't answer. Dan watched her face. She held her composure well, but a slight flicker in her eyes gave her away. George looked at Dan with questions on his face.

"You didn't know?" Dan said to Randall. "Two months ago, this beauty was dating a lab tech in Budapest. She was a college student there as well. It seems they stole some anthrax and then both disappeared. Now she shows up here. That's quite a quick shift from her previous circumstances."

George looked over at Wang. "Is this true?"

Wang shook her head but didn't say anything. She kept her eyes on Dan.

"Cat got your tongue? I know how to loosen it. We're going to go away, somewhere private to talk about things."

"You can't kidnap her. I'll call the police."

Dan turned his attention back to Randall. "You're in no position to call anyone. You're a two-bit drug dealer who is on the take from a cartel. *And* you have a Chinese spy for a girlfriend. I wonder how much pillow talk she's passed on to Zhōu Ming."

"You mistake me for someone else," Wang finally said.

"I'll take that chance." He shifted his seat to lean a bit forward. "Here's what we're gonna do. George, you're going to lie on the floor while I secure your girlfriend. I'll be leaving with her. What you're going to do after that will determine whether or not you continue to live. Like I said, others want me to be diplomatic."

He paused for a moment.

"You've got a sizeable amount of money off-shore. You're going to go to your boss, tell him you're burned out and you need to resign. At first, he won't understand, but he will later. You will leave the country. If I learn of you returning, there'll be a bounty put on your head. You'll be a hunted man and dead within days."

"I'm not leaving and you're not taking her."

"That's quite chivalrous sounding, but futile. I *will* take her and you *will* leave. Or, I can kill you now and take her. She goes. The only question is if you're going to save your own life."

"I'm not going with you." Her words came out flat and hard. Not at all like the coed that George was dating. He turned to look at her as if he'd never seen her before.

Without waiting, Dan fired a shot into Wang's right calf. She screamed and lurched forward to grab her leg. Dan stepped forward as George started to rise. He shifted his weapon to his left hand and swung his hand in an open karate chop across George's neck. He fell to the floor, stunned and out of commission.

Without hesitation, Dan grabbed Wang and threw her on the floor. He rolled her on her stomach and tied her wrists with zip ties. Then he turned her over and examined her leg. The bullet had grazed her shin and penetrated her calf muscle, ending up in the couch. He took a gauze pad from his pocket along with a wrap and bandaged the wound to staunch the blood flow.

That done, Dan turned his attention to George. The aide was beginning to come around.

"You're going to have a very sore neck for a few days. There'll be a bruise. I suggest you come up with a story. If what happened here tonight gets out, you'll prove nothing and you will just have put a target on your back. You'll be dead within twenty-four hours."

He grabbed George's face.

"Got it?"

George nodded groggily.

"Good. Now tomorrow you talk to Greely. Tell him you have to resign. You can't even give him notice. Tell him you're near a breakdown. Then you get out of the country."

"Where should I go?"

"I don't give a damn where you go."

"You won't get away with this."

"That's my problem. And if you want to live long enough to see if I do or not. Leave the country."

Late that night, two figures staggered out of Randall's townhouse. The shorter one had a coat thrown over her shoulders as she leaned against her partner. They looked like an amorous couple who had too much to drink. They made the three blocks without encountering any other pedestrians.

Once at Dan's car, he looked around. The street was empty. He opened the trunk and lifted the figure inside. Then he taped her mouth, closed the lid, and drove off.

Chapter 58

Six hours later, Dan pulled up to the hunting cabin. He got out and opened the trunk. Roland stepped out on the porch.

"What brings you back here?"

"Got a package for you." Dan motioned for Roland to come over to the car.

"Who's this?" Roland asked.

"Wang Li Xiu. She's the past girlfriend of Bela Mihok. He's the lab tech in Budapest who stole the anthrax. They both disappeared after the theft. Now she shows up here in D.C. I suspect poor Bela will never show up."

Dan grabbed the woman and hauled her out of the trunk. She let out a yell when he pulled the tape from her mouth.

"What are we going to do with her?"

"I think Jane would like to spend time interrogating her...with some specialists in attendance."

"Whoa, buddy. That's not my bag. I know Marcus suggested the water boarding, which worked. But we're not part of that team."

"What the hell?" Marcus stepped out onto the porch.

"Someone for you to babysit," Dan replied.

"This is getting pretty old," Marcus said.

"Tell Jane. She's the one parked you out here for now. Let her know you have Bela's girlfriend. She'll want to talk to her."

"What are you going to do?"

"Grab a cup of coffee and something to eat, if you can spare it. Then I'm off again."

"Where to?"

Dan shook his head. "Can't say. Jane'll be asking questions so the less you know the better."

"Fuck this. We get the shit job and you're going off the reservation. Jane isn't going to like this. If Henry finds out they'll be reeling you in."

"Maybe. Not before I do what I've got to do."

He grabbed Wang's upper arm and helped her limp to the cabin.

"She's injured?" Roland said. "So, we're nurses now?"

"Flesh wound. Just clean it. Triage like in the field and keep her leg elevated. She'll survive it. Not that she deserves the care."

Dan gulped down a cup of coffee and wolfed down a hunk of spam.

"Breakfast of champions," he said. "Gotta go." He stopped at the door. "And...thanks guys. I owe you one."

"More than one," Marcus said.

Dan waved and went down the steps back to his car.

† † †

After Dan left with Wang, George got up and poured himself a drink. His neck was sore, and he couldn't turn it to the left or right. *Who had attacked them? How did he know what he was up to? It had to be the CIA*. That insight was not hard to reach, but what could he do about it?

Despite what the man had threatened, he felt sure that Greely could blow up the CIA with this piece of evidence of their domestic operations. Which included kidnapping, threatening a congressman, a congressman's aide, and a personal attack on two innocent people.

He picked up his phone.

"What do you want? Do you know what time it is?" Greely's voice was a mixture of sleep and anger over this early morning call. George figured he was disturbing the man's sleep after a full night of action with his mistress, and Greely didn't like it.

"It's important. I was attacked tonight. By the CIA. We need to talk."

There was a pause on the line.

"Did you say the CIA?"

"I did."

"How do you know?"

"He knew things about me that one could only get through sophisticated surveillance. Both of me and my computer. I think my home has been bugged. Can I come over?"

"Shit. This is beyond the pale. I can't believe this is going on." Greely sighed. "Yeah. Come on over. I'll get some coffee on."

The line went dead.

A half-hour later, George knocked on Greely's townhouse in Georgetown. He entered and was led into Greely's study. Whether or not the mistress was still in the house was unclear.

"Are we alone?" George asked.

"We are. Tell me what happened."

George went over the events. It took some time to sort things out as the stress had caused some confusion in his mind. He finally could make enough sense of it, minus the information about his drug dealing, for Greely to understand.

James Greely sat there with a coffee cup in his hand. He had his head down as if thinking hard.

"So, what do we do with this?" George asked. "It's explosive and could bring some serious heat on the CIA, but there's some dirty laundry, so to speak."

"Your girlfriend? Hell, we can cover that. She's a student as you say. You're only guilty of dating young coeds. If one turns out to be a spy? Well, how the hell would you know? It would seem to be the CIA's job to know and to warn you. Them or the FBI."

George looked down at the floor.

"Is there something else? Something you're not telling me? George, if you have any shit hiding in your closet, you better show it to me. Otherwise, I'll get covered with it if it comes to light."

"I know you have an arrangement with Zhōu Ming. Hell, I help you remember your meetings."

"Those are business issues. He's a businessman and I and my family have business dealings with Chinese companies."

"I know that."

"And that has been known to most people for quite a while."

"I know that as well."

"So, what's the problem?"

"I…I…decided to get in on a bit of that action—"

"With Zhōu?"

George shook his head. "No, no." He paused before continuing. "But there are certain people who have an interest in the open borders we're pushing. They like the arrangement. I'm receiving funds from them to keep you on that course."

"Who?"

"Someone representing Alejandro Mendoza."

James sat there staring at his senior aide. The man looked like a dog that got caught eating off the table.

"*The* Alejandro Mendoza?"

George nodded without speaking.

"What the fuck? Are you stupid? You can't actually connect to them like that. You could blow up our long-term plans."

"It's quite low key. I don't interact with them. I just receive a payoff on a regular basis. Since things are going so well on the southern border, there's no issue."

"Where do you put the money? That can be tracked."

"Some of it is fed into your campaign organization, from a legitimate source. Some of it is run through a bunch of off-shore accounts. I don't keep any of it here in the U.S."

James continued to look at his aide with an angry expression on his face. "If it's the CIA, they can find it. Don't imagine it's safely tucked out of sight. With the money trail, they can sink you, and me as well."

"What do we do? Go on the offensive?"

Greely sat in his chair thinking while George sat nervously, waiting for what his boss would decide. He could distance himself and leave George hanging in the wind. The congressman would be damaged, but not terminally.

"I think I may put a call into the CIA. Talk to their DDO. I may be able to stir them up enough to shut this guy down, whoever he is. I can play it like he's a rogue agent, trying to attack me through you because I've been holding hearings. I can offer an olive branch to back off a bit, if he shuts this illegal operation down and commits to not pursue domestic action in the future."

Greely looked at his aide with a slight smile on his face. "We may be able to turn this into a win."

Chapter 59

"Where is Dan?" Jane's voice was sharp with anger.

"I don't know," Marcus said. "He showed up here with a Chinese woman who he says was the girlfriend of some guy in Hungary. He said you would know who."

"Bela's girlfriend?"

"That's the one."

"You have her?"

"Yep."

"How does Dan know it's her?"

"Hell if I know. You know more about all of that than Roland and me. We're just babysitters it seems."

"I've got to get hold of Dan."

"He's not picking up?"

"Don't get smart with me. I've got a shit storm brewing and I think he's the cause of it."

"I can't help you there, ma'am. We're just the—"

"I know, the babysitters. Just do that. But if Dan contacts you again, you tell him to get in touch or he's in some deep, serious shit and I won't be able to help him. He could ruin our whole division."

"I'll pass it on."

The phone went dead.

"That Jane?" Roland asked.

Marcus nodded. It's SHFT time in D.C."

"Maybe being out here ain't so bad."

"Better than making love to some gorgeous gal or eating in a fine restaurant? I don't think so."

"You don't like my cuisine? I'm shocked."

"We both don't, and you know it. And shepherding these two isn't much fun either."

"At least we're not getting shot at," Roland said. "Hey, why don't I go hunting tomorrow morning? I might bag a turkey or a deer. Then we'd eat better. Think you can handle our wards while I'm away?"

Marcus gave him a rude hand gesture but smiled at his partner. "I can. Can you actually hit something out there? More than trees?"

"You'll see, smart ass. I bag it, you clean it. Deal?"

† † †

Garrett Easton stormed into Roger Abrams' office. Roger, the head of SAD and Henry's immediate boss, was the key point of contact and insulation between Henry and the upper-level management.

James Greely had briefed Garrett on what had happened to his senior aide, leaving out some of the more incriminating pieces of information. Wang Li Xiu was part of the story, but she was presented as an innocent affair on the part of his aide. She might be a honey trap, but George was nothing more sinister than an official targeted because he was connected and single, vulnerable to her machinations.

Garrett paced in front of Roger's desk. That was never a good sign in Roger's mind.

"The top aide to Greely was attacked in his home last night. The attacker had detailed info on this guy. Information that could only come from an agency like ours. He was told to resign and leave the country or face lethal violence. On top of that the man's girlfriend, a Chinese student at GWU, was shot and abducted. Who knows what her fate is."

Roger just looked at his boss. He had heard nothing about this, but to protest at this stage would mean nothing. He needed Garrett to get the whole story out.

Garrett went on to describe the scene in some detail. From his picture, George was an innocent victim of an overzealous spy agency that needed reining in.

"What do you know about this?" Garrett finally asked after spinning out the story Greely had given him.

"This is the first time I've heard about any of it. It's certainly not an operation that I would sanction or authorize. We've been focused on the anthrax attack. Which, by the way, was successfully intercepted. It's taken the wind out of Greely's sails, don't you think?"

"I'll grant you that. But now we come up with crap all over us again."

"You think that's a coincidence?"

"What are you suggesting?"

"Greely's committee has found nothing. Now the public is happy someone is doing some sleuthing and protecting them from terrorists trying to infect and kill them. Then, all of a sudden, someone breaks into this aide's house and threatens him, and steals his girlfriend? Do we even know she's for real?"

"You think this is all made up? That would be quite a step to take. One that could backfire horribly on Greely."

"Maybe not if he can whip everyone up into a frenzy. Has he gone to the press?"

Garrett shook his head. "That's what's a bit odd. He wants to use this to make a deal with us."

"He knows his side is losing because of the attempted terror attack. He may be trying to save face. Makes me all the more suspicious."

He motioned for Garrett to sit down and stop pacing.

"What's he want?"

"Guarantee that there will be no more domestic operations and find the man responsible for the kidnapping."

"He wants him outed?"

"Not sure. Certainly disciplined and cashiered out of the service. I think he'll go along with doing it all quietly."

"And the hearings?"

"He'll wrap those up. He'll claim he got renewed personal assurances from me and the chief to not involve ourselves in domestic operations."

"Which is admission of guilt in a way."

"In an indirect way, to be sure."

"What do you want from me. I don't rate you coming here to personally deliver the latest news."

Garrett smiled at Roger's comment. "You're correct. I want you to give me a head to roll."

Roger thought for a moment.

"You realize that could destroy a whole center of operations."

"Possibly. But I have faith that our operational capabilities are not completely dependent on just one man...or woman."

"You'd be surprised. But that is what I protect you from." Roger sighed. "Okay. I'll look into it. Tell your congressman that we'll play along."

Chapter 60

Zhōu was disturbed. Li Xiu never missed a meeting with him. She was not sloppy. He had tried her cell phones, both the one he had given her, which was encrypted, and her more public phone, which a student would likely use. Neither phone answered. They were shut off.

Something had gone wrong. He thought about the ramifications of that. Li Xiu was a minor player in this operation, gathering small talk to glean for higher-level secrets that might be revealed. Yet she knew things from other operations, things that could be damaging to him. In this operations, as her relationship developed with the aide, he expected she could begin to exert influence. It was a redundancy he liked in his manipulation of Congressman Greely.

His frustration grew along with his worry that something big had gone wrong. He picked up his phone and called the congressman. It was time to connect. From the conversation, he might learn something.

Again, they sat in the Chinese restaurant deep in the Chinatown part of D.C. Again, Zhōu ordered for the congressman. It was always something not too unusual or adventurous.

"You look stressed. You should drink some of this green tea. It helps calm the nerves."

"It shows, huh? You could say I'm *dis*tressed. My aide was attacked two nights ago in his home. His girlfriend was shot and abducted. He was told by the attacker to resign and leave the country."

Greely paused to sip the tea.

"Can you imagine anything so bizarre?"

Zhōu shook his head. That explained Li Xiu's silence. "Who would do something like that?"

"You can guess. The CIA is my prime suspect. They must think the girl is part of a spy ring and my aide was a target, somehow."

"Will this come back on you?"

Greely shook his head. "I've turned it into a bargain with the CIA."

He knew he was beginning to say more than he should, but Greely needed to get his anger out and let someone other than his staff know how astutely he had turned a negative into a positive.

"You know I've been after them for suspected black ops. Now I've got evidence they've involved themselves in domestic activities. I can crucify them with that."

"And you don't?"

"No. I don't want to destroy them, just shut down their black ops. They've agreed to stop any activities that are going on and find the perpetrator. He'll be cashiered out of the service."

"So you will have cleansed the service, not killed it."

Greely smiled. "Something like that."

He knew that with the interception of the anthrax attack, both the FBI and the CIA were currently highly thought of. Popular opinion was that the intercept was done with the help of CIA information, even though the FBI claimed operational responsibility. This agreement would let him close down his hearings which were becoming unpopular with his leadership, and call it a win.

† † †

Roger walked into Henry's much more modest office and sat down.

"What can I do for you?" Henry asked.

"Tell me what the hell's going on. Garrett was just in my office telling me how someone broke into the house of a congressional aide. He apparently threatened him, shot his girlfriend, and then abducted her."

Roger went on to fill in the details, which Henry already knew.

"Tell me this isn't one of ours," Roger said.

"Do you want me to tell you what you want to know? Like you asked? Or do you want me to tell you what I do know?"

Roger sighed. He looked at his old friend. Someone who had fought the cold war with him in the clandestine arena. Someone who knew how to take the battle to the enemy, how to collect damaging information, and, just as important, how to deal out lethal blows when called for.

"Tell me what you do know."

"You're pulling back the curtain I've tried to keep between you and the ops I run, you know that."

Roger nodded. "Things are hot right now. We can play this out to our advantage, the congressman is willing to do certain things, but we need to get our people under control...if this is one of our people."

"Who's the congressman? Is it Greely?"

Roger nodded.

"He's not to be trusted. And why would he not shout this to the press and really put a noose around our necks? Why the deal making? Have you thought about that?"

"I just found out about this an hour ago. From Garrett. I haven't had much time to think it through."

"It might be helpful for us to do so."

"Start by telling me what the hell is going on."

Henry took a sip of his ever-present cup of coffee. He began the narrative of the anthrax thefts and how they looked coordinated. He spoke of the meetings between a Chinese agent named Zhōu, the Saudi billionaire, and the cartel leader. The conclusion drawn was that there would be an attack on multiple major cities in the U.S.

"Why didn't you go to the FBI?"

Henry looked down at his near-empty cup and thought for a moment. "You know they leak like a sieve. If we had told them what was impending, it would have gotten out."

Henry looked up at Roger. "How would you have liked to have New York, D.C., maybe Chicago and L.A. be thrown into a panic because the people thought they might be exposed to anthrax? That would be almost as disastrous as the actual attack in regards to disruption it would cause."

Roger considered Henry's response. "That would be a possibility. But you should have run that up the chain of command. That wasn't your decision to make."

"And if I had? It would have been debated for days. If anyone had the guts to go against the rules, other agents would have been assigned to the operation and they probably wouldn't have intercepted the terrorists in time."

"You don't know that."

"Roger, what I do know is that I could set my best agent on the trail with my best team behind him. That decision worked."

He slapped his hand on his desk.

"We go way back, but if you need a scapegoat, fire me. I'll take the hit. But leave my team intact. They've got terrorists not sleeping well at night because they know someone out there is hunting them. Someone very lethal. And now, we've disrupted another attack from this guy Rashid. He must be getting pretty depressed about how many attacks my agents have thwarted."

"I know how effective you've been. And if this had ended with the disruption of the attacks, that would have been fine. The FBI is happy to take credit and everyone is looking away from our role. We are suspected of helping, but no one knows for sure. Now someone attacks an aide and kidnaps his girlfriend and the shit hits the fan."

"I'll deal with that, Roger. I promise. But the girl isn't an innocent. She was involved with the theft in Budapest. She's a Chinese spy."

"You have her?"

"I'm in the process of getting her."

Roger ran his fingers through his hair. "Christ. This could backfire big time."

"No one will ever see her again."

Roger looked at his old friend. "Have you gone over the edge?"

Henry shook his head. "No. But I know what needs to be done, and so do you. So does my team. You know this is a messy game some times. Remember your time in the field. It was not always the gentlemen's game it's made out to be."

Chapter 61

Jane drove out to the hunting cabin. She wanted to interview the two people being held there herself. She had tried multiple times to contact Dan, but he had gone silent. Even Fred and Warren had not heard back from him after they had passed on their information regarding Greely's finances and the convoluted money trail his aide left behind. The last communication from Dan was to Fred to get someone into George Randall's townhouse and remove the bugs he had placed there. That, at least, cleaned up any possible direct evidence of spying.

"Glad you could stop in," Roland said, as he met Jane's car. She had labored up the long, potholed drive to finally come out on the grassy area in front of the cabin.

"That's some driveway you've got. You might want to do some work on it."

Roland shook his head. "No, ma'am. That's the way I like it. It deters strangers from venturing too far."

Marcus came out on the porch. "Are you here to relieve us of this babysitting job? It's getting pretty old."

Jane gave him a weak smile, although little else except for the takedown of the terrorists had given her much to smile about.

"This is quite a good location for a safe house. A good place to do heavy interrogations."

"No way," Roland said. "I'm not turning my hideaway over to you. This is *my* retreat. You find your own."

"Let's see your prisoners," Jane said. "Starting with the jihadist."

They walked over to the shed next to the house. Inside was a tractor with some implements, a walk-behind mower, various tools hanging over a bench, and, in one corner, a young man tied to one of the main beams. He was sitting with his hands behind his back, circling the beam. The rope was not so tight as to cut off his circulation but tight enough to not allow him any motion other than to sit where he was.

Jane walked over to the young man who glared at her. She grabbed a chair, pulled it in front of him, and sat down.

"He's spilled his beans. We sent you the info earlier. Still got an attitude, though," Marcus said.

"Jabbar," Jane finally spoke to him. "We all know how you worked with your uncle...your distant uncle. Jihad is messy sometimes. It is not the intellectual exercise with only polemics involved. For your fellow companions it is an ugly, messy business. As such, it sometimes must be dealt with in ugly, messy ways. That's what we're faced with here. I'm going to transfer you from these two men who you've gotten to know. I think you'll agree they're not bad companions for one to have and they are some of the finest warriors you'll ever come across."

Jabbar spit on the floor.

"However," Jane continued, "I'm going to transfer you to men who will not be good companions. Your world is going to be filled with pain and anguish. You will continue to divulge information in order to avoid the worst of the pain. And when we think you can deliver no more, they will end your life. You will be buried, without preparation, in an unknown grave, never to be found."

Jabbar looked at her with eyes that gradually grew more frightened. “I already told them everything.”

“Maybe. We’ll see. We’ll also see if you can prove useful to us in some more creative way. If you have a way to communicate with your uncle, or his men, and find out more of his activities, that would make you useful to us on a continuing basis. We could then make life more comfortable for you. In many ways.”

Jane stood up.

“I don’t expect an answer from you now. First the other men will take you away. Then you will experience your new life, the one full of pain. Then I will expect an answer.”

She turned and went outside, followed by Marcus.

“That was brutal, if you don’t mind me saying,” Marcus said as they walked back to the cabin. “You think you can get more out of him?”

“I don’t know. I’d like to think he might help us spy on his uncle. We can’t turn him loose, so we’ll have to find a way for him to do it remotely.” She waved her hand through the air. “In the end, he will just disappear. He’s not going to prison...anywhere.”

Inside the cabin, Jane walked into the bedroom where Wang Li Xiu was being held. She was handcuffed to a sturdy bed with her hands over her head. The wood looked like she had tested it for strength and found it stronger than her wrists.

Jane looked at her for a moment. Wang stared back at her without registering any emotion.

“Bring me a chair,” Jane said to Roland. “Then unhook her from the headboard so she can sit up. But keep her cuffed, behind her back.”

Roland did as she commanded without comment. Not only was Jane his boss, but he understood she was demonstrating her authority to the prisoner.

After making the arrangements, Roland retreated to the main room of the cabin.

"We know you were Bela's girlfriend. You worked with him to steal the anthrax. Did you kill him after, or did you have others do it?"

"You are a western dog. Not worthy of speaking to," Wang said in mandarin.

"And you are my prisoner," Jane replied in the same language. "And you will give us information or suffer much."

The woman's eyes widened in surprise. Jane suppressed a smile and just stared back at her. After a long pause, she spoke, now in English.

"We have pictures of you with Bela and ones with George. Your student act is impressive. Especially since you never enrolled. George is not going to use his influence to rescue you. He is hoping you never surface and that our recordings of you together with him never get revealed. You are alone. We know you were handled by Zhōu Ming, but he'll distance himself from you as well. He's probably out of the country by now, expecting that we're looking for him."

"What do you want?" Wang finally said in English.

Jane allowed herself a slight smile. This woman was not ready to give up valuable information. At this point, she was only buying time and trying to better understand her position.

"Simple. Everything you know." Jane smiled again at her prisoner. "But I don't expect you to tell me right away. At least the truth. That will take time. Hard time, painful time, for you. But I am a patient woman. I can wait until my men have brought you to the point where you tell only the truth. Then we'll have you tell all of it."

She got up and pushed the chair back.

"Wait," Wang said. "I will tell you now. As you said, Zhōu has gone. Abandoned me. I have no loyalty to him anymore."

Jane smiled at her. "That is correct thinking as you say in your culture. But it is not sincere. You must be tested to prove sincerity. And, as I said before, I am a patient woman."

She turned to go as Wang called out for her to wait and let her confess to everything.

In the main cabin, both Marcus and Roland were waiting for Jane.

"I have an interrogation team coming tomorrow to take both of them away. We do have a good site, not as good as this, but it will do. They'll take the two prisoners and both of you are free to leave."

"You mean you don't have any impossible missions for us to perform?" Marcus asked.

"Not at the moment. But when I do, I know who to call."

She smiled at the two warriors and went out to her car.

Chapter 62

After dinner with Greely, Zhōu understood why he couldn't get in contact with Wang. Then Greely called him, something the congressman never did. He asked outright if the woman had been an agent of his.

"I do not have agents under my control," Zhōu said. "I work alone, trying to make connections between people of influence here in the U.S. and those in power in China. That is my role...a facilitator, as you call it. I am not running a spy operation."

Greely was not sure he believed Zhōu entirely, but it served his purpose to agree with the man's statement of his role.

"You probably have heard that there was an attempted terror attack on some of our major cities. I'm sure it was the CIA that foiled it. However, the FBI is taking the credit. I think there was a breakdown in protocol and the agency lucked out by stopping the terrorists—all mid-eastern jihadist, by the way. Now the administration is happy to take a victory lap as the news gets out."

"What does that have to do with me?"

"Nothing. But I thought you should know that I'm closing down my hearings on the CIA. The sentiment has changed, both in the public's eye and with congress. My leadership wants to put this to bed."

“Does that change policy regarding the southern border?”

“No. We’re handling this as a separate incident, not connected to the border. As far as anyone knows, these terrorists came into the country legally. I think there will be efforts to support that claim in spite of other efforts to prove otherwise.”

“So, a standoff.”

“Something like that. Each side will believe their own, but our side is in power, and that counts.”

Zhōu figured Wang was in the hands of the CIA; it was most likely explanation. But how had they found out about her? It didn’t matter. If they had her, it would not be long before he would be exposed. He and anyone else she knew of. She was a tough, experienced operator but no match for any aggressive interrogation by the CIA. He would have to arrange to leave the country as soon as he could.

“I may have to travel outside the country shortly. I won’t see you for some weeks. My superiors will want to fully understand what has just happened, especially since it involves you shutting down the hearings.”

“Our deals are still going forward, are they not?”

Greely’s family had three pending deals with different companies in China. They all involved positions on the boards with sizeable payments as well as some stock options. They would translate later into significant short-term gains when the stock got sold.

“All that is above me. It will be reviewed by others. I will let them know how helpful you have been and continue to be, but I do not make those decisions.”

† † †

Dan drove back to D.C. He changed motels to another anonymous, blue-collar one in the western suburbs. It was time to find out the identity of the man who seemed to meet with George Randall. *Let's see how deep George is into illegal activity. I know he's doing some dealing. Probably these guys are supplying him.* Taking the leader would involve some level of violence. Men like that did not go without a fight. And he had gang members around him.

That night, Dan staked out the townhouse where he had last seen the men who had met with Randall. He watched as three of them came out and drove off. One was the man who had talked with Randall, another was his driver, and an unknown third man.

Dan was carrying his Sig Sauer P320XF-9. It was a full-sized version of the model holding seventeen rounds in the magazine. He decided to forego the suppressor, which added over six inches to the barrel length, making the gun awkward to use in a close-combat environment. *If it comes to shooting, do it fast and get the hell gone.* Dan just needed the leader; everyone else was expendable. He brought along a pair of nylon cuffs and duct tape. He wanted to capture the group's leader and find out about his relationship with Randall.

The men stopped at a small, self-storage warehouse in a business district in Alexandria. It was late at night. They used a code on the keypad to get into the gated yard. Dan stopped down the street to watch them enter. The office was closed; the place looked empty. The code-operated gate allowed tenants to come and go at all hours, provided they had a proper code. When the car disappeared around a row of units, Dan got out and climbed over the gate. He hid behind the entrance sign from where he could watch for the men to return. They would have to stop so the driver could punch in the code and open the metal sliding gate. That would be the point of vulnerability.

Ten minutes later, he saw the flash of the headlights as the car proceeded down the alley between the storage units. It turned the corner and drove up to the keypad located on a pedestal. The car was twenty yards away. The driver rolled down the window and started punching in the code. When the gate began to move, Dan fired.

His shot hit the driver in the head. Blood and brains spewed across the front seats, covering the passenger. Dan ran forward as the man next to the driver was pulling his pistol from his belt. He never got the chance to bring it into play as Dan's second shot hit him in the face, killing him instantly. The third man, the one Dan wanted to capture, dove out of the back door, and ran around the corner of the storage units.

Dan ran to the corner and then paused. He dropped down close to the ground before peeking around the corner. If the man had been waiting to shoot, he would have been aiming higher and missed, giving Dan a precious second to fire. He looked to see the figure nearing the end of the alley. Dan could have shot but held back.

He wanted him alive, which presented a problem if the man wanted to fight back. He might not be able to take him without shooting and maybe killing him. Finesse was called for something hard to manage in a gunfight and chase. Without going down the same alley, Dan headed across the rows in the direction the man had turned. At the next alley, he saw the figure starting to climb a chain link fence that was about eight feet high. Dan sprinted down the drive. The man twisted to fire a quick, unaimed shot and then turned back to climbing.

Dan reached the fence and leaped into the air, launching himself like a torpedo against the man's back. As Dan slammed into him, he let out a yell of pain and dropped his pistol. Dan got up off the ground and grabbed his waist, twisting him to one side. The man's grip loosened on the links. It was hard for him to hold himself on the fence along with Dan's added weight and pull. His fingers loosened, and he fell to the ground with Dan.

Dan rolled the man over and shoved him face-down against the grass. With a knee in his back, Dan grabbed one arm and pulled it behind him, then the other. He secured them with his zip ties and then stood up. He picked up the man's 9mm and put it in his pocket, then he pulled the man to his feet.

His captive glared at Dan as he struggled to regain his breath.

"You have the code to open the gate?" Dan asked.

There was no answer, only a hateful stare.

"I don't have time to fuck around with you. We have to leave. With the shots fired, the police will come shortly. If they find you here, they'll also find the storage unit and the drugs which I'm sure you have stored there, as well as the ones in your trunk."

He stepped up close to the man.

"I leave you here, you go down for the drugs. I take you out of here, you have a chance to not wind up in jail."

"I'll take my chances with the cops."

"I can't accept that."

Dan took out his Sig Sauer. He stepped to the side and placed the pistol against the man's hands.

"I'm going to destroy one of both of your hands, then I'll ask you again. If you don't tell me, I'll work my way up your arm. You don't get out of this without a lot of pain and jail time. Or, you can give me the code and we'll leave. I need to talk to you, so you're worth keeping alive."

He pushed against the man's left hand.

"Okay." He rattled off the code number.

"Let's hope you got it right."

Dan shoved the man forward and pushed him into an awkward jog to the end of the alley and the keypad. He punched in the numbers with one hand while the other kept a hold of the man's arm. The gate started rolling back, and Dan pushed his captive forward. When he got to his car, he opened the trunk and shoved the man inside. Then he put duct tape across his mouth and around his legs.

After closing the trunk lid, he drove off down the street. He heard sirens a few blocks away. *Probably headed here.* Dan turned onto Route 1 and blended into the still-present traffic.

Chapter 63

When Jane returned to the agency, she called Fred and Warren into her office.

"I want to know where Dan is. He's talked with the two of you. You've given him information. Now tell me where he is. He's not answering my phone calls."

Both men stared at their boss. She could fire them at a moment's notice. Possibly, even have them disappear. The thought had crossed both of their minds. Finally, Fred spoke up.

"We don't know. He only asked for information. He didn't say where he was. We assume he's in the metro area."

"Okay. Tell me what he wanted from you."

Warren spoke up and told her Dan asked for bugging equipment. Dan didn't say whose home he was going to bug, but when Dan told him to remove the bugs, he knew it was congressman Greely's aide.

"Great." Jane said. She slammed her fist down on her desk. "We get the terror attack intercepted. That looks great for all of us. We keep our role quiet and on the sidelines. Now Dan starts messing with politicians." She glared at the two researchers. "What was he looking for? And what was he going to do with it?"

Both men shook their heads. Jane was angrier than they had ever seen her. They were frozen by her agitation and how that might affect them.

"He wanted to monitor this guy. He had me download his hard drive and send the data to him," Warren said. "That's all we know."

Jane sat there in frustration. These two researchers were a valuable asset. Dan was using them to advance an agenda of his own. One she hadn't approved. One she probably would never approve of, which is why he went behind her back. She sighed.

Pointing her finger at both men, she said, "If he calls again, you are not to provide him any more information. You are to tell him that any action on your part must be approved by me. Do you understand?"

The two nodded.

"Your continuation in your positions depends on it." She paused for a moment. "Your continuation in life may depend on it."

With that, she dismissed them. It was a not-so-subtle point that she had made.

"Maybe we're in the wrong line of work," Fred said as they exited Jane's office.

Warren shook his head. "We just have to realize that we can't mess around, especially with our boss. Dan's a dangerous man, but Jane can have us disappeared."

"That's what I mean. I'm not sure I want to work for a boss that can do more than fire you."

Warren looked at Fred. "But you have to admit, it's exciting work."

"Maybe too exciting at times."

† † †

Dan drove to a complex of warehouses being constructed just south of the tank farm in Newington. They were south of D.C., just off I 95. He parked his car around back. The area was not patrolled, and it was late at night, with little traffic.

He got out and opened the trunk. Carlos looked at him as the lid came up. Dan reached down and cut the tape from his ankles. He pulled him out onto the pavement, then steered him to the car's passenger seat. Once they were inside, Dan pulled the tape off the man's mouth.

"Like I said before, I need some information from you. We'll start with your name."

"Carlos."

"You got a last name?"

"Becerra."

"Now, what's your relationship to George Randall? Why were you meeting with him?"

"Why should I tell you anything?"

"Because I'll hurt you if you don't."

"Vete a la mierda," fuck off.

"You don't believe me?"

Carlos shook his head. "I work for an important man. He can have my family killed. I will tell you nothing."

"You can be sure I can have *you* killed. With my own hands if I choose.

"So I am a dead man either way."

Dan tried a different tack. "You don't owe any loyalty to this guy Randall. Your relationship with him is over now. Tell me about your relationship with him. Your boss will never know."

Carlos didn't answer.

"You can tell him that people had started to investigate the guy and so you had to pull back. It happens."

Carlos looked over at Dan. "If I tell you what you want to know, you let me go?"

Dan smiled at his captive. “I won’t guarantee that. I could lie to you and say yes, but I want to be honest with you. I’m not sure letting you go is a good idea now. But talking to me is your best option right now.”

Carlos gave this some thought. Dan could see him weighing his odds. Pain now until he talked, then death against the possibility of being let go and the danger of dealing with his boss.

“Okay, I tell you. He’s an aide to Congressman Greely. I pay him money to have him influence Greely to work on keeping the border open.”

“You think they’re doing this for the money you pay an aide?”

Carlos shook his head. “No, no. They do it for bigger reasons. The money just helps us keep connected. My boss wants to stay close to those who make such decisions.”

“So that’s it? You sit down with him and give him his paycheck on a regular schedule. That’s all?”

Carlos didn’t answer.

“Tell me why then,” Dan continued, “was Randall dealing drugs to a small-time distributor in Baltimore.”

The look on Carlos’ face indicated he was surprised that Dan knew about that activity.

“I know a good bit. Enough to know when you’re holding back or lying. That will be painful for you and won’t help your efforts to remain alive.”

“He likes to play the...the bad guy, *mal hombre*, so we give him some drugs. His dealer is a minor one and stays in his territory. He doesn’t intrude on our operations.”

“Fentanyl?”

Carlos nodded. “Sometimes heroin, sometimes coke. Lately it’s been fentanyl. That is what the addicts want.”

“Anything else? He supplying coeds here in D.C.? Politicians?”

Carlos shook his head. "I don't think so." He paused for a moment as if considering how much to say.

"Remember, how valuable you are to me goes a long way to me letting you live."

"I provide him with women sometimes. Girls. He has a taste for the younger ones. He gets to enjoy them before sending them back to us."

"They work for you?"

"For the gang."

"And that's you. Or is there someone above you here in D.C.?"

Carlos just looked at Dan. He seemed afraid to admit to his leadership.

"We'll come back to that. What's he do with them, besides his own pleasure. He pimp them out?"

"No. He just uses them for himself. They often come back with marks on them. Like they've been tied up, really tight."

"You talk to any of the girls?"

"Only a few, the ones who looked like they had the hardest time. They said he liked to tie them up and rape them. He beats them sometimes."

"A sadist."

Carlos looked at him.

"Sádico."

Carlos nodded.

"What about Greely. Do you make any payments to him?"

"No." Carlos shook his head. "We expect Randall to pass on the payments to his boss. Of course, he takes some for himself."

"On top of the drugs and the girls."

Carlos nodded.

"Next question. Who is your boss?"

Carlos didn't answer.

"I can make some guesses. You're not a gang member, like MS13. You're a cartel member. You strike me as more organized, business-focused. Remember what I told you about surviving."

Carlos took a breath. "Sinaloa cartel."

"You belong?"

"Si." He nodded his head.

"So, your boss is Alejandro Mendoza."

Carlos nodded. His boss's leadership of the cartel was not a secret.

Dan thought for a moment. He added things up. Randall was taking money from the Sinaloa cartel, was dealing drugs from them to a minor gang in Baltimore, and was abusing girls that had been kidnapped by the cartel, some of them quite young, it seemed from what Carlos said. And to top it off, had a Chinese spy as a girlfriend.

"I'm going to take you to an abandoned warehouse. There's no activity going on there. It's the one where you used to meet Randall. You're going to be there for a while. I'll let you drink some water before I leave you. You'll be chained to an I-beam and your mouth taped. It won't be comfortable, but better than the alternative. After I digest what you told me, I'll deal with Randall and then come back for you."

"You kill me then?"

Dan gave him a steady look. "I may. I haven't decided. Your buddies died because they would have killed me if they could and I needed to capture you. If the rest of your gang get in my way, they will die and so will you. We'll just have to see how it works out."

"Maybe I call them. Tell them to not do anything but wait for me to come back."

Dan could see Carlos was looking for some bit of leverage that would tip the scales away from the easy choice, just killing him and dumping him in the river in a weighted bag. He guessed that was what Carlos would probably do.

Chapter 64

Henry sat in a chair across from Jane's desk. He had gone to her, not wanting her to be seen in the upper corridors. Now he had to get some answers, and she needed to give him all the intel she had. His main concern was Dan; where was he, and what might he do next?

"I want a complete download. Nothing held back. Now's not the time to shield me from anything. If I'm going to help save this unit, I need to know everything."

Jane looked at him for a long moment. "Someone lit your fuse?"

"Let's not be cute. Roger came to see me. Garrett talked to him. Shit runs downhill, so here I am."

Jane took a deep breath. She went over the events again, this time including both Fred and Warren, without whose help Dan would have been running around the Midwest blind. Jane talked about Jabbar and then Wang Li Xiu, the Chinese spy, and how she had them both in a safe house in the countryside. She would milk them for all the intel they had.

"After I get all that I can, I'll be coming to you," Jane said. "I'd like to find a way to use Jabbar to get close to Rashid. The woman? I can let you make the call. She may be of little use to us, certainly after we learn all she knows. I doubt we'll ever turn her, but you can weigh in on that."

She purposely emphasized the last. If Henry wanted to know everything, then she would tell him. She would also have him make some serious decisions about the fate of two people; a terrorist and a spy. *Let him take on the burden*, she thought.

She told Henry about the team's role in helping Dan bug the aide's home and then kidnap his girlfriend was chronicled.

"Where is he now? What's he planning next?"

"That's the problem. We don't know. He's gone silent and not taking calls. I told Fred and Warren they were not to help him if he contacts them."

"Is it time to bring the FBI in to find him?"

Jane shook her head vigorously. "No. Bad idea. You burn our most effective agent. At best, he'll be exposed and along with it, our operation. At worst, he'll be killed."

"So, you suggest we wait until he decides to let us know what the hell he's doing?"

"For right now. Tell everyone we will be disciplining the agent who entered Randall's home. But the female is a spy and we properly captured her and exposed her to keep someone near the centers of power, out of a compromising situation. We avoided possible blackmail."

"I can sell that," Henry said.

Jane shifted gears. "Tell me, why hasn't Greely gone public with all this? It could be very damaging to us."

"That's a question I asked Roger. He didn't have an answer."

"Let me take a wild guess. Wang is a spy. She's connected to Zhōu Ming. He seems to have played a part in the anthrax thefts and gotten the powder to the cartel. The cartel smuggled the anthrax over the border along with Rashid's jihadists. Zhōu and Rashid worked together on this plan. Now Greely's aide is uncomfortably close to the female spy and Greely's family is deeply involved with various Chinese companies—"

"I get it. He doesn't want all this to come out. His party is also looking for a way to shut down the hearings since they're not going anywhere. And we, the FBI, CIA, NSA, Homeland, along with the president, are taking a victory lap for stopping a major terror attack. Worse than 9-11. And we did it *before* anyone got killed."

Jane smiled. "You got the picture."

"That brings us back to Dan. Why doesn't he just call it a day and enjoy the amazing victory he pulled off?"

"That part I don't know. And that's what worries me."

Henry stood up. "We'll play it your way for now. But you have to get in contact with Dan. He has to know he's won and he shouldn't do any more. It's time to shut down the operation and let the heat dissipate."

After Henry left, Jane called Fred and Warren into her office.

"Have you heard from Dan?"

Both of them shook their heads.

"But he'll take your calls?"

"Maybe," Fred said.

"He may think we have some new information he can use," Warren added.

"What new information?"

"Well," Warren said, "he wanted to know all about Randall, then Greely. I found Randall's money trail and gave it to Dan. I also got him information on all of Greely's financial entanglements in China...him and his extended family. He may think I've found more."

"Oh no. He's not going after Greely, is he?"

Both men shrugged their shoulders.

"We don't have any idea of what he's going to do next. We had no idea he'd kidnap that woman."

"Make the call. Now. Keep your phone on hands free."

Warren punched in Dan's number.

After four rings, Dan picked up.

"You have new information?" he asked.

Warren looked at Jane. She leaned across her desk.

"I'm the one calling," she said. "I need to talk to you."

There was silence on the other end of the call.

"Don't hang up or go silent. You need to talk with me. You still work for the CIA and that comes with some responsibilities. One is to talk to your supervisor."

Again, there was a pause.

"What do you want?" Dan finally asked.

"I want you to come in. I want to go over all that happened."

"You already know everything that has happened."

"Look, Dan. You've done an incredible job and even if we can't take direct credit for it, as is always the case, it doesn't change what you and the team accomplished. Now the possible shit storm that your kidnapping could have erupted can be avoided. But you have to stand down...now."

Silence from the other end.

"Did you hear me?"

"I heard you."

"Then I expect to see you...today, in my office."

"You know I don't go into Headquarters."

"Well, then at my apartment."

"I've got a few things to finish up. Loose ends that I can't leave standing. I'll clean things up and be in touch."

"Dan, don't you go off on another—"

But the line had gone dead.

Chapter 65

Jane let out a string of curses that would cause a sailor to blush. Fred and Warren just sat there without a word.

She turned to them, mid-rant. "If you find anything out about where he is, you come to me right away. Understand?"

Both men nodded.

"Out of here," Jane snapped, waving her hand at the door.

† † †

Dan staked out Congressman Greely's Georgetown row house. The man's routine had become a bit disrupted by recent events, including, Dan was sure, his visit to his aide's home. There was an increase in security, evidenced by a patrol car parked a few doors down from the townhouse. Dan's facial disguise would allow him to walk by, but that was something he couldn't repeatedly do without drawing attention to himself. He was now dressed more like a young congress staffer. Such a look would attract little attention to him. Everyone in the neighborhood worked on or near the capital, either in government or its agencies. He would be just another bureaucrat.

He waited until the shift changed around 6 pm. The new officers would be on duty until around midnight. Near the end of their shift, the officer in the car would not be very attentive, getting increasingly sleepy and bored. Thoughts would turn to getting relieved and going home for the night.

Subsequent stakeouts revealed that during the day, from 10 am to 4 pm, there was no car on watch. The police figured that with the congressman at the capitol, there was little need to watch the townhouse. They went back on before he got home and were on duty the rest of the night.

The next afternoon, Dan parked two blocks away, near P Street, and walked back to Greely's townhouse. He carried a soft briefcase that fit his role as a staffer. He made his way down a parallel street to the alleyway going past Greely's residence. Dan walked up the narrow drive, and when he reached the backyard, he turned to the even more narrow walkway between back yards of the opposing townhouses. There was a stockade fence surrounding Greely's back property. Dan quickly picked the lock, lifted the latch, and stepped inside. He was now invisible to anyone in the alleyway.

Without hesitating, he walked to the back door and, taking out his lock pick, began to work on the deadbolt. This was the most dangerous moment. Anyone looking out from a second floor, across the backyards, would see him at work, and it would look suspicious. Dan felt the tingle of nerves course through his body. He kept his hands steady. The solution was to pick the lock quickly and get inside.

He felt the tumblers click and opened the door. Breathing a quiet sigh, he stepped inside and gently closed the door, listening intently for any sounds that would indicate something out of the ordinary. When satisfied that he had created no disturbance, Dan moved through the townhouse.

Greely would come home and, after hanging up his coat, probably go to the living room. There was a wet bar on one side with liquors and glasses and an under-counter refrigerator. The question for Dan was whether or not he'd have his mistress with him. In the end, it didn't matter to his agenda. He'd just improvise if she were present. He made sure the blinds on the windows and sliding door were pulled closed. Then he picked a comfortable chair and sat down to wait.

He had a balaclava mask with him that only had eye openings. He'd put that on when Greely came home. Dan carried his Walther P22LR pistol with a suppressor attached. It made only a whisper of a sound that would barely be heard on another floor, let alone outside the townhouse.

At around 8pm, the front door opened. Dan stood and went to a corner of the room, hidden in the shadows. James Greely came into the townhouse. Dan could hear him in the front hall, taking his coat off and putting it in the closet. There was no sound of another person. *That simplifies things.* Greely walked past the kitchen area and into the living room.

"Sit down Mr. Congressman," Dan said as Greely entered the room.

He turned and let out a gasp of surprise.

"Sit down and be quiet."

Greely just stood looking over at the shadowy figure in the corner of the room.

"Sit down!" Dan said it now more forcibly and stepped forward.

Greely sat back on the couch.

"What do you want? If you're here to rob me, I don't have much money in the house. But you're welcome to what I have."

Dan walked over to the chair he had been sitting in. He pulled it around to face the couch and sat down.

"First, this," Dan elevated his Walther, "is a .22 caliber pistol with a suppressor. It can't be heard much outside of this room, but it's a deadly weapon. A favorite of assassins, especially those who do their work close up."

"Are you going to kill me? Why?"

"I'm not going to kill you. Unless you make me."

"Then what do you want?"

"Congressman. I know all about you. I know about your financial entanglements with China. I know about your relationship with Zhōu Ming. I know about your family's investments in China. I even know about your mistress, a lovely woman. She's about half your age, isn't she?"

Greely didn't answer.

"I just want you to know that any protestations on your part about your innocence will fall on deaf ears. You've been a great advocate of open borders. You also have been attacking the CIA. One of the agencies that helped intercept and take down the terrorists that were going to spread anthrax in Chicago, D.C., and probably New York."

He leaned forward.

"Now listen carefully because you might not know that Zhōu was connected to that attempt. He procured the anthrax, gave it to a Saudi billionaire, and both the powder and the jihadists were smuggled into the U.S. across your open border.

"Your aide has been accepting bribes on your behalf from the Sinaloa cartel and dealing drugs in Baltimore to enhance his take. He takes a cut of the money before he passes it on to you.

"*And* we come to find your aide's girlfriend is a Chinese spy working for Zhōu. I've been following your activities and I can convincingly connect you to Zhōu. And he can be shown to be an agent of the CCP and complicit in the attempted terrorist attack."

Dan sat back. Greely didn't speak. He just stared at Dan with eyes wide with fright.

"Cat got your tongue? Where is the man with such glib tongue when it comes to immigrant rights, compassion for people wanting a better life? Is it compassionate to allow jihadists and criminals to come over the border along with all those seeking the riches of the U.S.?"

"What do you want?"

Again, the question.

"I'll spell it out for you. Tomorrow you're going to announce that you are resigning from congress, effective immediately. For mental health reasons. You will leave the country. You can go anywhere, but you are not to stay in the U.S. and try to make a second career out of being a lobbyist. You are going to depart the American political scene. Live abroad, enjoy your money, but have nothing to do with this country that you have so badly served with your greed and arrogance."

"I can't do that."

"You can and you will. You've been here through ten elections, twenty years. Time to go."

"I have responsibilities. Responsibilities to my constituents. I was duly elected. You can't thwart the will of the people."

"I won't argue with you. You are a fraud and are deceiving the people who voted for you. I wonder if they'd support you if they knew of all those activities? I wonder if your own party would not throw you overboard rather than be tainted with your stench? They may be just as complicit, many of them, but if you're the one who the spotlight focuses on, the one who's been picked out of the field, you'll be the one who's thrown under the bus. The one who has to atone in a way for his sins by leaving the field of action."

"But I can't."

"James. Like I said, I'm not going to argue with you."

Dan got up out of his chair and stepped to the couch. He leaned over and grabbed Greely around the neck with his gloved hand. With his other hand, he pushed his Walther up against Greely's temple.

"You either leave the field or you will die and disappear. I will see to that personally. Then leaks about your duplicitous activities will begin to surface, all to the detriment of your extended family."

Dan stood back and paused to allow Greely to digest what he said and evaluate his position. He didn't want to kill the man, but that would be the next step if he didn't make the right decision. Dan had other cleanup work to do as well. He made a decision.

"Here's what I'm going to do...going to offer. I'll give you two days to make your plans and announcement. Today is Wednesday. I'll expect it by the end of the day, Friday. That makes for a good wrap on the week. As I said before, you're free to enjoy your ill-gotten gains. Just not here in the U.S. and not in any position of power in public life."

He reached out his hand.

"Give me your phone."

Greely took it out of his pocket and handed it to Dan.

"I'll drop this in the alley out back. I'm going to leave. If you go to the front door and call out to the patrolman in the car on the street, I'll kill both of you. You will die, but you will also be responsible for the death of an innocent officer whose only job is to try to protect your sorry ass."

He stepped back to Greely.

"Do you understand?"

Greely looked at him and nodded but, this time, said nothing.

"I advise spending these two days preparing for your announcement and getting your affairs in order. If you spend them talking about my visit, you won't survive. There is no amount of investigation that is going to find me. Just as there is no amount of protection that can keep you alive. I can snatch the life out of you from a mile away, if I choose to do so. It's what I do."

He stepped back and went out the sliding doors.

"Do the right thing," he said, and exited the house.

In a few short minutes, he was at this car and got in. He listened with the window down but heard nothing. *At least he obeyed that part of my instructions.*

Dan started the car and drove off.

Chapter 66

After telling his boss about the kidnapping and threats against his life, leaving out the incriminating information that the assailant had somehow uncovered, George Randall tried to contact Carlos. He hoped that putting the gangster on the kidnapper's tail would be an effective way to neutralize the threat. His problem was that he couldn't connect with Carlos. This only increased his anxiety. Greely had promised to contact the high-level administrators at various investigative agencies to find a solution to Randall's threat.

"Did you get anywhere?" George asked his boss.

It had been two days since George had come to him and told him what had happened. Congressman Greely looked haggard and tired. He seemed to Randall to be under some stress. More than his problem would generate. Greely had seemed confident he could get someone high up to pressure the intruder to step back. He had assured Randall that if the intruder was a rogue agent, he'd be brought under control or neutralized. The agencies couldn't have assassins running around D.C. threatening congressional aides.

"I got all the players on board. The idea of an out-of-control agent running around threatening staffers shocked all of them. That would blow up so badly...so many heads would roll. Don't worry, it's handled."

George watched his boss's face. The stress was still there. It didn't match the reassuring words.

"Is there something you're not telling me? You seem stressed out, even as you tell me not to worry."

"I'm fine. It's just that the ground is shifting and I have to make the right moves to avoid getting knocked off my feet."

George thought about the words Greely used. He always spoke in the collective, the "we". Now he was speaking in the first person. It seemed odd to his ears.

"I'm the one who got threatened by some agency thug, but you're the one acting odd, even as you tell me not to worry. Hell, I got a lot to worry about. What if they can't find this SOB? He kills me and a shit storm comes down on whoever he worked for. They'd get crucified, yeah, but I'll be dead."

"I told you, don't worry. I've handled it!"

Greely glared at his senior aide. George stared back at his boss, almost in shock. He rarely snapped at him. Something else was up.

"Did you get threatened? Is there something you're not telling me?"

"No, damn it! I told you I'm fine. The anthrax attack, the demand to close the hearings, everyone jockeying for position as the accolades come in. I've got a lot on my mind."

He looked over at his aide.

"And right now, you're not helping."

† † †

Dan drove back to the abandoned warehouse near the Anacostia River, where he had left his prisoner. When he got inside, he unchained his captive and let him stretch his legs and take a piss. He gave him some water and then had him sit back down on the concrete floor.

He had taken Carlos' cell phone from him and placed it on a metal table in the corner. Dan retrieved it and checked the incoming calls. Five of them were from one number. Dan walked over to Carlos and showed him the number.

"George," Carlos said.

"Randall?"

Carlos nodded.

"I'm going to call the number back with the phone on speaker. If you try to warn him or even let him know you're compromised, I'll shut down the call and kill you on the spot. *Comprende?*"

Carlos nodded.

"Just find out what he wants and don't commit to anything."

Dan punched in the number.

"Why didn't you pick up?" Randall asked, when the call connected.

"I was busy. What do you want?"

"I need your help." George explained what had happened to him and that he needed Carlos to find and kill this guy. "My boss says the problem has been taken care of, but I'm not buying it. If you don't stop this guy, whoever he is, he's going to fuck up all our arrangements. Mine and yours."

"How am I supposed to find him?"

"I don't know. You're the goddamn gangster. You must have ways. This guy can't be operating in a vacuum. Have your men start searching for him. You know how to kill people. I'm asking you to get rid this guy before he destroys our arrangement. Your boss won't like it if something happens and you can't get to Greely.

Remember, you have to go through me. He won't meet with you."

"I see what I can do."

"Whatever you do, do it fast."

Dan ended the call.

"What are you gonna do?" Carlos asked.

"Not for you to know. You're going to stay here and I'll be back for you. My mind's still not made up whether or not you live. Try to think how you can be useful to me in the future."

After chaining Carlos back to the post, Dan left. He drove to Randall's neighborhood and parked a few blocks away. There were now two patrol cars in front of the townhouse with more officers on foot. Dan assumed there were men stationed in the back as well. He's better protected. *He thinks he can ignore what I told him to do. Increase his protection and wait me out until Carlos can get to me.* Dan smiled. A smile without warmth. It was going to be harder to get close to Randall. But he had another plan.

Chapter 67

During Dan's stake out of George Randall, he learned that the aide had no accompanying vehicles on his drive to and from the capitol where he worked. At work, the Capitol Police were responsible for everyone's security, and Randall felt fully protected. At home, the D.C. Police took over and had increased the number of men assigned to him. In between, everyone assumed he was secure, driving a locked car in D.C. traffic.

Meanwhile, Dan had staked out various buildings on Randall's route home. The man never varied his route, which was helpful; foolish but helpful. He picked out a three-story building at the intersection of Pennsylvania Avenue and Sixth Street. It was at the corner and had a good sight line to the road in the direction Randall would be traveling on his way home.

He could get to the roof from a fire escape in the back. He would park his car a block off of Pennsylvania and walk to the building through an alley where he could not easily be seen. It wasn't ideal, there would be so many people around, but it would have to do.

Back at his motel, Dan took out his M110A2, an updated version of the older M110. It featured a floating barrel and was fitted with a Sig Optics TANGO 1-6x scope. Dan had also fitted a Knights Armament suppressor. The rifle fired a 7.62mm round, and Dan had a box of subsonic rounds in his kit. The result would be a shot that would be hard to hear above the street noise. The impact would draw everyone's attention to his target, allowing Dan to depart the scene. Or so he hoped.

Late that night, he parked a block away from the building. After reaching the back through the alley, he started up the fire escape. It ended at a third-floor window. Standing on the rail, Dan could just reach the edge of the roof. He threw his backpack up on the roof. Then he pushed off with his legs and, with a huge surge of effort, pulled his chest up to the edge and then shoved his upper body over. From there, he slithered the rest of his body over and onto the top of the building.

He crouched low and walked over to the front corner that looked out over the intersection. He could snake his barrel through a notch at the roof's corner. It would be hard to see and only visible when the time came to use the weapon.

He'd have to stay there throughout the day in order to intercept Randall as he came home. He brought a camouflage tarp with him to cover both himself and his rifle from any notice by passing helicopters. It would be a long wait. He wore gloves and covered his body so no DNA would be left at the site. A bottle of water and power bars were in his backpack and would leave with him.

He thought about his mission. This would be a first. He would be crossing a big red line. Dan wasn't sure how Jane would react. She was already pretty upset at his not contacting her. Suddenly he felt his phone vibrate. Dan picked it up.

It was a call from one of the burner phones he had Marcus purchase.

"What's up?" Dan asked as he connected.

"That's what I want to ask you," Marcus said.

"You still babysitting?"

"No. Jane relieved us of that duty. Just in time after you added the second package. We didn't sign up for that crap. Now, what are you up to?"

"Jane told you to call?"

There was a pause. "I would have even if she hadn't asked."

"Asked or told you."

"Machts nichts. I would have called anyway. So, tell me."

"Better you don't know."

"Better I do know, partner. I've had to pull your fat out of the fire more than once. It's better to know what the hell is going on than to have to find out as I go along."

"I'm going to drive home a lesson and take a small step to end corruption."

"Sounds very noble. What the hell does it mean?"

"I'm going to dish out some retribution to a certain aide."

"You're going to take out some politician? Holy shit! Don't go there, man. That's going to mark you. Jane won't be able to work with you after that."

"He's not a politician. He influences one, though. And, most importantly, he's a piece of shit who's trying to get me killed."

"Seriously? You?"

"He thinks he's enlisted a cartel thug. I heard his instructions first hand. Now it's my turn."

"Dan, come on, buddy. Think this through. A civilian can't take you out, even if he tries to do it through a cartel member. You're too good for that."

"This will send a message to one actual politician, however. It's going to help him decide to retire from public life."

"Does Jane know?"

"I was wondering when you'd get around to that question. No, she doesn't. And don't you tell her. That will only screw things up big time."

"Buddy. I'm on your side. We've been through too much—you, me, and Roland. But I don't know."

"Pretend you didn't get through to me. Throw this phone away and check in with me tomorrow. Then you can say you called me and relay anything you want to Jane."

"You'll have already done the deed?"

"Just give me twenty-four hours. And get rid of that phone."

Dan ended the call and pocketed his phone.

Marcus thought about the call. They had been through so much together, and he trusted his life with Dan. He followed him into what seemed like suicide missions with no exit plan, something he and Roland always busted his balls about. But they always had improvised and had come through. Now Dan was more on his own than any other time he had known him. He and Roland could do nothing to help. And Dan seemed to not want to involve them in his crazy scheme.

Marcus sighed and went to talk to his partner. He'd advise that the two of them stay close to the D.C. area in case Dan needed help. In Marcus' mind, there was no doubt that he would help his brother-in-arms. It was what one did. He hoped it wouldn't become a fool's mission for all of them.

Chapter 68

Dan dozed at times. He had the whole day to wait. Randall would not be heading home before 7 pm. To leave any sooner would signal he was not dedicated to his work. Staying late was a mark of commitment. No one wanted to be the first to leave the offices.

Around 6:15, Dan took up active watch. He kept most of himself and his rifle covered with the tarp but with a good view of the intersection and the traffic upstream of it. His rifle was ready. It was not a long shot, and the scope was dialed in. If he was lucky, the light would be red. If not, he'd have to be fast to acquire the target before it went through the intersection and out of his field of fire.

At fifteen minutes after seven, Dan spotted Randall's car a half block from the intersection. He swung into action. He slid the M110 into position and acquired the target. As the vehicle approached, Dan fired the first shot. The windshield shattered into thousands of pieces. The car swerved, but Dan tracked it. He fired three subsequent rounds, each one hitting the driver's side of the front seat. The car lurched to the right and slammed into a utility pole; the driver slumped over the steering wheel, the horn blasting.

Pedestrians screamed and ran for cover. No rifle shot was heard, but the car's windshield exploding and then the vehicle subsequently hitting the pole on the sidewalk panicked the people along the sidewalk. A following car rammed into Randall's vehicle while another one, swerving to avoid the wreck, hit an adjacent car. There was pandemonium on the street.

Dan got up and stuffed the tarp into his backpack. He collapsed the stock on his rifle, slipped it into its bag, and stuffed it into the pack. After picking up the spent casings, he crouched and ran back to the edge of the roof where he had come up. Looking over, he didn't see anyone. No one was looking out of the few upper-floor windows that faced the alley.

Dan dropped his pack on the fire escape and swung his body over the edge. He looked down and dropped to the platform. Picking up the bag, he raced down the metal stairs, jumped to the ground, and walked quickly through the alley, taking off his hood as he went. When he reached the next street, he was just another pedestrian dressed casually with a loaded backpack walking home. He got into his car and drove off as the sirens headed towards the scene he had left behind.

The evening news had a late-breaking story about a congressional aide who was shot while on his way home. To the police, it looked more like an assassination than a car-jacking attempt. No one could say where the shots came from, and the police were going to have to reconstruct the scene, which meant the road would be closed off for the rest of the night and even through the next day. Locals grumbled about the disruption of normal activity and the burden it presented on them.

Congressman Greely watched the news that evening in horror. He placed some calls to the D.C. police. Using his position, he was able to speak to the Chief, who didn't have much more to say than what Greely had heard on the news. He did agree with Greely that it was most likely an assassination due to the circumstances surrounding the shooting and the recent threats Randall had encountered. The threats that Greely knew more about than did the Chief.

Hanging up the phone, he sat down in his Georgetown townhouse and poured himself a large Scotch. As he sipped, he thought about all the possibilities. Was this a message to him, using Randall as the unfortunate messenger? Randall had been given an ultimatum like he had. To get out of politics and out of the country. The man had said he didn't mind Greely enjoying the money he had accumulated, but he was not to try to get a lobbying job or use his money to influence politicians on China policies.

It was that...or the fate that had occurred to Randall. If the man could strike Randall down in the middle of the capitol hill area in broad daylight, how could he defend himself? Did he need twenty-four-hour protection? An armored car? Was he to be a prisoner in his home for the rest of his life?

Greely drained his Scotch. That was no way to live. But what would his wife say? He could explain to her but had to make sure the full story never came out. And the rest of his family? Greely wondered how well they would continue to prosper with the Chinese absent his influence. Should he meet with Zhōu?

Greely pushed that thought aside. Zhōu, in the end, would make decisions that were best for himself. He had seemed upset over the story of Wang's kidnapping. Perhaps what the kidnapper had said to Randall was right; Wang was an agent for Zhōu. Then Zhōu was, as Greely always suspected deep down, an agent of the CCP.

He picked up the phone and called his wife back in California.

Chapter 69

Henry called Jane into his office on Friday afternoon, the day after Randall had been shot. "Did you see the news?"

Jane waited for him to continue.

"Congressman Greely submitted his resignation effective immediately. He's resigning for health reasons and will be departing the country on an extended vacation. Ostensibly to recover from the stress."

"I did hear about this."

"It comes just after his aide was shot in what seems to be an assassination."

Jane nodded.

"So," Henry said, "what do you know about this sequence of events?"

"Right now, not much."

"Does Dan have anything to do with this? Either of these events?"

Jane took a deep breath. "I have Rashid's nephew in custody. I told you that before. I also have Randall's girlfriend in custody. She's the same female that befriended Bela Mihok, the Hungarian lab tech that disappeared after the anthrax was stolen. Authorities have never found him. But they have confirmed that his hand print and pass card were used to gain access to the powder."

"What do you plan to do with her?"

"Right now, we're letting her stew about her position. We'll interrogate her, out of the country, and see what she knows. She's connected to Zhōu, the Chinese lobbyist who comes around Washington and has a relationship with Greely. We've tracked payments to Greely that come from heavily disguised Chinese sources. We think Zhōu's involved. He met with Greely on a regular basis."

"This doesn't get to my question about Dan."

"I'm getting there. I now also just found out that Dan has added a Sinaloa cartel member to my growing list of detainees. I'm in the process of picking him up as we speak—"

"How does he fit in?"

"He's connected to Randall. Made regular payments to him, some of which were passed on to Greely. As I understand it, he also indulged Randall in drugs and women, young women, which Randall used to both increase his income and satisfy his sick fantasies."

"That's quite a rat's nest."

"Rat's nest of corruption."

"Again—"

"I'm getting to Dan. He captured both the female, Wang Li Xiu, and the cartel member. I think Dan gave Randall an ultimatum to quit and get out of the country. I think he also gave Greely the same ultimatum. Randall may have tried to fight back. From what I've learned, second hand so far, is that Randall enlisted the cartel guy to find and kill Dan."

Jane paused for a moment.

"Now, you know how Dan would react to such a pushback."

Henry looked at his subordinate carefully. "So you think Dan killed Randall? Be careful in how you respond."

Jane looked back at Henry. "You and I go way back. You set me up in this program and approved my first agent, Dan. We both agreed he was phenomenally talented in what he did. He's proven that over the years in many missions. He's also proven that he will extend or expand a mission as he sees fit and necessary. It infuriates you and frustrates me. Dan doesn't much care about political fallout. He works way out on the edge, where life and death hang by a thread. One wrong decision, one mistake, and he could never return from a mission, never be found."

"I get it. I've run agents before, remember," Henry said. His frustration was beginning to show.

"But you've never been where Dan has gone...repeatedly. It gives him a different perspective. Political fallout is a minor annoyance in his world, where death is so present. It doesn't register as important.

"*And*, to go on, he has maintained, over his career as a professional assassin, a strong sense of morality. He would not consider Randall someone worth saving or deferring to. Randall's seeming power is of no interest to Dan. His corruption, taking bribes, dealing drugs, and, I think this is more important than we realize, the man's involvement with young girls who are sexually trafficked, would offend him deep down. Randall could have continued to accept bribes, done the favors that such bribes demanded, and still been able to help such females. He could have been a damper on this Carlos guy. Instead, he participated in it, enjoying the benefits of their misery."

"So, he killed him." It was more a statement than a question.

"In the end, I think so. And, this is important, Henry, in what you decide from this point forward, I think it was justified. It eliminated a sick, traitorous individual, and presented Greely with a clear message."

"This was a message to Greely?"

"That was part of it, along with the other motivations I just told you."

Jane leaned over Henry's desk.

"Henry. Let this go. Dan's connection to this will never be discovered. Greely has resigned and it looks like he's departing the scene. I'm betting that was part of the ultimatum Dan gave him. If this goes further, not only will Dan get burned, it will re-ignite the hearings we just side-stepped. It will take us down and maybe many above us."

She sat back in her chair.

"And then the bad guys win. Right now, they're losing...because of Dan. Don't give the game back to them."

Henry put his head in his hands. "I've done some marginal things in my career. One can't always avoid it when one is in the field. Agents lost, what we call collateral damage, that euphemism for innocents getting hurt or killed. Opposing agents taken down and disappeared." He looked up. "But this goes much farther. We've broken so many rules this time—"

"And saved thousands of lives from anthrax poisoning, foiled another of Rashid's attacks, and maybe disrupted a Chinese influence operation that has dug itself pretty deep into our government."

Jane smiled at her boss.

"Henry, we won. Take the win. As you always say, we win in secret and lose in public. That's our lot and we accept it."

He looked over at her. A slight smile began to emerge on his face.

"And," Jane continued, "we have a connection that may lead to us uncovering more of the Chinese entanglements. We just have to mine the intel and find someone trustworthy in the FBI to turn it over to."

"Keep us out of any further domestic ops."

"Right," Jane said.

Henry sighed. "Okay. We'll play it your way. Roger won't make the connection, or if he does, he won't connect to one of our agents."

"It could be the work of the Chinese or the cartel. Maybe Randall crossed them."

"Plausible. And Roger won't see it much different, let alone Garret or Bill Gardiner."

"Better for those at the top. That's the premise we have always operated under."

Jane stood up.

"I better get back and work on housekeeping. Cleaning up any left-over elements."

"Do that. And I still want you to find Dan and get him off the street. I don't want anymore action on his part."

Jane saluted her boss and left his office. She felt a surge of relief. She had protected Dan and the operation. They could continue to function, and they could remain invisible, especially Dan. And they had new information that might enable them to strike back at Rashid; go on offense instead of playing defense.

Chapter 70

Dan arrived at the hunting cabin early the next morning. He was exhausted from the recent events. He pulled up into the front yard and turned off the engine. There was another vehicle, a four-wheel drive Land Cruiser, in the yard, indicating that at least Roland was at home.

The front door opened, and all six and a half feet of him stepped out on the porch. He held an M4 carbine at the low-ready position. When Dan got out, Roland smiled and slung the rifle over his shoulder.

"You here to bring me another prisoner? It's becoming like Grand Central Station here. Damn it, this was supposed to be my hideaway. Now I'm going to have to find another one. Everybody and their uncle knows about this one."

"Sorry about that. Just one more. I think the mission is completed. At least I hope so. I'll know Friday." He turned to the rear of his car and opened the trunk. After pulling Carlos out, he cut the tape from his legs and walked him forward.

"Who's this?"

"Meet Carlos. He's the D.C. head of the Sinaloa cartel."

"And you have him...why?"

"Long story. But I'm sure Jane will be happy to get her team to talk to him."

Roland kicked the ground in front of him. “Shit. This has got to stop. I’m not going to be a way station for captives.”

“Last one. Promise.”

Roland sighed and waved him forward. “Come on in. Marcus is out checking to see if his snares worked. He’s decided to become a trapper in his old age. I think he’s tired of Dinty Moore. You want some breakfast?”

“I’d love something to eat. I can even help make it.”

“Don’t trust my cooking skills?”

“I *am* a professional, you know. You shouldn’t look a gift horse in the mouth.”

“My you’re full of aphorisms, aren’t you?”

“That’s a big word, my friend.” Dan smiled at Roland and punched him in the arm. “You even know that it means?”

“Be careful sniper guy. You’re not ready for a round with me. And, yes, I do know what it means. I’ve been studying the dictionary.”

They went into the cabin. Dan took Carlos into the second bedroom and tied him to a chair. “Be careful with this one. Unlike the others, he’s more capable and will kill you given the chance. That, or take off through the woods and create a lot of work for us to recapture him.”

“Yeah. Don’t worry little buddy. We’re getting to be old hands at this prison guard business. We got it under control. Although I think I’ll bill Jane for use of my cabin. What do you think? A thousand a day for housing black op prisoners? That should fund a nice tropical vacation for me and one of my adoring ladies.”

Just then, Marcus came through the door with three rabbits in his hand. “Well, look who’s here. Just in time for roast rabbit as well. Fresh meat tonight!”

“You want me to skin them?” Dan asked.

“You offering? I’ll take it.”

Dan grabbed a filet knife from the kitchen and went out into the yard. He took a board from the shed and went to work. When he was done, he walked the entrails down the hill, well away from the cabin, and scattered them on the ground.

He came back with the skinned, gutted carcasses and the three pelts. "Four rabbit's feet. We can spread the luck around."

"Why is that considered lucky?" Roland asked.

Marcus shrugged as if to say, "Who knows?"

"It goes way back, I'm told. Seven hundred years BC or more. Rabbits were considered lucky in many cultures, so the foot could have become a talisman of that belief in luck, letting it transmit to the bearer of the foot."

"As always, the assassin-scholar has an answer."

"Just trying to help you guys gain more knowledge." He turned back to the bedroom. "You going to keep him locked up until Jane comes for him?"

"We'll let him out to do his business, but he'll be pretty much confined to the room," Roland said. "I don't speak much Spanish and I don't think we have many mutual interests. From what I know about the cartels, I'd probably get pissed off and deck him if we talked much."

"Jane'll be happy to have him. She'll think he might be useful," Dan said.

"Speaking of Jane," Marcus said, "are you going to contact her?"

Dan shook his head. "I'll wait until the end of the week. I may have more to do. I'll know by then."

"So, you're not going to check in because you have your own agenda, not Jane's, going on and you won't be done until Friday," Marcus said.

"That's about it."

"Jesus. You're going to be in hot water. I'll bet she'll be cutting you off for a while."

"Let's not go there."

Marcus threw up his hands. "Don't worry. I'm on your side. I just don't want to see you two get hurt. You make such a sweet couple."

"Fuck you," Dan said. His smile, though, conveyed his lack of anger at Marcus' jibes.

Friday morning, the three men were watching the news on a fuzzy, static-ladened channel of the cabin's TV. It was catching a weak signal from the outside antenna. Being located on a hilltop was the only reason there was any hope of a signal being acquired.

They watched in silence as the scene of Randall's shooting was displayed, including phone videos from on-lookers of the panic that ensued after the car crashed. The commentator only hinted at the possibility of the killing being an assassination, preferring to ponder how unusual it seemed for a carjacking or robbery to occur in such a busy intersection.

When the show was over, Roland turned off the television.

"That you, buddy?" Marcus asked.

Dan nodded.

Roland whistled. "That's a big red line. Way beyond kidnapping."

"He was a piece of shit. And he tried to get our friend in there," Dan motioned to the bedroom, "to have me killed."

"That's not a good idea."

"No, it isn't. Especially when I'm listening in on the conversation."

"Poor bastard," Roland said. "That was a big mistake."

"He made his choice. I told him about the consequences. He decided to not follow my instructions."

"And paid the price," Marcus said.

Dan nodded. "He also gets to send a message to a certain congressman. A message from the grave, so to speak."

"That what you're waiting for?"

Dan nodded.

That evening they turned on the TV again. They watched as the network played Congressman Greely's speech announcing his retirement and subsequent departure. Dan gave a big sigh.

"Mission over?" Marcus asked.

"Mission over."

"Now, call Jane. You owe her that."

"Yeah. That could get messy. I'll drive down to the village where I can get better cell phone reception."

"Just go up the hill. That works for me," Roland said.

"Take your medicine like a man," Marcus said. "Then get your ass back here to help with the roast rabbit."

Chapter 71

Dan walked up the hill behind the cabin to the rock outcropping Roland had mentioned earlier.

"Jane," Dan said when she answered his call.

"Where are you?"

"Out in the woods."

"Was that your work here in D.C.?"

"I think you know the answer to that."

"I want you here ASAP. I'm tired of you ducking me. It's way past time to come in and report."

"Not sure I can do that. What's waiting for me?"

"Only me. Do you think I'd sell you out?"

"I'm not sure anymore. I'm not sure of anything."

"Dan, I went to bat for you with Henry. He was ready to take things upstairs. I talked him out of that, not only to protect you, but to protect everyone around you. He's going to play it out like a foreign job. Maybe the cartels, since we can show the man took money from them. Everyone has their bad guy and the story gets neatly wrapped up."

"Okay, let's meet. But not in Arlington. That's too close for comfort."

"You're still invisible, but I'll meet you. Where?"

Dan gave her the name of a motel outside of Gainesville, just west of D.C. Three hours later, he pulled into the parking lot. Jane's car was at one end, in the shadows of the street lamp. Dan walked over and climbed into the passenger seat.

"I can get a room, so we can be more comfortable," he said.

Jane shook her head. "No room. I'm not in the mood."

"I didn't mean that. Just wanted to not talk in such a cramped space."

"Here is fine."

Her hands held a tight grip on the steering wheel, and her face looked forward with a grim countenance. There was a long moment of silence between them. Finally, Dan spoke.

"What do you want to talk about?"

"We can start by you telling me why you disobeyed my orders. I told you to keep me up to date on your progress when you set out to track down the milling machine."

The question drew Dan back to what seemed like an age ago. He was running blind, grasping at one tenuous lead, hoping it would lead to another one and the trail would keep going. He realized that back then, he had little hope he'd be successful. But following his mantra, he just kept going, working one step at a time. In the end, it led to overwhelming success.

"I felt I was on a fool's errand. You know how I am. Dogged. I just kept going, but at first had little hope my efforts would pan out."

"And when they began to bear fruit? You didn't think it important to inform me? When you enlisted my staff, you didn't think it important to inform me?"

Dan turned to her. "Jane. You said yourself that I was going to be invisible, on my own. No connection would be allowed to come back to the agency."

"You made the connection. You broke the rule of being on your own."

"And look at what it accomplished." He slapped the dashboard in frustration. Fatigue was making him short-tempered. "I'm not going to play this game—"

"And what game is that?"

"Second guessing me. I, we...Marcus, Roland, Fred, and Warren, found these guys and killed them. We even captured one of them for you to drain of information. I did my job. I did it with the help of your team and my combat mates. Don't start playing the bureaucrat on me. It's not a good look."

"And then," Jane went on, ignoring his outburst, "you threaten a congressman and his aide and kidnap someone in front of him. That requires a major sweeping to get put under the rug."

Dan just stared at her. She was angry, but she had never acted so officious towards him. This was a new side to her.

He took a deep breath. "I admit I went over the line. What I found out about Randall triggered me to act. He was poisonous and was influencing Greely. Greely was no angel but was partly acting out of a misplaced idea about espionage. He tried to keep himself cleaner by only interacting with Zhōu, who, incidentally, was helping him to get rich. But when the boys found out that Randall's girlfriend was the same woman that set Bela up...and probably killed him. That did it for me." He paused for a moment. "Did I tell you Randall was taking his pleasure with underage females the cartel owned? Seems he liked more than just money. I'm not sorry to have ended his shitty life. And, it sent a good message to Greely. Now we're rid of two corrupt political types."

"Two of many, unfortunately."

"It's a start."

Jane looked at him sharply. "We're not going there. If we're to continue this has to be an aberration. I can't cover repeated domestic actions. And Henry wouldn't stand for it."

"Don't worry. I'm happy to get back to my house and work overseas. I'm happier when I'm away from this swamp."

Jane turned back to look ahead without responding.

"So, are we okay?" Dan asked. He spoke in a quiet voice, almost tender in tone.

She shook her head. "I don't know. We've always been honest with one another. We realized up front that if we were to have any relationship beyond agent and supervisor, it had to be so. Now, I'm being honest. I'm confused and hurt by your insubordination. I know, I know, you got results. I'll grant you that. But you could have gotten them with me along. Not only for my help. I think I bring something to the operations side of the missions, but also so I wouldn't be blind-sided by what might erupt in my face."

"I'm sorry about that. I got on a charge and just took your words that night before I set out to be too inflexible...too unalterable."

"Maybe because that suited your purposes."

Dan stopped short and made no reply. Maybe he wasn't being as honest as he and Jane had insisted on between themselves.

Part of him wanted to move on, to keep justifying himself based on her words, some of which were his words put in her mouth. But that could damage the trust between them, which had already suffered from his actions. A part of him, the part that wanted to hold on to his grasp of humanity, of being connected to the community of human beings, knew that he had to atone for his actions.

He had chosen a lonely, dangerous path after the death of his wife, Rita, years ago. The vengeance he had wrought on those responsible had not healed the hole in his heart opened from her killing. His subsequent path as an assassin, turning that unhealed part of himself on the terrorists, had also not provided restoration. He did what he was good at, killing the evil men that threatened peaceful societies, particularly the U.S. But that didn't relieve him of the darkness that still lurked within.

Normal relationships were not possible. He had come to that realization with Christina, the pianist who had saved his life. He lived in a different world from normal society, and the two could not be reconciled. His relationship with Jane, who inhabited this same world, was a lifeline for him. It helped him maintain his grip on sanity and a sense that he remained a member of human society. Maybe it was the same for her. That they needed one another to remain human in this difficult fight they had undertaken. That quiet voice inside urged him to admit she was right; for the sake of their relationship and their sanity. If one was wrong, one had to admit it and acknowledge it in order to turn away and get back on the right path.

He took a deep breath. "You're right. It suited my purposes."

"Why?" Jane turned to him; with a concerned look on her face.

"Maybe I was worried you'd talk me out of any further action, either turning the whole intercept effort over to the FBI or Homeland, or talking me out of acting when I discovered the corruption going on under our noses."

Jane continued to look at him. She didn't smile, but her expression was now softer.

"That's an honest statement. I can accept that."

"Are we good?"

"Not yet. Let me have some time to digest everything, including what you just said. Without you being honest, I don't think we could go forward."

"At the risk of ruining things just as they are getting better let me ask, have you been honest with me?"

Now Jane looked away from Dan. A smile began to spread on her face as she paused for a moment.

"*Touché*. Everything I said was and is true. But I was pissed that my authority was being ignored...or disrespected." She continued before Dan could respond. "I know that's petty, but that authority is also important in our work."

"Understood. I forgive you that. Especially since I triggered it."

Jane turned her smile to him. "So, you expect we can just kiss and make up?"

"No ma'am. I think it may be a while. But I'm willing to give you all the time you need."

"Thank you for that. Now let's talk about what we do next."

"I get out of the country. I'll go down to the southern border. It's easy to cross. I'll get into Mexico and then fly back to Italy."

"Not going to see your sister?"

"Maybe. Do you need deniability or should I come clean?"

"No, leave it up in the air."

"I have a suggestion for you." Dan leaned forward and whispered in Jane's ear. It was not that he needed to do so, but more that he wanted to inhale her scent. He would carry it with him until they could reunite.

Jane smiled as he explained his idea.

"That might work," she said.

Chapter 72

A month later, Carlos showed up in Mazatlán, Mexico, at Alejandro Mendoza's offices. He had phoned Alejandro when he arrived.

"Why are you here? What is so important that you need to see me? You should be taking care of my business on the east coast."

Carlos stood in front of Alejandro's desk. Without a word, he opened his shirt to show his boss his chest. Alejandro stood up and gave him a close look.

"What is this? Who did this to you?"

"A *sicario*. He is the one who killed the mid-east jihadists. The ones we help smuggle into the states. I think he is the one who killed the congressman's aide. The man I worked with for our interests."

Alejandro walked around his desk to look closely at his lieutenant's chest. On it was tattooed the words, "I am coming for you." Underneath that short statement was *"Ángel de la Muerte"*.

"Why show me this? You can have this burned off. Why come all the way here? Is this person following you? Are you afraid of him killing you?"

Carlos shook his head. "No one is following me. I was told that I and my family would be killed if I didn't come and show you. The *sicario* said if I told you, you might not take the threat seriously, but if I showed you, you would. I felt it was wise to show you so you would protect yourself against this man."

Alejandro looked at his lieutenant with disdain on his face. "You are a fool." He waved his arm towards the door. "Go back to the U.S. Get back to making money. My uncle was careless. I am not. This man means nothing to me."

Carlos left the office. He got into a car with two of Alejandro's men, who drove off to take him to the airport. On the way, one of them got a phone call. They turned and went out into the desert, where Carlos met a gangster's death and was buried in an anonymous hole in the ground.

† † †

Zhōu got the call and traveled back to China. He was debriefed for two straight days by skilled interrogators. After, it was decided that, while he did a good job at obscuring the theft of the anthrax, enough unwarranted attention had been drawn to him to compromise his further work. The CCP also felt his presence back in China would taint them with this barely contained scandal.

His superiors knew his worth, so they decided he should serve as a recruitment agent for South America. He would be sent to Lima, Peru, which had a large Chinese community. From there, he could recruit not only Chinese immigrants but natives as well to spy for China. It was not exciting, but he accepted his assignment knowing the other options were not good for him. At least he could live in modest luxury from the money he had hidden from working with Rashid.

Rashid was a man that Zhōu felt he could work with again. He would be patient, satisfy his bosses, look for opportunities to prove his worth, and be repatriated back to the halls of power. His only sources of danger were offending his superiors and retaliation from whoever had disrupted the anthrax attack. That person was probably the same one that kidnapped Wang Li Xiu. That she would expose him to some extent, he had no doubt. And that man would be a danger to his survival if he ever discovered Zhōu's whereabouts. He knew this could happen someday and so resigned himself to a quiet life in comfortable exile.

† † †

Rashid heard no more from or about Jabbar. He had to assume the worst and took steps to protect his network, at least the parts of it that Jabbar knew about. He found himself snapping at subordinates, being cross with his family, and generally being angry and frustrated. This last effort to attack the U.S. had been foiled. He spent his days wracking his brain to devise a plan that could work.

How this latest plan had been uncovered eluded him. There were always possibilities along the way; someone linking all the anthrax thefts, someone finding out Zhōu had met with him, but locating and catching the men he had sent seemed almost impossible. In his ruminations, the thought came to him that he might be targeted. If this assassin was so successful, he must know about him at this point.

Rashid spent some time increasing his personal security. But this was not his mission. Hiding from a killer was not part of his vision of his future. His billions could surely be used to strike down the U.S., not just keep himself alive. Yet the knowledge that such a deadly man might be targeting him was beginning to give him sleepless nights.

He had to find out who this ghost was. He had to eliminate him in order to proceed with his jihadist vision.

The End

Afterword

Rogue Mission is the seventh book in the Dan Stone series.

If you enjoyed this tale, please consider writing a review on Amazon. Reviews do not have to be lengthy and are extremely helpful for two reasons: first, they provide "social proof" of a book's value to a reader unfamiliar with the author, and second, they help readers filter through thousands of books in the same category to find choices worthy of their investment in time.

You provide an essential service to other Amazon readers with a solid review. I very much value your support.

You can get access to behind-the-scenes activities and special features by joining my Reader List. Go to my website and scroll down the page to follow the adventure. No spam; I never sell my list and you can opt out at any time.

You can also follow me on Facebook at facebook.com/neesauthor

Other novels published by David Nees:

Jason's Tale book 1 in the *After the Fall* series
Uprising book 2 in the *After the Fall* series
Rescue book 3 in the *After the Fall* series
Undercover book 4 in the *After the Fall* series
Escape book 5 in the *After the Fall* series
Payback book 1 in the Dan Stone series
The Shaman book 2 in the Dan Stone series
The Captive Girl book 3 in the Dan Stone series
The Assassin and the Pianist book 4 in the Dan Stone Series
Death in the Congo book 5 in the Dan Stone Series

The Scorpion book 6 in the Dan Stone Series

Thank you for reading this book. Your reading pleasure is why I write my stories.

Printed in Great Britain
by Amazon

62181480R00245